The Sons of Hull

Book One of the Advocate Trilogy

Lindsey Scholl

ISBN-13: 978-1467990134

To Dad and Mom. You always believed in my writing.

ACKNOWLEDGMENTS

There are several people I would like to thank for helping with this book. First, Patrick and Laura O'Donnell (my mom and dad), who always said I could be a writer, and who had the patience to read all my efforts, good and bad. Dad, your artwork has helped me visualize my characters in a wonderful way; I have been gifted with a delightful family that is blessed with remarkable creativity. Dan Schaeffer, your friendship, experience, and enthusiasm for the book were a great help during my time in California. Lloyd Williams, you were my first young reader and I value your insights. Also, I'd like to thank Dave and Doreen Moore, friends whose knowledge about publishing and enthusiasm for this project were greatly needed at the time God provided them. To Clover and Rachel Carroll, for your encouragement, and Rachel, for your creativity in originally conceiving the cover art. To Shane O'Donnell at ThisDogJumps.com, for the beautiful final cover. And to my husband, John: you have patiently supported my writing and given me time to pursue it. I love you.

My greatest thanks go to God and to His Son Jesus Christ, who is my life.

PRONUNCIATION GUIDE

Amarian	Uh-*mare*-ee-un	N'vonne	Nih-*von*
Anisllyr	*Ahn*-is-leer	Obsidian	Uhb-*sih*-dee-uhn
Chasm	*Ka*-zihm	Patroniite	Pa-*troan*-ee-ite
Chiyo	*Chee*-yo	Prysm	*Prih*-zihm
Cylini	Sih-*lee*-nee	Relgaré	*Rel*-guh-ray
Destrariae	Des-*trair*-ee-eye	Rhyvelad	*Rih*-vuh-lad
Ealatrophe	*Ee*-luh-troaf	Telenar	*Tel*-ih-nar
Jasimor	*Jaz*-ih-more	Vancien	*Van*-cee-in
Keroul	Kuh-*rool*	Verial	*Vehr*-ee-uhl
Kynell	Kih-*nel*	Voyoté	Voy-*oh*-tay
Lascombe	Las-*cohm*	Zyreio	Zuh-*ray*-oh
Munkke-trophe	*Muhn*-kee-troaf		

PROLOGUE

"The day of the advocates always comes. Kynell will not sit silent in his house of Prysm. Zyreio will not keep peace in Obsidian. Ten thousand score of mornings and of evenings, then Rhyvelad will tremble again. Brothers will fight as enemies and one will die."

Book of Ages, Seventh Folio, First Line

The town of Win, South of the Glade possessed a scenic little schoolhouse, situated at the edge of a gentle wood and fronted by a crisp, manicured lawn. On this particular school day, twenty boys and girls sat attentively at their rude and uncomfortable desks. The studious children were literally sandwiched between small planks of smooth wood attached by a metal bar to stiff chairs that inspired good posture but little else. As a further benefit, every time a child squirmed in her seat, the desk would emit a tell-tale creak that drew all eyes, including the instructor's, toward the offender. The instructor, Mr. Ackburton, was a middle-aged man with wiry hair, sporting a shiny brass-framed monocle. He would grow irritable when one of these creaks interrupted his lecture. But in other respects he was an affable fellow with an impressive degree and a condescending willingness to enlighten these backwater students with his academic learning. He was currently lecturing them on religion, which happened to be his favorite topic. He loved to expound on the many exciting theories he had learned during his tenure in the city. The fact that his students failed to grasp even the basics of these theories bothered him not at all.

"So the question is," Mr. Ackburton proclaimed, tapping his blunted pointer on a board covered with chalk writing, "why does Rhyvelad need *two* gods? Why isn't one god enough?"

The boys and girls stared back at him. Some of them shifted

uncomfortably in their chairs, but none of them responded. He eyed them hungrily, excited by the vistas he was about to unfold. Finally, one student nervously raised his hand.

"But, sir, the Ages."

Mr. Ackburton shook his head vigorously, as if an annoying insect had crawled into his ear. His tussled dark hair shot out in every direction and his monocle nearly fell off of its perch.

"Come now, let's think about this. What are the Ages anyway? Let's review."

Just then, a boy burst in through the rustic, creaky door and hurried to his seat. He was about twelve cycles, with short hair as dark as Ackburton's. Tall for his age and keenly aware of his offense, he clumsily found his desk and commenced staring at his hands. The cuffs of his sleeves were damp.

"Amarian," Mr. Ackburton began, only half-concealing his exasperation, "this is the third day you are late. Do you have an explanation for your tardiness?"

The poor child looked around at his colleagues, who stared back at him with curiosity. "Yes, sir."

"And? What could possibly detain you for three days in a row?"

The boy flushed a deep red and shrugged. Water, or perhaps sweat, dripped from his brow.

The class burst out in giggles, causing the boy to blush even harder. Mr. Ackburton was not impressed. "*Shrugging* is not a reason, young man. If you are late tomorrow, I will have no choice but to give you demerits. Oh, and do try to attend class completely dry."

"Yes, sir." Another round of giggles.

"Now, then, where were we? Ah yes," he picked up his pointer again, "we were suggesting that there was only *one* god and that even he is probably better represented as an idea, rather than a personality. The Ages, we were saying, are flexible on this point, as we can see in the eighth line of the Fourth Folio, where it begins. . ."

As Mr. Ackburton droned on, subjecting line after line of the ancient book to his literary analysis, the boy named Amarian forgot his embarrassment and faithfully scribbled down notes on his slate. When the lecture was over, he was the first to raise his hand.

"Yes, Amarian?"

"Sir, if there's only one god and he's just an idea." Amarian stopped to work out his thoughts. "Then what happens to the Advocates?"

Mr. Ackburton laughed tolerantly. He was, after all, a kind-hearted man. "The point is, Amarian, that there never *were* any Advocates. This whole idea of the gods choosing a champion every five hundred and forty cycles is a metaphor. That means," he gestured to the class to take notes, "that it's not meant to be taken literally. The Advocates represent the idea of good

2

struggling against evil and of course, this process is cyclical."

Amarian was silent before the man's great learning, although something in what he said didn't feel right. When class was dismissed later that afternoon, he clamored out of his desk and walked thoughtfully outside with the others, who did not give the impression of being troubled by the day's lesson. Amarian couldn't help but envy their lightheartedness; everything Mr. Ackburton had told them had probably gone right over their heads.

To avoid further company and allow more time for thinking, he walked home through the woods instead of through town. His father surely wouldn't need him back immediately. He looked glumly down at his slate; normally, he would take the notes home and copy them onto the thin pieces of bark his father kept stored for that purpose. But today, he was repulsed by what he had written. One god? That's not what the Ages said, as he understood them. And what did "the idea of a god" mean? He scratched his head, trying to come up with an idea of something that didn't actually exist, but the best he could come up with was a rat with seven legs and a bushy tail. And even that was made up of things that *did* exist.

He scratched his head again and sat down on a tree stump, hopelessly confused by the instructor's lecture. His face was so puckered up in thought that he did not notice how the wind changed.

If the Advocates didn't actually exist, he reasoned, why did his papa keep telling him that they did? And why did he say that the time was coming when they'd be chosen again? And if it was all figurative about good and evil, how could the Advocates be brothers, born seven cycles apart as the Ages said? He thought about his own brother, Vancien, who was five cycles. He definitely *did* exist; his papa always said what a help he was, even at a young age. Even Amarian had to admit that, of the two brothers, Vancien was certainly better behaved. Such an admission was not as difficult for him to imagine as one might think: Amarian was an honest sort of boy and he knew his weaknesses. One of them was not minding as well as he should.

His mind wandered down the path that included his brother, taking him further away from Mr. Ackburton, the woods, and the wind. Vancien was the reason that he had been late that day and also the past two days. He had insisted that Amarian follow him up to the stream to go fishing. Since Vancien hadn't started formal lessons yet, he had no concept of Amarian's need to be at the schoolhouse, nor did Amarian feel the need to tell him. Besides, Amarian considered teaching his brother how to hook a worm a much more profitable experience than sitting in a stiff desk all day.

The trees were beginning to shudder from the wind now, but Amarian was too absorbed in his wandering thoughts to pay them any attention.

And what about all the other stuff the Ages said that the instructor hadn't mentioned? What about the brothers killing one another? What about the more than five hundred cycles when the victorious god would reign over the whole world? What about the stories he had heard of long periods of darkness over Rhyvelad? And even now, hadn't the world enjoyed five hundred cycles of peace?

The storm gathered strength around the boy, who only wrapped his thin jacket around himself tighter and thought harder. He remained in this position for a long time, brow furrowed as the wind stuck his hair up in short, dark tufts. He thought of Vancien again; how could he explain to him that Kynell was just an idea? How could an idea make worms: real, live worms that are meant to feed fish? And why did Papa insist that they both say their evening prayers to the god of the Prysm if Kynell didn't actually hear them?

Only when large drops of rain smacked against his head did he notice that the bright afternoon had turned dark; the sky through the trees was almost black. He jumped to his feet and started home. His papa would be certainly worried if he stayed out any longer. In fact, he was probably worried already. The thought made him break into a run, his feet pounding through the soggy fallen leaves. He almost fell twice, but his reflexes had always been quick and he was able to stop himself and his slate from tumbling into the mud. When he arrived home, however, neither his papa nor his brother were there. Hopefully, they weren't out looking for him.

Wet, cold, and tired, he fought back the shivers as he dumped his slate on the only table in the room and began to prepare a fire. It looked like the wood needed replenishing; he had no desire to go outside again, but all the other dry logs were out in the barn. Besides, he had to make sure the gate was properly shut. It wouldn't do for the milking cow to get out; fennels sometimes lurked in the woods and, despite the rain, Rita would make a tempting target for the over-sized, predatory cats.

So with a great sigh, he jerked his jacket up over his head and ran into the rain. The gate was already locked (Vancien's doing, no doubt) and the wood was in easy reach. Half a minute after he stepped out into the storm he was back again, ready to get dry and start the fire. He stopped, however, as he stepped across the threshold. The room was no longer empty. There was a stranger inside, sitting by a fire he must have started himself. He was dressed like a traveler, with his pants tucked into his boots, his hat dripping water in the corner, and a special cloak treated to keep off the rain.

Amarian started, dropping his logs, but the newcomer only looked at him, not nearly as surprised as he was. It seemed as if he was sizing him up. Amarian shifted nervously under his scrutiny, but when the man finally spoke, he sounded cheerful enough.

"Amarian, I'm glad you're here."

As the boy had no response and, indeed, had not moved, the stranger leaned back in his chair by the fire and made himself comfortable. He didn't feel any need to continue the conversation.

Amarian coughed to get his voice working again. "Uh, my father and brother will be back soon. If you have any business, you can wait where you are, by the fire."

The man leaned forward and stared into the flames. He did not look terribly old, but he certainly was not a young man. Amarian thought he had an unpleasant mouth. "I have waited, 'Ian. May I call you that? For a long time, I've waited. But it's not your father I want to talk to. It's you."

Amarian's back was getting wet from the pelting rain. The man did not seem interested in harming him, so he came all the way inside and shut the door behind him. "I don't have any business, sir. And how do you know my name?"

The man ignored the question and patted the seat of the chair across from him. "Please have a seat. I have a proposition to discuss with you."

Amarian took the seat, grateful to be by the fire but still suspicious. He didn't know what "proposition" meant, but he thought it might have something to do with chores. "I don't do work outside of the farm, sir. Don't have the time."

The man chuckled. "You're a funny boy, 'Ian. Did you think I needed your help for farm work?"

Amarian shrugged. "Don't know why you'd need my help for anything, sir. What did you say your name was?"

The man ignored that question, too. "You just came from class, didn't you? How was the lecture today?"

Amarian finally started to relax a little, happy to get his frustrations off his chest. "It was pretty confusing. The instructor thinks that god isn't a real person. He's just an idea. And that there aren't two gods, anyway, but only one. Then he said the Ages were a metaphor, or that the Advocates were. I can't remember which." He looked glumly into the fire, sour about the whole experience.

To his surprise, the man nodded knowingly. "Yes, I've heard that about Mr. Ackburton. But sometimes instructors can be wrong, you know."

"That's what I thought! My papa taught me that there were two gods and that they're real, as real as you or me. Papa says the time of the Advocates is coming soon. And he ought to know! He reads the Ages every night."

The man was still very agreeable. "Yes, he ought to. I guess he reads to you and your brother, as well?"

"Yes, sir. Every night. Vancien listens better than I do, but I like hearing about Kynell."

The man's smile was inscrutable. "You do, do you? Why him?"

"Oh, he's so powerful. He knows *everything*. And he's good, you know? He loves people."

"And Zyreio? What sort of god is he?"

Amarian poked a stick into the fire, warming to his subject. "He's not any of those things. He doesn't love anybody and Papa says he's probably not as strong as Kynell."

"Your father is wrong there."

"How do you know?" Amarian asked, startled at such a definite opinion.

"Just because Zyreio does not use his strength in the same way the god of the Prysm does, doesn't mean he's not strong. He's just smarter."

Amarian frowned, wishing that his papa would come back.

"But what if I told you there was a way to see for yourself?" the man continued. "What if I told you that your father was right, that the time of the Advocates has come?" He paused. "What if *you* were an Advocate?"

Amarian looked at him, as bewildered as he'd been all day. "Me, an Advocate? I'm sorry, sir, but .I've got to get back to my chores." He made to get up but the man grabbed him by the arm. His voice was hoarse with urgency.

"You are twelve cycles. Your brother is five. The gods have chosen you. *I* have chosen you."

Amarian was scared in earnest now. "Sir, I'm sorry, but I can't do whatever it is you're asking. I don't even know who you are."

The man did not release his grip. "I am Zyreio."

Relgaré whistled tunelessly, trying in vain to disengage an annoying hangnail. The man in front of him had been talking for the better part of the afternoon. The king was officially bored and hoped the long-winded priest would take the hint.

"Telenar, we've been over this. Go, do what you need to do. Haven't I given you my support?"

"Your Majesty, the support you have so generously provided is not enough. There is too much ground to cover, too many people to investigate. This is a long-destined time. It will not come again. It is our duty to do all we can to prepare for it."

The king leaned forward, intent on ending the tiresome interview. "I'm aware of the importance, Patronius. But I've spared all the men I can. These past cycles have been difficult in the Marches. The Cylini are encroaching and the border must be maintained. Besides, even if I gave you all the men in my kingdom, do you really know what you're looking for?"

Telenar, Patronius en preparatorium for the mighty realm of Keroul, clenched his jaw in familiar frustration. Relgaré was right, of course. His entire life studying the Ages and he still did not know what signs would indicate the boy, except that the firstborn should be in his second decade by now. Yet the king need only know the necessity, not the remaining questions.

"I shall know him when I see him."

"Of course." Relgaré's tone lacked confidence as he turned to a stack of waiting parchments. "Meanwhile, I have a kingdom to run. We must be diligent in *all* areas, lest this darkness you fear take advantage of us. That will be all for today, Patronius."

"Yes, my liege." With a courteous bow, the priest exited.

The two house guards paid him little attention as he swept angrily past them. These days, Telenar looked older than his cycles. He always seemed to be in a bitter mood and often chose to express it by storming down the chilly corridor, muttering to himself.

"Why are they so blind? Am I the only one who has counted the cycles? My life—no, the universe itself—has been leading up to this time and our noble king," Here, his tone lightened as he passed a servant, only to return to normal when the woman was out of range, "Is concerned about border wars! Now, even Patronius Supras does not listen to me."

He stopped before a massive portal. It was one of the largest doors in the palace, topped by a key stone inset with a pyramidal prism that reflected and transformed whatever light came through the corridor. The door itself was lined with pictographs, all of which represented the abstract ideas of honor, valor, and faith in one way or another. Telenar sighed. The tired old man would be within, devoted to his studies, but never understanding the urgency. How he was appointed Supras, Telenar would never know. Still, obedience and respect were required. The aging head of the fraternity was needed in this search. Besides, just because he didn't like the Supras did not mean he had to be rude.

His knock resounded down the hallway. On the other side of the door, he could hear the shuffling of feet. A breath later, an attendant's face appeared.

"Yes, Patronius Telenar?"

"Michail, please inform the Patronius Supras that I arrive with word from the king."

"One moment."

The door closed as Michail consulted with his master, leaving Telenar to wait impatiently for an interview he knew would be pointless. Several moments past his liking, the door opened again and he was invited into the chamber.

The patronage of the king had certainly benefited the Order. Clean rugs and rushes covered the floor, well-dressed servants hovered respectfully, and tinted windows illuminated everything in a kaleidoscope of color. Magnificent tapestries depicting legends of long, long ago guarded the room from chill. Here was Kynell planting the divine oastrada tree with his gilded hand. There was Zyreio burying his own tongue in the Plains of Jasimor, only to grow it back again and cause his buried part to infect all of Rhyvelad. Dragons warred with unseen enemies and gryphons flew with Destrariae to produce the mighty Ealatrophe: part glorious lion and eagle, part luminous cold-streak. All were great tales passed carefully through time to find their existence woven into the fabric of the Supras' chamber.

The Supras himself was less impressive. Reclining lazily on a collection of sumptuous Oragione cushions that was envied throughout Keroul, Patronius Supras Ganiedor had allowed old age and luxury to claim him. His clothes were coarse in obedience to the Patroniite Rule, but his skeletal fingers shimmered with glistening jewels and precious metals. Complacent eyes peered out from under shaggy brows at the newcomer. His voice was raspy.

"Telenar. Back so soon? How is the king?"

In response, Telenar knelt, covering his face with his hands.

"Arise, my child. What do you have to say to me?"

"The king is very busy these days, Supras."

Ganiedor's laugh was hollow. "The king is always busy, young Prepor. He knows little of these matters and cares even less. Do not worry about him."

"We must worry about him. It would be nice to have his men help search out the Advocate. Unless, of course, you have men to spare, Supras."

"Hm. You are straightforward, Telenar. But I think you are mistaken. The time may not yet be upon us. The interpretation of Kynell's timetable is a great concern for many of the patronii. Some scholars put the coming of the Advocate many cycles hence. To search for a champion who does not exist is a waste of resources that could be better used educating our country of Kynellian Lore."

Telenar could not hide his disgust, nor did he try. "Is that what they're calling it now?"

Ganiedor stiffened, allowing the speckled light from the windows to crown him with authority. "It is an appropriate designation. The Square has discussed it." He broke off with a dignified grunt. "It's not important. All you need to know is that we cannot spare the men. This urgency that plagues you, Prepor, is not shared by others. There are many in power who find your calculations incorrect." He tapped one of his jeweled fingers as if that decided the matter.

"And do you, Supras?"

The sunken old man averted his eyes to the tapestries. There his gaze lingered until Telenar understood his answer.

"Very well. I shall find the Advocate on my own. I trust I have the Fraternity's permission to do *that*, at least."

"Oh, come now, Telenar," Ganiedor remonstrated, pretending to be wounded. "You accept defeat so poorly. You can peek in to every little house in Rhyvelad, for all I care. Just don't make a spectacle."

"Of course, Supras. I shall not be a burden."

"Oh, and if you think you find this young Advocate, the Fraternity entrusts you with his guidance."

The meaning was clear: Patronius Telenar could expect no help from his brothers. He would be a lone priest whose search was recognized by neither king nor faith. Adventurous as that may sound, it had no appeal to Telenar. But perhaps Kynell would protect him, if the god of the Prysm could spare the time.

Covering his face and kneeling again, he bade farewell to the Supras in order to make his way to the Record Hollow to check the Ages once more. Perhaps he was wrong. Perhaps he was interpreting the text too literally. Perhaps he was taking the words of Kynell too seriously. Here he forced a smile and ran a hand through his thin brown hair. Let the others question and procrastinate. He, Telenar pa Saauli, knew the truth.

The boy trembled at the stranger's announcement. He didn't seem like some of the crazy people Amarian had seen in Win's few dark alleys. But a person would have to be insane to think that he was a god. He studied the man, who obligingly leaned forward, meeting his gaze.

If looks could kill, this one came close: the stranger's eyes were like two dark wells, threatening to pull him in. Through them he saw shadows, flames, and general scenes of destruction. But then there appeared a chair perched high on a cliff, unassailable from any angle but the sky. He, Amarian, was sitting in it, looking over all of Rhyvelad. He could see his house, with his father and brother working outside. And he could see horrible Mr. Ackburton, taking out his trash. They all looked so small. They were far away from him, but Amarian knew that he could make them do exactly what he wanted, if he chose to. Underneath him the stone was cool but strong. It was made of Obsidian. At that point, he noticed that he also held a mighty sword in his hand. Inexplicably, he started bashing at the chair with it, but it made no dent. The shiny black rock was invincible.

Then he was home again, next to the fireplace, talking to the strange man who was also Zyreio. Limbs shaking, he collapsed onto a stool. This *was* Zyreio. It had to be. He felt like he should bow or something, but his legs were so wobbly he couldn't even stand. Plus he suspected that his father wouldn't want him to.

The man shifted impatiently. "Do you know what I am offering you, Amarian? I am offering you a life of power. You could make anybody do anything you wanted." He gestured at the shabby room and then at Amarian's own tattered and wet jacket. "On top of that, you could help your papa and your brother. Wouldn't you like to give them a better life than this?"

The vision was fading. The chair on the cliff seemed a long, long way away. He did not want to go with Zyreio. From the toes of his feet to the top of his head, he did not want to go. But if he didn't go, what would happen to Vancien? The Advocates were always brothers. He knew that much, at least. If he and Vancien really were the Advocates, then they would have to kill each other someday. He shivered at the thought. As angry as he often got at his little brother, he could never hurt him. Not intentionally, anyway. Slowly the refreshing image of Vancien struggling to impale a worm on a hook began to erase the chair completely.

"Are you sure it doesn't hurt them?" Vancien often struggled with his r's. "Hurt" sounded much more like "hut."

"They're fine, Vance. Kynell made them to be bait for the fish."

Vancien wiped a grimy hand across his forehead and frowned in concentration. "They're too slippery."

"You're just not patient enough. Here."

Amarian took the hook and the worm, squelching the creature over the sharp point. Meanwhile, Vancien watched, his light hair flopping into his eyes. He brushed it away with great annoyance.

Fingers wrapped impatiently, jarring Amarian out of the memory. "Well?"

"What if I said 'no'? Would you find somebody else?"

Zyreio placed another log in the fire as the storm continued to howl outside. "I would make a visit to your brother. I'm sure he could be persuaded."

The thought of Vancien being confronted with this horrible man made Amarian break out in a cold sweat. That would never happen, not if he could prevent it. The poor kid couldn't even put a worm on a hook. How could he fight off Zyreio? The sight of Vancien so vulnerable gave him a surprising amount of courage.

"Stay away from my brother." His brave words sounded tinny to his own ears, and they must have sounded ludicrous to Zyreio, who had reached the end of his patience. He rose, looking more menacing than before.

"You do not tell me what I can and cannot do. What is your answer?"

Amarian looked around at his poor but cozy home. The rough table, the bunk beds against the wall, even the dirt in the corner all stood out to him with amazing clarity. He wished once again with all his heart that his papa would come home. Why wasn't he home? But maybe it was better. Zyreio could no doubt kill his papa or anybody else without much effort. But what would his papa do if he went away? How would Vancien ever learn to fish? He swallowed back tears, knowing that Zyreio was still waiting for his decision. To Amarian, it seemed like he was left with no decision at all.

Maybe it wouldn't be too bad. Maybe Zyreio wasn't lying when he said he could help out his family, maybe that chair was more comfortable than it looked. And maybe rats ran around with seven legs and bushy tails.

CHAPTER ONE

The air was surprisingly crisp for the late part of autore, Keroul's warm season. Usually the three orbs continued blistering the citizens until they literally smoldered in anticipation of cooler weather. But today offered a delightful respite from the heat. While thin smears of clouds drifted lazily across a blue sky, people basked in the orblight or else shivered in the shade. It was a happy day for the good people of Win, South of the Glade. All fifteen of the town's senior students had completed their exams and their formal education. The whole town had turned out to celebrate.

A woman with bright auburn hair was standing just in front of the old schoolhouse. Her clothes were homespun and ragged around the edges, but the vest she wore over the top of her frock was bright green. It looked like it was from the city and set off her eyes nicely. She was beautiful, although her beauty was not so much in her figure, which was about average. Nor was it in her hair, although it blazed red in the autore orblight. It was more in the laugh-lines around her eyes and her generous smile. At that moment, she was eating an uncooperative citrus fruit, which managed to explode every time she bit into it. Rather than get frustrated at the splotches forming on her green vest, she wiped them off with good humor and bent sharply at the waist, so that her next bite would send drops of citrus cascading to the ground instead of down her front.

After she finished the fruit, she wiped her hands on the matronly apron that circled her waist and walked over to a table that had been set up in the manicured lawn. There she pulled a young man out of a crowd of students. Although almost a full head shorter than his classmates, he was a sturdy, confident fellow who was well liked by most everyone he met. The lady, whose name was N'vonne, was his instructor.

While she cared for all of her students, Vancien was like a son to N'vonne. When she had first taken over the position of instructor from her predecessor, she had been young and nervous. Nor had her fear been helped by her predecessor's warning to watch out for the "Hull kid." Apparently, he was "as stubborn as his brother." After politely receiving the advice, she had tossed it aside, determined to make her own judgments. And she was right to do so. Vancien was quick, intelligent, and attentive: everything she could ask for. At only eight cycles, he had already been well acquainted with Kynellian Lore, though he objected to that name, Keroulian history, and various Rhyveladian cultures. When N'vonne had asked him where he learned all this, he had introduced her to his father, Hull, who had obviously taught his son a great deal. Through Hull, she learned that Vancien's mother had died in childbirth and the child had never known her. On top of that tragedy, when Vancien was five, his brother had been kidnapped, or else drowned. Nobody knew for sure what had happened: Hull was reluctant to talk about it. She had thought then that the boy had his fill of sadness, but when Vancien was thirteen, his father was killed in a farming accident. The whole town had mourned the loss.

But these thoughts were not in her head as she pulled Vancien away from the crowd. Today was no time for sad memories. Despite all of his personal tragedies, Vance had completed his education. His future could only be brighter than his past.

"Lady N'vonne! Did you see Henke's marks? The man's a genius at cross-way algorithms."

"Yes, Vance, I saw them. I graded them, remember?"

He smiled sheepishly. "Oh, yeah. But still, Henke's got to be the best mathematician in the class."

"He did score the highest marks in that area. But no one came close to your knowledge of the Ages and world cultures. Your parents would be very proud."

He blushed, kicking at the ground. His sandy hair matched the color of the dust he was disturbing. "I just wish he had been here, you know?"

"I'm sure he's watching from somewhere."

"I know. But it's not the same."

As they conversed, a short, portly man came trotting up. "Lady N'vonne! What a day! Hey, Vance! Congratulations!"

Vancien gave a cry upon seeing him, then wrapped him in a huge hug. "Uncle Naffinar! I didn't know you were here!"

"Wouldn't have missed it for the world, Vance. Came all the way from the capital city."

N'vonne did not have to feign curiosity. "How are things in Lascombe? I hope the king is well."

"Aye. And the princes are as healthy as can be. Fine lot of heirs, he has. Say, Vance, can I have a word with the lady?"

Vancien raised an eyebrow. "You came all the way from Lascombe to speak with my instructor?"

"And why not? You think you have the only claim on her?" He wagged a chubby finger at his nephew. "N'vonne and I have known each other for cycles. We go way back."

"Now gentlemen," N'vonne admonished while trying not to blush over the exchange. "Vancien, go help clean up the tables. Make sure they're folded and the leftovers are put away properly."

Vancien gave his uncle one more jealous look before jogging off. N'vonne waited until he was out of earshot to start the conversation. "This had better not be bad news."

Naffinar assured her that it was not, then allowed her to direct him toward her small office in the back of the schoolhouse, where he asked about the Vancien's grades, his activities, and how he was handling life without his father. "It's been such a long time since I've been back. I know what Hull said, but I feel responsible for the boy. Did you get my gifts?"

N'vonne pulled her hair back into a business-like bun. "They were the highlight of Vancien's term. And you should not have worried: Mayer's a good man. Though I don't think they have ever bonded, he's taken good care of Vancien and taught him his trade. Black-smithing is useful anywhere." She stopped, knowing that neither she nor Naffinar would be satisfied if Vancien decided to remain a blacksmith. "Besides, Hull knew you were needed at the capital."

"Hmph. *Needed.* The capital can run just fine without a court jester."

"Court jester? You're sounding as if your advisory position is less than appreciated."

Naffinar sighed, the picture of long-suffering. "King Relgaré goes his own way. He's been fighting these marcher wars for over twenty cycles and at no benefit to Keroul. What do we care if some barbarians steal a few stretches of land? Let them have it, I say, and pay attention to your treasury. The country's on the verge of bankruptcy, N'vonne."

She smiled, well aware of her friend's chronic financial pessimism. "I'm sure the king will come to his senses. How could he not with advisors like you? Now, what did you want to speak with me about?"

"Have you ever heard of Patronius en medio Telenar pa Saauli?"

"Telenar pa Saauli," she bit her lip, trying to recall the name. "It sounds familiar. He's a court Patroniite, isn't he?"

Naffinar adjusted his bulk in his chair, preparing to present his case. "Aye, although he's not been very active in court these past fifteen cycles. He's been too busy with his *search*." He placed great emphasis on the last word, in case she mistook it for a less significant search than it actually was.

"Search?"

"You haven't heard? Ah, I see you haven't."

"No, wait a moment. I remember hearing about it when I first came to

Win. Seems he was looking for a young boy."

"It was the strangest campaign I'd ever heard of. Claiming that he was doing what the Ages told him to do, he began advertising for some sort of young prodigy. He offered a large reward if a child was found that would fit whatever mold he had cast. For cycles, parents have been bringing him their young geniuses. But no one has been able to provide whatever it is he's wanting. Now he's become a bitter man and rarely sees anyone."

N'vonne wasn't quite sure where her friend was going with this. "I'm really sorry for him, Naffinar. But what does this have to do with me?"

"It doesn't have anything to do with you, N'vonne. It has everything to do with Vance."

"Vance? But Vance has never been to Lascombe." Then it dawned on her. "Wait a minute—"

"I have met Telenar on occasion," Naffinar rushed in before she could continue. "He knows me well enough to speak with one of my own."

"But Naff, he's already been accepted at Yartmuth. It's a prestigious institution and several of his friends are going, as well. We've spent two cycles collecting funds for his first-cycle tuition. What a waste it would be to go off to Lascombe in search of this dream of Patronius Saauli's!"

Naffinar's expression became unusually sober. "N'vonne, there's more for Vancien than an academy. This may all be a figment of Telenar's imagination, but I think it would be good for Vance to experience court, if only for a time. It certainly wouldn't hurt to put a bright lad like him in view of the king. The journey there would take less than a fortnight. If nothing comes of it, Yartmuth will still be waiting."

"And who would foot the costs for such a journey?"

"I have been saving for this for five cycles."

"You're joking."

"I'm serious. That's why I came. Vance can come back with me."

N'vonne ignored that last comment, choosing instead to express her concerns from a different angle. "And what if we get Vancien's hopes up for nothing? It would crush him to be rejected in such a way. And I hate the thought of his getting involved in court politics, especially when he's never even been outside of this small town."

"You underestimate my nephew, N'vonne. He is his father's son and stronger than you know."

N'vonne forced herself to look away before the sudden rush of emotion could show. "You should not mention his father so much," she whispered. "It will only bring up old pain for him."

He softened. "I know Vancien's not the only one who misses him."

Before she could stop them, tears flooded her vision. "He was so concerned for Vancien. Vancien was his life after Amarian disappeared. Kynell forgive me, Hull's been gone six cycles and I still can't look at his son without thinking of him." She closed her eyes. "Vancien must never know of this."

"I don't think it would make a difference."

"He must *never* know of this."

Naffinar quickly relented. "Of course. Whatever you want."

She straightened and reached for a kerchief. Her bun was beginning to fall out in wisps. "I don't see why his schooling couldn't wait for the spring term. Perhaps Vancien could go with you – as long as he is willing. I will go too. When he leaves, there will be nothing left for me here."

"What about your other students?"

"They will do just as well or better under another instructor. Do you understand, Naff? I have to go with him."

He had no serious objection to her coming, so he welcomed it with a broad grin. "Then I suggest we get all our affairs in order."

They emerged together into the crowded schoolyard, where it did not take long to locate Vancien and his friends. He was just dismantling the last table when Naffinar tugged at his sleeve, then whispered something in his ear. As soon as Vancien heard his name and the capital city in connection, he let out a whoop of joy that brought a perplexed mutter from his classmates and a surprised smile to Naffinar's face. But his face darkened when his gaze fell on N'vonne.

"I would love to come with you, Uncle. But I wouldn't feel right leaving everybody here."

N'vonne jumped in before he could continue. "You would be leaving anyway, Vance. It's not as if Yartmuth is right next door. But if you happened to be concerned about leaving a certain instructor behind, you shouldn't be. I've told Naffinar that I'm coming as well. I've always wanted to see the capital—"

But her words were cut off as he swung her off her feet. "Then it's perfect!" he cried, setting her down a little breathless.

Naffinar could not help but laugh. "Well, it's a plan anyway. But this does mean you won't be able to attend the academy this cold season. By the time hiverra comes, we'll be safe in the capital. I have a friend who is anxious to meet you."

"So that means," N'vonne interceded, "that we'll have to leave soon. Tomorrow, probably."

Vancien's joy was contagious. "Just tell me when. Hey, guys!" he shouted to his friends, all of whom had huddled nearby, trying not to look overly curious. "I'm going to Lascombe!"

Naffinar estimated that it would take them into the early part of the breach season, that turbulent time between autore and hiverra, to reach the capital. This was not the best time for traveling, as sailing was made dangerous by high winds and roads were made slick by frequent rains. Yet he was anxious to get back to his work and even more anxious to introduce Vancien to Telenar. The party was small, including only uncle, nephew, instructor, and Revor, the groom. It was consequently able to make good time even in inclement weather.

Their farewell to Win was brief. For Vancien, the town had mostly memories of loss, heart-ache, and the comfort of strangers. For N'vonne, the only strong tie she had to the place was traveling with her. She was happy to be wherever Vancien was.

The countryside through which they were traveling was both brutal and beautiful, particularly their route through the Eyestone Glade, an area of eastern Keroul well deserving of its fame. Though Win's official name included "South of the Glade" and the Glade offered the quickest route to the capital city, few of the town's inhabitants had journeyed through its ominous corridors. For the Glade consisted of row upon row of natural, sloping, shallow caves. Inside each cave was a variety of glistening stones that caught the light both orbrise and orbset in such a way that it reflected into the cave mouth opposite, creating a lane of illumination. Patroniites liked to claim that no better proof of a great architect existed: these caves shone perpetually, since the only time their interiors were darkened at all was when the triplet orbs were aligned directly overhead both midday and midnight. Even in the deep darkness of a Rhyveladian hiverran night they glowed. What little light the triple lunos offered, the stone drank and shared fully.

Only Naffinar had traveled through this region and although Vancien and N'vonne had heard of the great wonder, experiencing it was quite another thing. They gratefully accepted Naffinar's shadecloths, the only way anyone could travel through the Eyestone Glade without losing his or her sight. Revor the groom also bound the eyes of their voyoté: massive, canine beasts whose virtues as riding beasts are too lengthy to list.

After the first day in, the party selected a small cavern to camp for the night. A blind was erected to provide some darkness and the group began to shed the extra clothing they had donned as protection against heat-blistering. Four forms soon lay huddled under the protective shadow of the blind, three of them snoring gently. Only Vancien lay awake, gazing admiringly at the soft light.

What a fine architect you are, Kynell! he marveled, his heart swelling with excitement at this new adventure. *Why are you so good to me?*

He was not expecting a response. So when he heard the first distant howl, he nearly jumped out of his skin.

"Uncle! N'vonne!" he hissed, "Wake up! I hear fennels!"

But he quickly reprimanded himself. Fennels lived in dense woods, not in caves. Ashamed, he closed his eyes to sleep when he heard the sound again, this time much closer. Not bothering to wake his friends, he threw off his cover and crept past the blind to the edge of the cave. He squinted his eyes against the light. Could a fennel travel this far away from his habitat? Even as he considered this, he knew the howling sounded different than the fennel cries he had heard growing up. Holding his breath, he looked hard into the innocent glow.

"Vance!"

He turned just as a burst of cold light shuddered through him, knocking him off his feet. The howl was deafening. All around him the glow exploded like blasts of fire, freezing his mind and causing his ears to bleed. Everything went black. Only barely did he feel strong hands grasping his ankles and dragging him to safety.

The next day dawned brilliantly, oblivious of the night's suffering. Vancien lay on his pallet behind the blind, his eyes and ears mercifully covered, while N'vonne watched him twist and groan. She was afraid to ask that which burdened her most, and when she finally did, her voice was almost inaudible.

"Will he survive, Naffinar?"

He forced a smile, both to comfort himself and her. "The fact that he made it through last night is proof enough of his strength. I have no fear for his life."

"But will he ever see or hear again?"

"That only Kynell can tell us. The Destrariae so rarely leave their victims alive."

N'vonne shuddered again. When she spoke, her voice was low with grief and anxiety. "We need to get him out of this pit."

Naffinar peered miserably past the blind. The Eyestone Glade had become a weight upon them both. For all its brilliance, he was not willing to sacrifice his nephew to it. They would certainly move on in all haste.

"We'll wrap him in the blind cloth to protect him. There must be no light and no sound for him until we are out of the Glade and for the next several days. Otherwise, he may never heal. Revor can construct a litter between two of the voyoté." He met her uneasy gaze. "He will be all right, N'vonne. It'll be slow, painful going, but he *will* make it to Lascombe and there he will meet with Telenar pa Saauli."

No more words were spoken as they helped Revor put together a litter out of the cloth and poles of the blind. The voyoté were more than able to carry their added burden. Indeed, their great canine builds and durable coats made them ideal for any transport worth accomplishing. Obedient enough to follow their riders but intelligent enough to avoid natural pitfalls, they were used not only for civil journeys such as this, but for the Keroulian armed forces as well. Yet even their sharp teeth had been no match for the Destrariae. Shouldering the litter without complaint, they began to follow their masters. Two more days and one more evening in the blistering lanes, then the blessed release of a dark nightfall.

There was only one pass out of Eyestone Glade, and this night, one pair of eyes watched it carefully. The orders had been clear: do not kill the boy. Maul him, scar him, break him, but do not kill him. Patiently, these eyes had been watching day after day, waiting for the party to show itself. The creature had first thought to track them down inside the Glade, but no Sentry had ever survived that kind of light, and Tsare had not survived this long by being foolish. No, his master had said to stay here, and so he stayed.

Still, the wait had been a long one. His reptilian skin itched from the lack of water, his jagged teeth yearned to sink into soft flesh, and his eyes grew weary of the relentless orbs' light. Tsare knew there was rich land at the south end of the Glade, with plump musks and sleek creerats. But the north end was desert, and he had been in it for almost a week. The lizards provided little satisfaction for his ravenous hunger. Besides, even for his limited sensibilities, eating one's own kin was hardly desirable.

A noise interrupted his thoughts. Fanning his wide ears, he crouched and listened. Voyoté. He could hear their barking. One hundred paces into the Glade. They would be here in twenty breaths.

N'vonne almost cried in relief as they reached the edge of the Glade. Beyond the gap, she could just make out through her shadecloth some sparse hedges and a few scraggly trees. The sight was not welcoming, but anything was better than this brutal maze of light.

Naffinar was in high spirits as he stepped past the last trace of caveglow. The early evening was cloudy, an unlooked-for blessing that was a balm to the eyes. He knew they would now be traveling through a significant patch of desert, but wasn't concerned. Their water supply was only half used and it would be just a day's journey before they reached the beautiful Duvarian Range. After that, only a little while to the capital.

Spotting a small oasis, he ordered the litter to be put down by its shore. The water was brown but cool. It must have rained recently; he had never seen the waterhole so deep.

"We are out of the Glade, Vance," he whispered, knowing the boy could not hear through the padding on his ears. Vancien stirred in response.

"What did you say?"

Naffinar and N'vonne exchanged a startled glance. He shouldn't be able to hear through that padding. Technically, he shouldn't be able to hear at all.

"You can hear us?" his uncle said in a louder voice.

Vancien struggled to sit up. "Not with all this cloth wrapped around my head. Are we out of Glade? Why am I blindfolded?"

Naffinar looked hesitantly at the sky. The orbs were setting, so perhaps it might be all right.

"Vance, we're going to take away the cloths. Do *not* open your eyes."

As his nephew nodded, he reached over and slowly unwrapped the dark strips around his head. When finally exposed, the boy's face was pale but otherwise healthy.

"Without opening your eyes, can you tell if it's day or night?"

Eyes closed, Vancien cocked his head. "Maybe. Are the orbs setting? The breeze feels good."

"Then open your eyes slowly. Very slowly."

N'vonne let out a small, delighted shriek as her student's eyelids pulled back to reveal the same alert blue she had known. Naffinar was amazed.

"You can see, Vance? You can hear?"

"Yeah. You were worried?"

"Just a little bit. Here, let us help you off the litter."

Naffinar and Revor slipped their shoulders under his arms, but all three stopped when they heard a quiet tapping issuing from the bushes.

"What's that?" Vancien asked, squinting in its direction.

"I don't know," Naffinar replied, "but maybe we'd better get going. The desert has some strange creatures."

He turned his back, intent on dismantling the litter. Barely had his fingers undone the leather straps, however, when the tapping erupted into a ferocious snarling. It was a Sentry: a two-legged lizard the size of a man and Obsidian's most leathery, bloodthirsty class of henchman. Before anybody could react, it attacked Naffinar. The helpless man, never nimble and completely defenseless, was brought down without even a cry of protest. Then poor Revor, who had thrown himself upon the Sentry's back, was easily dispatched. At this point, the voyoté were putting up a vicious fight but they were no match for the large reptile's speed and intelligence.

N'vonne and Vancien watched the episode in horror. It all happened so quickly and yet they could only move in slow-motion. Vancien managed to shove N'vonne behind him, prepared to defend her with his life. But to his dismay, the creature flung him aside without any discernible effort. He landed hard on the ground, turning around just in time to see N'vonne waving a camp-knife in front of the Sentry's face. The Sentry looked amused at this, then roughly grabbed her wrist and wrenched it aside. Vancien jumped to his feet and charged again, but it was too late. The beast's sharp talons had already sunk deeply into N'vonne's flesh, forcing her to the ground. In a moment, she was dead.

"N'VONNE!!"

Only at the sound of his heart-broken cry did the creature turn to him.

"Vancien," it gurgled. Vancien shuddered. He had not expected it to be able to speak.

The two stood face to face, one pale with terror but resolute, the other confident of a quick victory. It stepped forward. "Come with—"

A brilliant light shot out of the Glades. Familiar howling filled Vancien's ears as the victorious Sentry suddenly vanished under the power of the Destrariae.

The scene was appalling in its stillness. Figures that had been living and breathing only moments before now lay in cold lumps, vacant eyes staring at the sky. Vancien stared, his mouth completely dry and his stomach lurching in alarming ways. Naffinar, N'vonne, Revor. Even the voyoté. All were gone in the space of a few whirlwind, terrifying moments. As the last of the orblight faded, his eyes stubbornly drank in the sight. Bitterness swelled in his chest, combining painfully with the freeze of the invisible Destrariae. Yes, they were his salvation, but his alone. And what use was that? It was because of him that they were on this journey anyway. Would that Naffinar had stayed in Lascombe! Would that Lady N'vonne had never agreed to come with them! Would that. What if. Why. Vancien bit his lip until it bled. If something like this could happen, what was the point?

Tears stinging his eyes, he bent over a bloody voyoté to dig out a small traveling shovel. He would bury his friends properly if it took him until hiverra. Then, after this morose honor had been observed, he would sit and allow death to take him. The wait shouldn't be too long, he reasoned as he mechanically scooped the first pile of desert sand. Blood covered the food rations and stained the oasis, so starvation would quickly become an option. It was a fate that a few hours ago would have been unthinkable and wrong. Now he welcomed it with grim resolve. Perhaps Kynell, who for some reason had not seen fit to stop this tragedy, would at least let him participate fully in it. The simple wish brought out a hollow laugh. Why should Kynell give him that mercy? He hadn't done so with his brother or his father. It seemed the Prysm god wanted him to be alone in this world.

CHAPTER TWO

Mid-lunos was approaching and the darkest hour was upon Keroul. It was the time when the three lunos aligned and the thrice-bright light was limited to one. The land seemed then to be submerged in shadows. A brightly painted plain became half blackness, while the valley that earlier had proudly displayed her trees to the sky now hid them in secret cavities. Where once three great lights shined upon a man, now he could move through the streets unseen.

Such a man moved thus. With an expression so dark it cast its own shadow, he slid from blackness to blackness, looking neither to the right nor to the left. His mouth was disfigured by a perpetual sneer. His nose was sharp, along with the rest of his features. He looked skeletal, as if warm food were a foreign concept to him.

The man soon reached his destination: a run-down tavern that glittered stubbornly against the darkness. *The Shattered Lantern* saw enough customers these days. Time was when the men of the town were occupied with their family and friends. Now, with the Cyliri battles stealing more and more of the country's youth, those who were left behind seemed to only have time to drink and revel in forgetfulness.

Business was consequently booming and the owner of *The Shattered Lantern* was enjoying the profits. There he stood, booted feet stamping on the table with impeccably inaccurate rhythm, a strip of flavored dried meat in his right hand, and a full jug of barley wine in his left. His shirt was brightly colored enough to be gaudy and its gold-laced ridges served the lowly task of absorbing whatever liquid fell from his mouth. In short, a bright but tasteless man, content to pour his ample earnings directly into his own product.

"Heya!" he whooped, finishing his song with a flourish of meat-stick. "And that'z how ye string a wench with words!"

His audience, at least those who could coordinate such an effort, applauded appreciatively.

"Thank ye, thank ye. I tell ye, tomorrow I'll yodel for the king!"

Amidst the laughter, a young voice called out. "Eh, I bet you will, Bokran! You'll sing yourself right into the royal dungeons!"

The uproar escalated as Bokran peered down imperiously from his rude perch.

"Eh? Who sez that?" His slurred speech, however, could not be heard above the celebrants, so he opted for a firmer, louder tone. "By th' plains of Jashimor, who sez that?!"

The furious demand silenced his customers. Bokran, who was often a jovial fellow, was also well-known for his temper. The night air was turning bitter in preparation for the early snows and no one was inclined toward forcible ejection from the warm tavern. As one, eyes lowered.

"Ah, I see how 'tis!" Bokran continued, aggravated further by the lack of response. "We have ourselves a coward in our presence! Speak, boy, before I kick ev'rybody out! It's as cold as the Northern Caves out there, an' I'd hate to close up shop early!"

At this, the noise began to regain its former level. When Bokran threatened to close shop, all knew the time to take the sodden man seriously was over. Individuals could be thrown out, but never the whole paying crowd. After a moment, the same youthful voice rang out again above the din.

"Why, Bokran, I just wanted to see how red your face could get! I declare, I've never actually seen it go purple." At last, a face emerged from the press.

"Corfe." Bokran spat. "I see yer back to yer old self. By the Plains, boy, get home to yer mother."

The young man of nineteen cycles smiled coldly as the tavern-keeper heaved his bulk down from the table.

"Leave my mother out of this, please. She'd turn over in her grave if she knew half the things you said about her."

Bokran was too hardened to apologize for his lack of tact. "Then go find a shop to rip off. I'm sure there's plenty aroun' to occupy yer time."

Corfe's smile disappeared. "I never took what wasn't rightfully mine."

"Ha! Don't preach that to me! I've a friend out fourteen athas because of ye."

"He lost in a game, Bok. And he didn't pay up. Besides, he could spare the money."

The keeper's eyes narrowed. "An' I can spare ye in my 'stablishment. Get out, Corfe. Find a hovel."

The youth was not intimidated. "I'll find myself a table. And maybe one of your serving girls."

Ignoring the drunken man's "bah!" Corfe turned on his heel and pushed his way through the crowd to a side table, where a drink was already awaiting him. With an oath, he dropped himself into the wobbly chair and glared at the wall. A blight on Bokran and all his worthless customers. Tomorrow, he was going to leave town and be done with the lot of them. He had more important tasks to do than drinking bad alcohol and insulting innkeepers. Tomorrow he would be on the road. Perhaps then the dust of the trail would blot out the strange coldness that had crept into his sleeping and waking hours. The man could not possibly find him here tonight, and before long, he planned to never be found again.

As he deluded himself, the door of the tavern opened wide, rocketing cold air into the room. The startled oaths were silenced, however, when a figure wrapped in a heavy black mantle stepped inside. He strode purposefully toward Bokran, taking no notice of the path that cleared before him.

Corfe watched in horror as the man reached the keeper and questioned him in a low voice. *No, Bokran. For once, be quiet.* In reply to the boy's silent entreaty, the intimidated fellow pointed a finger toward his table. Without another word, the stranger turned.

There was no escape and even if there were, Corfe's fear served only to freeze his limbs and his tongue. As the man drew nearer, his thoughts congealed into one improbable prayer: *Don't see me. Please don't see me. Don't see me."*

Then he was there, his sunken eyes pinning his prey. "Corfe," he said. His voice expressed no emotion. "Come with me."

Corfe shook his head but the man grabbed his arm and jerked him to his feet. Even in their drunken stupor, the patrons could not ignore the hysterical cries of the youth as the dark figure dragged him into the street. The door slammed, an awkward silence followed, and then came the sound of the impeccably inaccurate rhythm of Bokran's boot, pounding the table.

"A song! A song! For our dear departed son!"

To struggle against his captor was a waste of energy, as Corfe well knew. He soon cut short his cries for help.

The man would be his executor. Corfe was old enough to realize that no one crossed Zyreio's servant and kept his life. What a fool he had been to fall in with this serpent in the first place! If he had been wiser, he would have realized that no amount of hunger or need was great enough to justify what now awaited him.

Corfe had thought himself unassailable, secure in his reign of petty thievery and misdemeanors. There were even a few timely murders to which he could point in pride. So when this dark, hollow man approached him with the small chore of duping a Patronius, he had jumped at the opportunity to extend his talents.

The acting job was an odd one. If the man had come to ask his services for playing the part of a drunk, a thief, or a corrupt bureaucrat, the task would have been easy. Instead his new employer required something quite contrary to his personality: an innocent, or close to it. The role was simply a young man around nineteen who was intelligent (Corfe had that down), generous (he could work on it) and a pious slave of Kynell (a true test of his acting abilities). All of this was a cycle ago, and the months following the agreement had been filled with intensive study of Rhyveladian history and Kynellian Lore. He had brushed up on his manners, abstained from his day-to-day business, and practiced an innocent sparkle. The man had supervised him thoroughly: every grace had to be polished, every show of compassion made genuine. For a cycle, Corfe had abandoned his natural inclinations and donned the robe of purity and righteousness. Toward the end, even his own comrades were fooled. Poor old Bokran had gone so far as to ask if the boy was intending to join the Patroniite Fraternity. The plans of the dark man were succeeding and as the cool season of hiverra neared, there was only one person left to convince.

Patronius Telenar's small court was held three fortnights every cycle: two in the later breach season and one as the warm season of autore approached. The rest of the time the Patronius spent searching the land of Keroul and beyond, combing every city, every hamlet, every house for his prize. And each cycle he had discovered nothing. After broadcasting his search far and wide, he always returned to Lascombe to find hundreds of would-be Advocates, as he called them. None of them had convinced the priest, though Corfe had no doubt that his performance would be a success. Why? Because his mentor was flawless and exuded an awesome authority none could resist. Such a figure could only choose his students correctly. He would triumph over any force, let alone some Keroulian priest.

The young actor had consequently marched confidently into the small chamber. There, under a dusty window, sat the subject of many gossiping tongues: the famous, enigmatic Telenar pa Saauli. Corfe was not impressed. Where he had expected a towering force of a man, he encountered a short, stout scholar. And where he had anticipated a fierce expression and piercing eyes, he encountered quite normal features and eyes that were serious enough, but partially obscured behind small, wire-framed spectacles. Restless hands constantly found their way to a trimmed beard, a nervous habit formed from many cycles of anxious pondering. The billowy robes of the Patroniite Fraternity fit him well, however, and gave him some semblance of authority. Ultimately, only one characteristic of the man Corfe had expected proved correct: a face well-formed for laughter held no trace of cheer. Telenar was tired and discouraged. More than fifteen cycles he had been searching and it was rumored that time was running out.

A Patronius en preparatorium announced the young man's presence.
"A candidate, Patronius."

Telenar rose and dismissed the acolyte with a nod. The youth shuffled past Corfe without a word, closing the door on judge and defendant.

"Sit down, please, young candidate," was the judge's gracious welcome.

Corfe obeyed silently, having been ordered not to speak unless a direct answer was requested.

"You are the first candidate in a while," Telenar continued as he resumed his chair. "I had begun to fear Rhyvelad was running out of young prodigies. Do you think this is possible, young man?"

"No, sir."

"What is your name?"

There was no reason to conceal his identity. His home was a town many, many leagues from Lascombe and his name a common one. "Corfe, Patronius."

Telenar leaned back, studying the figure before him at his leisure. "When were you born?"

"I am nineteen cycles, sir."

"That's not what I asked, young Corfe. I asked when you were born."

So this was how the interview would be conducted: trick questions, double-sided answers. Well, this was something to which Corfe was accustomed.

"That would be 1,601 cycles of the Corruption, sir. I celebrated the day of my birth four days ago."

"And you are well-versed in Kynellian and Rhyveladian history, I presume?"

"All of my life."

"Let's talk about this Corruption, then, when Zyreio planted his tongue in the Plains of Jasimor and so corrupted all of Rhyvelad."

"What would you like to know?"

Telenar leaned forward, his watery gray eyes intent. "Can you tell me what was the chief of these corruptions that have stained Rhyvelad's great mantle?"

It took a moment for Corfe to recall his lessons and as he produced the answer, his palms began to sweat. "You are referring to deceit, Patronius."

"Very good, young Corfe. Indeed, I think you know this lesson so well that you are not only aware of the chief stain, but practice it on a regular basis."

Corfe started at the sudden accusation. "But—"

Telenar shook his head. "Do not waste your time on protests. I knew your colors from the moment you walked in the door. The only reason I have kept you is to ask you this: who sent you?"

Corfe swallowed. None of the training had prepared him for this, but he suspected that revealing his employer's identity would be a fatal disclosure.

Telenar noticed his panic and guessed accurately the cause of it. Rising, he stepped around his desk and seated himself beside the young imposter. His tone was compassionate.

"Are you so terrified of Zyreio's servant that you would gamble the wrath of Kynell?"

No response. Telenar raised his hands. "I would expel you as an impostor, only I can guess the price of failure from such a master. You should stay here, where you will be safe."

The gentle suggestion jerked Corfe into action. He rose hastily, knocking over his chair, then stumbled toward the door. It was bad enough that he had failed. All the worse if the Dark One found him hiding under the wings of a priest.

———————

They seemed to walk for an eternity. Corfe was not bound by chains, nor did he have any intention of escaping. To attempt it would be to foreshorten a life already ending. Not a word was spoken and the prisoner was told nothing of their destination.

The night around them was bitter. The cold winds off the sea seemed intent on attending their every step. Corfe wrapped his heavy jacket tighter around him, looked appealingly at the stars, and shivered. Never was there a lonelier time than late breach season night. The whole world seemed waiting to die in its embrace, forsaking all that was living and beautiful for snow and ice. Well, at least this would be the last bitter night he would know.

The man seemed to know his thoughts. "You are expecting death."

Chafing his cold hands, Corfe nodded. "Yes."

Still looking forward, the man continued. "Why are you expecting to die?"

"I have failed you and then I tried to escape you. Everyone knows you have no mercy."

If Corfe had been watching, he would have seen the man smile. His voice, however, showed no change. "You are right. I show no mercy."

They continued walking, the captor lost in his thoughts and the captive kicking himself for not playing his cards a little better for his last conversation. They were, by now, far outside of the small town and walking perilously close to the coastal bluffs. Corfe could not see the crashing waves at the bottom, but the sound of their attacks issued most ominously from the darkness. He swallowed and summoned his courage.

"You asked why I expected death. Is there another way?"

The man stopped, allowing the wind to stir his dark hair and add ice to his voice. "Do you know who I am?"

"You are a servant of Zyreio."

The man's eyes glinted in morbid pride. "*The* servant of Zyreio. I am

Amarian, Obsidian's Advocate."

"*You* are the Advocate?" Corfe repeated, clinging to conversation as his only hope.

"You forget your lessons already."

"So the time of battle has truly come again."

"How quickly you remember. I underestimated Telenar, but I did not underestimate my student. Your performance was pitiful."

As terrified as Corfe was, the blow to his pride stung. "I had no chance to give a performance. He suspected me as soon as I entered. The greatest of actors would have failed."

"You failed because you were empty of any qualities similar to my brother. I was a fool to think Telenar would be so easily misled."

Corfe fell silent, amazed at the amount of information the man had offered. Brother. Yes, the Advocates were brothers. He had read that in the Ages. So there must be another power equal to this man's. He looked again into Amarian's face and decided otherwise. No power could equal that of Zyreio's.

Amarian glared at the invisible sea. Perhaps he would spare this one's life, since some assistance may be necessary for what he was planning. He looked again at the boy and read not only fear, but awe that could be transformed into devotion. Yes, he would do.

"You ask if there is another way?"

"I do."

"There is. But it requires silence."

Before Corfe could cry out, Amarian clasped his throat in an iron grasp. Whispering strange words that sounded like a prayer, he looked up into the night sky and Corfe had the unpleasant sensation of his voice departing from his body. When Amarian released him, he could no more utter words than the silent cliffs on which they stood.

CHAPTER THREE

The desert orbs were rising as Vancien stared dully at his handiwork: three fresh piles of sandy clay, under which lay his three companions. Various lizards and dust rats scurried around his feet, unconscious of his great pain. He sat for an eternity thus, until his half-blinded vision began blurring the graves into one large mass. The mound began to pulsate until out of the dirt shot three arms, each one belonging to one of his dead friends. Vancien was paralyzed by shock as he watched the three limbs grope the dust, trying to dig the rest of their bodies out. From somewhere inside the mound, he heard the united voices of his friends crying for release. He jumped to their aid, but the sand turned hard as rock as he, too, became trapped in sandy grave. Shaking furiously, he succeeded in only lodging himself further until even his mouth was sealed.

"You're in trouble, yes?"

Vancien snapped out of his delirium. The desert orbs were indeed rising after a long, fitful night, but the graves were quiet. The dream had been powerful, but not powerful enough to force itself into reality. Nevertheless, sweat poured from his brow as he squinted to see his visitor. The creature was standing against the orbs' light, so he could only make out a shadow at first.

"Excuse me?" he whispered, his voice hoarse from lack of water.

"You're in trouble, aren't you?" his visitor insisted, stepping to the side and pointing a finger at the graves.

Vancien could see more clearly now, and made out a small, fuzzy animal as high as his waist, had he been standing. The creature was covered in short gray fur, except for its face, which held curious red eyes, a small nose, and a small mouth. It stood on two legs and its arms looked as if they could be used more for climbing than for pointing out gravesites. It was dressed in an elegant lizard-skin traveling tunic. Except for its expensive clothes, it reminded Vancien of the cheeky creatures swinging from the trees in regions he had read about as a child.

It spoke again and Vancien jumped to his feet, away from the eerie little beast. But its voice was deep and aristocratic, hardly what one expected.

"By the Plains, man!" it sounded again, taken aback by the movement.

A munkke-trophe, Vancien finally decided: a remarkable breed of primate known for its nomadic tendencies and its ability to comprehend various languages. Slightly ashamed, he held up his hands in submission.

"Sorry. You scared me."

The munkke-trophe was indignant. "I scared you? How do you think I felt, young man, when I rounded this bend here and stumbled upon three fresh graves and a living corpse?"

"Is this your territory?"

"This is the path I have chosen, yes." It stooped to pick up a short cane, which it had dropped when Vancien had so abruptly arisen. "And now, if you will excuse me, I shall be on my way."

"No, wait! You asked me if I was in trouble."

The munkke-trophe did not stop but called back over his shoulder. "Yes, I did. And I have my answer."

The past hours had evaporated Vancien's good humor. Before he could stop himself, he sent a sharp stone hurling toward the creature. The aim was true and the cane was knocked out of its owner's hands. A surprised oath accompanied the munkke-trophe to the ground.

"Well, I say," it snarled, casting about for its cane and brushing itself off. Vancien stood over it, watching silently.

"See here, young man, could you give an old 'trophe a hand up?"

"Yes, I could."

"Well then, by the orbs, do so!" The creature had found its support, but was unable to see for the sand in its eyes. The next few seconds were spent rubbing and blinking with great energy. "What, boy, are you still there?"

"Yes."

"Did you just pull that evil trick of knocking out my cane?"

"I did."

"Humph. Just as I thought. Dratted human youths thinking they can run all over other creatures."

Vancien could only laugh at its antics, forgetting his anger. He reached down and helped it to its feet.

"There you are. Can you see all right?"

"Well enough to see that you are not in any sort of trouble."

Vancien sighed as the tragedy came racing back to him. "I am in every sort of trouble. My friends are buried under those mounds, my food and water are spoiled, and I think Kynell has abandoned me."

The munkke-trophe gave him a brisk pat on the back. "But you have your health."

"A health I would sooner give up to join the others."

"Bah! Don't say that! The Prysm god spared you for a reason." It eyed Vancien's torn clothes and bloodied skin. "I assume."

"I doubt it. But what about you? What's your name?"

"What's yours?"

"Vancien pa Hull."

"So it is. I am Sirin"

Vancien extended his hand, which was received by an aging paw. "Well met, Sirin."

"Right. Lovely. A pleasure to meet you, Vancien pa Hull." Then he (for it was a he) turned to go.

"You're leaving?"

"That would be the general idea, yes."

The creature was insufferable. "Then you're a demonic little rodent!"

This caught Sirin's attention. His beady crimson eyes narrowed in hostility. "Now see here, young man. I did not pass this way to entertain a human bratling who was foolish enough to get his friends killed. Perhaps it has not crossed your mind that I have important business to attend to? I have no time to dawdle with impertinent youths!" He continued indignantly under his breath. "Demonic! I never!"

Vancien was not so easily intimidated. "Listen, rodent. You're a shame to your species if you leave me out here like this without any help at all."

"Stop calling me a rodent! I come from a long tradition of noble blood, great heroes, fearless warriors."

"And you're all there is to show for it?"

"Now you've gone too far, bratling!" His voice took on an animalistic squeal. "When I get to Lascombe, I'll report you to the civic authorities."

Vancien caught his breath. "Lascombe? You're going to Lascombe?"

The munkke-trophe was immediately wary. "Yes, although it matters little to you."

"Then I must accompany you."

"Ha!"

"If you don't accept me as company, I'll follow you anyway. You'll never lose me and never know when I'll show up next."

"Your threats are impotent. I know this desert like the back of my paw."

"And my father was a great tracker who taught me his trade." Vancien winced inwardly at the lie, but reassured himself with the knowledge that Hull had been pretty good at tracking cattle, at any rate.

"Bah!" Sirin exclaimed, unhappy with the arrangement but unable to see a way out of it. "Fine then. You have thirty seconds to gather your things and then I'm leaving."

It took less time than that for Vancien to scoop up his pack, collect all the money pouches, and bid a quick, sorrowful farewell to his friends. When he rejoined Sirin, the munkke-trophe's mood had not improved.

"Bratling."

"Rodent."

And so they marched into the rising orbs.

The day in the desert passed quickly and with little conversation. They had to cut sharply west, for although the desert was not wide at this point, it was long, piercing between the Duvarian Range and the flatlands to the south like the tip of a spear. They were north of the Glade now, but the Glade was a day's walk east of the only pass through the Range. Thus, they marched diagonally and hastily in order to get to the opening of the pass by nightfall.

Sirin was not accustomed to talking and walking at the same time, which was just as well, since Vancien was absorbed in morose thoughts. Where were N'vonne, Naffinar, and Revor now? Were they with Kynell? Or were they just sleeping? Kynellian Lore—or "the account," as he liked to call it— stated that the faithful dead slept until the next great battle. Then their spirits would awaken and aid the Advocate. When this task was finished, they would rise to Kynell's side, and remain there for all eternity. He was aware enough of the ten thousand score timetable to realize his friends would not rest for long. The cyclical battle of Prysm and Obsidian was coming soon. Vancien had only envy for the man who would receive N'vonne and Naffinar's companionship.

Eventually, after a seemingly endless march, the sand under their feet gradually began to turn to patchy grass. The Duvarian Range had been in their sights all day, and now they were finally in the foothills. He gazed around him, struck by the majesty. On his right, the mountains loomed like great slumbering giants. Perhaps there were gigantic men and women curled up under those snow-encrusted peaks, waiting for the time of their awakening. And the foothills would be their children, snuggled in bunches here and there, the green grass covering them like so many blankets.

Soon, he could see a split in the rocky wall. They were not too far now from the pass. As they stopped their westward progress and turned wholly to the north, he could see that some invisible hand had cleft the mountain in twain, leaving empty air where a peak should have been and a sheltering path to pass through. It was the only way through the range. The intact mountains were virtually impossible to traverse. Sharp rocks and dangerous cliffs were everywhere and sudden blizzards often swallowed the entire face. Many a traveler had also been lost to the treacherous sheetrock, where the seemingly solid surface was in reality only a handbreadth thick. Under the concentrated weight of a man, the sheetrock would break and plunge the offender into the hidden depths of the mountain.

Nevertheless, the beauty of the scene before them was undeniable. Despite his sharp grief, Vancien could not help but marvel at the precision of the great cleft. The Child's Pass, it was called, and its creation was a story Vancien had heard ever since he, too, was a child.

"Hey, Sirin," he said, trying to ignore the rawness in his voice.

The munkke-trophe turned, disgruntled at the interruption. "What?"

"Do you know the history of this place?"

"I don't care, actually. As long as it serves my purpose."

Vancien gritted his teeth. "I want to tell it to you."

The other began walking again. "You can talk if you like. Perhaps I'll listen."

So Vancien paused a moment to ponder the entire tale, using the distraction to help push the pain to the back of his mind. Then he began.

It was the early time and Kynell had just planted the divine oastrada tree. Everything was young and beautiful in Rhyvelad. Zyreio had not yet buried his tongue in the windswept plain of Jasimor. Peace was not a dream, but a reality, and man agreed with man. The range of Duvaria was stretching its mighty limbs, settling itself upon the mantle. It was a beautiful and ferocious place, and wise men knew not to go to the place where the snow and the cold had made their home.

The time soon came for Kynell to call upon the faithfulness of his people. Life had been simple and comfortable. Faith was easy. Kynell gave them all that they wanted. Zyreio, too, had a people, though few in number. They viewed existence much differently and only in their land was there strife. Indeed, they fed upon it. Their god watched over them, occasionally protecting their lives but never their minds. Then, one bright morning, Zyreio came to speak with the god of the Prysm.

"Your people are weak and faithless," he said.

Kynell did not become angry at this insult, for he knew that this was what Zyreio desired. Instead, he welcomed Zyreio and bade him be seated.

"How are your people, Zyreio?"

"They prosper."

Kynell knew this was not the case. He had watched in sadness as Zyreio's followers stole from and sometimes murdered their brothers and sisters. They grew fewer in number day by day and many had already crossed into Keroul, Kynell's land.

"Why have you come?" he asked.

"I have come with a request," Zyreio began. "Your men and women have it easy. They listen to you because you give them what they want. This is not love. This is convenience. My people do not get what they want. I test them. I probe them. I know they love me, because I do not make it comfortable for them."

"You want me to punish my faithful?"

"I want you to test your faithful and see how deeply their faith runs."

Enough was said and Zyreio departed. Kynell considered his request. He did not doubt his loved ones, but he knew Zyreio questioned their devotion. Perhaps if the followers of Obsidian saw the faithfulness and the peace of his people, they would abandon Zyreio's corrupt ways. Yes, this was good. This he would do.

The next morning, Kynell called his men and women to him. They came, as they always did, laughing and talking. Not one suffered and not one grieved. He told them of Zyreio's doubt, and asked if any would be willing to abandon their comfort and follow where he led. In this way, they would prove to Obsidian followers that they were a strong, devoted people. All came forward, but Kynell chose only five: a young man of great energy, a young woman of great warmth, an old man of great wisdom, an old woman of great courage, and a lame young girl whose family had recently come from Zyreio's realm.

The people wondered at this last choice but did not question Kynell's wisdom. Instead, they went to their homes to continue their day's work and pray for the five who would be traveling.

Kynell gathered his journeymen and women together and told them that what they were about to do was a great deed, one that would require energy, warmth, wisdom, courage, and. . .he stopped and looked at the little girl.

"What will you give?" he asked her.

She did not know, but she knew she was too weak and young to give what the others could give. "I will give you whatever I can," she finally said.

This pleased Kynell. But he knew the journey would be difficult. He would send them across the Duvarian Range, where the snow and the cold lived. There would be steep rocks and deadly cliffs. They must help each other and trust in him. All would be well.

He gave them everything they would need: blankets and gloves, water and food, and each a small horn to blow when they needed his help. Then they set out, the young man carrying the lame girl and helping the old woman, the young woman helping the old man. For a long time they walked up and up, occasionally stumbling on slippery rocks and narrowly missing some dangerous cliffs. But the young man would always press forward, the old woman feared nothing, the young woman encouraged them all when they grew weary, and the old man wisely pointed out which way they should go. The young girl was silent, enjoying her friends' company and admiring all that they did.

Sometimes they had to use their horns when a wall would be too steep or one of them slipped and was injured. Always Kynell showed them a path or mended a broken limb. Many times the way wasn't easy and the mending was painful, but they knew this trial would not last long. With Kynell's help, they made it across the Range to a land of great beauty, more fertile than any they had seen before and more spacious than any they had ever known.

"What a place!" the young man exclaimed. "I wish all of our families could come here!"

"It would be a long trek," the old man said. "It would take much planning."

"We could do it," replied the old woman.

"They would love it here," the young lady said. "It is more beautiful than anything I've ever seen. We must go back and tell them."

They all turned to begin their journey home, but when they looked at the Range, they found that a huge mountain had appeared behind them. The path they had taken had disappeared and all that was left was a smooth wall of stone.

The four who had spoken cried out in dismay. "How can we climb that?" they cried. "Are we trapped in this beautiful land, away from our family and friends?" All blew their horns, but there was no response. The mountain did not move, nor did they.

Finally, the little girl struggled down from the young man's shoulders and spoke to them. "You are strong," she said. "Courageous, wise, and loving. But where is your faith? Surely you do not think Kynell would abandon us here. Come, let us try."

With that, she approached the wall of stone and propped her lame foot upon a small rock, reaching as far as she could for a grip above her head. She slipped, but before any could stop her, she got up and tried again. All day she tried and no one could tell her any differently. "Kynell," she would whisper. "Help us get home."

That night she had no more energy, no more courage, no more love, and no more wisdom to find another way. She was tired. So as the others explored the great trees and rivers, she laid down at the foot of the mountain to sleep.

The next morning, she awoke to the sound of her friends laughing and crying tears of joy. She looked up and saw that at the exact spot where she had scraped her lame foot trying to climb the mountain, there was a bright green path.

"Kynell has cloven the mountain in two!" exclaimed the old man.

And so he had. He had seen the young girl's faith in him and rewarded it. The path was straight and wide, cutting right through the heart of the great mountain. So it was called the Child's Pass and so it was that Kynell's people built the city of Lascombe in the rolling hills north of the Duvarian Range.

———

Vancien's eyes were bright as he finished the story. It was one of his favorites, and now he was looking at the place where it had actually happened.

Sirin was less than impressed. "Hah!" he snorted. "A child's tale for the Child's Pass!"

"You don't believe it?"

"By the Plains, it's not even that interesting of a story. 'She laid down at the foot of the mountain to sleep.' How quaint. Bah!" He made a dismissive gesture with his paw.

"Then how else did the cleft get here?"

"The munkke-trophes dug it out with their bare paws. I don't know, bratling. I just know it's here and I'm using it."

Vancien shook his head. Rather than argue, he began to inspect what he could of the magnificent surroundings, for his story had carried them full into the mouth of the famous pass itself. Apart from the sleek walls, it was quite different than what he had expected. In his dreams, he had always pictured it as the same bright green path the girl had discovered. If he had given it more thought, he would have realized that it would be a main thoroughfare by now, since it was the quickest link between Lascombe and the regions south of the Range. Taverns, inns, and shops lining the canyon walls filled his vision. The activity was not that of commerce, however. Breach was upon them and in the Range, breach was just as dangerous as hiverra. No one stayed in the Pass through that season, since the snow could pile three times the height of a man. Everyone was breaking camp: women scurried about, collecting laundry and wages, men struggled with tent poles and rebellious voyoté, and children tried their best to get underfoot. Though the evening was fast deepening into night and many of the seasonal inhabitants had already departed, those who remained provided enough bustle to make the place look alive.

Sirin stopped in front of a tavern. "I am positively parched. We will stop here for the night."

Vancien eyed the place with suspicion. It was flat up against the west wall, squeezed between an tin-repair shop and another inn. Its windows were shut up tight against the coming cold with dingy pieces of wood. The paint on its exterior walls was peeling and the front door hung limply open, giving the travelers a glimpse of a dark interior

"It doesn't appear very safe."

"Bah! It's perfectly safe, boy. A few drinks in you and all Rhyvelad will seem safe."

There was no help for it. The old creature was already maneuvering his cane up the squeaky steps. With a sigh, Vancien followed him.

If the travelers had been fortunate enough to arrive at Child's Pass in early autore, they would have found *The Open Mouth* filled to the brim with boisterous patrons and loud servers. As it was, they stepped inside to find only a snoring man in the corner and a barman too busy to help customers.

All around were signs of boarding up against the coming snow. Tables were pushed into a corner with chairs stacked atop, crates of liquor awaited their journey south to warmer regions and even the fire was banked low to preserve fuel for the trip. As a result, the entire room was cast in shadows.

This did not affect Sirin. Intent on his drink, he strode as well as he could up to the bar and climbed onto a stool. "Greetings, barman!"

Positioned at the opposite end of the bar, the barman did not look up. "Bad timing you've got, Sirin. I'm plumb out of drink."

"You old fool, you're never out of drink! Come now, a splash of fine vintage for me and, uh, a jug of barley wine for the lad."

Vancien shook his head. "Water, if you have it."

The barman finally finished packing a case of glasses and walked resignedly over to the pair. Behind him, wooden shelves stood empty, bereft of their seasonal weight. A bottle of Lascombe Pure here and a jug of aforementioned barley wine there was all that consisted of the tavern's available store.

"I think I can handle the water, boy. And Pure's all we've got, Sirin."

The munkke-trophe sighed. "I suppose that will do, Stankley. And what of dinner? And a room?" He looked skeptically at Vancien. "Two, preferably."

Stankley's eyebrows drew together, making it obvious that he not pleased at this intrusion. He was a hefty fellow, with bristly hair and hairy arms. Vancien figured he didn't take his displeasure lightly, and prepared himself to be thrown out any minute.

But Stankley decided on a small dose of hospitality. "We've got some eggs we can cook and some bits of poultry. The rolls are cold, but they'll do."

"And a room?"

"You're lucky everybody's leaving town. Seven athas each for the rooms, ten total for the dinner and drinks."

"Ten for dinner and drinks! That's ludicrous! Why, when I was here last, I could get two *full* meals and better vintage than Pure for eight athas!"

Stankley shrugged his burly shoulders. "I've got to pay for my journey back, primate. You know that." He clunked two glasses on the bar, slopping the liquid over his hands. "Have a seat, boy. It'll be a while, as I'll cook it myself." Without another word, he disappeared through a back door into what Vancien presumed to be the galley.

"Are they this friendly all through the Pass?"

Sirin sipped his drink. "Well, it's the beginning of breach and tempers are sharp. But there's only a bit of town left, then Middle Pass. Not many people to annoy on the way, I fear."

"Middle Pass?"

"You're a useless bratling. All you know of Lore and nothing of geography. Do you think there's a comfortable tavern all the way through the

Pass to comfort your weary hide? You'll soon learn that not everybody's out to pamper you. There are two autore settlements on the southern and northern mouths of the Pass, but between those is one path, surrounded by fearful woods. Many travel there and survive. At least, if they journey through the day. During the night," his voice dropped to an ominous whisper, "mysterious things have happened. Dreadful things."

Vancien rolled his eyes. "Spare me the melodrama. What have you got against me?"

"Three things: you're a human, you're young, and you're stupid."

"Then perhaps I'd be better off without you." It was a surly suggestion, born of irritation, grief, and fatigue.

Sirin set his drink down. "I'm positive you'd be better off without me. I'm a nasty old primate." He leaned forward, widening his beady red eyes dramatically. "Leave."

Despite his dark mood, Vancien could not help but laugh. "I can't. I have to eat first."

Sirin hunched his furry shoulders, hiding his pleasure at the boy's response. "So be it."

Just then the back door banged open and in trundled Stankley with two steaming plates full of eggs and meat. Conversation ceased as the two travelers eyed their food.

"I had a second to heat up your rolls," the barman began gruffly. "No extra charge, but no complaints, neither."

Vancien thanked him profusely as Sirin inhaled a fistful of egg. Then the boy, too, eagerly began his first warm meal in days.

The rooms were small and sparsely furnished. Glimpses of rough-hewn wooden beams could easily be seen through threadbare rugs and scatterings of rushes. The pallets, supported a few handbreadths above the floor by scratchy timber frames, consisted of piles of straw bunched into thick woolen cases. There were no pillows, and each chamber was illuminated by a swinging candle-and-mirror, hanging dismally from the ceiling. When Sirin protested this crude lodging, their host gave a by-now characteristic shrug and mumbled something about preparing for his journey.

"Pay me now, or pay me in the morning. Whichever you like."

The barman's lantern scarcely lit the dark hallway as Vancien dug into a pouch and produced four coins. He handed them one by one into Stankley's waiting palm.

"There's a twenty-piece and a ten. The extra six should cover the service, I think."

In the flickering light, he could see Stankley's eyebrows rise in suspicion. He said nothing, however, except a short "good night" before he descended the creaking stairs.

Munkke-trophe and man were left in the darkness. Munkke-trophe spoke first.

"Trying to win my crusty heart, eh?"

"It was just in appreciation of having me along. Don't expect it to keep up."

"Oh, I won't, I won't. And don't you expect it in return."

"I never dreamed."

"Right. Tomorrow morning, then. If you sleep late, I leave without you."

"I'll be there."

After this pleasant parley, Sirin disappeared into his room. Vancien, too, stepped inside, locking the door behind him. With distaste, he stripped off his dirty, blood-stained shirt. Had it really only been that morning that he had left N'vonne and Naffinar's graves? Only last night his friends had been alive. Last night, he had known where he was going, what he was doing. Last night, he had believed Kynell favored him. Now here he was in this horrible tavern, the dependent companion of a belligerent munkke-trophe. Could things get any worse?

He sighed. Logic compelled him to admit that yes, things could get worse. He could be dead. He could be broke. He could be without shelter and a fresh change of clothes. He eyed his pack, dumped gracelessly next to the bed. Nothing fancy, of course. Naffinar had promised to buy him a new wardrobe when they arrived in Lascombe. Naffinar. N'vonne. He clenched his jaw. What a stupid journey. What a colossal mistake. It must be a sign or something. Some sort of vast tragedy to add to his other vast tragedies. His lot must be to stay in little Win until he, too, died. Great dreams and great cities were not for him.

Collapsing on the bed, he let his thoughts wander freely. Why was he continuing on to Lascombe? Surely he should have turned back and found some employment at home. But the thought of passing through the Eyestone Glade again made him shudder. Even worse was the mental picture of creeping back into town, blood and failure on his hands, desperate for work. He shook his head to dispel the image. He was determined to continue to the capital city, to find this friend of his uncle's. What was his name again? He seemed to remember Naffinar telling it to N'vonne. It started with an "m." No, an "s."

He was still pondering this when sleep claimed him.

CHAPTER FOUR

"And when I was fourteen cycles, I was apprenticed to the Patroniite School of Thought Over Fantasy, where I proceeded to gain the highest marks in my class."

Telenar stopped the discourse with an impatient flick of his hand. "Enough. Your marks do not concern me, nor do your accomplishments. But you are a bright young man, I can see."

The youth nodded at the compliment. He had traveled far to meet with this priest and he was determined not to waste the trip. Yet the man was not easily impressed.

"What would you like to know, Patronius?"

Telenar shook his head. Cycles of searching and he still did not know what questions to ask. For seasons, he had assumed he would just *know*. Now he was not so sure.

"Tell me about your home life. What was your mother like? Your father? Did you get along well with your brothers and sisters?"

The candidate concentrated hard, as if describing his family were just another lesson to plow through. "My mother was a wonderful woman. It was she who taught me all of the great stories of Kynell and Zyreio. My father was a tanner. He worked most of the day. I am an only child."

Telenar groaned. "No brothers?"

"Not that I know of, sir."

All of these cycles of searching, and he was finally beginning to get a sense of humor about it. "I suppose you haven't asked your mother?"

The boy did not catch the joke. "I assume she would have told me."

Telenar leaned back, assured that this lad, at least, was not the one. "Owahn, I'm sorry. The Ages are very clear that the Advocates are a pair of brothers."

Owahn's heart sank. Now all that was left to him was an assistant instructorship south of the Range. His mother had told him about it, assuring him that it was a good way to start in life.

Telenar noticed his disappointment. "Listen, I happen to know that one of the king's advisors needs an acolyte. It's only a run-and-carry job, but it will keep you at court, if that's what you want."

The boy brightened immediately. "Really? Oh, that would be wonderful, Patronius. But I don't want to be any trouble."

"Nonsense." He stood and rounded his desk. Opening the door, he called for a servant.

"Kerprack, take this young man to Advisor Naffinar's chambers. The Councilor is not due back yet, I believe, but see that Owahn is boarded and prepared as an acolyte for his return."

"Of course, Patronius."

Telenar turned to his candidate and smiled. "See? Naffinar's a friend of mine. Drop me a message sometime and let me know how he treats you."

Owahn was still thanking him as Kerprack directed the boy down the corridor into the Advisor's block, and Telenar smiled graciously until they disappeared. Once out of eyesight, however, he leaned wearily against the door-jamb. If time was short before, it was almost nonexistent now. The chosen one would have to show up on his doorstep within the next week for them to have time to prepare for the Dedication. Less than one cycle. That was all that was left. Surely, Zyreio's Advocate had been discovered and was in full training by now. Of course he was! The Ages were very definite about this: one brother was seven cycles the elder. Not the fairest of arrangements, but who can question Kynell? Indeed, Telenar already had a suspicion of the Obsidian servant's identity. That boy Corfe had been sent by him, of this he was certain. The presence of evil had stuck to the young candidate like a disease. As soon as he had entered, Telenar could sense it. Compassion for the pawn had overwhelmed him, but so had fear. If the enemy was so operational as to send a decoy, how could Telenar and Kynell's young Advocate hope to defeat him?

He heard his name called. It was the king's man, Chiyo.

"Telenar! I'm so glad I could find you."

Telenar was genuinely relieved to see the tall, lithe soldier. Chiyo was not native to Keroul. He had come from a land far west to serve what he styled "the only nobility in Rhyvelad." His loyalty was as unswerving as his manners and Telenar had soon found in him an understanding friend and confidante. Yet for all his poise, Chiyo was a fearsome warrior and had soaked his blade in a fair share of Cylini blood.

The man's pale, delicate features assumed an air of concern as he neared the priest. He stopped and crossed his arms. "You do not look so well."

Telenar slouched. He could be honest with his friend. "Time is running out, Chiyo. I still haven't found him."

"Ah. You mean he hasn't found you."

"Whichever way, we haven't connected. The Dedication is next breach season at the latest. It could even be in late autore. That gives me less than a cycle to find him, train him, and locate the site. Zyreio's Advocate is already active. And all the king cares about are those blighted Cylini! Doesn't he care about the next ten thousand score? If Zyreio wins, the next five hundred and forty cycles will be seasons of despair and war, with nothing to stop it." He paused for a breath, then added quietly. "I'm beginning to think that all he cares about is war."

Although Telenar spoke of his livelihood, Chiyo took no offense. The people of the West were known for their stoic manners. "War is an increasingly necessary evil, my friend. The king knows that. Perhaps that is all he cares to know at the moment. But come," he insisted, brightening. "The very same man wishes to see you on the East Wall. He asked that I come and fetch you."

"You're a good man, Chiyo," the priest responded, slapping his friend on the shoulder. "The king does well by you."

"The king does well by *you*, Telenar. More than he knows."

Chiyo waited as Telenar gathered his cloak, then the two began the short march from the palace to the East Wall. It was late afternoon and the pristine capital city pulsed with activity. The white-washed walls caught the light of the setting orbs and made the entire city shine golden as vendors put away their wares for the night. Entertainers were already beginning to stream onto makeshift stages and music wagons. Orbset was one of Telenar's favorite times: the air was filled with music and majestic rhetoric from Keroul's greatest creative minds. Plays from ten thousand score of mornings and evenings ago were performed with dramatic precision. Music from the age of Ruponi the Great drifted toward the heavens. The arts came alive during a Lascombe night, and this awakening was one of the few things that buoyed Telenar's spirits.

Behind them, the capital spire towered over the city. Not only did Lascombe house the finest of creative souls, but also the keenest of bureaucratic spirits. The Capitol School of Administrative Government was renowned from east to west, with many distant kings sending their best and brightest to study there. Under the great spire sat the Keroulian Square, with its four sides symbolic of the four different directions. Members of the Square were august men and women over forty cycles and wise in many areas. The elections for these five hundred and one positions (one hundred and twenty-five for each quarter of the country, then one capital-quarter representative) were highly competitive. The Square dealt mostly with quarterly issues and answered directly to the king, by way of bi-cycle reports. Though they had little say if the king did not agree with their suggestions, they could conduct a constituency-based vote of contention: this advised Relgaré that his subjects were displeased with a decision and were, perhaps, on the verge of massive revolt. If a vote of contention resulted in an overwhelming majority of disgruntlement, the king was advised to take serious pacifying action.

Telenar had observed this form of government all of his life and found it to be relatively successful. But his concern was not bureaucracy. It was the salvation of future generations. On this his thoughts settled as he and Chiyo wound their way through the city streets. Heads turned and bowed low as they passed. The priest and the king's great warrior were not rare sights to the public. Common though the vision was, the two of them walking together was an inspiring sight. Telenar was respected as a wise, if somewhat odd, man, while the tales of Chiyo's deeds in battle wove the materials of the greatest ballads. Two living legends they were, and the people of Lascombe revered them.

Chiyo pulled his cloak tightly around him. "It's getting colder. I can almost see my breath."

His friend nodded agreement. "How are the Marches doing?"

Chiyo stopped, surprised at the Telenar's insight. "Who told you?"

It took a few paces for Telenar to realize his companion was not beside him. "Told me what?"

"That's why the king wishes to speak with you. He is going to send you to the Marches."

Telenar froze in disbelief. "That's impossible."

Chiyo shifted his feet, as uncertain of his king's reasoning as Telenar. "He says there are a number of good men out there. It would be a good place for your search."

"He just wants me out of the city. He has never liked me, and I think in these past cycles he has grown even more uncomfortable with my presence. Well then, I'll go to his Marches. My fortnight will be up in one more week, and I suppose Marcher wars are as good a place as any to find an Advocate."

"You might have to leave a little earlier than that. A train of troops goes out in three days and he wants you to go with them."

Telenar shook as head as they continued walking. "No good. I can't leave before the fortnight is up. I'll go alone."

"I think the king sees it differently, my friend."

Telenar hissed under his breath and pleaded with Kynell for patience. The king was obsessed with these pointless Marcher wars. To go before the appointed time was ludicrous. What if the boy appeared while he was on his way to the borderlands? No, this order he would fight. The schedule must be kept. Consistency was the only way Telenar operated.

They soon reached the East Wall. More than merely a wall, the imposing edifice housed a number of residences, administrative offices, and even one grand kitchen. The king could often be found climbing the many steps of its grand central turret to gaze over his beloved city. Below him, his subjects danced and sang merrily, conscious of but not cowed by his presence. They knew he loved them, and had always treated them with the greatest kindness, so they sang his praises in everything from plays to tapestries to bed-time stories. He was past his prime, of course, but faithful Quinia had provided him with three strong sons and one marriageable daughter to follow in his footsteps. The House of Anisllyr would continue for another generation.

Relgaré wondered where his wife was at the moment: warning the young serving girls against vice in the lower chambers, perhaps, or strolling through the water garden north of the palace with their beautiful daughter. A smile crept over his weathered face as he pictured both headstrong women discussing anything from his latest politics to what an early hiverra could do to the redcup blossoms. His sons were probably out hunting or waiting to torment the same young serving girls. They were energetic, certainly, but not a rambunctious lot. Relgaren, his eldest, would soon reach his twenty-first cycle and was already well accomplished in the art of kingship. Farlone, his middle boy, would be a fine warrior and was anxious to depart with this next batch of troops. It had taken all of the king's persuasive powers to convince him to stay for one more round of training. Then there was Lors, his youngest. Relgaré frowned and ran a hand through his thick but graying red hair. Barely fourteen cycles and he was already going his own way. Still, the king thought he would make a fine Patronius and intended to broach the topic with him that evening. His bright mood returned at this, and his mind soon wandered back to the image of his wife.

It was these straying thoughts that the arrival of Telenar and Chiyo interrupted.

"Your Majesty." Telenar bowed low.

"Ah, Telenar! Chiyo was timely with his errand." The king nodded at his general. Without another glance at his friend, Chiyo gave a sharp salute and departed.

"Well, Telenar," the king began, sweeping an arm over the magnificent view of the city. "What a marvelous day! It began with good news and I hope it will end with the same."

Telenar took note of the hint, but chose to delay the topic for the moment. "What good news met you this morning, Sire?"

"Do you remember young Huran from the Ulanese kingdom?"

"Of course. A very likable young man from a noble realm. He was here last Lighting, I believe."

Relgaré stroked his beard. "Has it been almost a cycle already? I guess it has. Well, this Huran is his father's son: a strong ally, as well as a good leader. You know I have favored him for Dorylen?"

"I have heard so from the Supras. Does she favor him in return?"

The king could not contain his pleasure. "That's just it, Telenar! Dorylen confided in Quinia last night. She has been secretly communicating letters of affection to Huran for the past two seasons!"

"She has been communicating with another without your permission?"

"You know this is different, Telenar. I would much rather have it this way than have the girl protest. She is already intelligent for her age, but I also want her to be happy."

Telenar could not hide a wry smile. "So the princess shall be betrothed to the man she loves. What a pleasant scenario."

Relgaré looked out over the city, contemplating the idea. "Yes, it is. It will make things much easier for me. But what of you, Patronius?" He turned abruptly and fixed the priest with a probing look. "What of your search? I assume you have still not found the Advocate?"

"I would have told you immediately, Sire."

"I know of a place where you can continue your search."

Telenar kept Chiyo's information to himself and raised his eyebrows to encourage conversation. "And where is that?"

"There are a number of young men fighting in the Marches. Perhaps your lad can be found there."

There was no need to belabor the topic. A suggestion from the king was as good as an order. "When do I leave?"

"Three days from now."

Telenar eyed the king warily. What was his mood? How far would negotiation take him? "With Your Majesty's permission, I cannot leave so soon."

"That's when the troops depart. You will be spiritual advisor to Farlone."

"To do so would be an honor, Sire, but my fortnight does not end for another week. I cannot leave before the time, lest the Advocate appear."

Relgaré rolled his eyes. "Telenar, you have been looking for this Advocate for more than fifteen cycles. Do you really think a week will make a difference?"

Telenar modestly bowed his head. "This constancy is all I have, my liege. To abandon it would be too dangerous. Besides, I have traveled all over Keroul on my own. There is no need to fear for my safety. Indeed, I should like to journey there alone, lest I hold up the troops with a sudden discovery."

"Ha! Perhaps this Advocate will be sitting on the side of the road, whittling wood and singing praises to the Prysm god!"

Telenar wisely took no offense in the king's manner. "Whatever Kynell desires. As it is, I plead Your Majesty's permission to complete the fortnight."

The older man began to scratch his wrist, an unconscious habit that often surfaced when he was frustrated. There really was no reason to send the priest on immediately with the troops. He might indeed hold them up with his "discovery." It would be no surprise to find that Telenar had opted to stay behind once on the road, anyway, since his apathy toward the Marcher wars had always been apparent. Still, for some reason the presence of the priest rankled him now more than ever. The sooner he was gone, the sooner Relgaré could forget his existence and his "urgent" mission.

"You shall stay."

Telenar breathed a quiet sigh of relief, hardly able to believe he had so easily persuaded the king.

Relgaré drew himself up. "Yes, you shall stay. But after this fortnight, your search has ended. We will need a spiritual advisor on the field, and you have wasted enough of my resources on this frivolous endeavor."

Appalled, Telenar struggled to find his voice. End the search? Impossible! It was his life's work, chosen for him by Kynell. Of that he was certain. And resources! The only resources Telenar had used were his own money-pouch and the chambers regularly granted to a Patronius of his station.

"But Your Majesty, this cannot be rushed."

Relgaré turned toward the stairs, intent on finding his wife and perhaps a bit of dinner. "You heard what I said, Patronius," he called back over his shoulder. "One week. Then the Marches."

The desert wind billowed his cloak as Amarian gazed, unspeaking, at the scene: three shallow graves and no sign of his Sentry.

Obviously, the attack had failed. Amarian had guessed this when Tsare had not reported back to him. Two days had gone by, and then the Advocate decided to see the results for himself. Accompanied only by Corfe, he had ridden hard through the Eyestone Glade, cursing its light and resting only when his voyoté faltered. Now the beasts and the servant waited nervously as their master kicked the piles of sand and swore.

"It is what I feared. The boy's not even wounded."

Corfe, too, studied the graves. They were pointing north to south, which was a sign of reverence for Kynell. Certainly there was nothing left of the Sentry, though he only wondered what could have eliminated such a fearful creature with no trace of a struggle. For a moment, the possibility that one of Vancien's companions survived to perform the burial presented itself, but he quickly shook his head. No Sentry would mistakenly kill Kynell's chosen. The very idea was impossible. The appointed time had not come. The fact that Tsare was gone was proof that Vancien lived. Corfe shivered. Whatever it was that slew the Sentry and saved the boy did not come until after the attacker had done considerable damage. Though the Advocate may have been spared, his companions had suffered violent deaths.

Still what was done was done. It was nothing to him.

Amarian was already mounting his voyoté. "Quickly, slave. He has several days' advantage of us. We must not let him reach Lascombe."

As his servant scrambled to obey, Amarian smiled in anticipation. After long cycles of waiting, the hunt was finally on, and now his quarry was alone. Before long, fate itself would be captive in his hand.

By early morning, the merchants' town was well behind them. Vancien had insisted that they depart before the break of dawn, and for once, Sirin had not argued. The thought of combating with surly vendors for path space was not a pleasant one and he, too, was anxious to reach the capital city.

Above them, the trees of Middle Pass shimmered in the dark morning air. Despite what the munkke-trophe had told him the night before, Vancien found the forest enchanting, and was disappointed that they had no time to linger.

"This is the only way?"

Sirin nodded. "This is the only path, with the exception of some hunting tracks. Why? Are you complaining already?"

Vancien ignored him, choosing instead to study his surroundings. The path they were on was indeed well traveled. Wide enough for two large carts, it cut through the woods as if it, not the trees, had always existed. The ground was so well packed that little dust was stirred, while on either side of the road small channels carried off excess water to prevent flooding. The King's Road had been one of the great triumphs of Relgaré's grandfather's reign, and rulers from all over Rhyvelad had sent their civil engineers to study it before embarking on their own infrastructures. Vancien had remembered learning about the great project in school, but no mention had been made of the mysterious woods that surrounded it, or of the strange sounds that proceeded from them.

"Birds," Sirin had replied when Vancien asked him about the curious chirps and moans. "The birds are waking and the trees are creaking in the wind."

Vancien was not convinced, as there was not even a slight breeze in the morning stillness, but Sirin seemed to have abandoned his mystical attitude of the night before and there was no recalling it. Disgruntled, he fell silent.

They traveled in this sullen manner for the better part of the day. Occasionally, distant sounds of laughter reached them from behind. The merchants had begun their journey. Up ahead, there was nothing but the diverse sounds of the forest. Vancien was vaguely disappointed. After the past few days, one would think he desired a rest from adventure, but just the opposite. Among these trees existed a mystery, he felt certain, and he was eager to learn of it.

Sirin showed no such curiosity. "Keep up, bratling. Your peering stupidly into the trees is slowing us down."

"How long until the northern settlement?" Vancien asked as he obediently stepped up his pace.

"Long enough. We'll have to camp a night along the road. But we'll reach it in good time if you don't hold us up."

"Drop it, Sirin. Perhaps we should try to be civil."

"Why should I be civil to a tag-a-long? You're still a child, bratling."

"Fine. You're right, Sirin. I guess I'm still a child, even though I've been blinded in the Eyestone Glade, survived two Destrariae attacks, and suffered the deaths of three friends."

Sirin swiftly pushed his cane against Vancien's lips. The munkke-trophe's eyes were wide in surprise.

"Did you say Destrariae?"

Vancien pushed the cane away and continued walking. "No. I don't know. Did I?"

"Wait, bratling, this is serious! No one encounters a Destrariae and survives."

"Whatever you say, Sirin. You're the adult here."

Vancien had been prepared for any amount of sarcasm, but the primate's sudden screech startled him. Turning so quickly he almost suffered from whiplash, he beheld his cynical friend down on his furry knees, cane discarded and paws upheld.

"Great Kynell! Can it be true?"

"What are you talking about? Get up, Sirin, you're slowing us down."

The creature struggled to his feet and lurched toward him. "You said you survived not one, but *two* Destrariae attacks! Do you know what that means, bratling? Our great lord Ulras was slain by the mere chill of such creatures! Ruponi's son Meleazar was deafened for life when he heard their eerie howls. Even our own Relgaré fears them!"

"Well, I didn't really enjoy it." Sirin was beginning to scare him.

"But you survived it, boy. That makes you. . ."

"What? What does it make me?"

But his companion's mood had passed. "Never mind. Come on, step up the pace."

And the strange moment stood there, already almost forgotten. Sirin did not speak again until that night, and never again on that topic.

CHAPTER FIVE

"They will be close to Lascombe by now."

Amarian was in one of his moods. Although silent for days at a time, occasionally life would descend upon him and he would talk as if his servant could reply.

"The people fear me, Corfe," he confided one evening, after they had passed through the southern settlement of Child's Pass. "Did you see the looks in their eyes? I am a shadow to them. A ghost. Something with which to scare their children into obedience."

The night was cold and the wind howled eerily through the great crevice. They had found a site deep into the woods in Middle Pass. Corfe shivered, having never been so far north before, nor did he appreciate the eerie sounds echoing from the trees above them. But Amarian sat comfortably across the campfire, reclining casually to one side. With his dark clothes, only his face was easily visible: a somber canvas upon which the shadows of the flames danced. Though they had been traveling together many days and Amarian had not harmed him, Corfe was continuously intimidated by his presence. This was Zyreio's Advocate: Obsidian's chosen of all mankind, and one day he would rule Rhyvelad in a reign of intoxicating terror. The power seemed to vibrate from him.

"I have spoken with him once, you know. Face to face. I had to choose, Corfe. Did you know that?"

The young man shook his head as his master leaned toward him. "I chose evil. Do you know why? Because I hated the Prysm. I hate it still. One day my brother will feel the heat of my hatred, and he will burn beneath it." He leaned back. "But the time has not come. When the Dedication is completed, then will I move against him."

Corfe wanted to ask why they were chasing after him if nothing could be done, and Amarian seemed to read his thoughts. "Your mind is simple, boy. Of course Kynell will protect him until the Dedication. The failure of Tsare taught me that. But if I can keep him away from the priest and contain him until that time, who knows? We might just cheat—what was that?"

Corfe jumped at Amarian's sharp question. He had heard nothing in his increasingly drowsy state. But whatever it was could leave them alone for half a night.

"Get up, slave!" Amarian jerked him to his feet. "Pack up our things. We must move quickly." But the wind was beginning to circle around them, sweeping the air into a cyclone of fallen leaves and dust. The fire died and only the central lunos illuminated the two men. From the woods could be heard a strange groaning as the cyclone directed them through the trees and toward a slight clearing. Then it was gone and all that could be heard was the labored breathing of a dying animal.

It was a yemain, a lithe creature hunted for food and hide. Obviously, some hunter had declined to track down his prey, for here she was, wounded and alone. As the two watched, she struggled to rise, only to fall back upon down.

Corfe reached for his knife to put her out of her misery, but Amarian stayed his hand. Quietly, he knelt beside the creature. At the movement, the yemain raised her head and looked at him. To Corfe's amazement, it spoke.

"You are Amarian?"

"Yes." The Advocate evinced no surprise at this strange situation.

"You are called the Darkness of the World. Yet I die, and as I die, so shall your efforts to keep Kynell's chosen from his fate. *The brothers will fight as enemies and one will die.*"

Before he could respond, the yemain's head fell back, and her breathing stopped. Hissing under his breath, Amarian rose and pointed to his servant. "Skin this creature. I want to eat its flesh and burn its hide. Then we leave. There will be no rest until we find Vancien."

Lascombe. Finally!

The days of Sirin's surly company were fast coming to an end and Vancien could not have been more thrilled. The munkke-trophe had his moments, but by and large he was a very disagreeable character. The young man planned to part ways with the creature at the city gates, but to his surprise, Sirin objected.

"You are young and stupid. You will get lost in such a city. Why did you want to come here anyway?"

Vancien could not believe what he was hearing. "I thought you've been trying to get rid of me all of this time!"

Sirin shook his head and rolled his beady red eyes. "Once I let you out of my sight, you will go get drunk or killed or something dreadful. Not that I care. But I'd prefer not to have that on my conscience. Come. I will take you to the palace and deposit you with the rest of the lost boys."

"And if I don't come?"

"Then I will call the city guard and have them escort you to prison as a thief."

"I've never laid a hand on your belongings."

"You have stolen and wasted my time. I have a cousin in the guard. He could take care of you."

While Vancien pondered the image of a munkke-trophe city guard, Sirin shoved him past the large gateway and into the city. Then he disappeared, lost in the crowd. Vancien pushed forward, but the city was populated by giants compared to the thigh-high primate. Then there was a voice at his elbow.

"See? See what I mean? Useless. Now this time keep track of me."

It was hard to watch for Sirin and still keep an eye open to the magnificence of the capital city. Everywhere Vancien looked, giant buildings loomed, street performers danced, and living art mingled delightfully with static pieces. Occasionally, he would see a seemingly familiar face and his heart would sink into sober memory. But the brilliance of Lascombe was persistent, and he found it impossible to dwell in such darkness.

Twice he lost Sirin, and twice he was subjected to a condescending rebuke. After the second humiliating instance, he closed his vision to everything but the munkke-trophe. He consequently bumped into several people, provoking apologetic smiles as well as impatient shoves.

Rounding one corner, he bumped into a priest. Telenar's response was more distracted than annoyed.

"Watch where you're going, boy."

Vancien nodded and continued on, while Telenar shook his head. Crowds of people, he thought, and not one of them was right. He sighed, dangerously close to hopelessness. Tomorrow was his last day of the search, thanks to the king. Not that he would stop looking, of course. But now he would be forced to look among young, battle-eager soldiers, and he knew in his heart that the Advocate would not be found there. *Dear Kynell*, he prayed as he picked up his pace, *please let me find him. Please. I don't want to fail you.*

Vancien found the cousin of Sirin just as surly as Sirin himself. When he tried to explain his unusual situation, (Sirin had mysteriously disappeared into a pub after dropping him off with the guard) the munkke-trophe only asked again, "You're looking for whom?"

"A man. A friend of Advisor Naffinar's. I don't remember his name."

"The Advisor has many friends, boy. You'd better pick one."

The turn of phrase shook Vancien. "H-had, sir."

"What? Speak clearly before I throw you out."

"He, uh, he *had* many friends, sir. Naffinar was my uncle and he died on the journey here."

"You mean you killed him?"

"What?! You don't even know Naffinar, and you're accusing me of his murder?"

The guard had crueler streak than his cousin. He pushed Vancien lightly with the butt of his spear. "I know he had money. Come now, your purse is probably bursting with his treasure."

With a strangled shout, Vancien threw himself at the little soldier. But the munkke-trophe, who was expecting such an attack, easily swept him off of his feet and leveled the spear at his throat.

"Attacking the king's guard is a capital crime, boy," he growled.

"Guard!"

The munkke-trophe, still holding his prey, snapped to attention. "Yes, sir!"

Chiyo's tone was impatient. "What do you think you're doing? Attacking a citizen?"

"'Tis no citizen, sir. He's just a wanderer and he attacked me first. I had to defend myself."

Chiyo knew this guard's history and he didn't trust him. "Does this guard speak the truth, young man?"

Vancien's nod was almost imperceptible.

With an eye on both, Chiyo considered the situation. He disliked munkke-trophes, and this one in particular had a bad habit of picking fights. On the other hand, the boy had just confessed to the attack. "What did you say to him, Wark?"

Before Wark could reply, Vancien jumped in. "He wrongfully accused me, sir! He said I killed my Uncle Naffinar, when I didn't, and I was only trying to explain."

"Silence!" The soldier's hand shot up even as his eyes grew wide. "Did you say Advisor Naffinar was dead?"

Again, Vancien nodded.

"And how do you know of this?"

"I was his nephew, sir. We were coming here, when a Sentry attacked us outside of the Eyestone Glade. My uncle, instructor, and groom were all slaughtered. I only survived because the Destrariae saved me."

Chiyo's amazement was overpowered by a soldier's need to keep important information quiet. "You talk too much. Wark, hand him over to me and forget this incident. Go find your cousin. Yes, I saw Sirin in town. Make sure he doesn't offend any shopkeepers."

With a slight grumble, Wark saluted and departed. Chiyo waited until he was completely out of hearing range before he addressed his young prisoner.

"What's your name?"

"Vancien pa Hull, sir."

"You shouldn't have attacked a guard, son. No matter what he said to you."

Burning with shame and anger, Vancien only looked at the ground as Chiyo continued. "If I didn't know Wark's history, you'd be on your way to prison by now. But enough of this. I am very sorry to hear of Naffinar's death. He was a good man."

Vancien raised his head. "You knew Naffinar well?"

Chiyo managed a laugh. "Everybody knows Naffinar, Vancien pa Hull. Come with me. There's someone who knew Naffinar better than most and I'm sure he would like to meet his nephew."

As they pushed through the streets, Vancien pondered this turn of events with gratitude. He had already forgotten his comment on the Destrariae, but Chiyo had not. Indeed, it was all he could do to suppress the sudden hope that burst upon him as they made their way toward Telenar's chambers.

"Come in."

Telenar was just seating himself as two figures entered. They said nothing as they approached the desk, but the recognition was instant.

"Telenar," the first said. "Have you been expecting us?"

Telenar felt his mouth go dry as excitement gripped him. "I think I have."

"I hope I haven't arrived too late. The boy is not here."

The presence of Obsidian was overwhelming, but Telenar fought back his fear. "I trust in Kynell, Dark One. I do not fear you."

Despite his exhaustion, Corfe watched in fascination as his master's eyes flashed. "You should, priest. Kynell's protection does not extend beyond the boy. But you're jumping to conclusions. I'm not here to kill you."

As comforting as those words may have seemed, Telenar's confidence weakened. "Then what do you want?"

"That's a good question, Patronius. I mean, after all these cycles, your search has failed miserably. I wouldn't possibly want to use you for bait."

A knock sounded at the door as Amarian retreated into the shadows. "Or would I?"

Before Telenar could respond, the door opened and Chiyo entered with Vancien in tow.

"Telenar, I have someone for you to meet. Telenar?" He stopped, puzzled by his friend's alarm. As Telenar opened his mouth to speak, the door slammed behind them. The newcomers whirled around, suddenly conscious of other presences in the room.

"Chiyo, get that boy out of here," Telenar whispered hoarsely.

"Shut up, priest." Amarian spat, sliding out from behind the door and toward his brother. "Recognize me, Vance?"

Vancien shook his head at first. "No, I don't think so." Then he looked more closely. He didn't remember much of his brother, but after he had disappeared, Hull had commissioned an artist in town to draw up a likeness to help in the search for him. That likeness had hung up next to the fireplace for Vancien's entire childhood. "Amarian?"

Amarian smiled warmly, a change Telenar did not fail to notice. "You *do* remember me!"

"But what are you doing here? I thought you had died or something."

"You know him?" Telenar demanded.

Without taking his eye off Amarian, Vancien answered. "Of course. He's my brother."

Amarian's tone became even more affectionate and earnest. "I'm sorry to startle you. I didn't want you to run away before we had a chance to talk. Obviously, I didn't drown in the creek like all those fools said. Papa knew better."

"But where were you all those cycles? Why didn't you come back home?"

Amarian rolled his shoulders, warming to his tale. "I had some other things I had to attend to. I wanted to be there next to you, but I wasn't allowed." At this point, genuine grief flickered across his face. "But all that's over now. I came to find you."

Chiyo had already drawn his sword. Now he stepped forward menacingly. "I don't know who you are, but it's time for you to leave."

Amarian lazily drew out a small knife. "Come on, then."

Both Telenar and Vancien shouted for him to stop, but Chiyo had already committed himself to the attack. Amarian didn't even bother to raise his own weapon. Chiyo's blade struck true into his chest, but it bounced off as if it were made of rubber. Chiyo, on the other hand, dropped the weapon as if he'd been bitten by a snake. He moaned, crashing to his knees and clutching his hands.

"You should know better than to try to kill an Advocate," Amarian snapped. "Stand back!"

Telenar, who was rushing to help his friend, stopped instantly.

But Vancien was outraged. "What are you doing, Ian? You could have injured that man."

"He'll be all right," Amarian soothed. "I don't want to cause anybody any more harm. But they want to turn you against me, Vance. Me, your own brother!" He stopped, almost daring Telenar to speak. The priest held his tongue. "You know I'm the only one left for you."

Torn, Vancien's gaze moved to Chiyo and Telenar, then to Amarian, then back again. "I don't think," he responded, avoiding that last comment, "that you are all you seem to be."

Amarian nodded. "You always were bright. You're right: there's more to me than what you see. I have power, Vance. Power greater than you can imagine. And the gods have desired me to share it with you."

Vancien felt a cold ache stirring in his chest. As it grew in intensity, he was reminded sharply of the Destrariae. What was it the legend said? Once you survived them, they never left you? He shook his head, angry that the horrible things could intrude at a time like this.

"Where have you been all this time?"

"The gods pulled me away into their service. I cannot tell you more right now."

"Why do you keep saying gods? There's only one god."

Amarian's reply was cool. "There are two. You know that."

Now he was on solid ground. "There is only one for me, 'Ian. I do not recognize the authority of Obsidian."

His brother's loving guise began to slip as his loyalty took hold. "Then you're a fool, Vancien. Zyreio's power cannot be matched."

Vancien's gaze was level. "It can and it will be." Then his voice softened. "Maybe you can stay with me. You can serve Kynell. He is worthy of it. It'd be nice to have a family again."

If he had wanted to upset his brother, he could not have chosen better words. Amarian's face darkened as he stepped forward. He would end this now. "You are naïve, Vance! I would sooner die than serve your god."

Amarian reached out his hand just as Vancien felt the familiar ice burst from him. Both immediately fell to the ground with a groan, one clutching his arm and the other clutching his chest. For a moment, everything was quiet. Even the moans of the combatants were muffled. Then Amarian staggered to his feet, pale with rage or possibly even fear. Vancien was still lying prone on the floor, struggling to catch his breath. Amarian cast him a furious glance then stormed out of the room, leaving Corfe to scramble out in his wake.

Vancien still could not move, nor did he want to. The pain in his chest seemed to radiate into his stomach, his arms, his legs, and even his head. He lay there, eyes closed, not caring if he was alive or dead. When he finally did open his eyes, he saw the worried face of the priest staring down at him.

"This is him, Chiyo!" Telenar was saying. "Kynell be praised! We've found him!" Vancien did not bother to ask what he was talking about. Instead, he slipped helplessly from consciousness.

But the oblivion could only claim him for a few moments.

"Vancien pa Hull!" The name, more like a command than a label, brought him immediately back to himself again.

"Vancien!" Telenar called again, gently shaking his shoulder. "That is your name, isn't it?"

Numbly, Vancien nodded as he sat up. The cold in his chest was still there, burning and freezing at the same time. By now, though, it had at least receded from the rest of them. "My chest."

"It's the Destrariae."

"Yes," he whispered, "I know what they are. I'm beginning to hate them."

Wondering what the young man had already been through, Telenar leaned back on his haunches. "They saved your life."

"They have a nasty habit of doing that. Who are you?"

"Telenar pa Saauli, Patronius en medio. The other man was General Chiyo, my friend. I sent him for help." He stopped, eying his new student. Most of him still could not believe that he had found him and in such an extraordinary fashion! To have both Advocates revealed to him at the same time was a wonderful confirmation of his work, if a little unnerving. Amarian pa Hull, for now he knew their names, had been roughly what he expected him to be: a man eaten out by evil, cunning, pale, even skeletal. But this Vancien, Kynell help him, looked like just a regular kid. He was robust, if a little on the short side, with sandy, non-descript hair that appeared chopped, rather than cut. He also appeared recently orb-burnt, since his skin was glowing with an unnatural shade of red. Still, Telenar doubted he'd ever seen a more welcome sight. "I've been looking for you, young man."

As Telenar spoke, Vancien staggered to his feet. Despite this priest's obvious joy at his arrival, he couldn't shake the image of Amarian. "My brother. Is he gone?"

Telenar nodded. "He came to keep you from me and from your fate. Thank Kynell he failed in both."

Vancien rubbed his head vigorously. The cold seemed to have numbed his brain. "I don't follow you."

"I'm sure you don't. But you will. You are Kynell's Advocate. And I am here to train you."

———

Vancien was dumbfounded at the thought of being Kynell's chosen, but his new life at court was sufficiently busy to keep him from contemplating his fate in much depth. He staggered from meeting to meeting with an air of a man lost at sea. Telenar seemed to want him to do everything at once. He met the king, which was awkward. He met the king's family, which was even more awkward. In what was perhaps the most boring forty-five minutes of his life, he sat in on a session of the Square as they debated increasing import taxes on alcohol-based products. Through all of these encounters, he reeled from a mix of amazement, confusion, and grief. He had never been in a town larger than his own Win, South of the Glade. To be in Lascombe, surrounded by towering buildings and towering personalities was both overwhelming and exciting. One day, when he could catch a few moments to himself, he hid in the antechamber to the men's garder-robe (a fancy word for a waste house, he had learned). The small room was painted bright green, with two padded benches and three water pumps for washing one's hands, which was another trick he was told he had to learn. The sharp smell of the cleansing oil gave the room a medicinal feel. Still, it was the only place where Vancien could get some peace while admiring some of the clever details of the palace.

For Telenar had insisted that he stay next to himself, in the priest's hall, which was situated on the south side of the huge building called "the palace." Vancien learned quickly that the palace was more than just the king's residence; it was the central bureaucratic and ecclesiastical hub of the city, followed by the Square, which was right next door. The palace housed hundreds of residences and offices and was always subject to activity, even in the dead of night.

As for the priest's hall, it was literally a long corridor with several suites leading off from it. Vancien had first set foot in the corridor when he was following General Chiyo to meet Telenar. Though he had been worried at that point about the turn events were taking, the hall's lighting had caught his eye. It may seem odd for Vancien to wonder about lighting, but perhaps not when all the lighting he had ever known was candles and torches. The priest's hall, though it was well lit, had neither candles nor torches. Along both walls of the corridor, which were fronted with a sort of waxed timber, stretched a tube of glass, about five inches tall. Inside the tube was a narrow line of continuous flame, burning low and gently, filling the area with cozy light. Periodically along the tube, a narrower glass tube would shoot straight up along the wall and disappear into the ceiling. Vancien guessed that this was to let out the smoke, but he had still to figure out what it was that made the flame burn in the first place. How much better it would be to talk over these things with N'vonne, who had a knack for mechanical things! How much of the palace he wanted to show her, from the triangular central courtyard filled with lush foliage and man-made water features to the "chutes," which let in orblight to the interior offices of the palace, rooms which otherwise would have been kept in the dark throughout the day. These thoughts caused him such pain, however, that he quickly shoved them aside. Up to a few weeks ago, N'vonne had been the only person alive who was family to him, excepting Naffinar, whom he rarely saw. Now they were both gone. N'vonne, especially, would never be able to offer him guidance or comfort again. It was a gut-wrenching truth that he preferred not to think about.

Fortunately, Telenar kept the distractions coming fast and furious. If Vancien had loved books before, that love was tested under Telenar's tutorship. Every day, it seemed, he was in the study chamber, reading histories and pouring over charts of information he never knew existed. Surely, he thought, there was more to being an Advocate than reading. *A Chronicle of Kynell's Interventions* he could understand, but *Eighteen Ways To Cross the Trmak Desert*? If Telenar had his way, he would have to read every scroll in the scriptorium. Thank Kynell for Chiyo.

The general had insisted that an Advocate be skilled in warfare. Consequently, after his early studies, Vancien spent his mornings in the ring, learning to thrust, parry, duck, and dodge, both on foot and on a voyoté. Exhausted, he would then stumble in for a noon meal, then back to the scriptorium with an armload of Rolin's *Commentaries on the Rhyveladian Past: From the Planting to the Third Era*. His new instructor would often meet him with penetrating, irritatingly repetitive, questions.

Today was no different.

"Good afternoon, Vance!" he hailed as Vancien entered. Vancien's left arm was dangling limply at his side—a parting gift from Chiyo. With a grunt, he dropped into a chair. "How are you, Telenar?"

"Fine. Chiyo driving you hard, is he?"

Vancien eyed him sitting smugly across the table. The man must surely enjoy seeing him suffer. If Telenar had not been a priest, and if he didn't wear spectacles, he would have considered inviting him into the ring for some lessons in empathy. "Hard, but not unbearable. What do you have for me today?"

Telenar leaned forward, eager to test his new pupil. "We'll start easy. Give me a brief synopsis of the three eras, with dates and names."

Vancien opted for the bare minimum. After all, Telenar was not N'vonne. He deserved no special obligation. "Lost: Tryun and Grens. The first cycle. Lost: Varrin and Heptar, cycle 540. Won: Nejona and Erst, cycle 1080. Won: Vancien and Amarian, cycle 1620."

Telenar let him have his joke, then shook his head. "Overconfidence can kill. So can sarcasm. Try again."

Vance obediently began a second time, though he kept his monotone. "One cycle after Zyreio corrupted Rhyvelad, Kynell decided upon the boundaries for this new evil, which he nevertheless did not destroy. So he established a timetable, wherein the power of one would reign for ten thousand score mornings and evenings, or 540 cycles. Brothers were chosen to fight this battle, for only in fighting his brother could a man's faith truly be tested. The power of Advocacy was therefore never sought and often reluctantly accepted.

"Tryun and Grens were the first of combat. Tryun was the eldest and chose to serve Kynell. He did so faithfully, but Grens was evil from birth and Zyreio poured all of his might into him. Rhyvelad's first era was dark indeed. The darkness deepened with Varrin and Heptar, for Varrin slew Heptar the morning after Dedication. At the end of the second era, the fates of Nejona and Erst were kept secret from them. They both led quiet, uneventful lives before the Dedication, though those who knew Nejona knew he could not be trusted. He chose the path of evil for himself. The opposite was true for Erst. Their Dedications were separate, and neither brother knew his enemy until Nejona was slain in a duel he instigated. The truth was not revealed to Erst until afterwards, and despite this, he took up the reins of power well. This ushered in an era of light, which produced great monarchs, such as Ruponi, Natanya, and our own Relgaré."

"And Verial?"

"She was a captive of the first battle. Zyreio admired her beauty, so he preserved her youth and stole her freedom. It is said that she has been the unwilling mistress of every Dark Lord since." Vancien allowed himself a laugh. "Every Prysm Advocate has made it his duty to rescue her. Erst came close, but Zyreio retreated before he could succeed."

Telenar raised an eyebrow. "I take it from your manner that you have your doubts about Verial?"

"I haven't given it much thought. And if Tryun couldn't save her with his power, I don't have a chance. My focus should be Kynell, not some girl."

"You are right in that, although I wouldn't underestimate this 'girl'. Perhaps if Tryun and Heptar had focused more on the mission, they would have succeeded. So let's move on."

The young Advocate held up his hand to stop him. "Before we do, I have a question for you."

"Of course, Vance. What is it?"

But Vancien had turned nervous. He held his tongue, fingering a scroll in front of him, requiring Telenar to ask again what it was that he wanted. Only then did Vancien blurt out, "I was just reading Rolin's *Commentaries*, and he has an index of Advocacy powers." He paused for a sheepish smile. "Listen to me. I sound like I'm citing livestock accounts."

"You're also avoiding the issue. What did Rolin say?"

"He said that through all three eras, Kynell's Advocate has been given three gifts: the gift of a protected life until the battle, the gift of the Destrariae, and Grace."

The young man stopped again and Telenar had to urge him forward. "Yes?"

"Can you explain again to me what a Grace is?"

Telenar took off his spectacles and began to clean them. This was an easy question. "It is nothing short of resurrection, Vance. At the final battle, the souls who served Kynell rise up and fight with the Advocate. The same, of course, is true for Zyreio's servant. But to protect those who would help the Advocate until the Dedication, both Kynell and Zyreio have appointed their servants a Grace. If one of your comrades has fallen, he can be raised up before the battle to aid and comfort you. Obsidian's Advocates rarely use this gift. It's not often that they value their servants highly. But it's different for the Prysm, and I must tell you, Graces have been used very unwisely in the past. I believe it was Heptar who raised up his father, who then turned against him. One must be very careful with this gift. People rarely die without reason."

Vancien glared, annoyed at his instructor's brutal honesty. "And sometimes they just die."

Telenar's tone immediately softened as he recalled the Sentry encounter. "You're right, Vance. Sometimes they just die."

An awkward moment followed as Vancien considered how to voice his thoughts and Telenar considered how to change the subject. They both spoke at once.

"I want N'vonne back."

"Have you begun your next reading? Wait, what did you say?"

Vancien stiffened, ready for a fight. "I want N'vonne back."

Telenar tried hard to be understanding. "I know you miss her. But a Grace is very important. One must not be used unwisely or during intense grief. Your friends are at peace now, but I can see their memory still haunts you."

"N'vonne is the only mother I've ever had. Not only that, she is brave and wise. If I'm really going to be an Advocate, I need her help."

"No. It's too early and you don't know what will happen down the road. Once they are brought back, there is no guarantee that they will survive until the battle. I know it's hard, but we should wait."

With a scrape of his chair, Vancien rose abruptly. "You can wait. I'm bringing her back." He strode to the door before adding, "I know you think I'm being foolish, but I need your help. If I'm going to do it, I want to do it right."

"Vance—"

"Please, Telenar. Trust me on this."

Hands up in defeat, the priest rose as well. "Then follow me to the chapel. We will need to seek Kynell's wisdom."

CHAPTER SIX

Inasmuch as he was capable, Amarian loved a late breach season night. The cold winds and the bitter air seemed to vent frustrations for him. Those who offended him on a late breach season night were fortunate compared to those in autore: the howling gales slaked his thirst for vengeance and softened his bite.

This dark night, he prayed to Zyreio for a stronger storm than the one that raged inside. How could he have been so stupid? What kind of a child's trick was it to slam doors and tell lies to boys? To the Chasm with Telenar, that meddling priest. He should have executed both him and the soldier; then, at least, Vancien would be alone. Now the boy was under a Patroniite's leadership and growing stronger by the day. He sighed. All was not lost. Zyreio had warned him not to make a move before Dedication. Now that he had done so and failed, he would merely have to settle for preparation of the battle to come.

As his booted feet sounded upon the castle's entry, the Sentries snapped to attention. Ignoring them, he made his way through the narrow corridor and into the great hall. Keroul was not the only country in Rhyvelad to be a seat of power. The Eastern Lands were Obsidian's stronghold, protected on the west by the Trmak Desert and shielded in the east by the sea. They had become a refuge for Zyreio's followers, driven out of Keroul over the past five hundred cycles. As was his right, Amarian had occupied Donech, the capital city of the Eastern Lands, although in truth it was really no more than a formidable castle. The "people" of Donech were no more than the troops Amarian kept, along with their clinging families, if they had any. The Eastern Lands were not like Keroul, nor like the territory of the West. They had no major cities, no hubs of commerce. Amarian preferred it that way. In the past several cycles, he had even made it a policy to raise the taxes insufferably should any town begin to rise above its neighbors. Better to keep all Eastern settlements looking to Donech for protection and wealth. For all that, the lands themselves were quite beautiful. Except for a blustery breach season, the weather was temperate, if very windy, and the soil was so rich in minerals that cultivation was easy. It did not serve Amarian's purpose for his people to starve. He required a high level of tribute, certainly, but saw to it that his subjects were comfortable. Indeed, he desired them to be so proud of their quality of life that they saw little need for improvement. Dissatisfaction only made them less accessible to him.

Two Sentries opened the massive door, announcing his entrance. They were all there: clan chieftains, prideheads, and the five Sentry princes. Pounding their spear butts, swords, and mauls, they stood to greet him with a barbaric mix of fear and devotion. The chamber walls, burdened with dark tapestries and freakish statues, provided a haunting frame for this grisly company.

The chieftains sat at the far end of the tables, as they were the weakest and most prone to failure. Like all humans, they had a propensity toward evil and these few with their clans had followed it with abandon. Still, their skin was penetrable and their minds not always sharp. They were useful, and most importantly, expendable.

The fennel prideheads came next. Of all the three *galthis*, they alone had chosen to serve Obsidian, mostly because of their desperate need to feel rebellious. So Amarian was not surprised to see that, as they rose, they glared at him. Only half as large as a voyoté, their size was not remarkable, yet Amarian knew that little else on Rhyvelad matched their feline intelligence and agility. Theirs, too, was another gift: they could withstand the Destrariae.

At the head of the table sat his most effective servants. They also surrounded the room, standing faithfully by each door to watch for treachery. Sentries: five tribes of competent, vicious, powerful reptilian beasts all committed to serving him. The Mholi were the most numerous. Their strengths consisted simply of terrific physical stamina. The Urabi were night creatures and their ability to sink into any shadow (or make shadows sink into them) made them useful for gathering intelligence. The Aknat and Iu worked well together in battle: an Aknat could disappear for several breaths at a time while an Iu's speed dispatched the bewildered enemy. Often they patrolled in pairs, one disappearing while the other attacked, or one attacking and disappearing while the other distracted the prey. Finally came the smallest and most efficient tribe, the Neptim. It was a Neptim that Amarian had sent to capture Vancien, for he trusted their intelligence and endurance. Tsare had been one of the best. Unfortunately, the attack of the Destrariae was unexpected, although Amarian should have guessed that they would venture outside the Glade to protect an Advocate. If he had wanted to send a Sentry to die, he would have sent a Mholi.

All of the Sentries were armed with leathery skin, ridges of impenetrable scales, the infamous claws that tapped seconds before their attack and, most importantly, steadfast loyalty. Occasionally a human or a fennel would take it into his head to rebel and the Sentries could always be counted on to set them straight. As might be expected, such lessons were very painful.

He eyed them all with disdain until his gaze fell upon the woman sitting by his throne. She was beautiful, that one. Zyreio had certainly chosen well. Amarian had insisted that she wear a white gown for this evening's meeting. He enjoyed the disparity. What was life without contrast? Contrast. That was why he was here, after all.

She was watching him. Her blue eyes sparkled at his presence, he knew. Why wouldn't they? He was the first Obsidian Advocate not to force himself on her. The others were fools to make her their captive. Her hostility only made her a knife poised at their back. Besides, meddling in the flesh was not his concern right now.

By the time he ascended the dais and took his seat, the welcoming clamor had been replaced by an expectant hush. Even the humans, normally chatty, maintained their silence. None knew the specific instances of his failed ambush, but all knew that questions about the recent past were best left unasked.

"Lord," the prince of the Neptim began, rising humbly to his feet. "We are all gathered here as requested."

"Thank you, Tarl." He gestured for everyone to be seated, then leaned over to Verial. "You look radiant."

She nodded. "As you commanded, lord."

"Have the humans been troubling you?"

"No more than usual."

"I will kill any who do."

"So you've said and done."

This quiet parley was made without eye contact and none but the two heard it. The rest of the hall waited patiently while host and hostess examined the food placed before them.

"I saw my brother."

"I guessed as much, lord."

"I failed to bring him under my control."

Verial wisely kept silent as he continued. "But Corfe and an Urabi are watching them now. Ranti's not pleasant company. I wonder if Corfe will be of any use by the time they come back."

He watched for the quick blink of her eye and was not disappointed. More than 1,600 cycles of watching death's handiwork and she still occasionally felt pain for others. Amazing.

The company was trying its best not to fidget hungrily, so he made them wait a few moments more. Then with a nod, he ordered the food to be brought in. He was always careful to finish his meal before they began theirs. Watching the Sentries and fennels eat was an unpleasant experience, even for him.

When all had finished and the humans were scraping the last of their plates, Amarian rose. "Edgar!" he commanded, causing the eldest chieftain to stand. "What is your count of armed men and women?"

"Twenty-two thousand, lord. With another seventeen hundred ready by Dedication."

"That is good news. And the fennels? Where is Ssarb?" he looked down the table for the familiar gray face. Another feline had risen in his place.

"Ssarb was killed today, lord," it began, only to be cut short.

"Killed? By whom?"

Its yellow eyes narrowed as only a fennel's could. "A gryphon, lord."

Amarian grunted. Ssarb was not easily replaced. "And who are you?"

The creature nodded its head respectfully. "Koeb, Darkness. His firstborn."

"You are brave, Koeb, to tell me such news as this."

The fennel's hackles raised imperceptibly, but his tone was even. "I *am* brave, lord. You are wise to have such a servant."

Wretched felines. He would kill it for its arrogance, only the prides were growing slim, thanks to the gryphons. Every creature was needed for battle. Judgment for insolence could be given later.

"Your count, pridehead?"

"Seven hundred, Darkness. Another forty will be ready by Dedication."

"Then that leaves you, Tarl."

The Sentry's voice was raspy at any time, but compared with the silk of the fennel's, it was almost unbearable. "We have lost none since our last meeting, lord. Except one."

Amarian gritted his teeth. He did not need the reminder. "You should all know that the Prysm Advocate has joined with the priest from Lascombe. Telenar is a threat. He knows much. Corfe and Ranti are with them now. The rest of you will continue in drills and patrols. Our time to move is not upon us. We must wait in patience until then."

A few more commands, then Amarian gave control of the meeting to Tarl and left with Verial. Soon, they were in the quiet of his chamber and he could feel her trembling. Holding her by the hand, he leaned close. "I have a special assignment for you, my dear."

She did not speak.

"Go to Vancien."

Surprised, she stepped back and looked at him. Her locks shone golden in the candlelight, making the sight of her so beautiful he almost recalled his words. But dalliances would get him nowhere.

"Go to Vancien, beauty, and steal his heart. If there is anything that can distract a young man, it is you."

"You are joking, lord."

He admired her courage, but she was wasting time. "Have you ever known me to joke? You leave tonight. Edgar's son, Gair, will escort you. Once you are in Lascombe, Ranti will watch you to make sure you perform well." He began to pace as he plotted the strategy. "You will appear to Vancien as a lady-in-waiting, a seamstress, or some such lowly thing. He will, of course, instantly fall in love with you. Or lust, which would be better. But tread carefully, my dear. He will not be easily distracted from Kynell. Once his attentions are yours, you may do with him as you please. I have no doubt an innocent young fellow will provide a nice change for you."

Her face was a stone. "Of course, my lord."

"You are there as a distraction, Verial. Nothing more. I have spies enough, but I will check in on you from time to time. Any information you learn, particularly about his site of Dedication, I would be grateful to hear."

"My lord flatters me, to consider his servant so useful."

Raising her hand to his lips, he managed to catch her eye. "Tell me, Verial, do you love me or hate me?"

Her gaze was level and her answer honest. "I believe I am beyond both, lord."

"It is just as well."

N'vonne had never slept so well in her life. Now, as she awoke, she wondered how long she had been in that wonderful dream world. Or was it a dream? If it was, it was hard to let it go. But there stood Vancien, tears glistening in his eyes. Why was he crying? Had she been ill? Had something happened to Naffinar?

"Welcome back, N'vonne."

"Vance?" She sat up. "Vance, what happened? Where are your uncle and Revor? Why are you crying?"

"Shhh," he soothed, gently pushing her back down. "I will tell you everything in a moment. But first," He sat back, admiring Kynell's power. There was not a scar on her. When they had brought her body back, he had had his doubts, for several weeks of disfiguring decay had set in. Now, she was as fresh as on the first day of their journey. He would have taken complete joy in this moment, if only he didn't have to tarnish it with his tragic news.

"Did you sleep well?"

"I slept beautifully."

He nodded, undecided about how to tell her. His nervousness must have shown, for she asked, "Vancien, what happened to Naffinar and Revor? Are they all right?"

He took her hand. "They're dead, N'vonne. A Sentry attack."

"Gracious Kynell!"

"And you were dead too. But not anymore."

"I don't understand."

Vancien sighed, wondering how to best go about it. He had so much to tell, but where to start?

Telenar saved him the effort. Coming from the corner where he had been watching, he sat across the bed from his student and looked gently at the woman. With auburn hair encompassing her pillows and pale face fresh with new life, it was not a hard task.

"Lady N'vonne, we are pleased to have you with us. I am Telenar pa Saauli, Patronius en medio."

His voice was calming, as was the sleep that was beginning to reclaim her. "Telenar. I have heard your name before."

He smiled. "Naffinar may have told you about me. The old fellow knew what he was doing. Vancien has been found."

"Yes, I remember he wanted you two to meet. What do you want with Vance?"

She very much wanted an answer, but as Telenar answered, his words became indistinct and soon she lost hearing of them altogether. Breathing softly, she descended again into sleep, only this time she dreamed dreams of the living realm instead of the dead.

When she awoke the next day, Vancien was still by her side, but Telenar was nowhere to be found. She wondered if he was merely a figment of her imagination, but when she voiced her thought, Vancien only laughed.

"He can sometimes seem that way. Telenar is very hard to nail down. At the moment, I believe he's in the chapel, praying for guidance."

"Guidance for what?"

He stopped smiling and his voice took on a haunted quality she had never heard before. "It's time I tell you everything, before you fall asleep again. Are you well? Do you think you can walk?"

She nodded and he called in her attendant. Soon, instructor and student (in roles now strangely reversed) were in a garden, strolling among the redcups and blooming yarva vines, breathing in the fresh air. He told her all that had happened since she left: about the Sentry and Sirin, Lascombe and Telenar. He kept nothing back, for she must know everything. As he spoke of his Advocacy, her eyes widened, but she was not surprised.

"If an Advocate must be chosen, you are the only candidate I can see."

He flushed, stammering on to a vivid account of Amarian's appearance. Shuddering, she heard of Amarian's hollowed face and his attempt at fratricide. Shuddering, he spoke of the power of the Destrariae and how they had saved him again.

"They are a gift," he replied when she asked about their aid. "One of the three gifts of Kynell's Advocate. The second is protection from death, at least until the battle. The third has already been used." He looked meaningfully at her.

"Me? How am I a gift?"

"You are a Grace, N'vonne. Telenar says that all faithful souls will rise to help me at the great battle. But one of them may rise up before that time. I will need your help and wisdom, so I asked Kynell to call you back. And," he flushed again, looking hard at the ground. "I missed you. I wanted to show you Lascombe."

She didn't know what to say, so she stopped next to a sweet rosin tree, making a pretense at plucking its leaves. Finally, the words came, along with her tears. "Vance, you know you're like a son to me."

He, too, was fighting back tears as he wrapped his arms around her. "Don't leave me again, N'vonne. Please."

Telenar was stricken. From the moment he laid eyes upon the revived woman, he had felt it. Thus, his absence from her second awakening, their talk in the garden, and three days afterward. He had spent the time in the scriptorium, pouring over his rightful focus: the Dedication. Where would it be? How could they find it? How did she come to have gray streaks in her thirties? Had she ever loved another? Where was she now?

He shook his head angrily. To the Chasm with such thoughts! They were a ploy of Zyreio's to distract him, to be sure. At this most critical hour, his concentration must be complete. But how could someone so lovely be evil to him?

It was in this agitated state that Vancien finally found him.

"Telenar! Where have you been?"

"Shh! This is a study chamber, Vance!" was Telenar's hissed reply.

"Fine, then." Vancien lowered his voice as he approached a table covered with documents. "Where have you been?"

Telenar glared at him over his spectacles. "Studying. Searching. Praying. Like you should be doing."

Vancien was in too good of a mood to take offense. He had not felt this light-hearted since the Eyestone Glade. "Oh come now, Telenar. You know I've been looking and praying just as hard as you have. I've just found time for a little pleasure, too."

The priest's head snapped up from an old, marked-up copy of the Ages. "Pleasure? What kind?"

"The innocuous kind. The kind found in enjoying the beautiful waterfall behind the Palace. Or sitting by a fireside discussing Kynell's wonders. The kind you've been missing. Why, just today, N'vonne and I were talking about what we can see here in the city. You would be amazed."

"N'vonne! You haven't learned anything since she's been back. You even missed one of Chiyo's practices."

Bewildered and hurt, Vancien was tempted to snap back. But he forced himself to refrain. "You're not being fair. She's only been with us for five days. And Chiyo knew where I was. *He* didn't seem to mind."

Telenar finally relented, sinking his head into his heads. "I know, Vancien. I'm sorry. It's just that the time is drawing near. We still don't know where the Dedication is to be held and the Ages say nothing of how the Advocates discovered it. No two eras have been the same."

The young man leaned forward, smiling mischievously. "I have an idea: maybe Kynell will tell us."

"Now you're being simplistic."

"And you're being difficult. Where's your faith? Kynell's not going to let me miss my own Dedication. Keep praying, of course, but the Ages aren't going to tell us where to go. He will."

With resignation, the priest pushed the scrolls away. "Perhaps you're right."

"I know I am. But tell me, Telenar," Vancien's voice dropped conspiratorially. "What do you think of her?"

"Excuse me?"

"N'vonne! Isn't she marvelous?"

Suddenly preoccupied with the hem of his robe, Telenar broke eye contact. "She's great. But she's going to be a distraction."

"For whom? Me or you?"

"You! Who else? What do you think, that I—" he broke off, not himself trusting to go further. "You are young and quite naïve, Vance. She is a lovely woman, but I am a bitter old man who has a great deal of work to do."

"Then why haven't you shown your face to her?"

"*Because I have work to do.* Didn't you hear what I just said?"

Vancien nodded, dropping the issue. "Okay, Telenar. I won't argue further. Is there anything I can help you with?"

"Not at the moment." He stood to stack the scrolls and return them. After a short pause, he added, "But tell Lady N'vonne that we must all meet for supper tonight. I have some things I need to discuss with both of you."

Trying not to smile again, Vancien bowed respectfully. "I'll do that."

Supper was a simple affair, as it was supported out of Telenar's purse, rather than the king or the Patroniite Fraternity. Indeed, since his arrival, Vancien had only seen the king a few times. Relgaré had been respectful enough, but indifferent. The border wars were occupying his thoughts as always, and, although he would never admit it, he had little faith in Telenar. It was his quiet hope that soon the priest would cease presenting himself altogether. Since the boy had been found, his wish had almost come true.

Patronius Supras Ganiedor had been a little more curious, and one evening's dinner proved to hold engaging discussion on both Vancien's part and the Supras'. The Order had shown no more interest, however, nor was Vancien invited back.

Consequently, one servant served them one course each, complemented by plain bread and humble wine. Not being accustomed to finer fare, there were no complaints among the partakers.

Telenar had been the last to enter, and N'vonne and Vancien had risen to meet him. N'vonne spoke first.

"Patronius Telenar. It is a pleasure to see you again."

He bowed. "Lady N'vonne. The pleasure is mine." The words were stiff but the sentiment true. "I trust Vancien has shown you around the grounds?"

All sat as the meal was served.

"Oh yes. The Palace is marvelous indeed, Patronius. And Lascombe is," she paused, failing to find an accurate description.

"Brilliant?"

"It dazzles the eye."

Telenar began to eat. "I am afraid your guide may be lacking in experience, as he has only been in the great city a few months. Plus the cold has set in. You'll find fewer brilliant businesses open at this time of the cycle."

"Then perhaps you could show me the best ones to frequent, Patronius. I shall need more traveling attire before we get started."

The priest shook his head. "Please, just call me Telenar, Lady. And no, I'm afraid I won't be able to assist you in your shopping. There are more important matters to which I must attend."

Slightly taken aback, N'vonne tried not to sound disappointed. "Of course, Patronius. Sorry, Telenar. I'm sure Vancien will help me."

"Vancien is needed here. It would not do for a Prysm Advocate to spend time selecting riding skirts."

Vancien, who had quietly been watching this exchange, jumped to her defense. "Now see here, Telenar!"

"I'm sure one of the queen's attendants," Telenar interrupted, "will be happy to escort you, Lady."

By now, N'vonne's face was stony. "I'm sure that would be best. You are right. Vancien should not be distracted."

The rest of the supper was conducted in painfully civil tones, with Telenar questioning N'vonne about her past experiences and possible contributions, N'vonne replying with curt answers, and Vancien visibly attempting not to be furious with the priest. Only the servant seemed to be in a jovial mood, as the meal was cut short and he was allowed to go home early.

Later that evening, when the triple lunos cast a sober glow upon the palace grounds and the breach winds had picked up their howling, Telenar heard a soft tap on his office door. "Come in," he called, not bothering to look up.

N'vonne entered quietly, steeled for her mission. The hearth's fire was dying due to Telenar's inattention. Meanwhile, the candle on his desk produced little light and less warmth. She could not help but shaking a little. "Patronius," she began.

Upon seeing who it was, Telenar jumped immediately to his feet and gestured to a worn chair. "Lady N'vonne. Please come in."

His softer tone surprised her, but she did not waste any thought on it. "Patronius," she began again, only to be interrupted again.

"Telenar."

"Telenar, then. I just came to tell you that I love Vancien very much and I will do nothing to distract him from his mission. Perhaps you think that I am a shallow woman who cares only to buy clothes. I know that Vancien brought me back for a reason, yet I also know that he is young. If you, who are wiser and more studied in this holy mission, think that I should leave, I shall. And not a word to Vance."

As inappropriate as it seemed, Telenar chuckled quietly. "You must not know Vancien very well. He would go find you."

She nodded, trying not to take pride at the thought. "I know. But you could send me far away. Vancien will listen to you and stay here."

He shook his head, kicking himself for his earlier behavior. "Lady N'vonne."

"Just N'vonne. Please."

"N'vonne." As his eyes met hers, his well-intentioned resolve almost disappeared. Clearing his throat, he pressed on. "N'vonne, I have faith in Vancien's choice. He is wise beyond his cycles, as he should be. And I'm sorry about tonight." He feared that the admission would completely give him away, but he needed to say it nonetheless.

She bowed her head. "It is forgotten, Telenar. Rest well."

"Rest well." He watched her leave and then turned back to his scrolls. But there would be no more studying that evening.

CHAPTER SEVEN

Surprisingly, Gair was good company. The moment their voyoté set foot beyond the last of Donech's farm fields, he burst out in exultant laughter.

Verial was not amused. "I fail to see what is so humorous."

His eyes sparkled in a fashion most uncharacteristic of an Obsidian servant. "Nothing particular, Lady Verial. It's just that it feels so good to be out in fresh air! I've been trapped in that stuffy castle for three fortnights!" He stopped, realizing to whom he was speaking. "It must feel good indeed to get out of there after sixteen hundred cycles."

Jaded though she was, his exuberance was affecting. "Yes. I suppose it does."

"Tell me, Lady," he said, looking over his shoulder to make sure they were not being followed. "What is it like, living for so long?"

"I dare not speak of it."

His courage bordered on recklessness. "Why not? We're away from the Dark One. Powerful as he is, he can't hear you."

Foolish boy! He would get himself killed before they crossed the lower Trmak! "I think I would know the powers of the Dark One. They are greater than you think. And his Sentries hear very well."

He brought his mount closer to hers and whispered confidentially. "I don't fear him."

"Then you're an idiot," she whispered in return. "Kindly move away."

He obeyed, and they rode in silence for several moments. Though cold, it was a beautiful day. Zyreio had not managed to manipulate the weather since his last era of power. The crisp air stung her cheeks as the every-day depression to which she had become accustomed softened a little. The pale discs of the orbs were comforting. After a while, she almost began to relax.

"You are an unwise young man," she said suddenly.

Caught off-guard, Gair raised his eyebrows. "And why is that, Lady?"

"How is it that you do not fear the Dark One?"

His smile, which was quickly becoming characteristic, vanished as he eyed her. "I fear I spoke foolishly before, Lady Verial. Forgive me if I offended you, or your lord."

So that was it. The enthusiasm of earlier had settled into a cautious mistrust. And why should he trust her? She was the mistress of Zyreio's servant, exposed to every type of evil. Surely she had absorbed some of it through the cycles.

"Your excitement has cooled. Perhaps you have thought it wiser to hold your tongue."

"A good adventure always makes my words come quickly and perhaps, as you said, unwisely."

She almost regretted that part of him was retreating from her cold gaze. But did she dare speak freely? Or even kindly? It would be turned as a weapon against her. Amarian would hear of her affection for his servant and the boy would suffer for it.

"He is very powerful, child. Do not underestimate him."

"I will not, Lady. I promise."

His tone, subdued though it was, gave her hope. And this caught her by surprise, since hope had been an alien element for thousands of cycles. She sighed. Had it been so long? When Zyreio had first enticed her, she had been only fifteen cycles. Serving as a scullery maid in a minor lord's kitchen, she had jumped at the opportunity of playing such an exciting role in the epic battle. The day Grens had come to her was a memory that would never leave, and never did she recall it without a shudder. It was a spring day and she had felt particularly alive. There was a hillock not far from her small hut, where the trees blossomed with azure petals and the path wound round to a small, peaceful pool. It was there that she had directed her steps to dangle tanned and hardened feet in the cool waters. At that time, she had had long, full, brown hair, always pulled back in a cute, practical ponytail. Life had been difficult, but not enough to steal her carefree manner. She giggled to herself, picturing the several boys in town that had their eyes set upon her. All were rude and unworthy, of course. But she enjoyed their attentions. Especially Marta's sober green eyes. He was only a tanner's son, though, and she knew somehow that she was intended for a prince. So she sat, aware of the burgeoning nature at her fingertips, but dangerously ignorant of everything else.

He had approached her quietly, boots silent upon the moss. She felt him before she saw him. And when he spoke her name, she didn't start or run. It was as if her heart had beat fifteen cycles for this moment only.

"Little Verial," he said, resting a hand on her shoulder.

She swallowed, forcing herself to look at him. He was handsome, but that was not what drew her. If he had been wearing a butcher's apron, he still would have exuded an extraordinary, magnetic confidence. Dressed as he was in Zyreio's sable uniform, the young girl had had no defense.

If Verial had known how much she yielded to him that day, she might have resisted. Even now, though, she doubted if she would have succeeded. Of everything else that happened during that first encounter, one painful, completely unnecessary memory stood out to her: she remembered Grens pulling her gently to her feet and running his fingers through her hair.

"I've always loved blondes," he whispered.

She had followed his eyes, glancing down at the strand of hair he held between his fingers. With a cry, she realized that it was blond. All of her thick, warm locks had turned to silvery blond. Only then did it begin to dawn on her that she had made a terrible mistake. He must have known what was going through her mind, for he had comforted her, even made a pretense of watching out for her. But in the end he had forced her away from her parents, from her village, even from poor Marta. And he had changed her in ways much more horrible than the color of her hair.

These and other sober thoughts carried her through the rest of the day.

The next time Gair spoke to her was when they broke for camp.

"We'll be safe here, Lady. I am armed and the Sentries have circled us by now."

The question was out of her mouth before she could stop it. "Do the Sentries make you feel safe, young man?"

His surprised look contained a hint of warning. Earlier words regretted or forgotten, Gair was now highly concerned that they should be reported. "The Sentries are my lord's mightiest servants, lady. Nothing," his eyes gave the word emphasis, "can escape them."

There their conversation should have ended, for the Sentries could hear every word not whispered, and whispering would look suspicious indeed. But she could not help herself. Only a handful of times had she been away from the presence of darkness. During his lifetime, she was at Obsidian's side constantly, while all cycles between an era's completion, Zyreio submerged her into a troubled sleep. To be out under the night sky, with a figure of pleasant company by her side, was an experience to be explored, if not embraced. She wondered what tribe of Sentry her lord had sent and if they could be manipulated.

"Tell me, boy, have the Neptim all been sent for the battle's preparation?" She tried to keep her voice calm, but the path on which she was treading was unfamiliar. Never had she thought to deal other than obediently with her lord. Four lives she had led and she valued every one of them. Except this one. Something in the air or the company incited her to take a chance tonight, though she had no idea what she was hoping to accomplish.

Gair was disconcerted by her sudden insistence on conversation. "All but a few, Lady." Then he began to grasp what she was saying. "I believe we are accompanied by a Neptim and two Urabi. They should be very useful on our journey."

"You're right. But I wonder that they are still here. My lord would be most offended if they neglected their mission."

The cold shiver down her spine informed her that the Sentries were falling for the ruse. Two shadows flanked one grotesque figure as they stood just beyond the firelight.

"Lady Verial," the Neptim rasped as he bowed. "There is something you should tell us?"

She trembled as she spoke the words. "Darkness has provided me with further directions for you."

It was a unique sight to see a Sentry puzzled. "Lady?"

"Your assignment is to protect my person and my mission. But how can you do such a thing if you don't know what lies ahead?"

"But our lord has scouts."

"Our lord puts little faith in the fennels." Good, she thought. Stroke their vanity. "In order to preserve unity, he did not inform you of this in front of them. And so I am telling you now. You are required to scout ahead at least five leagues. Do not return until daybreak."

The Neptim shook his head. "Darkness would never leave his lady unprotected."

She allowed herself a trace of indignation. "Darkness knows whom he serves. And the one he serves offers me more protection than a battalion of you."

The Sentry looked at his companions, weighing her words. If she was incorrect—the thought of deception from the lord's mistress never crossed his mind—and they left, harm might come to her, and then a painful death would await them. Yet if these orders were truly from the Darkness, they risked their lives with disobedience.

Verial held her breath, waiting for them to question her further.

The Neptim faced her again. "Perhaps if one of us stayed."

"That would be one direction unchecked. Perhaps you doubt me."

The accusation hit its mark and all three bowed in submission. "As you wish and our lord desires, Lady Verial." Without another word, they vanished into the blackness to begin their search.

She turned to an astounded Gair. After a breath to assure they were far enough away, she spoke again. "We are free to converse."

"You are certain they will obey?"

Four lifetimes of experience served as her assurance. "I am certain."

But Gair still thought himself on shaky ground. "Lady Verial, I don't know what to say."

"I cannot promise I'll be pleasant," she interrupted archly. "But I desire to speak with you. And if you don't answer honestly, I will know it."

"It seems I have no choice."

"You do not."

With a sudden smile, he sat down next to the fire, relieved of the duty he was commanded to disobey. "Then ask, Lady Verial. I will answer as I can."

She sat less confidently, unsure how to proceed now that she had her opportunity. "I have not spoken freely for many cycles. But we don't have much time. You asked me earlier what it was like to live as I do."

"Yes, Lady. I did."

She traced a finger in the dirt, pondering the question. "There is a home for those who fail Zyreio. It is called the Chasm. Everyone has heard of it. All know that its inhabitants suffer endless torment for their disobedience or ignorance. Old wounds are opened, new wounds are made, and sleep is forbidden. They are never allowed to forget past indulgences, past mistakes." She stopped, not wanting to sound melodramatic, but wanting to speak the truth in this rare interval. "That is what my life is like, except that I can sleep. But that is no rest. When I dream, I dream of the Chasm."

Gair whistled softly. "I am sorry, Lady. I did not know."

"How could you?"

He hesitated to speak further, but her questioning gaze reassured him. "Can you tell me how it is that you are in this position?"

She broke eye contact again. "I made a decision when I was young. And I did not regret it quickly enough."

"Have you never thought of escape?"

"And have his henchmen find me? And then a living death in the Chasm? No. At least here I have the chance of a little warmth, occasionally found in the kindness of others. More often in the simple glow of the fire."

He bowed his head, not knowing how to respond.

She changed topics. "But what of you, young Gair? How is it that you are so foolhardy?"

He shrugged, but his smile was back. "I have a little hope."

"Hope for what? Advancement in the service of our lord? A word from me, and you may have it."

He shook his head. "No, my lady. No hope in that, although Father would like to see me do so. But my mother was not like my father. She taught me the ways of—" he stopped, fearful of saying too much.

"Go on. I can incriminate you with or without your words. You might as well speak."

"My mother was a follower of Kynell."

She started to hear the name. Visions of rescue attempts flashed before her: smiling but dying heroes whose love was completely ineffective.

"As am I," he finished, watching her carefully.

She knew he was nervous, but she could think of nothing to say. All she had known of Kynell were misdirected efforts and unfulfilled hopes. Tryun had tried to win her for the Prysm, but she had not wanted to be won. Even when Heptar, with his innocence, battled his way to her side, Varrin had been too strong for him. His violent fate had proved that he was no match for Obsidian. She heard once that Erst had tried to find her, but by then Zyreio's sleep had descended, and she was lost to him. Why would someone choose to serve a god of such little power? If Kynell had been strong enough and had wanted her that much, surely she would not be with Amarian now. But she could not bring herself to shoot down this young man's faith. Indeed, she would rather be sent to the Chasm than bring an end to his smile.

"Are you a spy, then, in my lord's service?" she asked teasingly.

He was beyond retreat now. "I suppose I am. And only Kynell knows why I'm telling you all of this. You hold my life in your hands."

Her heart leapt with this strange power. Before her was a spy of Kynell who was trusting her completely. Here sat a knife aimed at Amarian's heart. Could this young man be a thorn in his side? She wondered at the thought of giving the Advocate pain. Was it even possible? The idea fascinated her.

Gair was eying her closely, so she hastened to reassure him. "You were wise to bring me into your confidence, Gair. I will not betray you."

His grin spoke volumes. "I knew you would not, Lady Verial. But come on, we should get some sleep before the Sentries return. It wouldn't do for them to suspect us of chatting."

Breach season finished with a frustrated barrage of snow and ice: a suitable prelude to the harsh realities of a northern Rhyveladian hiverra. In Lascombe, Vancien studied with even greater diligence, while Chiyo's lessons were confined to strategy and armaments. The battle to come could take place on a random footpath, with two combatants only, or on the great plains to the West, with thousands of men and other creatures. Vancien must be prepared for either event and hundreds besides. Telenar continued to supplicate Kynell for a revelatory disclosure of the Dedication site, all the while studiously avoiding N'vonne, speaking to her kindly, but only when necessary, and berating himself for his ill-timed interest. N'vonne received these odd or absent attentions with grace and attempted to make herself as useful as possible. Vancien, at least, greatly enjoyed her company, so she satisfied herself with reminding him of more basic lessons on the mundane and natural world of Rhyvelad. These, she assured herself, would be helpful in the coming days.

Amarian prepared for war. His legions were strong, faithful, and growing every day. Discontent was inevitable at the end of a Prysm era. Evil, so long pushed into the corners of society, demanded a more prominent place, feeding its subjects with hopes of power, pleasure, and revenge. Dissolute men and bloodthirsty creatures flocked to the Obsidian banner, causing the very sky above Amarian's stronghold to be stained with the campfires of the degenerate.

Above, beside, beneath, and throughout were Kynell and Zyreio, by whose power these movements were executed. They watched with occasional pleasure, occasional pain, and constant interest. Both knew the taste of conflict. They had experienced it without ceasing since the planting of Zyreio's tongue. Neither did they shrink from the climax that approached, for their confidence in their Advocates was complete.

CHAPTER EIGHT

Another snow-laden day. When it was not blocking the roads to make them impassible, it was melting, making everything a dreadful mess. The officers in charge of transportation and pathways shook their fists at the gray sky, but to Vancien it was enticingly beautiful. The hiverran paths seemed to summon him out beyond the palace grounds, beyond Lascombe itself, and into the magnificent Duvarian Range.

Several fortnights had passed when he decided to embark on his adventure. Not surprisingly, Telenar did not approve.

"You're insane. You can't go into the mountains in the middle of hiverra by yourself!"

"But I wouldn't be alone! You and N'vonne are welcome to come."

The priest shook his head, annoyed at the boy's carelessness. His office was stacked high with scrolls and letters in preparation for the Dedication. Each ceremony in the past had been different, so there was little information to rely upon, but the searching gave Telenar satisfaction. He would be prepared for everything within his power. He believed this approach to be the practical side of faith. Vancien agreed, but the palace was stuffier than ever, especially since he was confined by the snow and Relgaré's orders to stay out of sight. Even Chiyo was off on an expedition to the Marches. The young man felt that if he studied another folio of the Ages, he would go mad.

"Telenar, I've got to get away. I haven't been outside for any length of time since Chiyo left. The snow's not expected to fall for another week and it's surprisingly warm outside. A three-day expedition. Tops."

"No." Telenar said, then changed the subject. "Did you know the king has denied us an army?"

Vancien nodded. From Relgaré's treatment of him, he was not surprised. "I figured as much. He's got it in for me, doesn't he?"

Telenar did not look up as he perused the responses of the various sub-kingdoms. Chiyo's homeland would help, but their forces were few and highly specialized, plus they wanted to meet Vancien first. The provinces north of Keroul were too caught up in their own petty arguments to help and their men were weakened by two decades of battle. He had even (Relgaré would have his head if he knew this) dispatched a secret envoy to the Cylini, since this was a struggle beyond territorial disputes. A response had not come, but he was expecting it soon. It was a few moments before he replied to the question.

"He doesn't have it in for you, my boy. He just doesn't believe you. He's bought in to the figurative cycle theory, so he thinks he has more time than we're giving him. To the king, you're just a young man living off the palace's expenses and getting a free education."

"But hasn't he been watching Amarian? A giant army lurking past the Trmak Desert would be cause for alarm, I should think. Doesn't he—"

A knock at the door prevented him from completing his question. At Telenar's abrupt command, a servant stepped in and handed him a small, sealed piece of parchment. "For you, Patronius."

Telenar took the letter, thanked the man, and sent him away. As soon as they were alone again, he cautiously broke the seal and surveyed the contents.

"What is it?" Vancien demanded as Telenar's face fell.

"It's from Chiyo. It seems our king is well aware of the existence of Obsidian's army. Indeed, he's funding it."

"What?" Vancien took the letter and scanned its incredible contents. At Telenar's urging, he read it aloud. "Greetings to you, Telenar, from the Cylini front. I am afraid I cannot send you any news that would bring you joy. The army the king has prepared to face the Cylini is not what I expected. I know you have no interest in border wars, but I believe you should know this: there are two companies of Sentries here, one brigade of fennels, and many more men who have not been trained under Relgaré's banner. That these are mercenaries from Amarian's camp, I have no doubt. The king, I have recently been informed, has signed an agreement with Obsidian's general, who calls himself Hull in a half-hearted attempt to disguise his identity. Should we have victory, Amarian's reward for this aid is control of Keroulian forces for himself, and land and freedom for the troops (many of whom have been convicted of multiple crimes). I risk my life in telling you this. As a friend, I warn you to be careful. Escape. The jaws are closing more quickly than you think."

The two stood in silence, Vancien in shock as the news sank in and Telenar in wonder at the foolish monarch.

"We've been betrayed," Vancien finally said.

Telenar shook his head as he retrieved the letter from his pupil's limp hand. "He was never with us. The king thinks of nothing but the Cylini."

"But what did he mean by escape? Surely the king wouldn't arrest us."

"He could do the equivalent: send you to the front and send me in the opposite direction. Then Zyreio would have you right where he wants you. When the time comes, Amarian could accuse you of treason, and this great, climactic battle would be nothing more than a public execution. Your fight could be over before it begins."

"What about Chiyo?"

Telenar rolled his shoulders. It suddenly felt as if the weight of the world were pressing down upon him. "General Chiyo has taken an oath to serve the king and he does not take that lightly. Perhaps he would step in, but more than likely, Amarian would make sure he was out of the way. This," he held up the letter, "is all the help he can give." He threw it into the fire. "Go get N'vonne. Perhaps we'll take a vacation into the mountains after all."

N'vonne was relieved to get out of the palace, but she was less certain about spending that much time with Telenar. When Vancien came to her with the news of their journey, her reaction was mixed.

"The mountains, Vance? But the Pass cannot be traveled at this time of the cycle."

"We won't be taking the Pass, N'vonne. Telenar has heard of another way."

"Has heard? He's never been?"

Vancien shook his head. "We can't go east. Amarian's army is beyond the desert. West, we go right into Relgaré's men. Nobody would follow us into the mountains."

"That's because there wouldn't be anything left to find."

She was being uncharacteristically petulant and Vancien knew why. Telenar had been, as usual, surly to her and he suspected she didn't cherish the idea of his constant company. But now was not the time for petulance. If they didn't move quickly, Amarian would set another trap to frustrate Kynell's purposes, a thought the growing Advocate within him could not abide.

"Pack your things please. We're leaving tomorrow morning."

His tone was chastising and she received the message. "I'll be ready, of course. Who else will be going?"

"As few as possible. Only us three."

They departed before dawn, in the frigid early hours of a day that promised no warmth. So cold was the air that Vancien clutched his chest, reminded forcefully of his personal tormentors, the Destrariae.

Telenar was speaking quietly with the stable's head groom, trying to persuade the leathery man to part with three of his best steeds. So far, little progress had been made.

"No deal, priest. The money you offer wouldn't buy a dying nag. And you want three of my best?'"

Telenar shook his head, frustrated. "I wouldn't ask this of you if it were not important. You know the work I've been doing, Trun. If this young man is harmed, it could be the fate of Rhyvelad."

Trun grunted, unimpressed. "Where'd you say you were going?"

"I didn't. The less you know, the better."

"Then I can't help you. These steeds're destined for the front. The king would have my head, an' my job besides."

"There's nothing I can do to convince you to part with them?"

"Nope." The man turned away, but not before hesitating a little.

"What? What is it?"

"Well," He kicked at the snow before he continued. "Word has it that you and General Chiyo are good friends."

The priest held his breath. Implication of Chiyo in this matter was out of the question. "Go on."

"For several cycles now, he's been buying my steeds and then getting 'em killed in battle. Now he's paid me for every one, but it just tears at my heart to see him take those fine voyoté and spear 'em on some Cylini's blade. If you could put in a word for me, askin' him to take better care of my stock, then I might be able to see my way to loaning you three fine beasts."

The ease of his request was deceptive. Relieved but wary, Telenar agreed. "I will put in a word for you, certainly. Now then, may we have the animals?"

"'Course. Right this way."

They followed him through the warm stables, grateful for the reprieve from the cold. Around them, voyoté of all shapes and sizes greeted them with the hoarse coughing sound that was their trademark. They were all fine examples of Keroulian breeding, but Trun paid them no attention as he trudged to the king's end, where the mightiest of the voyoté were housed.

"You got a couple of choices 'ere," he began in the manner of a condescending teacher. "Here's Kate. She's a fighter, an' she always wins. Best for tearing out Cylini throat. Nagab over there will take you to the Plains of Jasimor and back without a night's sleep. He's a bit off in a fight, but he does the trick. Then the twins, Cetla and Lansing. They watch each other's back and are as loyal as they come. Cetla here took a blow for her brother that knocked her down for three fortnights. But she's on the rebound and Lansing hasn't left her side. There're a couple more, but these are the best."

Telenar eyed them all carefully. A lifetime in the service of the king and the friendship of Chiyo had served him well. It only took a glance for him to see that these were indeed fine animals. Another glance told him which ones he wanted.

"We'll take Nagab, Cetla, and Lansing. We're not looking for a fight, so we'll leave Kate to the army. Saddle them up, please, Trun, and we'll meet you out front."

"Right. And I'll expect payment with interest when you return."

Telenar did not protest. He should have known not to trust the wily groom. Still, he and Vancien were hoping to return in triumph. If they did not, a debt to the stable would be the least of their concerns. He waved for Vancien and N'vonne to follow him outside. As they waited, stamping their feet, he issued his few orders.

"I'll take Lansing and N'vonne will ride Cetla. Vance, that leaves you Nagab. I don't know how far we'll be going, and if Kynell desires you to separate from us, then you don't need one of the twins. Each voyoté gets a fair share of the provisions but Nagab will carry the Ages as well. If anyone needs them, it will be Vance. Today, we're going east of the Pass. There's an old camp about halfway up. Barring any difficulties, we can make it there by orbset."

Any further words were forestalled by the approach of Trun and their steeds.

"All right then, priest," he announced, handing over all three pair of reins to Telenar. "Take good care of 'em."

"I will do my best."

"An' don't forget about General Chiyo. I'd like to see 'im come back on the same animal he left with."

"I promise to tell him next time I speak with him."

Trun nodded and stepped back. "I suppose that'll do."

They mounted and set off for the nearest gate. A few eyes gazed at them with curiosity as they passed, but most were fixed on finishing their pre-dawn chores and getting back to warm houses. For a moment, Vancien envied them. For him, all that lay ahead was cold night after cold night. Yet this was what he wanted, he curtly reminded himself. Just yesterday he had had a warm bed and cooked meals and was not content. Today, faced with a cold, dreary ride toward an unknown destination, he felt more at peace than he had since the attack at the Glade. At least now he was doing something for Kynell more than just reading and play-fighting.

The jingling of the harnesses made little more sound than the padded step of the voyoté as they crept through the morning. The entire world seemed to slumber around them and N'vonne was certain that the pounding of her heart was the only disturbance to be heard. An unusual sense of alarm had gripped her. What if, during the course of this journey, Vancien were to leave her? Even after several fortnights of civility with Telenar, she did not trust him. Indeed, she barely even knew him. If Vance were to be called away, she would be out in the wilderness, alone, with a man who despised her. The possibility of such a situation made her long for Hull, whose image had begun to arise more and more frequently before her. What would he be like on such an adventure? How graceful and easy he would sit atop Lansing, which would be a stark contrast to the upright but sullen figure of the priest. His arms, she knew, would encircle her protectively against any danger and his dark eyes would look on her in love, not the scorn she imagined of Telenar. Her body and soul instinctively sought the warm days of his friendship, and when a sudden burst of cold air sent a shiver through all of them, it struck her particularly hard. Under her bulky hood, she struggled against tears.

A day of hard riding brought them to the foot of the great mountain chain, but Telenar had underestimated the effect of the weather on their mounts. The cold slowed them all down as the voyoté had to plow through high snow drifts and pick over rocky paths made slick with ice. As night drew near, Telenar realized that his proposed camp was still a morning's ride off. But to continue up the mountainside after orbset would be fatal. Camp had to be made, whether he liked it or not. He and Vancien chose a location under a protruding ledge, which obligingly protected the ground underneath it from most of the snow. Circling the voyoté around them to conserve most of the heat, they started a small fire with a bundle of wood brought from Lascombe. A warm meal would be had tonight, but there was no telling what tomorrow would bring.

"This wood will last only a few days," Vancien sighed as he eyed their stock.

"I know," Telenar replied. He was weary after the day's ride and frustrated with himself for not gauging their progress correctly. "But we couldn't bring a forest with us, could we? The voyoté can only handle so much."

Vancien looked at the beasts, just beyond the fire's glow. He knew their habits, and knew also that soon one would disappear for the hunt, leaving the other two to guard the camp. They would thus take turns until each was fed, though what they would find out in the snow to eat was anyone's guess. He wished them all success. He was grateful to them already for fighting the hiverran winds with heavy loads and tired riders weighing them down. Kynell had been kind, despite the mounts' inability to carry several bundles of wood.

"Come on, Vance," Telenar's voice cut through the wind. "Why don't you lead us in a prayer of thanks before we eat? Then we need to catch some sleep. It's been a long day, and tomorrow might be longer."

Vancien nodded and slid one hand through each of his companions'. Telenar and N'vonne, without looking at each other, cautiously joined hands as well and bowed their heads. Then the three knelt on the cold ground as the Advocate began.

"Lord Kynell, mightiest of all above and below. We kneel here in gratitude for your kindness, awe of your power, and supplication for your favor. Help us in this mission, throughout which you are our Champion, and through which we endeavor to serve you May we do so in love. Thy cause alone."

"Thy cause alone," they repeated as they raised their heads.

"Now, then," Telenar resumed, jumping to his feet with renewed vigor. He loved to hear the prayers of the Advocate. Although Kynell listened to all, he always felt especially blessed when Vancien called upon the Prysm. Partly as a result of this fervor, and partly because the day's journey had weakened his defenses, he turned to N'vonne.

"Lady, would you mind taking the first turn preparing dinner? Vancien has told me you are a good cook, but I would like to see what you can do with hard bread, cold cheese, and meat sticks."

Startled at his playful tone, N'vonne smiled involuntarily. "Of course, Telenar. I will do my best."

Vancien grinned as well, grateful for Telenar's banter. Nothing would please him more than to see these two closest of his friends enjoy each other's company. "I'd be careful, N'vonne. If we like what you do, we might make you cook every night."

"But if you cook as well as you eat, then it would be a disservice to Telenar if I deprived you of the chance."

While Vancien tried to look hurt, Telenar chuckled at her wit. "Be careful, Vance. You're in her line of fire."

Much to her surprise and chagrin, N'vonne felt herself blush at the comment. Quickly, she turned her head and started rummaging for their dinner. But the damage was already done. In the blink of an eye, frustration gave way to fascination, resentment started to fade, and a second image, though dim, began to take shape beside that of Hull.

The next day was as bitter as the day before, but a night's companionship and rest had renewed their spirits. The climb began as soon as they broke camp, with Telenar following Larsing on foot, N'vonne doing the same with Cetla in the middle, and Vancien bringing up the rear. The path to Telenar's base was almost completely covered, so that Telenar prayed with every step that he would not lead them all onto the deceptive sheetrock, and thus to their ends (at least for himself and N'vonne). The voyoté were more than able to carry them and would be more wary of natural traps, but the way was often so vertical that riding any beast proved impossible. Every creature, two legged or four, had to find the footing for himself.

Communication between the three was confined to signaled directions and shouted questions: the wind tore away everything else. Heads tucked into their hoods and frozen hands clutching the tails of the voyoté before them, they struggled and scrambled forward until they reached the relative quiet of Telenar's camp. The small cave was warm enough with all three voyoté crowded inside. Exhausted, they collapsed in a deep slumber from which they would not awaken until the night's fall prevented further progress.

The three sleepers could not have known they were being followed. The snow erased their footsteps as soon as they made them. For Corfe, it was a frustrating continuation of his task at Lascombe. Seeing without being seen. Not a simple undertaking in any situation, but nearly impossible in a mountain snowstorm. The company of the Urabi Sentry made it doubly unpleasant, though Ranti was very effective.

"They have camped for the night," the creature hissed, sliding into their small shelter.

Corfe nodded, choking down the revulsion he always felt at Ranti's presence. With a sigh, he prepared to sleep, knowing the Sentry would watch them through the lunos hours. In the morning, he would disappear, presumably to rest, although Corfe doubted the creature needed any such human luxury. Then he would take up the watch himself. He occasionally wondered what Amarian would do if his mute servant were lost, deciding every time that Darkness would find someone else just as, if not more, useful, without bothering to discover his fate. It was an unpleasant job any way one looked at it, but the perks were undeniable: unlimited funds and the promise of unparalleled power were two temptations Corfe could not resist. He had an especially covetous eye toward the lord's mistress. It was obvious Amarian cared nothing for the Lady Verial and did not even bother to benefit from her. . .attributes. He crossed his arms over his chest. If the Dark One could not find a use for her, maybe his servant could. These thoughts and other unmentionables warmed him through the freezing night and on into the next morning, when his struggle of surveillance began again.

CHAPTER NINE

Thousands upon thousands of humans, all armed to the teeth, mounted on the fiercest of voyoté, and wearing Keroulian blue. Amarian smiled at the sight. Things were going well. Good King Relgaré had been more than willing to form an alliance. Anything to stave off those dreadful Cylini. Amarian almost laughed out loud. Dreadful Cylini. Nothing more than a ragtag group of swamp dwellers who presented the king with a useful distraction. All of Keroul's resources were being wasted on insignificant border wars. Nothing could please Amarian more.

He allowed himself a few more laughs these days. Obsidian's Advocate though he was, he still enjoyed the bright orblight of the lands west of Lascombe. It had been a tedious journey leading his forces over the Trmak desert, across the southern end of the Kingdom of Ulan, and through the farm fields of eastern Keroul. The journey, already long, was made longer still by the fact that he had to send emissaries ahead to the Ulanese royalty, assuring them that he was only passing through on Keroulian business and meant them no harm. The Ulanese had a difficult time believing his tale, given the past hostilities between their kingdom and the Eastern lands. In the end, it took a special dispatch from Relgaré to sort things out. The city of Lascombe had at least been forewarned of his coming, though even then he took the long way around, stringing his forces north of the city, through the trees, so as not to alarm the good people of Keroul.

Travel went more smoothly after he joined up with the king. Together, they had passed out of Keroul and into the barren no-man's land that divided Keroul's eastern border from the northern cities of the Mein peoples, more commonly referred to as the people of the West. The scenery was broad and desolate: wet but not fertile, flat but not smooth. Still, thanks to recent activity, it was now in the hands of King Relgaré. The Cylini had been driven out of their northern expansion, forced back across the mighty River Preshin into their cramped little swamp.

As Amarian rode out for inspection, the troops fell to ranks in front of him. Humans. Sentries. Fennels. All under one puppet banner, all under Obsidian. His thoughts turned toward the future as he passed the lines. When young Vancien rides out from his Dedication, Amarian told himself, he will look for an army and none will be found. There will be only the risen souls of Kynell to help him and those, Amarian was certain, would be no match for his own undead. He could already feel their fury kindled against the detested Prysm, the power responsible for their imprisonment. The Chasm was a harbor from which they could watch their enemies flounce their righteousness. But soon, the Chasm would open its gates, the vengeance and hatred of ten thousand score mornings and evenings would spill out, and all of Rhyvelad would be stained with its wrath.

"Good morning, Commander Hull!" hailed Relgaré as Amarian approached him. The king was in a fine military mood. The battle yesterday had given him control of Taggershack's Loop, an important tradeway as well as a strategic fortress. All that was left was a bit of cleaning up on the northern end, then the army could proceed south into the marsh in one final, destructive sweep. The king had every reason to be content.

"Good morning, Sire." Amarian nodded respectfully, but his insistence on staying mounted placed them on even ground. Relgaré noticed this obstinacy, though he did not remark on it. If the sullen commander wanted to have his quirks, he did not mind. He had just inherited an entire army.

"How are the Sentries doing? Have they recovered from their losses?"

"All three of them, yes. The Sentries are quite accustomed to battle, you'll find. The loss of so many is exceptional. But the Cylini were numerous, as Your Majesty surely remembers."

"Hm, yes. It's hard not to. But our men were brave, eh?" Relgaré treated him to a comradely slap on the back, which Amarian took with a frosty smile.

"Yes, Sire. Very brave. The combination of our forces is mighty indeed."

They were just finishing this gratuitous conversation when another rider joined them. Relgaré greeted him openly.

"Ah, General Chiyo. We were just talking about our fine achievement yesterday."

"And with reason, Your Majesty," Chiyo responded with forced enthusiasm. "It was certainly a memorable event." Yesterday was a massacre, he knew. The Cylini were no match for the combined might of the Keroulian forces, Sentries, and fennels. The first charge had scattered their ranks, and the second was nothing but a blood fest. He was sure the tribes had regrouped, but was just as certain that they would cause no trouble until the confrontations in the south. There would be a small period of peace, but at a great price.

Amarian did not fail to notice the general's coolness, nor had he forgotten his brief encounter with the man in Lascombe. "You seem less than elated over yesterday's victory, General Chiyo. Tell me, why is that?"

Chiyo's response was logical and formulaic, a strategy he had learned quickly after the arrival of Obsidian. Any disdain or antagonism would be quickly recognized and he did not want to provoke a confrontation yet. He still had some services to render, so he would aid Kynell by just staying alive for the moment.

"The policy of Keroul is always victory without bloodshed, if it is possible, Commander. Sadly, in this instance it was not. It is still allowable in the Ages, Second Folio, line three hundred and forty seven, that a general can grieve within reason for any loss of life, even that of his enemy."

Gutsy, quoting the Ages to Obsidian's Advocate. But this was a non-controversial piece of evidence and Relgaré would stand by him on it.

The king was watching with amusement. "He's right, Commander. If General Chiyo is a little soft of heart, he is still a fine soldier. Let him have his grief."

Amarian nodded. "Of course, Sire. Perhaps we should proclaim a day of mourning for the lost Cylini."

Relgaré laughed, taking the Amarian's comment as barbed sarcasm and enjoying it. "Indeed, Commander, indeed! But I think I'd rather feast than fast! I'm sure the Cylini won't mind that. Chiyo, stop this sober nonsense and call all the generals. I want a meeting in my tent by noon."

Chiyo saluted, grateful to be sent away from Amarian's presence. "Of course, my liege. We will be there." With a nod to both men and a smart turn, he rode off to fulfill his orders. As he left, he muttered a quiet prayer for patience.

Amarian did not hear his supplication, but he suspected it nevertheless. That one, he had long since decided, would be a problem.

"General Chiyo is a faithful soldier, I can tell," he commented casually.

Relgaré agreed. "He is my best. Chiyo's service is more distinguished than any other man's under my banner."

"Have you ever had any trouble with him?"

The king was not so taken in by the Commander's aid as to not be suspicious of his words. "Just what are you implying?"

Affecting surprise at Relgaré's tone, Amarian shook his head. "Nothing, Sire. I want only to be more informed about my fellow commanders. These days, a completely faithful man without ambitions of his own is a rarity. But it is obvious that General Chiyo is an exception, or else you would not place so much confidence in him. Forgive me if I have offended you."

Relgaré was not appeased by his fluid words. "You've offended one of my own, so you offend me. I trust that this will not be common practice between your men and mine?"

Amarian had to fight to keep his calm and appear subservient. With a respectful bow, he apologized. Relgaré accepted it gruffly, riding away without another word. The distasteful conversation soon disappeared from his mind as he prepared for the move south, but the shadow of misgiving remained.

Verial despised hiverra and it was becoming obvious that it despised her. She and Gair were well into Keroulian lands by now, and the reports of the Sentries had directed them toward the Duvarian Range instead of Lascombe. When she heard the news, she was incredulous. How did Amarian expect her to play the seductress in a blizzard? Their journey had already taken them through the southern leg of the Trmak desert and now were camped in the woodlands south of the Eyestone Glade. If it wasn't for the hiverran weather, the remaining portion of the trip would have been easy going. As it was, every day was a battle against cold and ice. And now they had nothing to look forward to at the end of their journey but more cold and ice. What beautiful symbolism for her life, Verial commented inwardly. Hiverra upon hiverra, as far as the mind could see.

Gair was breaking camp. A few more days and they would be at the Range. Then he would probably leave her. She would miss his company. The Sentries had taken their bait of night scouting so seriously that they now had every evening to talk as they willed. She was truly amazed by his optimism and energy. It seemed that the further away they journeyed from the fortress of Donech, the more he was inclined to share about his love of Kynell, as well as his affection for home and family (including his father, who was fully involved in Amarian's service). He even discussed how he hoped to fall in love one day with some village girl. These were all amusing topics for Verial and all were just as far beyond her scope of understanding. Lust, maybe. Curiosity, often. But love? She did not care to know it.

It was their last evening before entering the Duvarian foothills when Amarian met them. Riding in quietly, he dismissed the Sentries (fortunately for Verial, they had not disappeared for the night) and ordered Gair to make his camp somewhere else. Gair hesitated, unwilling to leave the lady alone with such a beast, but he was given no choice.

"What, young man? You do not trust the lady with her master?" Amarian snapped, sensing his reluctance.

Gair quickly recovered. "No, lord. It is not that. I just wondered if I could be of further service to you before I left."

"You may not. Now go."

Gair saluted and departed. Kynell would have to protect his lady, for he could not.

Verial was not surprised at Amarian's arrival, only curious that he took so long. "My lord, welcome to our camp. Have you dined?"

He let out a bark of laughter. "Have I dined? That's a strange question from a lady who has gone so long without seeing her master. But perhaps," he paused, so she could get the full impact of his meaning, "I'll dine later on tonight."

The words were not lost upon her, but she thought it an empty threat. He would not go this long without touching her only to start now, so close to the Dedication. She watched as he made himself comfortable around the fire and beckoned for her to sit next to him. When she had obliged, he leaned toward her, his arm gentle upon her shoulder.

"So, how goes the journey? I hear you are closing in on your mark."

She nodded, adopting the submissive manner to which he was accustomed. "It goes well, my lord. I am sure you know they are in the mountains."

"Yes, Ranti keeps us all well-informed."

"Then you know too that there are three of them."

He raised his eyebrow. "This concerns you?"

Staring steadfastly at the fire, she shook her head. "Of course not, my lord. I have no doubt your plans will succeed. I only wonder that they might suspect me. Or at least that Telenar will."

"What do you know of Telenar?"

"Only what the Sentries tell me. That he is very suspicious."

"Suspicious but human, my dear I am sure your performance will convince them all."

She did not respond, but the thought struck her that even if Vancien fell for her, what good would it do? After the Dedication, he would be barely human. How could she hold the attention of a man bordering on the divine.

As if reading her thoughts, he answered. "It is possible. He will still be fallible and your powers have been honed over generations. You might even convince yourself that you're in love with him."

That was something she did not expect. "You expect me to betray you?"

"You are beyond love and hate, and you are beyond the ability to betray me. If you fall in love with him, he will undoubtedly do the same with you. And that is all the better. The last Advocate who loved when he fought was Heptar; his fate is well known. But I will not be a fool like Varrin. I'll bide my time and live long enough to see my success." He stopped, picturing the love-sick Heptar struggling desperately to save the lady sitting next to him. The Dedication notwithstanding, the hero had found a higher cause than Kynell, and thus abandoned, the protection of the Prysm abandoned him. Oh, what a sweet day that would be, if only he could recreate it!

The woman beside him was silent, as always. It was obvious that she gave no thought toward his vision. He wondered if she gave any thought at all. Four lifetimes of physical and mental oppression could certainly dull the senses. Still, there might be enough of a spark left in her to resist, so he added, "If you decide to thwart my purpose by appearing hateful to him, he will care for you all the more, as a shepherd does for a lost, rebellious lamb. By the Plains of Jasimor," he leaned back, kicking a stick into the blaze, "that's a sickening picture. But that too will be the end of him: he'll sacrifice the care of many for the coddling of one."

She did not trust herself to look at him. "And if I do not make it into his presence?"

He did not miss a beat. "Then I'll assume your escort failed in his duty and have him thrown into the Chasm. Alive."

Her knuckles were white as she struggled not to show a reaction. It was impossible to do that to Gair. A person thrown into the Chasm suffered the worst of fates: a body slowly eaten away by the Darkness and a spirit that felt every possibility of rescue ebb away. Any dead soul there deserved its punishment, as she would no doubt know someday. But a living servant of Kynell thrown in the Chasm? Could Amarian even do such a thing? She was certain that he could and would. The image of Gair alone, weeping because he would never be able to reach his god, almost caused her to faint.

"My lord has considered every possibility," she whispered. "But I must assure you that I have had no thought of betraying you."

His fingers tightened on her shoulder even as his gaze softened. "Of course not, my dear. But as you say, I must consider every possibility. This is not a game I intend to lose."

"If there is anyone who can succeed in this, it is you, lord."

She tried not to stiffen as his hand moved slowly from her shoulder, across her back, and to her waist. "You would flatter me more, Verial, if you began to show some affection," he whispered.

Cycles of obedience took over as she moved to kiss him, but instead of a welcoming response she felt closed, cool lips.

"Very good," he whispered. "But see that you show Vancien more warmth." Then he was on his feet and striding toward his voyoté. "I shall not speak to you again for a while," he called back. "But you might tell Gair that the Sentries don't need to go scouting at night. I have plenty of spies out for that."

Torn between indignation and relief, she watched him disappear. He had been the first—the first!—to decline her embrace. She had no power over him at all. And now she was forced to not only sacrifice herself to Zyreio, but all that was good in Rhyvelad as well. There was just enough humanity left within her to hesitate at this thought. Still, she would rather annihilate the faceless masses (including Vancien) than give up Gair's warmth, which she was beginning to know so well.

He found her the next morning, alone and shivering next to a dead fire. With a cry of alarm, he hastened to tear off his cloak and warm her. She submitted quietly to his ministrations, responding only when he hissed a question in her ear.

"What?"

He moved back enough to search her face and repeated his question. "Did he hurt you?"

"Of course."

His sudden reaction startled her. With a face first pale, then red with rage, he jumped to his feet and unsheathed his sword. He was mounted before she could stop him.

"Gair!" She grabbed his reins. It took all of her efforts to gain his attention. "Gair, get down! He'd kill you without a thought."

"I don't care!" he shouted, loud enough for the entire forest, and certainly the Sentries, to hear. Then he bent down to her. "Any man who treats you like that should be punished."

Only then did she realize what exactly he was avenging, and how her unthinking answer had almost got him killed. "Gair, listen to me. He did not touch me."

He waited, impatient to stop the monster but relieved that he had not failed so drastically in his duty. "You said he hurt you."

"His very presence hurts me, Gair. It is the same with him as it has been with all of the Advocates." Making sure she had his attention, she added, "Only he has not touched me."

He bit his lip, still frustrated at his own helplessness. "That is something, at least." Then he was down off the saddle and holding her close, much like a father would his scared child. The move was the final of many surprises that long night and morning. Her defenses failed, her eyes filled with unfamiliar moisture, and in detached wonder, she began to cry.

The Sentries watched as the two stood there, freezing in the wind but unable to let go. In eager expectation of a feast, their grisly heads turned toward their master. His face was expressionless. With a flick of his wrist, he could destroy both of the traitors, but he did not. So the girl had finally found some comfort. Well, let her have it for a bit. Gair could do him no harm. Indeed, because of scenes like this, Verial would be sure to complete her mission.

Noticing the hungry eyes of his servants, he shook his head. "Not yet, boys. But soon there will be a feast that even you will not be able to stomach."

He wasted not another thought on the couple. Instead, he urged his voyoté back through the hiverran forest. The great pines pierced the sky, their boughs laden with the unforgiving snow. He knew this area of the world well. In truth, he was only half a day's ride from his home town of Win. The thought brought him no pleasure. He hated anything that reminded him of his childhood, anything that whispered in his ear of the true reason he had decided to serve Zyreio. Though he had not forgotten his brother, he had forgotten his brave, boyish desire to protect Vancien at all costs. It was an understandable oversight, since Zyreio had a vested interest in making him forget.

Amarian was now deep in the woods. As his voyoté plodded along, he was suddenly overtaken with the desire to be alone with his god. He needed clarity. He also needed comfort, to know that he was not alone. Only Zyreio could offer him those things and so much more besides. So after several paces, he allowed his voyoté to meander to a stop. Dismounting quietly, he picked his way through the dead underbrush until he found an area clear enough for him to kneel. He dropped to his knees, ignoring the wet snow, and pressed his face to the ground. Arrogance was required of him with all the inhabitants of Rhyvelad, but when he faced Zyreio, humility was all he could offer. All of his schemes and plots seemed to rush upon him, only to retreat with equal haste. What were his plans anyway? Chaff before a mighty god. His lord would have his own way, and none could say otherwise. Even he, the most powerful man in the world, was only a pawn in Obsidian's game. With a groan he sought out the Darkness for the power he needed. May Obsidian keep him in its palm and hold him through the coming trials. Power would come. Victory would come. And he would rule. But he would always be a servant. So be it. That was what he had chosen and that was how he would perish: a master of all and a slave to one.

He lay there for most of the day, conscious only of Zyreio's presence. When he finally rose, the orbs were setting and night was closing in. All the creatures of the woods were silenced, either by death or slumber. The only sound he could hear was his own labored breathing. His hands were white from exposure and his knees could hardly move. Stumbling to his sleeping voyoté, he shook it awake, welcoming the warmth of its fur.

"Take me to the king's camp," he rasped, knowing that the direction of his hands, not his voice, would guide it. Still, it was of some comfort to speak with another living thing.

The voyoté obeyed as he slumped onto its back, cold and exhausted. Instinct would guide it out of the forest, at least. After that, he would take control once more.

CHAPTER TEN

Telenar's voice, husky with sleep and cold, woke them up for another day.

"Get up, everyone. Quickly! We've lost a great deal of time."

With a rebellious groan, Vancien curled tighter into his blanket. "Go'way, Telenar. It's not like we've got anywhere to go."

Telenar sat back on his haunches, glaring at his pupil. His annoyance was magnified by the fact that while Vance was warm in bed, he had been saddling the voyoté and breaking camp. Consequently, the news he delivered was tinged with macabre satisfaction.

"Of course, Vance. We've nowhere to go. I'll just go tell Corfe that we'll be in for a while."

Vancien's reaction was even better than he could have anticipated. With a strangled yell, he sprung from his covers and began yanking on his boots.

"What? Where? Who is it? How close is he?"

"Shhh." Telenar soothed, for N'vonne too had jumped up and was looking around frantically. "Look, you startled N'vonne."

She hastily shook her head. "I'm fine. Who is following us?"

Vancien interrupted before Telenar could respond. With rumpled hair and tunic askew, he looked young and boyish to a fault. "There's no one here. He was just messing with us to wake us up."

He was countered with a glare. "On the contrary, Vance. His name is Corfe and he's just a couple hundred paces behind us."

There were times when Vancien's Advocacy was not as apparent as his tutor could have hoped. Eyes wide in expectation, he ran to the edge of the cave and peered out. "I don't see any signs of a camp."

Telenar jerked him roughly back. "Of course you don't, fool! Get back in here before he sees us."

Such a flare of temper shattered the relative camaraderie of the morning. An awkward moment followed as Vancien struggled to regain his dignity while Telenar debated between berating him or apologizing for his outburst. Behind them, N'vonne quietly arose and began packing her bed.

In the end, Telenar did neither. "Pack your bed," he grunted. "He might be upon us soon."

Vancien clinched his teeth and nodded. But shame at the reprimand still burned as he silently went about his chores. Telenar had lost his temper before, but never so unapologetically and never in front of N'vonne. He felt like an ignorant schoolboy. Curse Telenar, for treating him like that, and curse his own stupidity!

Respect for Telenar kept N'vonne's mouth shut. Were it any other man, she would have torn him apart for demeaning her student. But Telenar was as close to a father as Vancien had at the moment and they would have to work it out themselves. Nevertheless, the incident hung like a cloud over them for the rest of the day.

By late afternoon, they had journeyed past the most dangerous regions. The blizzard that had assaulted them the day before was nowhere to be found. Their greatest difficulty now was pushing through the waist-deep snow. If Corfe was behind them, he did not show himself, and by evening's fall, Vancien was beginning to think Telenar had been mistaken.

They were almost to another small campsite when N'vonne's voyoté stopped and began to whimper. Vancien and Telenar were a few paces ahead, lost in their frosty silence. N'vonne had to call to them twice before they turned.

"What is it?" Telenar replied, alarmed.

"It's Cetla. She won't move forward and she's whimpering."

Both men dismounted and started to come to her when Cetla began to bark and snarl at them.

"What's going on?"

"Shhh, Vance," Telenar hissed, stopping immediately. "She's telling us to stay back."

Indeed, both Lansing and Nagab were eying their comrade with concern but still keeping well away. N'vonne's pallor matched the snow as she watched her friends watch her.

"What should I do?" she whispered.

"Nothing," Telenar responded. "Just stay on her and wait. She feels something around or underneath her. Don't worry, she'll know the best way to make it out."

His words did little to comfort her as she listened to the voyoté's whine. Cetla seemed as unsure as her rider. After a few seconds, she slowly allowed one paw to push forward through the snow, then another.

Telenar watched anxiously. "It's sheetrock," he whispered. "See how she's moving? There's sheetrock under that snow and it could give at any moment."

Vancien held his breath and prayed as he watched the pair inch slowly forward. They could now hear the groaning of the ground beneath them. Then the groaning turned to a muted roar as the mountain began to open up. Snow rushed past Cetla's hind end as she slipped into the cavity, N'vonne with her.

"Grab her!" Telenar yelled, springing forward and landing on his chest, arms clutching the panicked voyoté's neck. Vancien slid past them to the edge of the crevice, furiously groping for N'vonne. Thankfully, she was still there, clutching Cetla's waist. Below her there was nothing but empty air a hundred paces down.

"Vance!" she cried, legs swinging in vain for something to support her.

"Hold still! There's nothing around you to stand on, and if you swing, you'll drag Cetla down."

Obediently, she hung still. "I can't hold on too long, Vance. My shoulder's hurt."

"Shh! It's okay. We'll get you."

"Vance!" Telenar shouted from the animal's head, his voice muffled and terrified. "Is she there?"

"Yes, but I can't get her! Pull Cetla out!"

A few grunts could be heard, but the voyoté didn't move. Then again from the head, "I can't! She's too heavy. And she can't use her back legs to push."

Meanwhile, all three animals had begun a pained whimpering that only made communication more difficult. Vancien turned backed to N'vonne.

"Okay, how are you holding up?"

She shook her head. "Not good, Vance. It's my shoulder."

He stretched out his arms, but he could only grab her clothing, which would tear easily. And he couldn't risk her hold on Cetla by grabbing her arms. Restraining an exclamation, he ordered her to hold on and slid backwards past Telenar.

"What are you doing?" Telenar barked as he saw him. "You're leaving her?"

Vancien did not respond as he ran to the other voyoté and tore through their packs until he came up with the rope he wanted. Lashing it first to Lansing, then to Nagab, he tied it around his own waist and ran back to the edge of the chasm. . .and over.

N'vonne screamed as he fell past her, instinctively throwing out her arms to catch him. The rope tautened as Lansing and Nagab held their ground, and Vancien just barely caught her by the waist as she tumbled by. They hung there in a second of stunned silence as Cetla, suddenly free of her burden, scrambled to the surface. They could hear Telenar swearing and shouting from the ledge. His head appeared as nothing more than a dark circle against the clear sky when he peered down.

"Vance! N'vonne! Great Kynell, are you there?"

"We're here!" Vance shouted back, clutching N'vonne with all his might. "Pull us up!"

Telenar's head disappeared as he hurried to urge the two voyoté forward. Slowly, the distance between the surface and the danglers shortened. In a few moments, they were only four handbreadths from the top when the pressure of the rope and its weight against the remaining sheetrock forced it to give way a second time.

Both of them screamed as they plummeted further into the abyss. With a surprised yelp, Lansing and Nagab were jerked backwards, almost into the cavity themselves. Training and strength rushed in, however, and they regained their footing enough to stop the plunge and pull forward again.

Beside himself with fear, Telenar rushed to the edge. "Vance! N'vonne!"

Twenty feet below the surface and swinging wildly, the two did not at first respond.

"Vance! N'vonne! Talk to me!"

Struggling to keep a hold of N'vonne, Vancien could only manage a muffled "Busy!"

Telenar almost cried in relief. "Okay! The boys have their footing! We're pulling you up!"

Soon, the only sound that could be heard was the hiss of the rope over now-solid rock and the growling and grunting of the voyoté as they strained.

In a few more moments, Telenar was grabbing N'vonne by the waist and hauling her to safe ground. Vancien managed to scramble up without help, but N'vonne was almost unconscious from the pain in her shoulder.

"It's dislocated." Telenar whispered, hastily laying her down and wrapping her with his cloak. "Are you okay, Vance?"

He managed a nod.

"Good. Because that was a stupid stunt you pulled back there. You almost killed yourself *and* her."

Vance couldn't believe his ears. "It was the only way, Telenar! I couldn't reach her from the top and there wasn't any time."

But it was too late. His friend's terror was voicing itself in unreasonable anger. "Shut up, Vance. You saved N'vonne, but you were foolish. Don't you ever do anything so dumb again!"

"You won't have to worry about it." Vancien snapped, getting to his feet. Without another word, he stalked off, incredulous at Telenar's behavior. But Telenar paid him no attention. N'vonne was getting paler by the moment, and if he failed to do something, she might go into shock.

Shaking her good shoulder, he leaned close. "N'vonne! N'vonne! Come back to us."

She began to shiver. "Vance?"

"Vance is fine. He'll be back soon. How are you?"

Her lips were beginning to turn purple. "I'm cold. And my shoulder won't move."

"I know about your shoulder. It's dislocated." He paused, deeply regretting what he would have to do. "We need to do something very painful to fix it."

She nodded and even smiled. "I know, Telenar. I know it'll hurt. Go ahead."

The sight of her laying there in such agony, yet managing to smile, made him love her even more. He nodded resolutely and adjusted his spectacles.

"Okay." Placing one hand on either side of the joint, he caught her eye again. "Ready?"

Another nod and he began to count. "One. Two. Thr—"

It was done before he finished the count, but not before her scream echoed out over the snow.

Vancien stopped his angry march. He knew what was being done and knew Telenar was the man for it. N'vonne was in capable hands. Shaking his head, he wrapped his cloak more tightly around him. He couldn't take being around anybody at the moment, let alone his unreasonable instructor. The day's events were taking their toll. Now he sought only the presence of Kynell and the snowy mountainside. Telenar would call his action stupid, but he didn't care. He needed to get away. Now. The Prysm would guide him.

N'vonne tried not to sob uncontrollably, but Telenar was holding her close and whispering soothingly in her ear. So she let the tears flow freely as he rubbed her shoulder, praising Kynell and reassuring her with any words that came to his mind. All the frigidity that had characterized their early days was disappearing rapidly into the snow.

"Shhh. It's all right. You're safe now. Vancien's safe too. It's all right."

She nodded against his chest, vainly wiping away the tears and trying to recover her composure. Finally, she had her voice again. She sat back and looked at him. He, too, retreated, unsure that in seeking to comfort, he had not overstepped his bounds.

"Where is Vancien?"

He sighed, remembering his harsh words. "He went for a walk. I was too scared for you to be of much help to him."

Through her tears, she arched an eyebrow. "Scared for me? But he's the Advocate."

"Exactly. Kynell wouldn't let *him* fall."

It was a textbook answer, but she sensed something else behind it. "Is that it, then? You had to be scared for somebody. It couldn't be him, so I won by default?"

Her words were harsh, she knew, but she couldn't allow him to retreat so easily. Even so, she was surprised that his expression showed real horror.

"Of course not! Without you, who knows what Vancien would do? You're the only family he has. And without you, I—"

"You what?"

He stopped, unsure of how he had planned to finish his sentence. He could change the subject. However rude it might seem, he would not have to reveal the truth just yet. But he had treated her rudely long enough and Kynell valued honesty.

Springing to his feet, he started to pace. Instead of confession, however, he opted for interrogation. "Why do you think I would have kept you at such a distance and avoided any unnecessary, er, contact with you? I would have thought your woman's intuition would have picked up on how I feel."

Was he saying what she thought he was saying? "Feel what?"

He himself could not believe the words he spoke next. After nervously adjusting his spectacles for the second time, he sat down again, took her cold hand and placed it between his own. "N'vonne, there is a reason I avoided you at first. There is a reason I haven't welcomed you into our camaraderie as the laws of Kynell would command. I couldn't believe that such a thing could happen, but according to all I have read it's not strictly forbidden. Others have certainly done it."

She removed her hand and looked at him pointedly. "Telenar, you have something to say. Say it."

His gray eyes were a fascinating blend of fear and resolve. She had never seen him so vulnerable.

"Lady N'vonne, the Ages do not forbid a priest to marry."

"Go on."

He took up her hand again. "That means that they do not forbid a priest to love."

Love? Suddenly, Hull was there, just back from a day's work, smiling with satisfaction. His eyes sparkled as he swung her off her feet. So who was this stern man, gazing fixedly at her? He was not Hull, and never could be. Never *should* be. But she could not deny that he was strong in his own way.

The shoulder and the snow were forgotten as they stared at each other. He did not know what else to say. All was out and she had not responded. Had he just made a fool of himself? Had he condemned the rest of their journey to uncomfortable conversations? She began to shiver again so he hastily tightened his cloak about her. In doing so, his hand brushed her arm and she sighed involuntarily. The sound was slight, but was enough to bring down the last of his restraint. Not daring to wait for an invitation, he turned up her face and, for the first time in his life, kissed a girl.

The kiss was awkward but sincere. He pulled back, abashed. "I'm sorry. I don't know what came over me. I'll go find Vancien."

"No, Telenar, it's okay." Before she could stop him, he had stumbled off into the darkness. But in a few moments he had returned, even more shame-faced than before.

"I, uh, well, it's starting to get dark. I know Vancien's protected, but I'm not." He sat down as far away from her as possible. "Wouldn't do for me to get myself killed."

His demeanor was so bashful that she could not help but be charmed. She patted the ground next to her. "Why don't we make camp? And we can talk while we work."

He obeyed and they began to talk. She told him about watching Vancien grow up, about her fear for Vancien's life at the Eyestone Glade, about the first few moments of the Sentry attack. She even told him a little bit about her reckless youth. And about Hull. In return, he shared some bits of his childhood with her, his entry into the Patroniite Fraternity, and his concerns about where the priesthood was heading. A few hours passed in this pleasant manner. Finally, as the fire burned bright in the little cave they had found, Telenar noticed N'vonne struggling to keep her eyes open. With renewed confidence, he placed his hand gently on her cheek and kissed her forehead.

"Good night, Lady. May Kynell give you a good rest."

She murmured a response, drifting off to sleep as he crept to the other side of the fire. But he did not sleep. Instead, he stared at the fire and dreamed of a future beyond the coming battle, of mundane things like a having a wife, a home, and children.

Night had descended in full upon Vancien as he pushed his way through the snow. He was freezing, but he could not admit as much to himself. He had to think, had to pray, had to be alone, and the cold was a small price to pay for the opportunity. Telenar might be worried, but Vancien spared little thought for his mentor at the moment.

He stopped to catch his breath and survey his surroundings. The three lunos were almost full, and the Range was both stark and beautiful. Thanks to the brilliance of the lunos, he could see peaks stretching into the distance on either side of him. The view was so majestic that it touched a chord within him. N'vonne's pain, Telenar's irritation, his own failures. Everything seemed trivial when compared with the brooding peaks, witnesses to all of Rhyvelad's past. Here among such massive formations, did his life really matter? Perhaps all that he had read, all he had believed in, was really nothing more than a fantasy. What was more, maybe the Supras Patronius was right. Maybe Telenar misjudged the dates. Or maybe they had all been deceived. He grit his teeth at the thought. Surely it was a little fantastic, if not self-centered, to believe the world's fate rested on his own young and very human shoulders. Maybe it would be better to call this whole adventure off, go back to Lascombe, and consider things rationally for a while.

Shaking his head, Vancien tried to dispel the persistent doubt. Telenar was well-educated. He knew Keroulian history and the Ages better than anyone in Lascombe. He was also cynical: if he had had any doubt, surely he would have expressed it by now. And then there was Kynell himself, who had been with him through so many trials, from the disappearance of Amarian to the death of his father to even now. But perhaps even this was his imagination. He had never seen Kynell, never heard his voice, never touched his hand. What proof was there of his existence?

Telenar's voice, quoting a section of the ninth Folio, instantly arose in his mind: "For when I was there, you doubted. I saw the doubt and did not leave. Still I was there." Vancien smiled at the oddly repetitive observation. He actually had very little reason for doubting, considering all that Kynell had done for him. To give his doubt free reign would be ungrateful, especially since no argument and no rationale compelled him to do so. Nevertheless, it was there, and Vancien doubted if anything short of Kynell's physical manifestation would remove it.

Beating his hands together to keep warm, he tried to weigh his options. He could go back to Win, South of the Glade, let Relgaré wage his war, and leave Telenar and N'vonne to finish out their lives in peace. But that would mean betraying their trust and for what reason? Because he had doubts. Or he could swallow them for the moment, press on, and see what happened. At the very worst, he would waste his own life as well as his friends'. On the other hand, this could be the most remarkable opportunity to see Kynell at work. If Telenar's reading of the Ages was correct and he actually was the Advocate, then to turn back now would be disastrous. With this thought, he gave the stars one last look before retracing his steps.

Corfe had watched Vancien leave his friends, following him as discreetly as he could. He was rather displeased to note that the Sentry was following *him*. The abominable Urabi were remarkably unsettling, as they were hardly ever visible. In the mountains, even the telltale click of their claws was muffled by the snow. He had tried his best to forget the unsavory creature. This strategy had worked only long enough for him to be startled anew when Ranti reappeared every few days. He sighed quietly, aching to rub his hands in the cold but wary of attracting the attention of Vancien, who was only a score paces away. Not that Vancien appeared easily distracted. The young man was staring at the stars and mumbling to himself. A prayer, no doubt. Corfe raised an eyebrow. If Kynell were paying attention, what would the god of the Prysm say to Amarian's right-hand man witnessing this private spiritual moment?

Why would you care what Kynell thought?

The unwelcome voice boomed inside his head and for a moment Corfe wondered whether Amarian had acquired telepathic abilities. It sounded like his master, but there was something else. Something even darker, if such a level of darkness could exist.

It can.

Was that his own voice? Or was Ranti speaking in his ear? He shook his head to clear it, but the words felt like they were burning into the back of his eyes. He would have cried out, if he had a voice.

Look at him. What you see is not peace. What you see is weakness. Look! He shudders at my night sky and cannot bear my biting cold.

Involuntarily, Corfe thought to himself, "*I* shudder at your sky."

But to his relief, the voice had gone, leaving him to continue his lonely mission.

CHAPTER ELEVEN

When Vancien returned, Telenar was awake, allowing N'vonne to sleep as he sat protectively beside her. He looked up as Vancien came in, his face glowing with more than just the reflection of the fire.

"I am sorry I snapped at you, Vance. Have a seat. You must be freezing! There's some dinner left."

Vancien gratefully accepted the peace offering, and after biting into the meat, looked inquiringly at his chatty mentor. "Did you miss me?"

Telenar laughed nervously. "Of course. But N'vonne knew you were in Kynell's care and I happened to agree."

Vancien nodded thoughtfully. "How's her shoulder?"

Telenar started. Amidst all the vistas that had opened up to him since earlier that evening, he had almost forgotten about the incident with the sheetrock. "It was a simple dislocation. It popped into place quickly enough." His brow furrowed. "I was sorry to have caused her such pain, though."

So vulnerable was Telenar's demeanor that Vancien was tempted to pay him back for the past several weeks of surliness. His better part won out, but he could not resist an accusatory question. "So what went on afterwards?"

Telenar nervously poked a stick into the fire. How much did the boy know? "Nothing 'went on,' as you put it. We talked."

"Uh-huh."

Was Vancien teasing him? He looked sharply at his young charge. If Vancien had been opposed to the match, then there would have been no question: his own attachment for the lady would have had to take second place. Awkward as it may be, he had to know. "Judging from your attitude, I conclude that you are of aware of a mutual interest?"

Vancien could not stop a laugh. "How could I not be? You haven't been the same guy since she woke up!" He shook his head. "No, I saw this one coming a while back. You're good for each other, as long as she's okay with it. Besides, in a little while, I won't be much company."

"I assure you I have been completely honorable and will continue to be so." Then Telenar quickly switched gears as he realized what Vancien had said. "'A little while?' Why do you say it like that? Do you feel something coming?"

Vancien shook his head. "No, I don't feel anything. That's kind of why I'm suspicious. Before, I felt bold and confident. Now, so many doubts are attacking me that it can be only one of two things: either I've finally realized that this is all child's play or Zyreio is purposefully weighing heavily on me, trying to distract me."

Telenar's silence was thoughtful and not a little impressed. Kynell was becoming clearer in this boy every day. "Which do you think it is?"

Vancien didn't have a straight answer, so he didn't offer one. "I don't know, but we're going to pretend like it's the second option and keep on going."

"That could be all he's asking of you."

"I hope so, because at the moment, I think that's all I can give."

Travel for the next few weeks proved uneventful. Before long the small party could see the foothills with their soaring pines, broken only by small, dim clearings. The days, though growing warmer, were also getting wetter as hiverra began to give way to the early rains of autore. Despite the daily soaking, however, the three travelers were in cheery company. In front of them was freedom and warmer weather. Behind them, the Duvarian Range loomed, many of its threats exposed and overcome. Perhaps the old Range welcomed the departure of such undaunted guests. Whatever the case, it did nothing to stop them as they squelched their way down to lower altitudes.

It would be dishonest to say that Vancien participated in the excitement of the season to the same extent as Telenar and N'vonne. The two lovebirds were caught up in their own world, which consisted chiefly of quiet moments, spontaneous laughter, and occasional rounds of poorly hidden angst. It was this last demonstration that Vancien found especially hard to stomach. Whenever one party registered an offense, the other would engage in a half-hearted attempt to forget the crime, all the while sulking until the offending party pleaded first for explanation, then forgiveness, then restoration. Until all three were requested and granted, the day was tense and decidedly unpleasant. As a further complication (though Vancien was ultimately grateful for it) neither Telenar nor N'vonne felt that it was appropriate to share their concerns with him. He consequently went from beloved son and student to distant outsider in a matter of minutes as they privately worked through their personal struggles. Fortunately, such brooding only lasted a few hours. The tiffs, if that is what they may be called, never extended from one day to the next.

For the rest of the time, both N'vonne and Telenar were excessively thoughtful toward each other and toward him. The love growing between them had apparently opened up channels of affection neither one of them had known existed. N'vonne now embraced Vancien openly, telling him repeatedly that she loved him as a son. Telenar, meanwhile, reiterated how grateful he was that Kynell had sent him such a smart, easy-going Advocate. Encouraging as all this fondness was, it was a little upsetting. Vancien found himself taking more and more walks by himself in order to think, pray, and give them some space.

One night, after a day's heavy rain had lifted, the two romantics were being particularly sentimental, making Vancien the unfortunate witness of many secret glances and chaste blushes. Telenar was simply going out to collect firewood, but the way they carried on, it looked as if he was venturing forward to slay a dragon.

"Maybe there's a reason priests often remain single!" Vancien finally groaned. "How can you serve Kynell if you can't even focus long enough to get firewood?"

Telenar stopped mid-hug. "I'm sorry. Are you volunteering to go fetch it?"

Mildly annoyed, Vancien jumped up. "Well, sure! I did it last night and the night before, but I could use the exercise." Ignoring Telenar's sincere protests, he marched into the thin trees to look for fallen timber and hopefully a water supply. The wood was easy enough to find, but the search for a stream took him beyond hearing range of the camp. Soon all around him was quiet. There were no settlements around this area. In Vancien's time, Rhyvelad was still a young and thinly populated world, much of it undiscovered or unsettled. Thus it was possible that he was treading upon tree roots that had never yet felt the foot of man. It was a strange thought.

As he went, another worry began to turn his stomach. The past few days, Vancien could feel the atmosphere getting thick with the tension of the coming Dedication. The very air seemed to take on an electric force, as if particles of sky were deliberating about whose side they should take on the day of battle. Every flower appeared to have a dark side to him, as absurd as that sounded. The increasing presence of evil did not scare him for his own sake, since he knew his day had not come. Yet Obsidian would only be too happy to strike at Telenar and N'vonne. Especially if that Corfe fellow were still following them. Suddenly, finding a water supply did not seem as important. They had enough to last through the evening and into the morning, anyway. After gathering up an armful of kindling, he started to hurry back toward the camp.

Just a few resolute steps later, he heard a faint sound drift across the melting snow. He stood still, listening. It sounded like a human, possibly a woman. She was crying. He shook his head, dismissing the interruption as the beginning of Zyreio's tricks, and resumed walking. But the crying nagged at him: the lady did not sound hurt, but she definitely sounded upset. He found himself wondering why a woman would be alone in the sparse snowy woods, crying. Had she been abandoned? Bereaved? Finally and inevitably, he departed from his path and plunged in the direction of the voice.

She was by a stream (this he noted with detached irony; good thing he had brought a bucket) and she was indeed alone. Gently setting down the bundle of wood, he took a few cautious steps toward her.

The crying was not contrived. Ever since Gair had been so unnervingly kind, Verial had been sobbing uncontrollably (in her view, at least, which amounted to a normal woman's occasional tears). Her sobs intensified as he approached. He hated the trap she was about to lay and knew her tears only lured him further. But what could she do? This was the only way to save Gair, although he had told her before he left that he did not fear Amarian. But he was very naïve. Kynell's powers of protection were uncertain and foreign to her, while Amarian's cold ability to extinguish anything good and alive was all too familiar. Earlier the habit of detachment had helped her, but this time she knew such a safe reaction could not be relied upon: the very thought of such a fate for Gair made her tremble. It was for him that she cried as Vancien respectfully drew near.

"Excuse me?"

She heard him, but did not respond. For the ploy to work, she must not appear too eager.

"Ma'am? Er, my lady? Are you all right?"

He was now only a few feet away, looking at her with a mix of concern and impatience. He kept glancing over his shoulder as if he had to get back to something. Slowly, she pulled herself together and looked fully at him. He seemed so very young. How could such a child carry so much responsibility?

"May I help you?" she finally said.

Vancien drew back, disconcerted. "No, I just thought that *you* might need some help."

Her laugh was hollow, giving Vancien the unmistakable impression that she considered herself beyond anyone's help. Well, he did not have time to find out. N'vonne and Telenar were waiting.

"I'm sorry to disturb you. I heard crying and thought I could be of some assistance. If you're all right, then, I should be off." He turned to gather his things.

Verial jumped to her feet, taken aback by his abruptness. "You're leaving?"

Vancien did not stop, but answered over his shoulder. "If you're okay, there's really no point in me staying around. I must get back."

Her mind raced. He couldn't leave! What would happen to Gair? And beyond that, her vanity was a little bruised. She was good enough for four Dark Lords and a few Prysm Advocates. What was this boy's problem? The crying had obviously failed. Perhaps she should change strategies.

"Don't leave so quickly. Please. I have indeed lost my way. Perhaps an able young man like yourself could guide me?"

Blushing at the compliment, he stopped and turned. "I am sorry to hear of your trouble. Where are you going? Perhaps I can point you in the right direction."

Where was she going? Not to Lascombe. He had just come from there. And there were no villages around here for leagues. She had to go in his direction, but where was he headed?

Jasimor.

She shook her head at the sudden mental intrusion. Was that her own voice or someone else's? "Maybe I should ask you where you are going? If it is along the way, we could walk together."

Vancien noted the woman's anxiety. "We're actually not going anywhere in particular. Just out. Anywhere away from Lascombe."

"You crossed the Duvarian Range just to go 'out'?"

"Look, miss, it's hard to explain. I'd better get going."

Miss? What happened to "my lady?" This stripling could use some manners.

Jasimor!

Whose voice was that? It sounded like Amarian, but it wasn't. Amarian was powerful, but he could not project his thoughts into people's minds. That only left one possibility. No, that couldn't be. *He* never spoke directly to anybody. He used the Advocate as his mouthpiece. Why would he suddenly start talking to her now, after all these cycles?

ASK HIM ABOUT JASIMOR.

The unmistakable voice thundered in her head, bringing her to her knees. "No!" she cried helplessly, "You never do this! Let me be!"

Vancien watched in surprise as the woman crumpled before him, sobbing and clutching her head. What had happened? He stepped toward her, but she struck out at him like a cornered animal.

"Go away! Quickly! He sees you here!"

He sprang back. Was this a trap from Amarian? "Who sees me here? My lady, who are you?"

She collapsed in the snow without responding. He rushed up to her, relieved to see that she had only fainted, nothing worse. Instinctively, he moved to pick her up and take her back to camp. But what had she said? What if this *was* a trap?

He hesitated, uncertain. Then he heard Telenar calling. Marking his long absence, the priest must have decided to go looking for him.

"Over here, Telenar!"

In a few moments, Telenar was there, staring with him down at the unconscious woman. Vancien related all that had happened while Telenar let out a low whistle.

"She must be from Obsidian. Perhaps your brother sent her as a ploy?"

"Send me a woman as a diversion? I suppose he might think that way, but surely he would know me well enough that I will not be distracted by a prostitute."

Telenar grimaced at Vancien's haughty tone but decided not to address it. Instead, he knelt down and brushed away the woman's hair. She was pale but beautiful. Her clothing spoke not of prostitution but of royalty. He shook his head. Surely not. Not even Amarian would send out his mistress. Well, maybe he would. Sitting back on his haunches, he pondered the idea. How often had the Prysm Advocates fought for Verial and how often had they been defeated because of it? Now Amarian was sending the distraction

108

to them, instead of waiting for them to come looking for her. It was certainly possible that Vancien might fall prey to her charms. He looked again at her. From what Vancien had said, it appeared that she was undergoing some type of rebellion. This one might still be claimed for the Prysm, but at what cost? Her turn of heart coupled with her beauty would undoubtedly capture Vancien's attention. And then what would happen?

"Telenar?"

Telenar abruptly jumped to his feet, brushing the snow off his legs. "Leave her."

"Excuse me?"

"She will indeed be a distraction. We must leave her here."

Vancien could not believe what he was hearing. "Abandon her? Just like that? She might be a prostitute, but she deserves to be treated with kindness."

Telenar caught him by the arm before he could pick her up. "She's not a prostitute, Vance. This is Verial."

It took a moment for the name to process. Even when it did, Vancien did not show the concern Telenar was expecting. "Really? I kind of doubted that she existed. But this is her? How do you know?

"Look at her clothing. She's dressed like a queen. Amarian knows you well enough not to trouble you with a mere prostitute." The last word was a mimic of Vancien's earlier scornful tone.

"But why would he think that I would be tempted by *her*?"

Telenar saw his chance, but even as he seized it, he knew it would not work. "He obviously does not know you *that* well." Propelling Vancien gently away, he added, "Don't worry, Amarian won't leave her out in the cold for long. We have to get back to N'vonne."

But Vancien would not be swayed so easily. "We can't just leave her! If she was sent here on a mission to deceive me, what will happen when Amarian finds out that she has failed? What will he do to her?"

"What will he do to Rhyvelad if *you* fail? You cannot be concerned about her right now. Perhaps you can rescue her after you've won."

Vancien's look was hard. "You mean after Kynell's won. It's his battle, remember? And he's in charge. Besides, what's the point of fighting some great battle if you allow casualties like this along the way?"

Telenar clenched his teeth. "Casualties like this? She *chose*, Vancien. A long time ago. And she can choose to leave any time she wants."

"And where would she go? Amarian would find her. She's only

protected if she's around me."

"Which is exactly what he wants! It's like inviting a spy and a thief into your house! She'll tell him all we do and try to steal your heart, as well."

"I'm sorry, Telenar, but I will not leave her here. Look, she's starting to wake up."

It was consequently under both Verial's and Telenar's protests that all three of them went back to camp. N'vonne had decided to collect her own firewood, so she had some sort of meal prepared upon their return.

"Who is this?" she asked curtly, noticing a fourth and unwelcome party.

Vancien winced at the steel in her voice. Hospitality must be the first casualty in such tense times. He did not answer, but directed Verial toward the fire and gave her a bowl for the stew. Telenar, meanwhile, headed straight for N'vonne and whispered something into her ear.

"Verial!" The cry tore through the still night with all the gentleness of an avalanche. Ladle in hand and red hair blazing in the firelight, N'vonne marched over to the newcomer. "You think to come here and steal Vancien away from us? Trollop! Did that Corfe fellow send you?" She suddenly turned towards the mountains. "Corfe!" she shouted, still brandishing her ladle. "Come out and get your filthy leftovers! We don't want her!"

Nobody answered. Vancien, meanwhile, rushed to Verial's side.

"N'vonne, it was I who brought her here! But if Corfe has had any trouble tracking us, he'll sure be able to find us now. Besides, she didn't want to come. And Telenar didn't want her to come. So leave her alone!"

N'vonne withdrew the ladle and glared at him. "Why did you bring her here?"

"Because she needed help. And I didn't want her to go back to Amarian."

"Well, she can't stay. I'd sooner feed her to the voyoté than have her poison us all."

This time it was Telenar's turn to react. "Enough, N'vonne!" Then to Vancien, "By the Plains of Jasimor, Vance, you've put us in quite a spot."

As if struck by lightning, Verial jumped to her feet. "Jasimor!" She looked wildly at Vancien. "You must go. . .must not go. . .to Jasimor."

Casting one last wary look toward N'vonne, Vancien took the frightened woman's hand. "It's all right. Calm down. Which is it? Must I go, or must I not go?"

"You're going to listen to her?" Telenar interjected.

"Why not? We don't have a Dedication site yet."

But Verial had withdrawn her hand and sat back down, mumbling to herself. "He's going to kill Gair. No, not kill him. Destroy him, little by little. All is out. I have made everything open and he won't like it. But maybe he will."

"Vance," Telenar raised his voice above her ramblings. "I don't think she's quite right in the head."

But Vance was kneeling beside her, treating her as if she were a scared kit. "Shhh, Verial. It's all right. Who is Gair? Is Amarian going to do something to him? What won't he like?"

Verial's beautiful face was tear-stained and her eyes were red, but when she spoke, her voice was even. "I hate him. I've hated all of them. All they do is use me. He's using me now, no matter what I do." She looked sharply at him. "I should leave you, but if I do, he'll torment the only person I care anything about. I can't let that happen. I do not know you and I do not care about you."

Vancien was still for a moment, wondering what he should do next. What would Kynell have him do? What she had said convinced him more than ever that she should not leave. At least, not in this state. "If you go, he will hurt you and Gair. If you stay, he will probably still hurt Gair."

She shook her head. "No. Gair is a knife leveled at my throat and yours. Once he is thrown into the Chasm, there is little else Amarian can do to him. He sits now on the edge of the abyss, every day looking down into it and knowing, as I know, that his life is in my hands."

"Who is this Gair?" Telenar snapped, finally feeling that it was safe to let go of N'vonne.

She sighed, hoping no Sentries were close enough to hear but certain that it would make little difference anyway. "He's one of Amarian's guards, but he's different. He does not worship Zyreio."

"He is of the Prysm?"

She nodded miserably. "That makes him a traitor. Do you know what Amarian does to traitors? The only reason he's alive now is because of me."

Vancien looked at Telenar. A spy in Zyreio's camp? Maybe the situation was not so bad after all. "If he is a servant of Kynell, then he is under much better protection than any of us can offer. Kynell won't let him be thrown into the Chasm."

If her experience with Gair had warmed her to the idea of good in the world, the presence of these Prysmites simply galled her. Vancien was as thick as only a boy of nineteen cycles could be. "Really? I've seen many a kind man thrown in there before. What makes Gair so different? Kynell's power does not extend so far."

But Vancien cut her off. "Kynell's power extends everywhere, Lady. Everywhere."

She didn't have a response. Instead, she ate the food N'vonne shoved at her in silence, more certain than ever that Kynell didn't stand a chance.

Ranti and Corfe watched the scene with amusement. Then Corfe sent the detestable creature off to report to Amarian. That would give him a week or so of relief. He sometimes wished Sentries moved a little slower. The fact that they could run three times as fast as a human meant that Ranti would be back by his side all the quicker. He returned his gaze to the girl. What was Verial thinking, spilling her guts out to the enemy? She had gone soft, and very quickly. Corfe wondered who Gair was. He had never met him and could only presume that such a turncoat had already received his reward. A servant of Kynell in the lord's service? What stupidity! As soon as this turncoat was out of Verial's sight, Amarian would undoubtedly teach him a well-deserved lesson.

He shivered from his hiding place. How long was Amarian planning to keep him on this assignment, anyway?

CHAPTER TWELVE

Gair had indeed just left Verial when the Sentries began closing in on him. He swallowed hard, not relishing the upcoming interview.

"We are under orders not to kill you yet," one of the creatures wheezed. They were words of small comfort, considering what followed. He attempted to fight back, but what man alive can take on three Sentries? Soon a pair of claws sunk into his arm, sending stabs of pain up to his shoulder, followed quickly by another set of claws in his leg. Kynell help him, this was going to hurt. He had fainted away by the time the second Sentry descended on him.

He awoke a few times during the painful journey, but not completely until he was lying on a stone floor, both his arms and legs horribly mangled. Surveying the damage a little closer, he had to stifle a cry: his left leg had been severed below the knee. Where his calf and foot should have been, there was only blood-stained floor. Unclean bandages and a tourniquet had been haphazardly applied to stop the bleeding but were in no way conducive to healing. They were meant only to keep him alive.

Then he noticed that Amarian was standing over him.

"Welcome back, Captain."

The two of them were in a small cell, clearly intended as Gair's new residence. It had a sloping, barrel-shaped ceiling that came down so low against the wall that Gair's head bumped it from his seat on the floor. A bit of hay had been thrown in the corner to serve as a bed. To complete the nakedness of the room, there was no window. The only source of light was from the torch in Amarian's hands. Gair watched it greedily, trying not to wince from the pain.

"Oh, please, go ahead and grimace. I know it hurts. You know it hurts. That's the whole point." Amarian then lazily kicked one of Gair's supporting arms, sending him crashing to the ground again. The scene made him smile as he settled himself on a short stool to watch the entertainment. But Gair whispered a prayer for help and forced himself to sit up again and meet his gaze.

"You were praying, weren't you?"

"Yes."

"Do you know that I can tell when *his* name is mentioned, even thought, in my presence?"

"You can't make me stop." That was a bit of bravado. But Amarian only laughed.

"Why would I? Pray away, my friend! Pray away! Pray to that great god of the Prysm! He will surely deliver you. Of course, you will have to suffer a little, but what is pain to a martyr?"

Gair looked down, disconcerted that his captor knew his thoughts so well.

"Don't be surprised, little one," Amarian continued. "Your thoughts are not original. Many have thought them before and many will think them again. If I cannot enter your mind and pluck them out, then I can read your face like a book. A very boring, poorly written book."

"Why am I still alive?"

"Why indeed? I should have thrown you into the Chasm hours ago." Amarian waved his hand at the wall as a black splotch started overtaking the stones. It grew wide, swallowing everything, even the hay, into its darkness. And as it grew, sharp cries, many of them human, began to fill the room.

Gair gritted his teeth. Kynell would be faithful, Kynell would stand by him, Kynell would deliver him.

"Kynell, Kynell, Kynell. *Please* stop saying that name. It grates on my ears so. And besides, he cannot hear you. You are in enemy territory, my friend. Deep, deep into enemy territory."

"There is nowhere I can go that he will not follow."

Amarian leaned back on his stool as the sounds of the Chasm grew louder. "Will he follow you into there? Does he like keeping company with Obsidian's dead?"

Gair was silent.

"Not so confident now, are we? After all, where does it say in the Ages that no Prysmite will be lost? Even great Kynell has to take a few casualties.

But at least you have the comfort that you went down for a noble cause. Feel free to tell that to your fellow believers in the Chasm."

Now that was too much, even for an Advocate. Gair could not abide such treatment of the Prysm. "I will tell them that, sir, when I see them. Perhaps you would like to toss me in now and get on with business."

"Tempting. But I'm afraid you're of more use to me outside the Chasm than in it. There is a reason I didn't have the Sentries kill you."

From outside the door there came a chorus of tapping.

"Hear that, Gair? They are waiting to finish you off, leaving only enough of you to throw into the Chasm, of course. They stay back only at my bidding."

"Then let them come."

Suddenly, Amarian cracked his knuckles in frustration. "Do not be so eager to die, fool! I was in the middle of divulging my wicked schemes."

"I don't want to hear them."

But Amarian's patience was at an end. In half a second, he was kneeling next to Gair, knife blade flashing. "You don't have to live with your tongue! Perhaps I can relieve you of it so it won't get you into any more trouble."

Gair wisely took the hint and remained quiet.

The blade disappeared as Amarian resumed his cool demeanor. "As I was saying, you are alive only to keep a certain somebody on good behavior."

The shot hit its mark. Verial. What had he gotten her into? She would try to succeed in her mission as long as he was alive, and if she succeeded, then what would happen to the Advocate of the Prysm? He suddenly lurched toward the Chasm's opening. If he could just keep himself from being a pawn, he could help untangle this mess.

Amarian watched him reach the opening of the abyss, then watched him crack his head on the unforgiving stone. "Don't be in such a hurry to leave. There is still much left to be done, and I would like you to see it."

Biting his lip, Gair tried not to swear at the illusion. "You can torment me all you like. I probably deserve it. But what has Verial ever done?"

"Done?" Amarian looked mystified. "Why, she hasn't *done* anything. She won't have to. As long as she's her wretched self, things should work out just fine."

The next morning, tempers had calmed considerably among Vancien and his companions, although all three, including Vancien, watched Verial with caution. She tried to ignore their suspicion, knowing it was fully justified. There was nothing she could do. For Gair's sake, she had no choice but to stay with them. All the same, it was awkward being with such average humans.

As the small company broke camp, Telenar wondered aloud which way they should go. Vancien's answer was short.

"We are going to Jasimor."

Telenar tried to be patient as he saddled the voyoté. "Are you still convinced of that? You know that Zyreio is probably speaking through her, don't you? No offense, ma'am," he added hastily.

Verial did not respond. She had no reason to. The priest was right. It had been Zyreio's voice in her head yesterday and although she would not welcome it, she could not be certain that he would not return. It was best for them not to trust anything she said.

Vancien mounted Nagab, searching the sky for the orbs. "Yes, I'm convinced. Do you have any better ideas?"

Telenar helped N'vonne onto Cetla before he turned to study Verial, who had not moved from her place next to the burnt-out fire. "Other than not taking advice from the mouth of the enemy, no. But it's always been my instinct that when Zyreio says go west, we go east."

Vancien smiled despite himself. "Sound thinking. But in this case, I think we have not been misguided. His motivations are of course unreliable, but a Dedication is a Dedication. What place would be more fitting than the Plains of Jasimor, where it all began?"

"More fitting than the wellspring of evil? Hm. Let me think."

N'vonne ignored both of them, steering Cetla over toward Verial. She held out her hand. "It's probably best you ride with me," she said gently.

Verial reluctantly climbed on and N'vonne could not help but feel a surge of pity. What was it like, all those cycles of forced companionship? She glanced at Telenar, who readily smiled back at her through his argument, and shuddered. She must remember to be kind to this woman, no matter what her past or her future.

Telenar was losing the debate. How does one argue with an Advocate, especially such a bull-headed one? Of course, stubbornness may come with the territory. He sighed. Perhaps all the Advocates had been like this. "All right, all right. We'll go west. If Relgaré has moved the army south, we'll have to avoid them, of course. The whole region will be crawling with Amarian's troops."

"Think of it this way," Vancien called over his shoulder as he urged

Nagab on. "If Zyreio wants us to be there, he'll make sure his own armies don't trouble us."

Telenar snorted. "But Relgaré's might. We could arrive there in pieces, you know." He glanced again at Verial. How connected was she to Amarian? Did he know her thoughts? Quite possibly. They would be wise not to mention that they had an ally in the king's army, if only one. Zyreio could find out about that as he pleased.

————————

Chiyo was growing more impatient with the king every day. The march south had been swift, as if the Cylini were some major threat to Keroul. By the Plains, they had already passed the western foothills of the Duvarian Range! Did Relgaré think the nomadic tribe was going to sweep east ahead of them, then cut north and cross the mountains just to sack Lascombe? The old soldier shook his head. No, they were in retreat. The army had broken this small nation and any stand in the south was going to be the Cylini's last, valiant gasp. From atop his voyoté, he surveyed the troops' encampment at the meeting of the Yrghennum River (or in Keroulian, the Ergana) with the Preshin, the Ergana's fierce tributary. Already one river separated them from Lascombe, for they had needed to cross the Ergana north of the Range for their earlier engagement. Now they would be crossing another, since the Preshin was the northern border of the Cylini's stronghold and their last natural defense. Beyond its mighty current lay a scraggly world of marshes and plains with few resources. The Ergana, running along the territory's eastern edge, had turned the many floodplains into huge, useless, and soggy tracts of land. How the Cylini managed to live in such a place, Chiyo could not guess. Nor could he fathom how such a poor people could amass such a troublesome army. In the beginning, they had been a great threat, but all the king had to do was turn his full attention on them and they were soon reduced to the border raids that had driven Relgaré crazy these past few cycles.

He turned his attention back to the defenses. His men had set up fortifications as usual, digging a ditch along the outer perimeter and placing the pikes just outside the dry moat. Any voyoté jumping the pikes would break its legs on the steep wall of turf and then have to stumble up the sharp incline to face a timber wall and more pikes. All in all, a very useful defense system, but against the Cylini, it seemed like more grand theatrics. They were not so foolish as to attack the camp. Perhaps once, many cycles ago, they would have been able to charge the fortifications and win. But not any more.

117

His gaze moved past the Keroulian men to the soldiers brought by General Hull. The sight made him groan. They spread out like a blemish on the land: a vast, moving infection that the king had invited along. Where would these troops go when the Cylini had been finally cowed? Would they quietly march back home to Amarian's stronghold in the east? Not in Kynell's lifetime. First they would turn on the Keroulian soldiers, then decimate whatever army Vancien may have acquired. He shook his head as despair gripped him. He knew his own countrymen would fight for the Prysm once they had seen the Advocate. But they alone were no match for this dark army. Plus, Chiyo was absolutely certain that Amarian had more troops waiting back home. The fight would be no more than a rout, and all because Relgaré insisted on beating down the wretched Cylini.

"General?"

He snapped out of his frustrated reverie to see a young aide at his knee. "What is it, Bren?"

"The king requests your presence. Commander Hull is returning soon."

"He gets around a lot, doesn't he?"

"I'm sorry, sir?"

"Commander Hull. He always manages to be where we don't want him. Oh, never mind. Tell me, Bren, before I go and see the king, how do you think the men are holding up?"

The aide shifted nervously. He was a conversational person by nature, but he had only been in General Chiyo's service for a brief time. He had not expected the general to engage in such direct conversation. "Well, sir, they seem to be doing all right. It's just that, " he stopped, unwilling to offer a critique.

"Go on."

"It's the others, sir. The ones that aren't men. I like all sorts of things and creatures and such. A good friend of mine is a munkke-trophe."

"Get on with it, Bren. I know you are a fair-minded."

"Hull's soldiers just don't get along with our men. They fight well enough, but they always look as ready to kill *us* as to kill *them*."

Chiyo saw no reason to soften the truth. "That's because they are, boy." He leaned forward so only Bren could hear him. "Never trust them. Their fight is not with the Cylini, Bren. It's with the Prysm."

Bren's eyes widened at the revelation. "The Prysm? They want to fight the Patroniites? Why would they bother with priests?"

It was a naïve response, but Chiyo did not mock it. "The priests are not the only followers of the Prysm. There will soon be a time when Rhyvelad will be divided in two. Be sure you're fighting on the right side."

With that curt advice, he rode off to the king's tent. He found Relgaré inside, giving orders to a captain. Upon Chiyo's entrance, he dismissed the officer and offered his friend a seat.

"Have we set up our defenses?" the king asked idly, pouring a drink for them both.

Chiyo did not respond to such a needless question.

"Ah, well, I see that we have. Make yourself comfortable, Chiyo. We have much to discuss."

"We do?"

Relgaré pretended not to notice his tone. "Yes. Much. As I'm sure you know, Commander Hull is coming back soon."

"So I've heard."

"Yes, Bren would have told you. A good aide, that young man. We shall keep him around awhile. It will be a pity to make him a soldier, won't it?" He tried a laugh, but he was too nervous to make it sound convincing.

If possible, Chiyo was beginning to get more worried. "What is it, my liege? What is wrong?"

"Wrong? Nothing's wrong. What makes you think something is wrong? The men are settled. Hull's soldiers are behaving themselves. The Cylini are weak. Hull's coming back soon."

"You've already said that. Does his return worry you?"

Relgaré slammed his cup down on the table, spilling some wine. "Watch your tone, Chiyo! Why would I be worried? He's an ally."

"We are useful to him at the moment. He is not an ally."

"Chiyo," the king's voice wavered for a moment. "I don't know that I want. . ."

". . .him to return?"

"I didn't say that! It's just that, well, he *is* an unsettling man. But he is useful to me."

"What did you call me in here for, my liege? You know how I have judged the general."

"*Mis*judged." Relgaré added weakly.

"Perhaps. But I doubt it. The men don't trust him, sir, and they don't have reason to. Do you honestly think Hull is here for the Cylini? Can you not see what's on the horizon?"

"I see a bunch of thieves and raiders, ready to die for their greed!"

You see nothing, Chiyo thought but did not say. How it must fit into Zyreio's plans to have such a blind king at the end of ten thousand score! He drew a deep breath. "Why did you summon me?"

The king grew nervous again, fingering the covering on the table and avoiding Chiyo's gaze. "Our army is very strong, Chiyo. Too strong for the Cylini. But I don't want to be surprised. They may still come up from the southwest and that's our weakest side."

Chiyo was grateful to be talking strategy, although he knew Relgaré was about to say something he would not like. "They will not cross the Preshin."

"Even so, I would feel better if we had an advance battalion down there to check things out."

"That's easily done. I'll get one my captains to organize a scouting force. They can be ready by dawn."

Relgaré hesitated. "Wonderful. Thank you. Just one more thing."

Here it comes. "Yes, my liege?"

"I think you should lead it."

Chiyo was not surprised. He had known this day would come, but he was determined to put up a fight. "I disagree, sir. I have many capable captains who would be more than willing to do this task."

The king was shaking his head. "No. I've given this a lot of thought. You're the man for the job, and now that I think about it, I rather doubt you'll need a full battalion. Perhaps half, or even a quarter."

"Let's cut through the preamble. How many men are you willing to send with me, old friend?" Chiyo's voice was icy. Anybody in the camp but the king would have heeded the warning. But Relgaré's mind was set.

"I can spare fifty."

"Fifty men? With all due respect, Your Majesty, I fear you've gone mad. The Cylini are weak, but not *that* weak! What do you expect me to do with fifty men? Whet their appetite?"

"Enough, Chiyo! Your tone is offensive. We have fought too many battles together for you to be petulant now. If anyone can handle the Cylini, you can. Besides, it is clear that you do not get along with Commander Hull and I cannot have dissension in my camp."

"So you send me away."

"I entrust you with a valuable mission."

Chiyo stood, furious but trying to keep his voice level. "Then I must get my men ready. My hand-picked men."

Relgaré had won his battle and was not about to fight another one. "Of course. Whomever you want. And take plenty of supplies."

Because I'll be gone a long time, Chiyo muttered inwardly. Without waiting for a dismissal, he strode to the door of the tent. Then he stopped and faced the king. "There's one thing you should know before I leave."

"Oh? What's that?"

"Commander Hull is also called Amarian. He is Vancien's brother."

"Who is Vancien?"

"Telanar's student. The one you made so welcome at the palace."

"Oh, that boy. What does it matter that he has a brother?"

Chiyo gritted his teeth at such willful ignorance. "He is a follower of Zyreio."

"To each his own. What's that to me?"

"Just bear that in mind after you've beaten the Cylini. You might not get rid of him as easy as you like."

"You're dismissed, General."

"I'm already leaving."

The men watched as Chiyo stormed out of the king's tent. While barking an order to his first captain, he almost ran over young Bren.

"Watch where you're going! Oh, hello, Bren. Excuse me. I'm in a hurry."

But Bren was not so easily deterred. Instead, he composed his gangly limbs into a salute. "I'm sorry, sir. But I heard what you and the king said."

Chiyo's look was blistering. "You should be whipped for spying. How did you get past his guards?"

"I, uh, that is, I'm very small and quiet, and there's one spot where, if you can get between the tent poles, you can hear really well."

"Never mind. Did you want something?"

"Well, it's just that I heard that, well, you would be leaving and going south. I thought that maybe you would like some help. Someone to help you. Like I said, I'm small. If you were to need help, I could help."

"If you're going to be a soldier, Bren, you're going to have to learn to speak clearly. Get back to me when you have your thoughts formulated." Without another word, Chiyo went to compose his small army, leaving Bren to fight back embarrassed tears.

By dawn, fifty armed men were mounted and prepared to leave. They would strike west first, then cut across the river. The air was cool and moist. Hiverra ended quickly in the marshes. By noon, undoubtedly, there would be torrential rain, a depressing prospect for all involved. Their leader considered paying his respects to the king, but decided against it. Relgaré wanted a hasty departure and he would get it.

Chiyo had just opened his mouth to command the march when Bren appeared again at his knee.

"Yes, Bren?"

"The, uh, th-the king, sir. He's not wanting you to go alone."

"What do you mean?"

"It's just that you'll have about five Sentries following you, sir, to, uh, make sure you behave."

Chiyo growled under his breath then instinctively glanced over his ranks. No, they wouldn't be there. Sentries don't like to be seen if they can help it.

Bren was still at his knee.

"One more thing, sir."

"Make it quick."

"I was wondering if I could come too, sir."

Chiyo stared at the boy of no more than eleven cycles and wondered distractedly if Relgaré would count him as a man. Probably not.

"Very well, Bren. You know what kind of mission this is, don't you?"

"An unsafe one, General."

For the first time in many days, the old soldier smiled. "Then go get your things. We leave in few moments."

Before the orbs had completely risen, the company had departed from the camp. Chiyo rode at the head, but he was soon joined by his first captain and fellow countryman, Hunoi. They rode in silence for a time, Chiyo watching the horizon and Hunoi watching his general. When he spoke, his words were carefully selected.

"I see that the king has made his choice."

Chiyo did not answer, keeping his eyes on the trees as they grew thicker.

"When will Commander Hull arrive?"

"Call him Amarian. That's his true name and that's the name he'll use when he sets up his reign."

Hunoi winced. He had never seen his friend in so dark a mood before. "You are certain that this is the time?"

"Growing more certain every day."

"And you do not think the Prysm will triumph?"

"No."

"You think Kynell's strength depends on men and horses. But you know the Ages better than I. There must be something else."

Chiyo did not look at him. "Kynell has used men and horses in the past. Kynell has lost in the past."

"Perhaps he chose to lose."

"Perhaps he just lost."

Hunoi shook his head. "I can see there is no talking to you."

He began to slow his voyoté, but Chiyo grabbed his arm, still gazing ahead. "Hunoi."

"Yes, General?"

"I want those Sentries dispatched by nightfall."

"They'll be gone by mid-day, sir."

CHAPTER THIRTEEN

The four had finally made it through the foothills, leaving the last of the chilly mountain air behind. Finally! Vancien rubbed his arms. Although it was still late hiverra south of the Range, it would be nice not to have to sleep in a fetal position. He glanced over at his two friends. Verial's presence had suppressed some of their growing romance, but Telenar still made sure to point out every scenic or historic spot to his lady. N'vonne, meanwhile, was intent on keeping the priest's side warm every time they stopped for rest. Compared to those two, Verial looked like a thin, watery icicle. She had not said much since they had embarked, nor had anyone urged her to speak. Vancien did wonder, though, what she was thinking. Were they her own thoughts? Amarian's? Zyreio's? A collection of memories from all Obsidian's Advocates in the past? If that were the case, he pitied her. Of course, he reminded himself, he pitied her already. Why would Kynell allow such a creature to suffer? He sat silent for a moment, then turned in his saddle to see Telenar pointing out a charming little waterfall to the ladies.

"Telenar, how long until the Plains?"

The priest dropped his arm and thought for a moment. "Autore will be upon us fully in a few weeks. We'll have to go through the southern half of the marshes to avoid the army and that could take many weeks. Jasimor is in the southern tip of Chiyo's country. It will be a race to get there by breach."

"Where are we now, exactly?"

Telenar raised an eyebrow. "Forgotten geography already? We're a league south-west of the Child's Pass southern gate. We'll swing west when we get into Cylini territory. It will be unpleasant, and of course we'll have to ford the Ergana, but we have to avoid Relgaré. It's best, too, if we stay off the main roads."

Vancien nodded, welcoming the distraction from Verial. Telenar was right: geography had never been his strong point. Neither was he terribly excited to spend weeks in the marshes, shut out from the orbs, battling off insects the size of birds. He wondered how the voyoté would do in such conditions. They had been fine beasts so far, but would their paws grow moldy walking through water and slime day after day? An interesting question, but not interesting enough to keep him from glancing surreptitiously over at Verial.

N'vonne tried not to constantly keep her eye on Vancien, but she was worried about him. Ever since the day that she and Telenar had reached their understanding, he had been the third wheel by default. She was growing fonder of Telenar every day, of course, although they had not repeated that first, awkward kiss. Yet Vancien was still her priority. She had seen the way he treated Verial, as if she were both a helpless infant and a curious toy. If they were not careful, simple numbers and convenient arrangements could encourage something more than detached fascination. Two men and two women traveling together could result in, well, natural divisions. But that could not be allowed to happen. Vancien was not just any man and Verial was not just any woman. If Vance were to fall in love with her, the battle could be lost before it was even fought. Kynell forbid!

Behind her, she heard a soft sigh. The sound was beginning to irritate her. Did that woman ever do anything but sigh? In a valiant attempt to be civil, N'vonne turned her head slightly and asked if her if she was all right.

"All right? If you mean that I am warm and well-fed, then yes, I'm all right."

No time to settle things like the present. "Well, I meant a bit more than that. Do you mind if we ride ahead? I'd like to talk with you."

"Do not trust anything I say."

"I won't. But if there's anything you want to say, you'd best say it now."

Heeding the tap of her rider's heels, Cetla jumped forward a few paces. Telenar noticed, but did not comment. Vancien noticed, too.

Once they were decently out of hearing range, N'vonne jumped right in. "Tell me, Verial, are you feeling any better since you have joined us?"

N'vonne felt her shrug. "I don't know. It's been so long since I've tried to feel anything. I feel Amarian watching me. He might even know what I'm thinking. And if he does not, then Zyreio does."

"Still, there have been no Sentries. Amarian can't be everywhere."

"But Zyreio can. And he would know if I were not accomplishing my task."

"So why don't you? If you're supposed to charm Vancien, you're doing a poor job of it."

The retiring Verial quickly vanished. "I can do as I please when I please. Vancien's as easily charmed as any man."

N'vonne was not intimidated. "You have charmed Amarian, then? So well that he sent you away?"

"Darkness is no mere man. He has no soul, no desires, except to serve Obsidian."

"It's hard to believe he's so focused before the Dedication. It sounds as if he is consumed already."

"He is not easily swayed. And after Zyreio takes him completely, nothing will touch him."

N'vonne glanced back at Vancien, who was absentmindedly picking at Nagab's fur and trying not to watch them. Although he may not look the part, she had complete faith in him. "When the time comes, Amarian will meet his match."

Vancien, meanwhile, chewed his lip, deep in thought.

"What's on your mind, Vance?"

Vancien smiled nervously at his inability to answer. "I'm not quite sure. I think I was thinking about Kynell, or maybe some other things."

"Verial?"

Vancien started. "No. Why? Well, maybe. It is curious, isn't it, how she shows up on our doorstep? Do you think it was only Zyreio who had something to do with it? Maybe Kynell put her there, as well, and he's using this situation."

Telenar eyed him. "She was placed there by Amarian, Vance. *Amarian.* He only wishes you harm. Remember the Ages? Tryun and Heptar? They fell for her, too."

"I haven't fallen for her. I'm just curious at this turn of events. What would happen if she were to choose the Prysm?"

Telenar was still uncomfortable with the Vancien's line of questioning, but if this was what he wanted to talk about, then he would go along with it.

"I honestly don't know. There aren't any prophecies about her. She just kind of shows up from time to time, usually as a nuisance."

"Do you think she has much choice in any of this?"

"I think she used to have choices and she made the wrong ones."

"You're wrong there. She still has a choice, but I don't know what she'll choose."

This was getting exasperating. "Don't you see? It doesn't matter what she chooses. In fact, it would be almost better if she chose Zyreio." He saw Vancien grimace but continued. "Why would you waste your attentions on a servant of the enemy? But despite yourself, you would love a convert to the Prysm. And that particular love could kill us all. She's not the only one whose life is stake, Vance."

Vancien resumed his plucking at Nagab's fur. "But what about her soul?"

"Her soul is important, yes, but it's not in your hands. *Your* task is simply the culmination of ten thousand score."

"But what if she's some sort of culmination? What if her choice represents the final ten thousand score?"

Telenar could not accept this. "That's heresy, Vance, and you know it. There may be more to her than first appears, but the fight is between you and Amarian. If you forget that, then Zyreio has already won."

Vancien nodded as if he had not really heard the warning. Seeing his words so lightly taken, Telenar impatiently kicked Lansing in front of Nagab's path and forced Vancien to look into his eyes. When he spoke, his voice trembled with rage.

"Vancien pa Hull, you are considering treason. May Kynell slay you now and find another Advocate if you refuse to take your burden seriously. Do you hear me? *Do you hear me?*"

Vancien's jaw was set as he returned his friend's fierce gaze. "I hear you, Telenar. But you are not the only one I hear. You have the Ages and I have them, too. But they are not everything. *Kynell* is everything. I march on his orders, not yours. He does not want me to abandon Verial and I doubt that he would look kindly upon you charging an Advocate with heresy."

Telenar was furious, but he could only watch helplessly as Vancien pushed past him and rode up to visit with N'vonne and Verial. What had gotten into that boy? How much damage could he wreak before the Dedication? And what happened when an Advocate of the Prysm became consumed with his own pride?

The sky was rumbling, causing Amarian to nod in satisfaction as he gazed out the window. Rain would be coming soon, which was all the better.

The sea of campsites surrounding the castle was beginning to stink, sending wave after wave of stench up to his private chamber, which was situated at Donech's highest convenient point. Such locations were hard to come by in the Eastern Lands, which were mostly flat and windy, with few trees and fewer hills. The fortress itself mirrored the landscape. It was flat, no more than three stories, and sprawling: thick walls formed an oblong pentagon that housed only the barest necessities: a sparse kitchen, a cavernous great hall, and Amarian's most trusted servants. At the extended point of the pentagon, sticking up like a thorn, was the tower that housed Amarian's chambers. Except for a suffocatingly close servants' access, it was accessible only by a narrow staircase leading to an iron-barred door. Though he did his best to ensure loyalty among his followers, Obsidian's Advocate knew better than to rely on such a tenuous virtue.

From his vantage point, he could look down on the rest of the fortress, as well as the surrounding encampments. He had made certain that all of his marshaled forces were gathered at the western point, within view of his tower. If any settlements were found outside of his scope of vision, they were summarily and roughly moved to a more desirable location. It was also equally important that all of his forces could see him, or at least a reminder of him. His high chambers were perfect for such a purpose, providing an aura of omnipresence and inaccessibility at the same time.

He stretched, gathering his thoughts as well as his robe around him. He would need to leave soon if he was going to reach Relgaré's army before they forded the Preshin. With one last look at the cloudy sky, he glanced around to make sure everything was prepared, including the empty suit in the corner. He needed to look like a commander, after all. This particular breed of armor was a specially tinted dark gray, easily hidden in the mist, lightweight, and quiet when he moved. Not that he would need armor for a while. Zyreio would protect him until the Dedication, but it helped to look the part. With a nod to his servant, who was busily packing up the various metal plates, he wandered down to the stables in the courtyard to observe his magnificent new steed.

Rhyvelad was full of marvelous beasts, some of them friendly to humans, some of them not. In Amarian's time, many of them had gone into hiding, having been driven away Zyreio's manifold corruptions. Only a few of them had become bold enough to show their faces (or whatever served that purpose) along the outskirts of the world's civilized population. Gryphons had occasionally been spotted in the peaks far north of the Eastern

Lands, where only outcasts and ambitious Ulanese travelers went. With a fennel body and the head and wings of a bird of prey, they were fierce creatures but quite rash, headstrong, and not well-suited for human companionship. Ealatrophes, meanwhile, verged on immortal: their gryphonic heritage made them aggressive, but their Destrariae blood was said to have flowed straight from under Kynell's throne. As Vancien had already experienced, Destrariae cold pierced through any living thing. Priests labeled it *klathonus*, as bright as the Prysm's truth and as unchangeable. Such a peculiar combination of *klathonus* and gryphon produced a valiant, holy creature scarcely accessible to humans, unless like Kynell himself, it decided to restrain its glory and allow a mortal to approach.

Neither of these creatures were suitable for Amarian's purposes. But there remained one beast, one holdout that smacked of Rhyvelad's earliest days, when giants were common and voyoté were just a twinkle in Kynell's eye. Like the gryphons and Ealatrophes, these creatures were holdovers from the days before Zyreio's deceit had captured the hearts of men, the days when, for all creatures, Obsidian was just a dark stain on the horizon. It was a time when men could be trusted with beasts and vice versa, so Kynell had created with abandon, instilling all his creation with a level of power, beauty, and swiftness that mirrored his own qualities. Only much later, when Zyreio had drawn many men and beasts to himself, did Kynell withdraw most of these great beauties from Rhyvelad's mantle, leaving behind only those that begged to stay. (In order that man might not be alone, however, in work and companionship, he created *galthis*, or helpers. The most versatile and least intelligent of these is the voyoté, but there is also the fennel and the munkke-trophe. Since that time, many fennels have fallen in bondage to Obsidian. Theirs is a dark history, but not as dark as the Sentries, which is a history for another time.)

Of the three early giants that remained, the only ones that could now possibly be of great service to Obsidian were the dragons. The Patroniites called them *eiresa* because after Zyreio's great deception, the few remaining dragons of Rhyvelad had offered to serve as emissaries between the Prysm and Obsidian. (The term *eiresa* means simply 'one who chooses,' implying that one chooses repetitively and poorly.) Kynell declined their offer, but Zyreio greedily accepted. So for many cycles, the dragon ferried messages back and forth between Zyreio's men and Kynell's. It was an unpopular job by any measure, earning the distrust of both parties and meriting reward only from Obsidian. Though occasionally followers of the Prysm would use their services, Kynell never officially sanctioned the dragons' self-appointed role.

Over time, the beasts grew bitter that Kynell dismissed and condemned their virtuous labors. They decided to take their pay for themselves from the flesh of Kynell's men and women. Such an outrage had never been done in all of Rhyvelad and punishment was swift. In righteous fury, Kynell robbed the offenders of their speech and cast them into the great subterranean caverns of Bar-norak. There their wings were effectively clipped as they drifted from cave to cave and rift to rift, forbidden from seeing the light of orbs until they repented of their heinous action. But they did not repent. Instead, they waited for the time when Obsidian would be powerful enough to release them. Sadly, the day of release of never came. Obsidian either forgot about its former employees or did not have the power to deliver them. So they continued to fly the deep shafts of the world, silently waiting for freedom.

It had taken Amarian a great deal of time and manpower to track down Bar-norak. It took even longer to discover a way inside. But eventually he managed both. Through the aid of Zyreio, he released one beast from its black imprisonment before closing off the entrance. He did not, after all, want an entire race of dragons. One was enough.

As he neared the yard behind the stables, he watched the handlers prepare the dragon for her flight. Ovna was fairly young for her kind: her grandsire had just cut his teeth when Kynell threw the dragons into Bar-Norak. Robbed as she was of speech, she had no way of communicating this to Amarian, nor did she care to. Rather, she seemed content to watch the men scurrying around her with brooding eyes that were slowly adjusting to the light. Like all dragons in those days, she was gritty black: the exact shade of the cavern walls of her prison. Her hide was not glorious nor particularly tough, but her reflexes were quicker than any beast aboveground in those days. They had been honed over a lifetime, for the vengeful dragons, not having anything else to do, frequently made war on each other in the dark.

Her tail flicked patiently, hoping to catch one of those amusing "men" beneath it. When the mood struck her, she used to lazily stretch out her long neck and nip at a passerby. Since her nips were often fatal, such a practice had not only decreased the number of her handlers but had increased their carelessness in strapping on the harness. Much to his annoyance, Amarian had almost fallen off during a test flight because of this haphazard treatment. Although he punished the neglectful handlers, he also realized that their service would not improve unless they could work without fear of sudden dismemberment or worse. So he had taken Ovna aside one day. Although no one in the camps or the castle knew exactly what happened in that interview, she rarely indulged in such playfulness again.

Today would be her first public appearance. In anticipation of his plan, Amarian had long ago sent out his bodyguard and the regiments he intended for the western front. Although they had left more than two months before, Ovna's speed would put him there in two weeks' time. He would arrive the same day as his troops. Then Commander Hull would make an appropriately grand entrance, sufficiently impressive to awe that idiot king and hopefully intimidate that troublesome general into submission. Amarian himself would take no satisfaction in the petty display: it was only a prelude to the main event. In a matter of days, Relgaré's Cylini would be defeated. That task Ovna could accomplish all by herself. In the meantime, the king would die tragically in battle, and he, the grief-stricken commander, would assume control of the armies. A simple plot that would proceed without a hitch, especially if General Chiyo were also to disappear. That minor chore would be satisfying.

Ovna screeched in protest as the men tightened the straps, but refrained from attacking them. Meanwhile, the servant who had been packing the armor scurried into the yard and gave his package to the handlers for loading. Soon all would be ready. Amarian turned to his passenger.

"Isn't this exciting, Captain?"

The chains scraped painfully on Gair's already mangled flesh, but he tried not to let his voice show it. Instead, he watched the dragon with profound disgust. "What purpose does it serve to take me?"

"Perhaps I want the company."

"I would be poor company for you. Why would you want a Prysmite breathing down your neck?"

Amarian laughed, involuntarily batting at the back of his neck. "We both know you're harmless. Besides, what if Ovna wants a snack on the trip?"

Gair shut his mouth. The man had a response for everything.

A handler appeared, dodging Ovna's tail. "Darkness, your ride is prepared."

"Then let's go. I don't want to keep the good king waiting."

CHAPTER FOURTEEN

Relgaré was irritable as he inspected his troops. The messenger had said his commander would be there by morning, but the hot autore orbs were by now beyond the horizon. He growled low in his throat: he had a strategy to consider and it did not involve Hull's tardiness. The engineers had already finished the bridge, leaving the way into Cylini territory temptingly open. Now with the morning roll call of the officers almost finished, they had to plan for the next big attack before the Cylini used the bridge against them. Where was Hull?

A trumpet blared from the eastern watch, causing Relgaré to look automatically in that direction. A dark line had formed on the horizon and soon three regiments of fennels, humans, and Sentries came into view. By mid-morning, they would ford the river and reach the camp, but Relgaré sought Hull's banner in vain. He asked a nearby officer if he could see the commander.

"No, my liege. Perhaps he has sent his troops on ahead."

The king disagreed. Hull had said that he would be there in person: Relgaré intended to hold him to that commitment. Perhaps he was with the rear guard, or he had come another way. Just as he was about to allow his frustration and confusion to overflow into words, a screech pierced the air above them.

"Dragon! To the ballistae!"

Relgaré looked up to see a large, black dragon folding her wings for a dive. Dear Kynell, she was going to attack! He shouted hoarsely for the giant crossbows to fire, but before they could, he recognized the rider.

"No, wait! Call off the men! It's Hull."

At the last possible moment, Ovna pulled up from her plunge, fanned her wings, and drifted quietly to the ground. The men gave her a wide radius, purposely keeping the over-sized crossbows loaded. Relgaré approached as the dragon settled, ignoring the fact that she was eying him hungrily. His fury was such that, had she tried anything, he would have given her a worthy struggle.

Amarian jumped down and patted his mount appreciatively on the neck, then bowed as the king stormed up to him.

"My liege! I am sorry for my late arrival. Ovna here had to stop for a snack."

Relgaré fought to keep his temper in check. It would not do to show dissension in front of the men. "Commander Hull. How glad we are that you could join us. I see that you've acquired new transportation."

"I have indeed." Amarian turned slightly as Gair was helped down by some brave soldiers. "And a new servant. Both, I think, will be useful in the fight before us."

Relgaré did not bother to look at the bedraggled man. "I am happy to hear it. Would you mind accompanying me to my tent? We have a meeting with the generals soon and I would be grateful to have a word with you in private beforehand."

Amarian bowed low. "It is my honor. Gair, see to my mount."

With help, Gair reluctantly re-boarded Ovna to seek a more spacious landing place. Amarian watched him go, then followed Relgaré into his tent. Once inside, the king dropped his reserve.

"What in the Chasm were you thinking? Did you see what that beast did to my men?"

"I'm not quite sure what you mean, my liege. I believed that a show of power would be appropriate."

"A show of power? We want *our* power, not Zyreio's!"

Amarian helped himself to a glass of wine. "Power is power. Now they know who is on their side."

"What if they don't want that kind of power on their side?" Relgaré had begun to pace. "Who wants to fight on the side of a dragon? And where in the Chasm did you get it?

"That's not important. And those who fight alongside a dragon are those who want to win."

"We will have victory with or without your theatrics."

Amarian sipped his wine. "My liege, I think you're making too much of this. She's just a dragon. I've instructed her not to harm any of your men."

"Many thanks."

Amarian did not appreciate Relgaré's sarcasm. Did he suspect how numbered his days were? "I am sorry, Your Majesty. I did not realize her presence would be so unappreciated. I'll have Gair send her away."

Exactly as he had planned, the king shook his head. "No, no. She's already here so we might as well use her. I trust she'll find her own food?"

"Of course. Perhaps soon she'll lunch on the Cylini."

"Hopefully by noon tomorrow."

Now that the tense encounter was over, Amarian pulled up a chair. "Yes, I saw that your bridge was finished. How soon are we crossing over?"

"Tonight. The generals are coming any minute to discuss it."

"I see. And what about General Chiyo? Will he be heading up the charge?"

But Relgaré coughed nervously and began to rub his wrist. "Chiyo has been sent on a separate job to explore the marshes. He will not be back in time for the main attack."

Amarian received the news impassively. So the great Chiyo had fallen out of favor. While he was amused at the king's fickleness, he was displeased to hear that the one general who might cause him trouble had slipped beyond his observation.

"I'm sure he will accomplish his task in a timely manner. Did he take many with him?"

Relgaré stared absently at the canvas walls. "No, not many. I allowed him to select fifty and he also took with him a young aide. The Sentries should be back to report on their progress any day now."

"You sent Sentries?" Why had he not heard of this? Why hadn't the Sentries reported immediately to himself?

"Yes, just to help us keep tabs on him. They're fast messengers, as you know."

The man's ignorance annoyed Amarian. A few Sentries against fifty armed men? It was a stupid waste of resources. Chiyo would have ordered them killed by noon the same day. "My liege, may I say something?"

Relgaré jumped to his feet at the sound of approaching footsteps. "Make it quick. The generals are coming."

"I do not know that it was wise to send Chiyo out alone. After all, he is one of your best men. Can you really spare him?"

The king's answer was clipped as he moved back the flap of canvas to greet his officers. "Why not? I've got you now."

It had been harder to slay the Sentries than Hunoi had anticipated, but there were no casualties in the minor fray except, of course, the reptilian watchdogs. The first captain shuddered. Those things were pure evil and although he took no joy in their death, neither did he feel any remorse. No matter what the king thought, the Sentries were never allies. But now his attention was occupied by concern over his general. Ever since they had left camp a few days ago, Chiyo had not been himself. The only person he would speak to was his aide, Bren, and even then only in sharp commands. Hunoi could only wonder what the king had said to him in their final interview. He had asked his friend several times, but each time he was rebuffed. This evening, however, he was determined to crack the shell. They had just forded the Preshin and were about to enter the marshes far west of the Ergana; the men would need their leader if the Cylini decided to engage them.

He found Chiyo gazing into the fire by his small tent, long limbs folded in contemplation. Chiyo had never acquired a proper officer's lodging, since his conferences were often held in the field and he considered himself a man with minimal need for sleeping space. Hunoi's arrangements were similar to his leader's, but as long as they had pack animals, he had not seen the point in denying himself a cot and a small table and chair. Chiyo always sat on the ground. Whether he was setting a good example for his men or merely being stubborn, Hunoi had yet to decide.

He stood at a respectful distance. "General."

Chiyo did not look up. "Yes, Captain?"

"May I request a word, sir?"

"You may request it. Speak all you want."

Hunoi tried not to be annoyed. Chiyo was his general, yes, but also a man who was being purposefully difficult.

"May I sit, sir?"

Chiyo finally looked up, his face the blank mask that Hunoi had dreaded. "Of course, Hunoi. For goodness' sake, sit. Have you had dinner?"

"Yes, sir."

Chiyo glanced around as his friend lowered himself onto a fallen log.

"Enough. You don't need to call me 'sir' in private. Why did you come?"

"To speak with you."

"Is something wrong?"

"There will be if you don't change your behavior."

Hunoi was dismayed to see that Chiyo's expression was not altered by the reprimand. How depressed had he become? He leaned forward, forcing Chiyo to look at him.

"Chiyo, what is wrong? You look as if you've given up."

"And if I have?"

"You had no right to."

"Hunoi, you have been with me a long time. Too long, I suspect. Remember when we came to Keroul? Relgaré was only a boy then and we were little older. But he was so energetic, quick both to act and to take counsel. We were proud to serve him first as our prince and then as our king. He made us forget even our longing for home. We have fought many battles under his banner, but this new threat is different. The Cylini are nothing." Chiyo stopped and then said something completely alien to his training. "And Relgaré is nothing, except he is being a fool and delivering our brave Keroulian army into the hands of Zyreio himself. When Vancien comes back from his Dedication, what army will be there to greet him? If the gods choose an open battlefield, who will be there to fight?"

Hunoi stretched his arm in the direction of their men. "There are these. They would fight."

"Fifty against thousands? There wouldn't be enough for a rout."

"You sound like you doubt what Kynell is doing."

"I doubt very much what Kynell is doing. He has lost before."

"So you've said."

"What's to keep him from losing again?"

"What's to keep him from winning? I thought you were a faithful servant of the Prysm. Surely you remember that our mothers and fathers sent us because they *knew* we would die before abandoning Kynell. If they had thought us weak, would they have let us go? They sent us because, young though we were, we knew that Kynell's power does not rest on men and arms."

"Then why did he allow Tryun to go to battle in ignorance? Why not give Heptar a chance to fight, instead of letting him be brought down in his sleep? What if he has such a fate in store for Vancien? Then what would become of our high ideals?"

Hunoi was not a priest and his answer was not eloquent. But he suspected that a scholar in the high towers of Lascombe would not disagree with his response. "His Advocates are not sorry to give their lives for him.

Perhaps he chose to be defeated."

Chiyo snorted. "For what reason? To plunge Rhyvelad into a thousand cycles of misery?"

"Perhaps. But think of it this way. If he were truly defeated, then why didn't Zyreio destroy him? Obsidian had plenty of opportunities and ample motivation. Do you think that, if given the chance, Zyreio would have allowed a remnant of the Prysm to survive?"

Chiyo was silent for a moment as he remembered the many atrocities he had witnessed in his lifetime: the brutality of war, the madness caused by grief, and the bittersweet taste of killing. He shook his head. The work of Obsidian was thorough. There was no mercy for the innocent or the brave.

"I see your point. Keep talking."

Hunoi eagerly took his cue to express an idea he'd been rolling over in his head for months now. "Think about it, Chiyo. It has been the opinion of some priests that there exists a great balance in our world, that Zyreio has not been annihilated by Kynell because Kynell doesn't have the power, and vice versa. But no true believer in either the Prysm or Obsidian believes this. If the battle will continue for eternity, why fight at all? Somebody *must* win out in the end. Such a victory would result in the complete destruction of 'the balance.' The Ages say that Kynell conquers all. But how can he conquer all when he loses twice? Unless he has chosen to lose. Unless he has a plan that we do not know about. We either believe in him fully or not at all, Chiyo."

Chiyo's fog began to clear as he reluctantly entered the debate. "So if Kynell can conquer all by himself, why does he use the Advocates?"

"To allow us to help in the victory? To give evil the chance to repent? I don't know. But I do know that if Commander Hull, or Amarian, wins this victory, it will not be because he has the greater army. It will be because Kynell did not bring Vancien success and he did not forbid Amarian triumph."

The fire crackled as Hunoi waited for a response. Finally, Chiyo stood. "You will make a fine theologian someday, my friend."

Hunoi stood as well. "If I am so ordered. But for now, your men need a leader."

Chiyo nodded. "That will be all."

Hunoi disappeared into the darkness. Chiyo watched him go before entering his tent. They would be in the marshes by tomorrow evening. This could be their last sleep on dry ground for some time. Hopefully, his men would enjoy it.

The lunos were bright as Relgaré's battalions silently tramped over the bridge. The waters of the Preshin rushed under their feet, causing several of the younger soldiers to watch the waves suspiciously. It was said that the river was guarded by sea-beasts whose razor teeth could slice a man to pieces, that occasionally they would jump from the water and snatch their prey from dry land, or in this case, a dry bridge. Of course, as the men looked around at the fennels and Sentries who accompanied them, they could not forget that the real threat marched by their side. Not a few of them wondered what had possessed their king to invite such unwelcome guests.

The first battalion had just set foot on the opposite shore when the Cylini attacked. Their war-whoops filled the air as they emerged from the trees guarding the southern bank and swept down upon the troops. The army was too well-disciplined to panic, but there were still two full battalions bottlenecked on the long bridge, and the battalion already across was heavily outnumbered. Flaming arrows rained down, threatening not only to decimate the trapped soldiers but to ignite the bridge itself. The officers in charge hesitated to respond. If they ordered a full retreat, they would give the Cylini a swift victory that could only encourage them. If they ordered a charge, the bridge might very well burn down around their ears and leave whatever soldiers had crossed at the mercy of the enemy. Such an order would sacrifice too many men and accomplish nothing. A trumpet sounded the retreat.

Amarian watched the disaster from the air. He had known the Cylini would attack and known the bridge was a foolish idea. Yet he had not argued with Relgaré, who was now stupidly pushing his way to the front of the fray, shouting at his men to press forward. In a few seconds, the moment would be perfect. Just let him set foot on the shore. . .there. Amarian barked a command to Ovna, who obediently folded her wings and dove straight into the battle.

At the cry of the dragon, both Keroulian and Cylini men looked up in terror. Relgaré ignored her, slashing at whomever was in his way in a mad dash to get to the archers before they torched the bridge. A small company followed him. They had almost made it to their goal before Ovna was there, her teeth and claws tearing into the enemy and catching a few unfortunate Keroulian soldiers, as well. The Cylini archers tried bravely to bring her down but she was too quick for them. Helpless, they fled, but both dragon and king relentlessly pursued them. The men on the bridge, seeing their enemy

retreat, shouted a victory cry and surged forward to complete the massacre.
Ovna could not make it far into the woods, but she stalked its border, picking
off any who fled in her direction. Amarian let her have her fun while he
dismounted, seized a nearby voyoté, and raced after the king. Though
Relgaré was already deep into the dark, soggy trees, he had no problem
following the bellows of his murderous rage. He soon found him wading
through ankle-deep water, beating the bushes stained with Cylini blood and
shouting for another challenger. Relgaré had also dismounted. Except for
his voyoté a few yards off, he was quite alone.

Amarian approached slowly, noting the bodies at Relgaré's feet. "My
liege, where are your men?"

Relgaré stopped his call for blood and focused on the figure riding out
of the shadows. "Hull? Is that you? Curse them all, they were taken by
another ambush. The Cylini jumped out of nowhere and," he surveyed the
damage around him, "my men put up quite a fight. I was able to finish off
the few they left alive."

Amarian now emerged fully into the lunos-light, his glinting armor
showing no signs of a fight. "Are you hurt?"

"No." Relgaré put down his sword. "But you look like you haven't
fought at all."

"By the time Ovna finished her dive, there was little fighting left to do.
Besides, I was so intent on seeing to your safety, I did not have time to chase
after stragglers."

The indirect criticism was not lost on the king. "They had to be finished
off. Tonight."

"Of course." Amarian dismounted and picked his way over the bodies
until he stood directly before Relgaré. "Your men will be worried about you.
It is easy to get injured tearing off into the trees like this."

"You can see that I've been protected. Kynell be praised."

Amarian nodded. "Indeed."

Despite his brave words, Relgaré began to get nervous. Commander
Hull appeared a little too patient for his liking. "Well, we must be getting
back. There will be quite a bit of clean up, I'm sure." He whistled for his
voyoté.

"Kynell's protection is great, is it not?"

Now that he was mounted, Relgaré felt a little safer. "It is perfect."

Gentle splashing interrupted their conversation. Amarian allowed
himself a luxurious stretch, then jumped back on his voyoté and began to ride

away. "You will have to tell me sometime, my liege, what you mean by 'perfect.'"

Relgaré, now completely unnerved, started to follow him but was blocked by two dark reptilian forms. They were Neptim, two of Obsidian's finest. It was a king, after all, whom they were about to dispatch. Amarian did not look back as he heard the sounds of struggle and Relgaré's cry for help.

Now that the king was out of the way, Amarian could get to the real fight. He wondered where Vancien was. It had been a few days since Ranti's last report. Of course, now that he no longer had to keep up this ridiculous ruse, he could send out whole regiments to stalk his brother's small group. He pondered that option, then considered it too obvious. It was far more effective to strike at the Prysm in subtle, even sensuous, ways. He pictured Verial. Despite herself, she would do her job well.

CHAPTER FIFTEEN

Four days after Verial had joined their troupe, the companions stood on the riverbank, looking sullenly at the marshes beyond the waters. The Ergana was both calm and shallow at this point. Crossing it was the least of their worries. Nevertheless, all expressions registered dismay as they beheld the heavy mist hovering around the gnarled trees of the marsh, and inhaled the stifling vapor of the orb-moss that grew there. It was called orb-moss for precisely the opposite reason that one might think. Rather than needing the light, it shriveled instantly in the heat, exuding as it did a noxious odor. On the marsh's edge, where the orbs shone at mid-day, the fumes were particularly offensive, for the moss grew quickly in the night only to die by noon. Thus there occurred a futile cycle of daily generation and decay. Telenar assured them, however, that the stench was only on this side of the marsh. It would be less fragrant when they had gone deeper into the trees and further from the orb-light. It was such a small comfort.

They had intended to move south along the river's eastern edge before entering, but Vancien wondered if some soggy paths and stagnant pools would be a fair exchange for a reprieve from the smell. When he suggested as much to Telenar, Telenar had solemnly informed him that far worse dangers lay within the swamp than wet boots. By virtue of being such an unpleasant place, the marshes harbored all sorts of tree and water-dwelling creatures that might otherwise have been stamped out in the light of the orbs. Instead, they had found a refuge from man's civilizing hand, growing larger and more fearless with each cycle.

Vancien shuddered. "No wonder Relgaré wanted to approach the Cylini from the north. No man in his right mind would send an army through there."

Telenar nodded his agreement. "Which is why we'll be safe, at least from the king. Even the Sentries dislike this place. You would think it would be their perfect environment, but apparently they are little match for its inhabitants."

"Sounds lovely," N'vonne chimed in as she joined them. Sneaking an arm around Telenar's waist, she announced that dinner was ready. The men happily abandoned their distasteful conversation and followed her to the campfire where Verial was seated, stirring the broth. She did not look up as they approached but silently handed them their meals, took her own, and excused herself. Telenar grabbed Vancien's arm as he started after her.

"Vance!"

Vancien shook him off without a word, following her to the tree-line, out of hearing range. Although she must have heard his footsteps, she did not acknowledge his presence until he spoke.

"It'll be dark soon. Do you intend to stay away from us all night?"

She nodded, not taking her eyes away from the marshes. "I have done so before."

"Yes, but now we're in dangerous territory. Telenar says that the marsh-creatures are to be treated with caution. It's not wise to go off alone."

Verial sighed as she pondered how she should treat this opportunity. Now would be a perfect moment to set the bait, if she were so inclined. Was she so inclined? Would she ever be? Probably not, but her disinclination would not help Gair.

"Perhaps it would be wise for me to court danger. If it finds me, it will save you and your friends a great deal of trouble."

Shaking his head, Vancien lowered his voice unnecessarily. "That is foolishness. You are one of Kynell's creatures, just like Telenar and N'vonne and me. You have a responsibility to preserve your life."

"Ha! If you only knew how much trouble my life has caused, you would throw me into the marshes yourself!"

Telenar's warnings to him, never very pressing, were now as far away as the Eastern Lands. He turned her face up towards him, holding her chin firmly in his hand. "I *do* know what you've been through. But I also know that Kynell has spared you for a reason. Your life is not your own. It is his."

He spoke with such intensity that she could not help but meet his gaze. What she discovered there was surprisingly familiar. Suddenly she was taken back to that day thousands of cycles ago, when another young man stood before her and offered her a longed-for life. She had succumbed then and the results had been unspeakable. But this time, the power was different. While still frightening, it shielded her with a jealousy that no servant of Obsidian had ever displayed.

Vancien saw the fear in her eyes turn to awe. She had involuntarily taken a step back, but he followed. There was some communication passing between them, something he could not put his finger on. He held his breath, heeding the urge to close the gap that separated them. Here was a creature of Kynell, a jewel caught up in a perpetual dungeon. From her prison, she had effortlessly made Prysm Advocates fall. But Kynell still suffered her to live, to breathe, to be beautiful. This last he could not deny. Her fair hair caught the setting orblight, framing a face that was too young to bear such burdens. If she would only realize how much Kynell desired her, what freedom she could experience! He took another step closer. This time she did not step back. How many dark nights had she suffered, how many cold hands? Had she known any warmth at all? If there was no hope for such a woman, then Rhyvelad would never be saved.

Telenar watched nervously as the two figures in the distance spoke, then appeared to cease speaking only to look at each other. What were they doing? Would Verial succeed in her treachery so easily? As he saw Vancien bend his head down to kiss her, he almost leaped from his seat. N'vonne pulled him back, although she too was watching with anxiety.

"What does he think he's doing?" he sputtered. "Fool! Does he think this is a game? Does he think that he alone of all the Advocates has the strength to dally with that woman?"

N'vonne had to use all of her force to keep him from charging like an enraged fennel. "Telenar, please! We cannot stop his actions and if you rush over there now, it will only turn him against you. Kynell sees it, too. Remember that it was he who allowed Verial to come to us."

Telenar allowed himself to be restrained but did not calm down. His face had flushed a deep red. "How can you say that? You know what happened to the other two."

"I know as well as you, Telenar. But we have to trust Kynell."

"So it's our job to stand by and watch him ruin us?"

"Of course not!" Her green eyes sparkled with all the indignation that he was feeling. He sighed and took her hand.

"You are handling this too well, N'vonne. If I recall, you were the one who attacked her with a spoon."

"But I know Vancien better than you do. If you bully him now, you will only push him away. But he'll come to you in time. He loves the Prysm too much to linger in disobedience without it eating away at him."

Telenar watched as the new couple separated and began walking toward the campfire, awkwardly keeping apart yet clearly fighting the urge to draw together again. "I hope you're right, N'vonne. But how long will it take before he comes to his senses?"

The next morning, they forded the river in silence. There were a few lame jokes ("What does the orb-moss do in the night?" "Spit at the sky," a joke which has befuddled scholars to this day), but any attempt to lighten the mood didn't work. Everyone knew that the next several weeks would be unpleasant. This knowledge, combined with Telenar's frustration with Vancien and Vancien's awkward attempts to engage Verial, made for a very uncomfortable start.

The Ergana allowed them to pass with no objection, as if happy to send the vexing travelers on their way. Soon their voyoté were picking their way through soggy turf, sneezing if a particularly strong scent of orb-moss drifted across their nose. For a while, the marsh was as silent as the intruders, but as they made their way deeper into the moist darkness, they began to hear unfamiliar sounds.

"Don't suppose those are birds?" The question was N'vonne's, but the hopeful thought was shared by all, even Verial.

Telenar shook his head. "I wish. Everybody watch out for pools like the ones over there. They may be shallow, but the mud at the bottom will suck you down. Vance, trust Nagab. Don't try to steer him. He knows what to avoid."

Vancien obediently loosened his grip on the reins, biting his lip to keep from retorting. Instead, he urged his mount up next to Cetla, where N'vonne and Verial were attempting to fend off an onslaught of insects.

"You two all right?"

N'vonne batted away a large, predatory wampa beetle. "Right as we'll ever be. Didn't we bring any nets to protect against these things?"

"Unfortunately, no. All we have are the shadeclothes in case we passed through the Glade. But they're not much help here."

She tossed her auburn hair, casting out at least four more beetles. "Hm. Poor planning on our part. Did you hear that?"

Vancien had, although he wasn't sure what to make of the noise. It was a loud, deep, croak. From the sound of it, its owner had to be at least the size of a voyoté. Worse, it seemed like it was coming closer. Cetla and Nagab stopped, allowing Lansing and Telenar to catch up. They all waited as the sound grew near.

"Perhaps," Vancien whispered, "we should move while we have the chance."

"And stumble into a pool or something worse?" Telenar replied. "But you're right: we should keep moving. Slowly."

Harnesses jingled as they resumed their journey, but soon the croaking was directly in front of them. They stopped again, but couldn't see anything except the leaves shaking from the sound. As N'vonne and Telenar looked at each other, wondering what to do next, Vancien impatiently dismounted and moved toward the source of the disturbance. Before the others could stop him, he tore away the foliage to reveal a small frog with bright orange eyes. It stopped mid-croak as Vancien scooped it up with one hand.

"Vance, are you insane? It could be poisonous!"

Vancien waved away the objection. "It's all right, Telenar. I remember reading about these guys in school." He triumphantly held out the frightened creature. "N'vonne, do you remember teaching me about this little fellow, whose bark is worse than his bite?"

"Not really, but it's been a while. You might want to put him down, just in case I taught you incorrectly."

Telenar nodded his enthusiastic agreement and ordered Vancien to remount so they could continue. This Vancien did, more because Nagab was starting to nervously paw the turf than because of Telenar's imperative. With a confident grin towards N'vonne and Verial, he allowed Nagab to take the lead. So they traveled until dark, when they made as dry a camp as possible and spent an uncomfortable night's sleep. This pattern was repeated for several monotonous days, with occasional interruptions to note a fascinating swamp creature or avoid a dangerous one. By the end of the fourth day, they were all cranky, wet, and nostalgic for the foothills. On the afternoon of the fifth day, it began to rain. By the end of a week, the waters were rising to a dangerous level.

Telenar groaned as his voyoté sloshed his way through the trees. "Any more of this and we'll have to build a boat."

Vancien couldn't hear him through the downpour, but imagined all too well what he was saying. If the rains didn't let up soon, they would be in trouble. Already he had seen the smaller critters climbing the trees, trying to escape drowning. He might have considered following their lead, except the voyoté were poor climbers and he had noticed some not-too-small, vicious-looking beasts finding refuge in the trees, as well. Better to be washed away than devoured at a high altitude.

N'vonne was pondering similar options when she saw something move in the water next to her. This was nothing new. Many fish and amphibians were enjoying the rising flood. But a second look showed that this something was not moving ahead or falling behind. It was keeping pace. She turned and called for Vancien, the only one of their group with a sword.

"Vancien! I think we may need your help. There's something swimming next to us."

He nodded and splashed over by her side. But when he looked where she was pointing, he could see nothing. "I don't see anything. Are you sure it wasn't your imagination?"

Verial's scream answered him. He looked up just in time to see her pulled off Cetla into the dark water. With a shout, he jumped off Nagab and splashed around, sword out, in the waist-deep filth. N'vonne, too, started in alarm, but she remained mounted. Telenar raced over to join them.

"What happened? N'vonne, where's Verial? Vancien, what are you doing? Get back on your mount! We don't know what else is out there!"

Both of them ignored his questions and commands. As N'vonne anxiously scanned the water's surface, she thought she saw a glimpse of color. "Vance, over there! Quick!"

Wading as quickly as he could in the direction she pointed, he soon saw Verial's heel and dove for it. For a breathless moment, N'vonne and Telenar watched the surface, now disturbed only by an occasional splash. Then Vancien was up again, with a half-drowned Verial in tow. "I got her! Quick, take her before it comes back."

"You mean you didn't kill it?" Telenar demanded as they hastily helped the drenched woman back onto Cetla. As soon as she was safely aboard, Vancien called for Nagab.

"No. There wasn't time. I just cut off whatever part of it was holding on to her."

"Then it's going to be angry. We had better hurry."

Vancien nodded. "Yes, we had better. Come on, boy." Before Nagab took two steps, however, the water swelled next to voyoté and rider, and out of the wave emerged a large, flat head.

"Vance, watch out!"

But both Vancien and Nagab were under water before Telenar finished his warning. This time, they did not surface.

N'vonne's scream was punctuated by Telenar's cry of dismay. But it was also interrupted by something else: the whizzing of arrows.

Telenar was incredulous. "We're under attack?" But even as he said it, he noticed that the arrows weren't meant for them. Instead, they sliced through the water where Vancien had disappeared. Soon it became difficult to tell where the rain stopped and the arrows began. But they had their intended affect. The dead body of large, flat-headed triple-tooth soon floated to the surface, bleeding from multiple wounds and clutching both of its victims between its three rows of razor-sharp teeth. Blood from all three stained the water.

Hurriedly dismounting, Telenar waded over to his student's limp body and tried to pry open the rubbery mouth of the beast. N'vonne and Verial appeared next to him and tried to help, but it was no use.

"Is he dead?" The question had to have been Verial's; N'vonne would have known better. But Telenar's answer didn't sound as certain as he would have liked.

"He can't be. It's impossible. He can't die. N'vonne, keep his head above water! Verial, see if Nagab is alive. How do we get this mouth open?" His orders were hissed through tears of frustration. Try as he might, the jaws of the beast were clamped tightly around Vance. Every movement of the rescuers only sunk the teeth deeper into his flesh. "Where's his sword? Maybe we can chop its head off."

N'vonne's gasp was not the response he wanted to hear. "What is it?" She pointed mutely at Vancien's left arm: his sword arm. From the shoulder down, it was almost completely severed, and the rest of the limb, as well as the sword it had clutched, was flopping around somewhere in the beast's mouth.

"Nagab is alive!" Verial shouted from the other side of the head. "His hind end is in bad shape." Then she gasped.

"What is it?"

She pointed up to the trees. "Are those friends of yours?"

Telenar followed her gaze to see a handful of roughly dressed humans descending into the marsh. "I don't think so. The only humans in these swamps are the Cylini."

He watched as they silently approached. There were only six of them, armed not only with bows and arrows, but short swords and some nasty, curved type of knife. Without saying a word, they surveyed the scene. Then one of them barked an order, and two of them pulled out their short swords, reversed their grip, and started pounding on either side of the beast's jaw. Soon two sharp cracks resounded above the downpour. As the Cylini warriors expertly pried back the broken bone, Telenar had the impression that they had done this sort of thing many times before. The leader then issued another order and two of the warriors lifted Vancien up and out of the mouth, while the other three struggled with the much heavier, semi-conscious, Nagab. The leader concluded the grim ceremony by saying something to the dumbfounded travelers and wading west. His men followed, carrying man and voyoté as well as they could. Vancien's sword splashed into the water as they passed; the Cylini took no notice, but Telenar stooped to pick it up.

N'vonne appeared at his elbow. "Could you tell what he said?"

"I didn't catch it. My Cylinic is too rusty. But we have to follow them."

By the time the bedraggled company reached their destination, the rain had let up. Night was falling, allowing N'vonne to barely make out the nature of the strange camp ahead of them. Torchlight hovered eerily above what appeared to be floating wooden platforms, bound together by vines and held above the water by hundreds of inflated rubbery sacks. N'vonne didn't have a chance to get a close look, but the material from the sacks looked similar to the skin of the three-tooth. The platforms were lodged in-between the trees, cut roughly to the shape of the open area, so the trees themselves served as posts to prevent floating away. Branches were trimmed back so the platforms could rise with the floodwaters, but as long as the trees stayed put, so would the campsite. Each floating surface was surrounded by a tall fence. She shuddered to think what creatures these barriers were meant to keep out. Inside the fences, however, was more than just a military camp. It was a village, spread out across several platforms and connected by an impressive system of gates and bridges.

As they neared one of the fences, their leader shouted a greeting and a gate immediately swung open. To N'vonne's surprise, children flocked to the opening, chattering happily and gaping at the new arrivals. The leader, who up to this time had appeared stern, instantly dropped to his knees and hugged a boy of about three cycles. Then the women joined them. In the excitement of the homecoming, the visitors were almost forgotten. But an older woman who had nobody in particular to greet soon noticed Vancien's wounded shoulder. With great authority, she questioned one of the warriors, who shook his head, said a few defensive words, and gestured toward the swamp. Still glaring at him, she hurried into the crowd and started pulling the women away from their loved ones and toward Vancien and Nagab. Man and beast quickly disappeared under a series of ministrations while a brave handful of souls tried to lead Cetla and Lansing to an appropriate shelter. At first, the voyoté had no intention of leaving their fallen comrade in the hands of strangers. But in the end, weariness, hunger, and Telenar's reassurances took their toll and the two exhausted beasts trudged off to their dinner.

Meanwhile, the three remaining visitors were hurried into a warm hut, where they were given food and dry garments, then left to their own devices.

Telenar looked politely away as the ladies changed from their soaked attire into warm Cylini clothes. As soon as they had done the same for him, they all sat down around the central fire, warming their hands and wondering what to say. N'vonne and Telenar, of course, had plenty to say to each other, but Verial's presence discouraged lively conversation.

N'vonne spoke first. "Verial, you're not hurt, are you? That monster got you, as well."

Verial held up the tattered remains of her sleeve. "He had hold only of my shirt. I was not harmed." She relapsed into silence.

N'vonne nodded, satisfied. "I hope they take good care of Vance."

Telenar reached out to rub her shoulder. "I think they will. They didn't bring us this far to kill us, although our clothes and speech must have told them who we are. They've probably been tracking us for a while."

"Thank Kynell for that! Imagine what could have happened otherwise. Did you see the children?" Her eyes sparkled in the firelight. "I bet this is a side of the Cylini the king hasn't seen."

"Even if he has, I doubt that would change anything."

N'vonne had to agree, and she was just about to say as much, when Verial started out of her pensive trance. "Your king is Relgaré?"

Telenar was immediately suspicious. He was still irritated at her for being the cause of all the day's trouble. "Of course, but that's of no concern to you."

"He is dead."

"Excuse me?"

Verial ignored his comment and turned to N'vonne. "I am sorry, but your king is dead."

N'vonne looked hard at her. She had no attachment to Relgaré, but why would this girl know anything about him? "Are you certain? How do you know?"

Verial did not answer at first, only looked into the fire. "I've been told to tell you."

Telenar ground his teeth. Having this woman with them was becoming far too dangerous. "Who told you? Zyreio?"

When she nodded, he jumped to his feet and started pacing. "We should have seen this coming. We *did* see this coming. It was only a matter of time before Amarian dispatched him. That means we've lost the armies. And that means that Ch—" He stopped and turned hastily toward Verial.

"Has he told you anything else? Can he read your thoughts?"

She nodded again. "He knows all, priest. But he hasn't told me anything else."

Her answer was insufficient. He crouched in front of her and took her face roughly in his hand. N'vonne watched nervously, unsure of the limits of his patience. But he did not strike her. Instead, he forced her to make eye contact. "Does Amarian know what you know?"

"If Zyreio allows him to, yes."

"Can you stop him?"

"Probably not. Why would I?"

Telenar wanted to strike her, but it was wrong to hit a woman, even Verial. "Why wouldn't you? Do you *want* him to win?"

She shrugged, causing him to turn away before he lost his temper completely. "I don't care who 'wins', as you say," she responded. "What are five hundred cycles to me? Besides, Amarian has never harmed me." This last statement was not entirely true, but she was getting impatient with these imbeciles. Was this how Kynell conducted his battles? With a crew of idiots?

N'vonne only stared in disbelief, but Telenar was furious. "How many cycles have you lived?" he demanded, his face turning a crimson red. "How many deaths have you seen? Tell me, has Amarian used you to send souls to the Chasm? Has he allowed you to participate as he tortures his own followers, then kills both them and their families? How many times have you watched a good man suffer and done nothing about it? Your heart is made of stone, lady! And after thousands of cycles of watching men die fighting for your lord or die fighting for you, you're still nothing but a spoiled girl sitting by a pond, hoping for something better to come along."

Until that last comment, his speech had had no effect on her, but she flinched when he mentioned the pond. "How did you know about that?"

Her question caught him off-guard. "About what, the pond?"

She nodded.

"Don't you read the Ages?"

Now she was uncharacteristically flustered. "Yes, of course. A little. It doesn't matter. My life is in the Ages?"

"How could it not be?"

"All of it?"

Telenar wasn't quite sure how to respond. "The parts where you come into contact with the Advocates, yes. I don't know what they leave out."

She started to fidget. "But how is that possible? There was no one there except Grens and myself. No one to see. . ." Her voice drifted off.

Telenar began to soften. "Kynell sees everything, child. No one escapes his notice. Not even you."

It was meant as a comfort, but Verial spat and kicked at the fire.

"Kynell! You're all obsessed with him! If he's so powerful, why does Obsidian know your every move? Why did he allow his Advocate to be eaten alive by a swamp creature? And his king to be Amarian's pawn?"

Telenar was about to remind her that Obsidian knew their every move because there was a spy in their midst and that the only reason Vancien was attacked was because he was rescuing her, but N'vonne interceded.

"Shhh, child. Be careful what you say."

Child? Why did they keep calling her child? She was older than the Ages themselves! Beside herself, she stormed out the door of the hut, only to run into an old Cylini man who was just about to enter. With a shrill, "Out of my way!" she pushed him aside and disappeared into the night.

The visitor looked at them uncertainly, but neither Telenar nor N'vonne felt any compulsion to go after her. Telenar nodded at him to come in.

"Far'an lur, 'eloi."

"I thought you didn't speak Cylinic."

"I said I was rusty." Then to the newcomer. "Pratsa twy am tehn nequrra, 'eloi. Preto, ga'an." He indicated the recently vacated seat next to the fire. The old man returned the thanks, and sat. He smelled of wet leather and mold, but his long beard was combed and his teeth clean.

N'vonne could understand nothing of the halting conversation that followed, except that Telenar appeared to be complimenting the Cylini on their living arrangements and discussing recent events. The names Relgaré, Hull, and even Amarian surfaced several times. When they were finished, the man smiled graciously at N'vonne, bowed to Telenar, and left.

"What did he say?"

"He said that Vancien won't be able to travel for several days and even then Nagab won't be able to carry him. But he is going to get together a few warriors to escort us through the marsh to the west when we're ready. He also says that he likes your hair and that if he didn't have a wife, he would make you stay here."

"Hm. How nice." She could not decide if she was put off or flattered by the compliment, but considering all that these people had done for them, she decided not to take offense. "What did you tell him about Relgaré and Amarian?"

Telenar moved over next to her, pleased that Verial's sudden departure had finally given them some time to be alone. "Nothing he did not know already. His scouts have told them that the Keroulian army is now controlled by Commander Hull, who rides a dragon. That means that Verial was right, and Relgaré is dead."

Her brow furrowed. "A dragon? How in Rhyvelad did he find a dragon?" She looked at the door. "And what are we going to do about Verial?"

Verial's plight was the furthest thing from Telanar's mind at the moment, but she was right. Something would have to be done. She was probably in with Vancien right now, casting her spell. The thought irritated him so much that he forgot about the romantic mood he was had been attempting to create.

But N'vonne did not. Leaning into his shoulder, she gazed at the fire as she spoke. "Maybe she'll just leave and not come back. Would that be so bad? I feel sorry for that Gair fellow she keeps mentioning, but Kynell will take good care of him. And if she doesn't go on her own accord, maybe we could leave her with the Cylini. That old man might like her hair better than mine."

Telenar chuckled low in his throat. The deep sound made her even more relaxed. "I doubt that, my love. Besides, she found us once and she could find us again. And Vancien wouldn't understand. As you said before, it's better to keep an eye on them both than to alienate Vancien because of her."

She looked up at him. "I said that? How very clever of me."

Her face was very close to his. He could smell her breath, which, despite all they had been through, still a had a touch of mint. He had to fight hard to keep the jovial mood. This was neither the time nor the setting for anything more serious. But he couldn't keep from stroking her hair.

"Of course it was clever, dear one." He hesitated, painfully aware of how rare moments like this were. "You're very precious to me, N'vonne. You know that."

She nodded and began to stare into the fire. "I know."

But he tilted her head upward, marveling at what he was about to say. "I mean, when all of this is over, I don't want you to leave me."

She sat up slowly, watching him. He couldn't tell if it was a good look or not, but he pressed forward anyway. "I mean, I don't want you to ever leave me. I want you to be my wife."

"You're asking me to marry you?"

"When this is over, yes."

So this was it. She had thought about this moment often enough, but now she had difficulty believing it was finally happening. She looked harder at him, not wanting to make him wait but wanting to be sure of her decision. Hull was still a part of her, but he would never come back. Not for her, at any rate. And Telenar was here in front of her, alive. She loved him like a brother. No, more than a brother. Much more. In truth, she had known how she should respond for a long time now. When all of this was over, she still wanted to be able to spend every day with him.

"Yes, Telenar. I would love to marry you."

His eyes lit up. "Really? You would? Then can I kiss you?" He flushed, remembering his first awkward attempt.

She nodded. His second kiss, though unpracticed, was encouraging. The third was better still. He was just about to try a fourth time when the door banged open and Verial entered. She did not say a word, but crept into the corner to sleep. Her presence was nevertheless an effective safeguard against further attempts. They sat there for a moment, smiling foolishly. Then Telenar, needing to do something with his elation, commented that it was time to check on Vancien. N'vonne decided to stay with Verial, so he left her to her hopefully pleasant thoughts.

Stepping out into the cool night air, Telenar caught the elbow of the first person he saw. "Uche go brunert 'nthro?"

The young lady stared at him for a moment, then pointed to the next hut over.

"Pratsa twy, 'elai." He let her go, then moved quietly to the next door and opened it a crack. "Vance? You awake?"

An inarticulate noise assured him that his student was somewhat conscious. He stepped inside and saw Vancien laid out on fur-covered table, his shoulder thickly bandaged and his arm in a splint. Although that was the worst of his wounds, his left leg was also gashed and his face was still swollen from his underwater beating. Telenar's heart ached for him. What right had he to propose to N'vonne when the Advocate was suffering the next door down?

Vancien read his tutor's guilty expression and tried to smile. "Don't worry, Telenar," he croaked. "I deserved it."

The comment brought Telenar back to his old self. "Of course you did. What right did you have to go plunging around after her? You may not get killed, but you can do a lot of damage in the meantime."

"She came by, you know."

Telenar pulled up a stool and sat. "I figured. Did you talk?"

Vancien shook his head, then winced at the effort. "No. She thought I was asleep. So I just kept quiet and let her talk."

"What did she say?"

Vancien thought about keeping some of her comments in reserve, but decided against it. She may be a creature of Kynell, but Telenar was his mentor and close friend. The man's loyalty to the Prysm was complete. "She sounded out of sorts, as if she had just come from a fight. What did you say to her?"

Telenar looked away, recalling his words. "I was too hard on her. Let's leave it at that. Did she mention the Ages?"

"Yes, quite a bit. But she was ranting as if she'd never read them, swearing that Kynell had no business to intrude on her life, cursing you, and calling the wrath of Obsidian down on everybody. If she's trying to seduce me, she's doing a poor job of it."

Telenar swallowed his sarcastic reply. "She thought you were asleep. But I don't think she knows what she's trying to do. One minute she's crying over Gair and asking about Kynell, the next she's acting cool or invoking Zyreio's name. Obsidian still has a strong hold on her, Vance. Don't forget that."

"I won't, Telenar. I promise. And I'm sorry for ignoring your warnings. Very sorry."

Telenar could tell he was remembering that kiss by the Ergana. "It's done, Vance. We will start anew with her. Cautiously."

"But with love."

The admission was more difficult than Telenar expected. It was a long moment before he spoke. "Cautious, *very* cautious, non-romantic, guided-by-Kynell sort of love, yes. I won't lie: in my mind, she's just a tool of the enemy. But," He paused, staring at the floor. "it might be possible to love our enemies."

Vancien nodded. Telenar turned to leave, then stopped at the door. "I thought you should know that I just asked N'vonne to be my wife. And she said yes."

Vancien grinned as widely as his bruised face allowed. "Congratulations, my friend! May Kynell bless you!"

Telenar let himself a smile, as well. "Pretty amazing, isn't it? I mean, she's so. . .well, anyway."

"You two are a good match. I've already said so. Give her a hug for me." He paused, then wagged one of his good fingers at him. "But behave yourself."

"Of course! I wouldn't do anything inappropriate. The Ages say with no uncertainty that a man and a woman are to remain pure."

Vancien dismissed his objections as well as he could. "I know, Telenar. I was just teasing. Now I think I'm going to get some more sleep. But could you keep Verial away for a bit? She's not exactly restful."

"Absolutely."

CHAPTER SIXTEEN

Amarian's distaste for his new army was obvious. After the victory at the bridge and the death of their king, the Keroulian troops had become fidgety. Many a high-ranking soldier had come to him with petitions from their battalion to return to the capital. The king, they insisted, deserved a proper burial attended by his wife and children. Now the generals were here again with the same monotonous demands.

"I'm sorry, General, what did you say?"

Tengar, the senior officer of the delegation, impatiently repeated his statement. "King Relgaren has already been crowned in Lascombe. But the troops won't budge until prince Farlone arrives. And even then, they have no enthusiasm for chasing the Cylini into the marshes. If you won't let them return home, then they at least want to see their king and bury him in a proper manner."

Amarian tried to adopt a conciliatory tone. "I told you, my men could not recover his body." This was not entirely true. The Sentries had done their job a little too well. No one who had seen Relgaré's corpse would think that it was the work of the Cylini. "It's those barbarians. They've butchered your king and burned his remains."

Tengar shook his head. "Some of the troops are saying the barbarians are not in the marshes, but fighting beside us. And what should I tell them? That the Sentries and fennels they've been raised to hate are suddenly allies? That they're trustworthy? You've seen the fights between your troops and ours, Commander Hull. One of your Sentries tore a man in half last week.

How am I supposed to convince my men that the Cylini, not your hordes, are the enemy?"

The other officers nodded their agreement. Amarian's patience began to wear thin. He rose, planted his hands on the camp desk, and looked sternly at his insubordinates. "Do you think I've brought my army halfway across Rhyvelad to destroy my own allies? Do you think I don't have a stake in annihilating the Cylini? They sit there, plotting their raids against civilization in that infested swamp of theirs. They're a knife lodged against our back and now they've murdered your king. If we don't wipe them out now, they'll think us weak, that we're loyal to only one man instead of to a kingdom, to a civilization. I know that our men do not see eye to eye, and that Sentries can get out of hand. Trust me, those who have acted inappropriately have been punished. Hate them all you want, but we have to finish this. Once the Cylini have been wiped out, once every last woman and child of them has been shown what real civilization, real strength looks like, they'll either submit or die."

Tengar shifted uncomfortably. "You're talking genocide."

"I'm talking preservation. I'm talking about a life free of border wars and niggling little conflicts. You know as well as I do, general, that any Cylini man, woman, or child left alive will only stir up trouble for our children and grandchildren. The only way is to uproot them completely. To do that, we must fight together."

One of the younger officers cleared his throat. "The king would never have approved this."

"The king is dead. Obviously his policies weren't thorough enough. Gentlemen, we do not have a choice here. If we turn tail and go home, then all of our battles have been for naught. Please, consider other options. You may go."

Tengar grimaced at being dismissed so lightly. He turned to the officers behind him. "Gentlemen, please allow me a word with the commander."

They obediently went out, murmuring, and he redirected his attention to Commander Hull. "I would like to remind you, Commander, that until the prince arrives, I am in command of the Keroulian army and I do not answer to you. And when the prince arrives, he will be in command of our men. You may exercise complete control over those monsters you call soldiers, but our troops do not budge until I tell them to. And I will not send them into the marshes until I hear the command from Prince Farlone himself. Is that clear?"

Amarian thought about killing the man then and there, but decided it would be wiser to bide his time. It would be better to win Keroul, not destroy it. "General, you mistake my intentions. I have no desire to usurp your authority or the prince's. I ask only for your aid. Forgive me for dismissing the officers so abruptly. I meant no offense. But I'm glad you sent them out, because I need to tell you something."

Although not appeased, Tengar's curiosity checked his anger. "What do you have to tell me that you could not tell the others?"

Amarian eyed the man, wondering how familiar he was with the Ages. It was a chance he'd have to take. "There is going to come a time, probably in the middle of our marsh campaign, when I'm going to have to leave for a while. It will only be for a week or so, but I want you to know that I'm not abandoning you. I have some reinforcements that I won't be able to muster until breach season."

"Why are you telling me this now?"

"Because I trust you, Tengar. I know that while I'm gone, you will be able to persuade Farlone that I'm not deserting him. Plus, I wanted to give you plenty of warning."

Tengar nodded, still wary. "And these reinforcements? Who are they? Why can't they come sooner?"

Amarian rose and walked over to the map of Rhyvelad hanging on the tent wall. It was marked with various red slashes, indicating battles, and blue lines, indicating troop movements. "They're in preparation already, but it will take a while for them to get here, since they're coming from beyond General Chiyo's homeland."

"The Far West? I thought it was pretty desolate out there. And why would these troops care about our problems? What do they want from us?"

"Nothing really. They are in my debt and I'm simply requesting repayment."

"Well, that sounds all right. Just let me know closer to the time. And remember what I said about the prince."

"Of course, general. Now it's getting late and there's much to do tomorrow."

Tengar nodded and exited the tent without another word. As he left, Amarian shook his head. Now that the man felt himself in Hull's confidence, he would be less likely to stir up trouble. Still, he bore watching. He held up his hand and an Urabi emerged from the shadows.

"Keep an eye on him. And send somebody to find General Chiyo. Tell

158

them to stay alive this time."

The Urabi nodded and slunk off into the darkness as Amarian turned his thoughts to Verial. Corfe had returned with Ranti several days ago to report that the group was entering the marshes. The young man was now making himself known to the generals, in preparation for Amarian's imminent departure. Unfortunately, only one of the Sentries he had sent after Vancien and Verial had returned. The rest had managed to get themselves eaten by some brainless swamp creature. The last he knew, the same creature that had taken out his scouts had attacked Vancien's party, as well, only to be killed by some Cylini warriors. This night, he imagined that Verial slept among the Cylini, wet, tired, and probably hungry. He closed his eyes and pictured her frustration at being trapped with such shabby company. Frigid as she was, Verial was nevertheless accustomed to deference. One day, her arrogance would undo her. Whatever was left to be undone, that is. Meanwhile, she had managed to capture young Vancien's attention and get him wounded in the process. Well done, lady.

The following days passed quickly and pleasantly for the four travelers. Although she could not speak the language of the Cylini, N'vonne was enjoying getting to know their customs, leaving Telenar to both practice his Cylinic and inquire into their spiritual traditions. Verial remained in their hut for much of the time, surfacing occasionally to visit with Vancien or to shadow N'vonne. Vancien, meanwhile, still had very limited use of his sword arm, but at least he was up and on his feet. He often joined Telenar in his discussions with the Cylini priests, many of whom had a working knowledge of the Keroulian tongue.

One evening, as Vancien seated himself around the fire, Telenar was deep in conversation about Cylinic history. He looked up as Vancien drew near. "Have a seat. We were just discussing the Ages." He waved his arm in the direction of the aged priest, who was perched like an old, withered bird on the edge of his mat. "Did you know that these people only have one copy to share among their tribes? One copy! I've got copies in five different languages back home, one of them Cylinic. I should send it out to them when I get back."

Vancien nodded respectfully to the holy man. "How do you know the accounts, then? How do you teach your children?"

"We know many things without pages or scrolls, young man. We know your language. We know Kynell's."

Telenar was so stirred by this pronouncement that he actually wriggled in his seat. "That's what they call the accounts: Kynell's speech! It's fitting, if you think about it. But then that raises question of other types of divine communication. Tell me, brother, do you call all of Kynell's work his speech?"

The man nodded. "Yes, all of it. There is no difference between words on paper and words on the heart."

Vancien couldn't help jumping in, painfully adjusting his wrapped shoulder as he did so. "But the Ages are written with ink: they have not changed since the time of their writing. Surely the heart can be deceived."

Again, the man nodded. "Certainly. The Dark One's tongue infects us all. But Kynell knows the right and wrong of it, and that is all we ask."

Vancien was uncertain of how much he should reveal but could not see any reason to hide it. "Do you know who I am?"

The priest gazed thoughtfully at him before rising and stepping into the darkness. Telenar was just about to reprimand Vancien for being so forward when he returned with a small leather bag, out of which he removed a cut piece of polished clearstone. As its sharp angles caught the firelight, his weathered face turned intense. "This is only a stone, but it captures light very well. That is what prisms do, no?" He looked directly at Vancien. "Kynell has shone his light upon you. And he will shine through you in the dark times to come." Now he turned to Telenar. "We, too, have counted the days. We know what is coming. Yet our chiefs have foolishly sought war, as have yours. We are killing our brothers when we need them most. Kynell is displeased."

Telenar had to agree, but he felt some compulsion to defend Relgaré. "I do not think the king knew of your faith. He would not quickly attack known followers of Kynell."

The priest shook his head. "No, but he was quick to fight alongside Obsidian." Out of the same bag, he pulled a chunk of the unpolished black rock, holding it up to the firelight. "Look. It allows no light to pass and takes for itself whatever light it receives. It is a nothingness that swallows all good that comes upon it. It has swallowed your king. If thing continue as they are, it will swallow our chiefs."

"But our hope does not lie in kings and chiefs," Vancien reminded him. "Our hope lies in Kynell."

There was a silent moment as the man gazed at him. The mature wisdom that had characterized his appearance up to that point was beginning to fade, until soon he looked simply tired, old, and wrinkled. "Yes, young man, you are right." He sighed, dumped the rocks back into the bag, and rose. "You are right, you are right. But how many souls will Kynell lose to the Chasm before he answers our prayers?" He did not wait for an answer but bade them good night and left.

"That wasn't the response I expected."

Telenar watched the man go. "Even old holy men get tired of watching their people became strangers to the Prysm. He has seen many a soul fly to Zyreio."

"Because of this war?"

"More than the war, I think. Wars only separate men's souls from their bodies. Obsidian has bigger plans than that. Dead men are no good to Amarian unless he's already won their hearts and minds. And you can be certain that is what he is trying to do with the remainder of Relgaré's army. I wonder how our good friend is holding up."

The scout was soaking wet, but then, they all were. The rain had not let up for several days. The grumbling of Chiyo's men was beginning to turn into bold complaint. Some of them even postulated that they had contracted skin disease from over-exposure to moisture. Hunoi wanted to discipline them for their whining, but Chiyo had only laughed, merely assigning them an extra load to relieve the voyoté.

Despite the scout's report that he had not seen any Cylini, and despite his suspicion that he was leading his men into a trap, Chiyo felt optimistic. Perhaps it was his relief to leave behind the king's unwelcome ally. Getting as far away from Amarian's smothering presence as possible had become the general's secret mission. By now, he had no intention of returning his small band to the main force. Let all of Keroul be deceived by Commander Hull. He and his men would fight the good fight while they could. Of course, that still left the problem of what to do in the meantime. Sloshing around in a swamp full of enemies was a waste of time, though Chiyo would much rather brave the Cylini than Amarian's forces. So they had adopted a course that led them gently west, through the marshes but in the direction of the plains preceding the Plains of Jasimor.

There was a polite cough from Hunoi. "Yes, Captain?"

"Sorry to disturb you, sir, but another scout has returned. He says he's found some sort of village just southeast of here. It's Cylini, of course. He says that—" A soft thwack interrupted his sentence, causing him to look down. To his surprise, an arrow protruded from his chest. He felt his extremities grow cold, heard Chiyo's cry, and then, with a moan, slid to the ground. Half a second later, the wet sky was filled with Cylini arrows.

Chiyo wheeled his voyoté around. "Shields up, swords out! Stay together!"

The men did not need to hear the orders to obey. Soon the officers' voyoté had scattered into the trees until they could be of more service, while cavalry and infantry combined to overlap their shields. The result was two tortoise-shells, impenetrable from a distance and deadly at close range. The formation was both effective for offense on an open battle field and useful for buying time in tight quarters. The marshes, however, were unforgiving, and the troops could go nowhere with the water up to their thighs and the enemy closing in. The arrows battered against them for what seemed like an eternity. Did the Cylini have an endless supply of them? Chiyo knew that without reinforcements they would shortly have no choice but to surrender or be slaughtered. He pondered it for a moment. Better to yield sooner than later. They had already lost several men in the initial barrage. He waited until a break in the onslaught, then thrust out his arm through the shields and plunged his sword into the mud and water. The hilt was hardly visible above the sludge, so he waited a few breaths until the symbol could be recognized. Then he stepped out with his hands raised high.

"Mercy!"

Several arrows continued to whiz by. Those Cylini who had crept close looked tempted to take advantage of an unarmed, high-ranking officer. But it did not take long for one of their commanders to acknowledge the gesture. He barked an order and his men began to form a restless circle around the troops, who maintained their defensive position. Pointing to the two shells, the commander addressed Chiyo in stilted Keroulian.

"Do they give up, too?"

Chiyo nodded and shouted back to the ranks. "Lower your shields! We surrender this time!" As the shells obediently disintegrated, he turned back to the commander.

"We surrender. What are your terms?"

The Cylini leader eyed his enemy through the downpour. When he finally spoke, his demand was unconditional surrender. Chiyo nodded, ordering the Keroulians to hand over their weapons, which the marsh warriors took eagerly enough. Stripped of their arms, he and his men were led in the direction from which the second scout had come.

It was a long, depressing march. The vision of Hunoi disappearing beneath the water kept replaying in Chiyo's mind. It had all happened so quickly. One minute, his captain was speaking to him, the next, he was dead. Chiyo shook his head. He could not process or grieve over Hunoi's death right now. That would have to wait until he had secured the safety of those still alive.

Before long, they arrived at a village. Chiyo eyed its fenced platforms with concern. Surely the Cylini would not have resources for almost fifty prisoners. Had he ordered his men to surrender only to face execution? He had no time to consider this possibility before the gate to the compound opened and their captor exchanged a few words with a man inside. Even with his decent grasp of the Cylini language and the lightening rain, Chiyo could only pick out parts of what the men were saying. What he did hear, however, startled him.

The Cylini word for Keroulians was "Nwcherov" or "the winded ones," referring both to the high winds that could race across the region north of the Duvarian Range and to the extensive (and uncalled for, to many minds) spread of Keroulian culture. The Cylini commander mentioned this term a few times while he indicated captives, but to Chiyo's surprise, the other man repeatedly pointed inside to the "Nwcherov." Were there other Keroulians here? Chiyo assumed that his band had been the first scouting mission Relgaré had sent into the swamp, but maybe he had been mistaken. He watched with interest as a priest joined the discussion, began to vigorously shake his head, and pointed like the other man to the huts behind him. Meanwhile, the Cylini warriors were growing impatient: standing guard in the water when warmth and rest were only a few steps away was beginning to make them irritable. Finally, the triumvirate at the gate made some sort of decision. Chiyo and his men then were led to up onto a smaller, adjacent walled platform. It was empty of any comfort or furniture, but at least it was dry. As the Keroulians clamored inside, several surly guards remained to ensure their good behavior.

As curious as he was about the other Keroulians in the camp, Chiyo first had to concern himself with his men. The ambush had taken its toll. Three dead, including Hunoi, one arrow wound in the thigh, one in the shoulder, a nasty slash on the arm, and some scratches where arrows had almost made their mark. Still, given the nature of the attack, Chiyo was surprised that more of his men were not killed: the Cylini must have been more interested in captives than corpses, although why, he had no clue. Still, if they wanted living prisoners, they would have to provide more than just a dry surface to lay on.

Holding the gaze of the closest guard, he rose slowly to his feet. Then he pointed to his wounded and asked, in Cylinic, if he could request medical help for them. To his indignation, the guard shook his head.

"Paran?" If the normal rules of war were not going to be observed, Chiyo wanted to know why.

The guard did not answer, but he neither did he object when Chiyo ordered some of his men to staunch the bleeding and field dress the wounds. The man's indifference revived in Chiyo's mind the unpleasant vision of a staged execution. But mass executions were not usually the Cylini way, unless Amarian had managed to taint them as quickly as he had the Keroulian leaders.

Chiyo was again trying to push that option out his mind when the guards snapped to attention. He looked up to see the same Cylini commander who had captured them. The man gruffly ordered him to rise and follow, which Chiyo did, but not before establishing a second-in-command. Then he followed the commander across a narrow swinging bridge to the nearest large platform, then to a small building on his right, where the man gestured for Chiyo to enter. Chiyo nodded, approached the ill-fitted door, and knocked. A young girl immediately opened it, bidding him to come inside and sit by the fire. This he did most willingly. His clothes were soaked from the marsh and the rain. Except for the fire, himself, and the girl, the room was empty. But the moment he had seated himself, the door opened a second time, and the figure who entered was wonderfully familiar.

"Telenar? What are you doing here?"

Telenar adjusted his spectacles and peered into the shadows. The late afternoon light was fading fast, but he wanted to see the source of the voice before he confirmed its identity. "Chiyo?"

In response, Chiyo bounded to his feet and rushed his old friend. "You're alive! You must have received my message. Where's Vancien? How did you get here? Are you prisoners like us? Do they mean to execute you, too?"

Telenar eagerly returned the embrace, but he had a hard time keeping up with the questions. Chiyo was more animated than he had ever seen him. What must he have been through, Telenar wondered, that the sight of a friend caused him such relief? Aloud, he begged Chiyo to sit down again by the fire and get warm. Then he called to the servant girl.

"Elai, tra'oon tai 'nthro bertra frau verstra."

She nodded, running off to perform her errand. Satisfied, Telenar sat down next to a grateful but amused Chiyo.

"I don't need new clothes, Telenar. These will dry soon enough."

But Telenar was pleased to offer the small favor. "It wouldn't hurt to have a change. Besides, some Cylini clothes may come in handy."

"I notice you've found them to your liking."

Telenar glanced down at his own rough garments. "They're better suited to the climate. Besides, ours weren't much good, what with the blood and all."

"Blood? I guess we had better start with your story first. Vancien is well?"

Nodding, Telenar briefly recounted what his small group had been through. When he had finished, Chiyo told his tale. By the time all the news had been exchanged, the dry clothes had arrived and Chiyo was feeling much better, although the news of Relgaré's death hit him harder than he would have thought.

"He was a good king. For a time."

Telenar nodded.

"Now Amarian's in charge of the army. That dragon of his has probably eaten half our voyoté. Plus he has brought the Sentries." He stopped. "My men! They must be half frozen by now. Do you think you can talk the Cylini into giving them a fire and some food?"

"Of course. But then we must speak with the priests: we have to convince the warriors on both sides that this fight is no longer between the Keroulians and the Cylini. Vancien's going to need us fighting together."

Chiyo shook his head. "That'll be a challenge, but we don't have a choice, do we? Now that my men and the Cylini have seen what Amarian can do, hopefully they won't see an alternative either." He pulled his cloak tighter around his shoulders. "But our first step should be to get out of this wretched swamp."

Telenar smiled. "It's not so bad. But yes, we'll have to leave soon. Vancien has healed well enough to ride, though Nagab is not ready to bear him. Were your men mounted?"

"They were until the attack. The voyoté fled under the arrows, but I'm sure they've regrouped somewhere nearby. As soon as we're on the move and they sense it's safe, they'll return."

"Good enough." Telenar stood, brushing off his robes. "Would you like to come see the others?"

———————

It took some work to convince the Cylini not only to let scores of Keroulian soldiers go free, but also to send some of their own men to fight with them. Their hesitancy deepened when Telenar had to admit to the council that he would be taking the small force to the Plains of Jasimor. Several burly chiefs crossed their arms and protested loudly. What if Commander Hull attacked while the warriors were away? Who would protect the women and children? The people of the West had never treated the Cylini with kindness: why would that change now? Telenar had no good answers to any of these concerns, although Chiyo vouched for the welcome—or at least a cessation of hostilities—on behalf of his homeland.

In the end, the chiefs refused to actively commission a fighting force, but agreed to let any volunteers depart with the Nwcherov. This announcement produced a doubtful murmur among those Cylini present at the meeting. With the threat of Commander Hull and his dragon lurking over the swamp, understandably few warriors were willing to leave their families unprotected. But Telenar did secure a small diplomatic victory: upon assurances of the native priests that Vancien was indeed the Advocate, the chiefs unanimously agreed that they would be ready to march with Vancien when he called upon them, provided Hull had turned his attentions elsewhere.

With such success, the meeting dispersed. Chiyo departed to prepare his men and round up the few Cylini who had opted for this new adventure. Telenar accompanied him, suspecting that he had more on his mind than the council's decision, and as he suspected, Chiyo soon stopped on a swinging bridge, far outside of anybody's earshot. Telenar waited patiently for him to start the conversation.

"I don't want to speak ill of any in your company, Telenar, but I'm grateful you forbade that Verial girl to attend the council."

Telenar nodded in agreement. "She is Obsidian's eyes and ears."

"Then perhaps we should blindfold her and stop her ears."

"Not a bad idea. Not at all. But Vancien insists that we not treat her like an enemy. He pities her."

Chiyo grunted. "Vancien may be the Advocate, but he's also a young man who sees a chance to help a pretty girl. A woman. A spy. Surely Kynell does not expect us to aid and abet the enemy?"

"I wouldn't think so. But if we alienate her, we alienate Vance, which is bad both for him and for us. The Dedication is coming up quickly. I need to keep track of him as long as I can." He stopped to watch Chiyo scrape a piece of bark off the wooden railing, then toss it into the water. "All the same, we must be careful what we say. Even Vancien doesn't trust her."

———

Vancien had been delighted to hear of Chiyo's arrival. His enthusiasm doubled as the plans were finalized for the Keroulian troop to accompany his small band. It helped that he had also made several friends among the young Cylini warriors, some of whom had jumped at the opportunity to leave the marsh. Though he would never admit it, Vancien missed his classmates from Win, South of the Glade. He had the companionship of Telenar and N'vonne, certainly, but they were more like parents than colleagues. Not to mention the fact that Telenar could not tell a joke from the hole in the ground. At times, Vancien even missed ribbing old Sirin, whom he had not seen since that first fateful day in Lascombe. The rambunctiousness of his new comrades was therefore a welcome change. Day after day, as his shoulder healed, he had watched them swing from the trees, throw each other into the marsh, and ruthlessly pull pranks on unsuspecting targets. As soon as he could manage it, he was up there with them, sneaking orbmoss into the young women's seat cushions and learning how to tell a solid branch from a "fewchan"—a limb that, despite its strong appearances, would readily send you tumbling.

If Vancien had feared his welcome would fade after his new friends learned of his advocacy, his fears were unfounded. Though they were at first surprised, the news only fed their eagerness to both tease and enlist him. Still, the language barrier was significant. For conversation, he found himself turning to young Bren, Chiyo's aide, who filled him in on all the details of a soldier's life (what little a boy of eleven cycles could experience), the arrival of Hull and his dragon, and the ambush that had brought them to the village. Vancien drank in everything, remembering his days of training with the general and wishing his fight could be as direct as Chiyo's. When he shared this thought with Chiyo himself, though, the general only laughed.

"Your fight will soon be direct enough, young Vancien. And my time of fighting is over, at least for the moment. Now we must bide our time, make new allies, and await the Dedication."

"Will you be with us all the way to Jasimor?"

Chiyo nodded vigorously. "If Kynell allows, we won't let you out of our sight."

Vancien was no coward, but Chiyo's determination was comforting. He had often thought that Kynell might make him carry out this battle on his own, which was a prospect he was ready to consider but did not want. As he watched the army forming around him, he wondered how Telenar could think it insufficient. For Vancien, it seemed like a force large and loyal enough to take on anything Zyreio could throw at them.

The waters receded after a few more days and they were on the move again. Chiyo and Telenar rode lead, then Vancien and Bren, then N'vonne and Verial. The final two said very little. After Verial's disclosure that Zyreio saw, heard, and spoke through her, no one had much inclination to engage her in conversation. Chiyo's jest that she be blindfolded was carried out at the insistence of none other than Vancien. Telenar did not argue, although he suspected that Vancien was being too charitable when he claimed that the blindfolding would be for the girl's own protection. Behind the six rode forty-seven Keroulian soldiers and twenty-three Cylini men.

None of them noticed the blotch in the sky far above them. Such a small force, the Dark One thought as he hovered far above the thinning marsh trees. It was not difficult to estimate their size from the air: the Keroulians with their bright armor and the Cylini with their loud talk made the entire group painfully conspicuous. With a nudge, he urged Ovna toward the ground, a safe distance away from the diminutive army. They were already on the edges of the marsh and would be well into the western plains by the next day. It would be an easy thing to slip Verial away from her companions. He needed a diversion before the little prince came.

CHAPTER SEVENTEEN

Gair watched his jailer with less malice than one might expect, given his weak and humiliating situation. With hands bound to a tent pole and another set of bruises marking his face and body, he hardly looked the swaggering hero who had once tried to protect Veral. If pressed, he would admit that his current condition was entirely his fault. As soon as Amarian had left to take Ovna on a hunt the day before, he had attempted to escape into the Keroulian troops. His attempt had been brought to a discouraging end, thanks to the arrival of Amarian's human servant, Corfe, who bore a note from Commander Hull himself that granted him authority in the place of the absent commander. Unfortunately, he had been in the process of showing this document to General Tengar when Gair had attempted to crawl from Hull's tent. Corfe, undoubtedly informed by his master of Gair's treachery, recognized him immediately. But whether the sound beating he had received was a result of his escape attempt or Corfe's predetermined hostility toward him, Gair couldn't tell.

Now this strange mute was pacing the carpets like a caged fennel. From what Gair had gleaned from Tengar's conversation, the young man had arrived from east of the Ergana, bringing with him information about some people who had escaped Lascombe many fortnights ago. Now he was in charge of the army, although he couldn't have been older than Gair himself. Gair wondered if the poor fellow was up to the task.

"They say that it was Amarian who took away your power to speak. Is that true?"

Corfe ignored him, pausing to look over some maps.

"They also say that you tried to impersonate an Advocate. One of the men remembers seeing you at the Capital."

Again, no response.

"That means you've met the priest, Telenar. Is it true that he's a bitter old man? I wonder if he still is, now that he's left Lascombe?"

His chatter was cut off by a blow to the mouth. He cried out in pain, but Corfe only put a finger to his own lips in gesture of silence before walking back to the maps. Trying not to make a sound, Gair squeezed his eyes closed and bowed his head. He was being rash, he knew. Why would Kynell protect someone who kept looking for trouble? He needed to keep his mouth shut. The truth was, he was beginning to give up hope. Here he was in the midst of good Keroulians and he was trapped with yet another monster. Had Kynell even heard his prayers? Pain he could handle, but what good was he doing tied to a post? He had to get out, had to find a place to heal, had to—

To his surprise, he felt a wet cloth on his mouth. Corfe was back again, dabbing away the blood he had just caused to flow. When he had finished his nursing, he patted Gair condescendingly on the cheek, and left the tent. Gair stared after him in astonishment. Perhaps enforced silence had driven his captor insane.

Corfe, for his part, *was* beginning to feel a little insane as he stepped outside to wander around the vast military base. He had placed his tent in the camp of men, ostensibly to keep an eye on the wretched villains, but more so because he didn't want to sleep with the Sentries. Not that he had received any welcome from either group: as Amarian's servant he was hated by all and feared by few. Even that miserable little Gair had felt safe taunting him, although Gair had learned his lesson. Or had he? Corfe shook his head, recalling his brief ministration. What had come over him? He should have left the prisoner to bleed, not mothered him. Such foreign impulses had been stealing over him during the past few days and he was losing the power to resist them.

He paused, watching the movements around him. Camp was always a constant bustle of activity, though little was actually being done. The generals rightly believed that the ground troops needed activity to keep them from mutiny. But surely even Keroulian soldiers would realize that polishing the sharp ends of wooden stakes was a colossal waste of time, even if the points did gleam prettily in the orblight.

Corfe turned his attention to the clear sky. Amarian had said he would return the next day, although he would only stay long enough to welcome Farlone and ensure the prince's loyalty. The time of the Dedication was drawing near. Soon he would be flying west, to Jasimor. Despite the warm day, Corfe drew his jacket tightly around him. He shuddered to think of his master's return from the Plains. They said the Advocate became possessed after Dedication, and what he had read in the Ages only confirmed the rumors: the first thing Grens had done after his return was brutally execute his second-in-command. Given his current position, the story was very much on Corfe's mind, nor had he found any reasoning behind Grens' action, despite frantic searching. The man had simply been in the wrong place at the wrong time. Although Corfe was determined not to repeat the poor fellow's mistake, he had no idea how to avoid it. His only hope, and a slim one indeed, was that Zyreio would value Amarian's characteristic restraint and see fit to maintain it. Besides, they were all dead men anyway. When Amarian defeated Vancien, the whole of Rhyvelad would be plunged into a reign of terror. If any man survived the initial carnage, he would be living only to die another day.

Corfe frowned as he watched a young soldier struggle to patch his tent before the Keroulian prince's arrival. The boy stopped and saluted as he walked by. While Corfe returned his salute, he couldn't help but think that he and that young man would be sharing the same dark fate. How much would he give right now to be back at *The Shattered Lantern*, teasing old Bokran? But those days would never return. He had chosen poorly that night on the cliff: death would surely have been preferable to watching the world go down in flames. Still, he mused as he kicked at the dirt, it was better than being on the losing side. With that comforting thought, he turned back to check on Gair, the one man more pitiful than himself.

Vancien and Bren were the first two to clear the trees of the marsh and step out into the bright orblight. With a whoop, they urged their voyoté into a run and tore across the grasslands. The beginnings of the western plains stretched out in front of them like the sea, with stretches of prairie grass beating upon the trunks of isolated trees, just like the waves of the Osai crash against its lonely islands. It was a beautiful sight, welcome to everyone who saw it. Even the Cylini were relieved to feel dry, firm land under them once again. That night, they camped out in the open, soaking in the lunos light and swapping stories as much as cultural barriers would allow. Verial sat silently among them, guarded by Cylini warriors not because they feared she might slip away, but because Telenar had no desire for her to be around Keroulian speakers.

Her guards watched her diligently for a time, but soon one excused himself for nature's call and the other's attention wandered over to the campfires and the laughter. Verial did not notice his lack of attention, of course, since she was still blindfolded. But she did notice was the thump of something large hitting the ground, then a touch on her arm.

"Vancien?" As soon as she said it she knew she must be mistaken. Why would Vancien sneak up in the dark and take out one of his own men?

Her suspicions were confirmed as the grip on her arm tightened. So Amarian had come again to check on her. Without a sound, she rose and followed as he guided her away from the sounds of merriment and into the quiet darkness. Only when they had walked for several minutes did he stop to take off her blindfold. Still, she chose not to look at him.

"Why have you come, lord?"

Amarian said nothing as he brushed the hair away from her face. Her fear, which was poorly concealed under a veneer of indifference, made her all the more enticing. He looked back toward the camp.

"Have you tired of their company?"

"They are provincials. Even the priest. And Vancien is very young."

He grunted, still watching the camp. "He is indeed. Yet he outshines every one of those dogs."

"My lord?" It was odd to hear him speak with warmth about anybody, let alone his brother.

He looked at her. "We two have been in poor company these past fortnights. You with rustics and I with stuffy, self-righteous generals."

"Yes, my lord."

"But we are used to dealing with inferior beings, aren't we? We should never bother to look for equals. Our equal always turns out to be our enemy."

What was he talking about? "I am neither your equal nor your enemy, lord."

"Neither are you a servant. Or a friend."

"I am whoever my lord wishes me to be."

"And who were you to Grens?"

So that was why he had come. To remind her of who she was. "I was young." *And foolish*, she thought.

He leaned forward, softly kissing her first on the forehead, then on the mouth. "Yes, you were. But you are mine now. Not Grens'. Not Vancien's. Mine." He twisted his hand cruelly on her arm. "And I don't want you to forget it." Then he released her and stepped aside, confident that his little reminder would keep her in line. The more unsettled she was, the better.

The lunos were high in the sky before Vancien decided to check on Verial. He felt somewhat guilty for isolating her, but Telenar was right: she was a grave liability. Still, she must be famished, so he spooned her up a bowl of stew and headed toward her campsite. A few moments later, incensed and afraid, he was back at Telenar's fire.

"She's gone! One of the guards is missing and the other unconscious. Quick, we have to go find her!"

N'vonne jumped to her feet, as did Bren and Chiyo. To Vancien's exasperation, only Telenar stayed seated. His expression, however, was not without concern.

"It's all right, Vance. Sit down. I'm sure she's in good hands."

"Good hands? You mean Amarian's hands? He's a monster! What if he kidnaps her with that ghastly dragon of his?"

By now, the others were confused as to what was the appropriate response. N'vonne sat back down by Telenar, but as long as Chiyo remained standing, Bren stood uncertainly behind him.

Telenar eyed them all coolly. "Vance, sit down. You're causing a scene. I didn't mean Amarian's hands. I meant Kynell's. Besides, she's run off before, hasn't she?"

Vancien began to pace. "And left a fallen guard behind her? Do you suppose she managed to knock him out while she was blindfolded? You stay here if you want. I'm going after her." With that announcement, he turned on his heel and marched back into the darkness.

"Vancien!" N'vonne started again to her feet, and she and Bren were almost gone before Telenar managed to stop them. In truth, he could not explain why he felt so detached from this new turn of events. He knew as well as Vancien that Obsidian's servant lurked beyond the firelight, and he was even more certain that Vancien would soon be out of his hands. His only concern now was to keep his small band together. And with the look N'vonne was giving him, that would be no easy task.

"Let me go! You're going to let him go after her alone? What's the matter with you?"

Trying to be as gentle as he could, he steered her back toward the fire.

"N'vonne, listen to me. He's out of our hands now. Kynell won't let anything happen to him. Ow!"

Her well-placed heel against his metatarsal caused him to loosen his grip. Before he or Chiyo could stop her, she was gone in Vancien's direction.

The general watched in some amusement as Telenar hopped around on one foot. "Does your fiancé always treat you like this? Should we go after her?"

Telenar spat, swore, and did a few other un-Prysm-like things before he answered. "We don't have much of a choice do we? Bren, grab a torch. These women will be the death of us."

When Amarian left, Verial was more confused than she had ever been. In a daze, she started to wander back toward the camp. Her arm stung, but that was not what was upsetting her. She could still feel his lips upon hers, and to her dismay, she had liked it. Could she actually feel warmth for Amarian? She had thought herself completely beyond such an emotion, especially for him. Had she betrayed Gair? What about Vancien? Such was her disorientation that when she first beheld the flash of light and felt the biting cold, she thought it was only a trick of her disturbed mind.

But the vision before her was no illusion. It stood only a few steps away, dull fur and feathers barely hiding hints of brilliance underneath, and a large fennel body that looked braced for a fight. Its beaked head was lowered menacingly. She had never read the Ages, but she had heard enough legends to know that this was a mythical creature. As mythical as Amarian's dragon, at any rate. It was an Ealatrophe: part gryphon, part Destrariae, and entirely offended by her presence.

With a shriek that split her ears, it lunged at her and would have torn her to shreds had not Vancien shouted, stopping its attack.

"Verial! Where are you? We need you back at the camp. By the Plains, what is that?"

He stopped several yards away, instinctively clutching his chest. Visions of the Eyestone Glade and Telenar's office flashed unwelcome through his mind.

"Verial!" he shouted again, trying to avoid the creature's brilliant gold eyes. "Are you all right? What are you doing with this thing?"

Unwilling to draw the Ealatrophe's attention again, but eager to make herself known, she managed a small "I'm here."

He nodded, unable to go to her because of the beast but relieved to hear her voice. The Ealatrophe, however, had an obvious distaste for her. With one eye on Vancien, it screeched its protest and batted at her hopefully with a hind paw.

Vancien returned its gaze, wondering if the creature would listen to him. "Verial, give him a wide berth. Back up, walk far to my right, and go back to camp."

Verial nodded and gladly obeyed. The frostiest of welcomes from the priest and N'vonne would be preferable to staying around this dreadful new arrival.

When Vancien was sure she was out of harm's way, he approached the animal, talking softly as he did so. The creature stared at him, interested but unmoving.

"So you're an Ealatrophe," Vancien murmured, "and the legends are true, after all. What are you doing here? Are you here for me? If you are, then maybe you can warm up your Destraiae blood for just a little bit. How can I come near you if I can't breathe?"

In truth, Vancien was almost paralyzed by the cold. But he was now an arm's length from the creature, who showed no trace of the hostility it had so recently exhibited against Verial. Instead, as Vancien tentatively reached out his hand, it bowed its great head and knelt.

Vancien stopped, weighing his options. Surely it would be foolishness to ride the beast, although that appeared to be what it was inviting him to do. But could he just leave it? That was out of the question. Ealatrophe do not drop from the sky for nothing. Still, more out of curiosity than intent, Vancien took a step back, as if to return to camp.

The Ealatrophe's response was immediate. Screeching, it jumped to its feet, took a few steps toward him, stopped, and bowed again. Clearly Vancien had not followed the appropriate protocol. The creature's strange blend of grace, confusion, and determination made him smile. With a protective hand over his chest, he slowly assumed a seat on its back, just behind the drab feathered wings. To his surprise and delight, the icy burst he was expecting did not come. Instead, the cold began to warm until it felt like pure, rushing energy, uniting beast and rider into one unit. Trembling, Vancien leaned forward and whispered for the Ealatrophe to fly.

Verial had just come into N'vonne's sight when both women saw the brilliant flash. N'vonne blinked as Verial grabbed her arm.

"What was that?"

Verial shook her head. "It's an Ea—Eela—"

"An Ealatrophe." Telenar's voice sounded just behind them, giving the ladies another start. "And I bet Vancien's on it." He shrugged, trying to hide his distress in the torchlight. "That's the last we'll be seeing of him for a while."

Vancien had never felt so alive in his life. The Ealatrophe shot through the night sky like an arrow, reducing the campsite to a bright spot on the dark surface of Rhyvelad. He let the creature take its lead for a long time, since it obviously knew where it was going. As dawn approached, though, he began to worry at the length of his absence. Telenar and N'vonne would not have slept a wink all night, he was certain, and besides, the haste and hostility with which he had departed weighed heavily upon him. He should go back and apologize.

Reluctant to bring this glorious night to an end, he nudged his the creature with his right knee and leaned to the left. An Ealatrophe was not a voyoté, but surely it would take the hint. In response, it cocked its head, curious at the interruption, and continued flying straight. Vancien tried again with more force and received the same response, this time accompanied by an annoyed squawk. Trying to fight down a swell of panic, he tried a third time. By now thoroughly displeased, the Ealatrophe folded up its wings and entered a dive. It was all Vancien could do to hold on as they rocketed toward the ground. Just as it seemed they would crash into open grass, it pulled up, fanned its great wings, and landed gently on the turf.

With a prayer of gratitude, Vancien tumbled off, lurched a few paces, and was sick. It took him a few minutes to recover and a few minutes more to find a stream where he could wash out his mouth and attempt to wake himself up from this dream he was having. Surely he hadn't just spent several hours exploring the skies, thoughtlessly abandoning his only friends in the world and leaving them in the presence of Obsidian's Advocate. Telenar and N'vonne must be beside themselves by now. And Verial. What if she hadn't found her way back to N'vonne and Telenar, but to Amarian's arms? He sucked in his breath. There was no hope for it. He had to go back.

Getting stiffly to his feet, he swung around only to collide with the sturdy shoulder of the Ealatrophe. It had crept silently up behind him. Strange, only the night before, he had felt its burning *klathonus* cold several paces away. Now, either the flame had expelled itself or he had been devoured by it. If the latter, perhaps it would be better for him to stay away from human contact for a while. Rubbing his sore forehead, he eyed the beast with a mixture of chagrin and amusement.

"Well, my friend, it seems you have kidnapped me."

The Ealatrophe only stared at him with bright eyes.

For lack of anything better to do, Vancien began to pace and start a one-sided conversation. "Yes, sir. I'm going to assume you're a 'sir.' Correct me if I'm wrong. We're out here in the middle of nowhere, far away from any humans, and me without a thing to eat. I don't suppose you would let me go back and get my things, would you?"

His companion had no answer, but its resolute gaze followed him as he strolled back and forth.

"Don't suppose you have a name?" He stopped to ponder the idea. What would be an appropriate name for such a magnificent creature? All the animal names that came to mind seemed childish and demeaning. After a little more musing, his lessons with Telenar began to tug at his memory. Heptar had been the only Prysm Advocate known to ride an Ealatrophe, but he had been killed by Varrin immediately after the Dedication: an untimely murder that had caused all Rhyvelad to slide into a second era of darkness. Maybe the beasts weren't such a gift, after all. Looking at his new mount, he could hardly believe this to be true. Heptar had been caught unawares. The Ealatrophe had had nothing to do with it. It had been *thelámos*. Kynell's inscrutable will.

Vancien snapped his fingers at the old Patroniite word. That was it. The coming of the Ealatrophe, his inability to return to his friends, even the entire drama about to unfold between himself and Amarian: all of these events were *thelámos*. And in getting back on this wild but holy creature, wouldn't he be fully submitting himself to Kynell's will?

He allowed himself one more splash of water in order to buy time and build courage. Then he approached his ride. "All right, Thelámos. Where are we going?"

Thelámos flapped his wings, bowed his head, and made no reply.

CHAPTER EIGHTEEN

The time was drawing close. Amarian could feel the power well up within him as he flew Ovna over the camp. Some of the soldiers looked up at his approach, but most went about their business. Far from feeling slighted at such indifference, Obsidian's Advocate was well-pleased. Only a few fortnights ago, any good Keroulian man would have grabbed the nearest bow for a shot at a dragon. Now, they were so dulled to the presence of Zyreio's forces that nothing shocked or appalled them. Besides, they had other things on their mind. Today was the arrival of that fledgling prince, Farlone. The thought of obsequiously greeting the boy was not pleasant, but as much as he'd like to root out all of Relgaré's brood, he had to admit that they might still serve a function. Farlone would be no different than his father.

Trumpets blared as Ovna landed, but not for him. The prince had just arrived. The captains, as brightly polished as the stakes that surrounded the camp, lined the main thoroughfare with fierce rigidity, and the figure that rode before them was just as rigid. It was Farlone, second son of Relgaré, heir to the noblest blood in Rhyvelad, and the fighting hand of the House of Anisllyr. He was riding astride the largest voyoté north of the Range, which put him several feet higher than even the mounted officers. The height gave him confidence, a quality he rarely lacked.

On the day of his arrival, he had every reason to be self-assured. Though his elder brother, Relgaren, was now king, his father had left Farlone a campaign that was all but won and an ally with unprecedented strength. Plus, the soldiers revered him. He had spent most of his young career in the military. Riding, fighting, and bleeding with the men now standing at attention had given him a unique caché among them. Though he had not been in the fray the night Relgaré died (he had been called to Lascombe on state business), none held it against him. To a man, the Keroulians were simply glad to see a representative of Anisllyr's house among them again. And if the prince also accomplished the expulsion of Commander Hull and his hordes, so much the better.

Amarian knew their thoughts but was not troubled by them. Instead, he dismounted and watched as the entourage approached the generals, who stood as tall as they could, particularly since the prince remained mounted while addressing them. Much to their embarrassment, however, Farlone soon excused himself and rode boldly up to Ovna's snout. General Tengar, although officially dismissed, walked beside him to perform the introductions.

"Commander Hull," he barked, determined to maintain his authority. "Our lord prince has arrived."

Amarian stepped out from behind Ovna's wing, where he had been casually inspecting a harness strap. "I see that, General. And I daresay the prince needs no introduction." He allowed himself a gracious bow.

Farlone nodded in response, then signaled to a man in his party dressed in Patroniite robes. The young man, whose face was still full of freckles, came forward to scrutinize Amarian, much to the Advocate's annoyance. The Patroniite then dismissed Tengar and asked Farlone to dismount. Soon, only the three figures stood under the shadow of Ovna's bulk. The priest was the first to speak.

"Look, brother, how he stares us down. Perhaps he thinks to brainwash us as he did our father. Does he think the House of Anisllyr so weak?"

Amarian's smile was cold. Who did these two pups think they were? "I assure you, your holiness, I did no such thing. Your father's will was his own."

Farlone's hand rested lightly upon his fancy sword hilt. "Lors thinks differently, Commander Hull. And though he is young, he is very wise. Tell us again why we shouldn't send you and your hordes back to the Chasm from which you came."

Amarian ignored the bait and repeated his bow. "My princes, you have misjudged me and you have slandered my soldiers. We did not start this war of yours, only come to help you finish it." He stopped. Perhaps he should call their bluff? "If you desire, we will pack up and leave at first light."

Lors began to nod enthusiastically at the plan, but was stayed by Farlone.

"There's no need for such a drastic withdrawal. Keroul appreciates the sacrifices that your. . ." He searched for the right word and came up with the wrong one. ". . .*men* have given in our fight against the Cylini. Please stay and finish the struggle."

Amarian nodded, not a little mystified at the man's indecision. But before he could reply, Farlone continued.

"But we are not ignorant of your true identity and we will not be allied to Obsidian any longer than necessary. My young brother would gladly break all ties and declare you our mortal enemy, but then, what can you expect from a Patroniite?"

Lors was openly offended at Farlone's speech, but held his tongue as his brother finished.

"You and I are men of the world, Amarian, and we know there's little room for idealism. Our paths are joined for the time being. *Redayo et lo redayo sun lon heiro.* 'The enemy of my enemy is my friend.' So we shall be friends under those pretenses and none other. Agreed?"

Amarian was so pleased by this pompous speech that he allowed himself a third bow. "Agreed, my prince." He then turned quickly toward his tent, trying to hide his pleasure. The princes watched him go, Farlone trying not to show his annoyance at his departure and Lors staring in open exasperation at his brother. Neither said anything as they remounted and followed Tengar to their accommodation.

Corfe did not take note of prince's arrival, nor did he dread the appearance of his master, mostly because he was pre-occupied by a crushing realization: he was going mad. He turned the events of the preceding day over in his mind and found that insanity was the only explanation for them. The incident with the prisoner had not been his only moment of weakness. Later that day, he had remitted an execution sentence of a treasonous Keroulian. Even this morning, he had spared a fennel—a fennel!—the punishment it had deserved for insolence. What was happening to him? He shook his head, nervously pacing from one end of his tent to the other, stopping only when a shadow fell across his path.

He turned and bowed.

Amarian seated himself at Corfe's camp desk, gazed at his servant for a moment, then spoke.

"You were not present to greet the princes."

Corfe smirked. The lordlings were of no interest to him.

Amarian seem pleased by the response. "It is just as well. The only thing you missed was a show of bravado. Farlone will be no trouble. Like his father, he thinks only of the Cylini. But his brother will bear watching."

Corfe nodded at the assignment, well aware of what a useful spy he made. After all, if he were caught, what amount of torture could overcome his disability?

Amarian continued. "I leave tomorrow for the Plains. Only Obsidian knows when or if I'll be back, so you must keep the army in readiness."

Again Corfe nodded, but the gesture was not unaccompanied by surprise. Was it possible that Amarian did not know of his recent behavior? He must not have taken time to talk with the Keroulians: after yesterday's reprieve a whole battalion had set about rejoicing in their good luck. Corfe had to send Sentries to quell the demonstrations.

Amarian rose, calling an end to the one-sided conversation. "Tell me, Corfe, are you afraid of my return from the Plains?"

Yesterday, Corfe would have nodded reflexively at the question. But the change that was working in him prevented him from giving an immediate response. In truth, fearing the Dark Advocate was becoming secondary to fearing himself and what he might be becoming. His confusion was so distracting that he forgot to answer the question.

Amarian took note of his hesitation. "I did not expect such indecision. Perhaps you have found someone else to fear?"

Finally gathering his senses, Corfe hastily shook his head and, for good measure, bowed obsequiously. Whether Amarian was mollified by this response he could not tell, but he left without another word. Corfe watched him go, trying to ignore the sinking feeling that, yet again, he had not done himself any favors. The sooner Amarian departed for the Plains, the better. Besides, there was always the small hope that Obsidian's greatest servant would fail to return. He cringed at his audacity. No one was ever sure if the Advocate could read minds, but if telepathy truly had been a gift of Zyreio's, Corfe was certain that his master would have returned to kill him immediately for his treason. Yet he remained alone in the tent. Perhaps Amarian's powers were more limited than he had suspected. This curious thought attended him throughout the day and into the night. By the time Amarian took his leave the next morning, though he could give it no logical explanation, Corfe felt as if he were breathing freely for the first time.

The farewell assembly was brief and cheerless. Amarian mounted Ovna, bade farewell to the generals and the princes, and promised he would return soon with reinforcements enough to wipe out every last man, woman, and child of the Cylini. The generals were pleased with his little speech, as was Farlone, but Lors only glared. After waiting for dragon and rider to disappear over the horizon, he pulled his brother aside.

"Do you realize he's planning on murdering all the Cylini?"

"Of course. He is Obsidian's Advocate. Do you really think he's squeamish about genocide?"

Lors could have suggested that perhaps it was *they* who should be squeamish about genocide. Instead, he said curtly, "His intentions don't surprise me. It's your reaction to him that I'm worried about. Do you honestly believe that after he returns, he'll help you with the Cylini, and then go off to fight his little war somewhere else? He means to use us, Farlone. And then dispose of us. I really don't think that—"

He was cut off by Farlone's sharp look. Amarian's second, the mute called Corfe, was approaching, accompanied by a Sentry. The young man looked even more haggard than usual. Nevertheless, he gave a shallow bow as he drew near, then held out a sheet of parchment. Farlone seemed reluctant to have any contact with him, so Lors received it with a polite nod and read it aloud: "Majesties, it is my great regret that I cannot vocally deliver my salutations. This brief note will have to suffice. As you know, Commander Hull has left me in charge of his forces, a command in which my effectiveness extends only so far. I have consequently appointed the chief Sentry, Tarl," (the Sentry nodded at the mention of his name) "as operating commander. Should you need to discuss anything, you should speak with him. All decisions must meet my approval."

Lors tucked the parchment into his vest. The man before him was a committed enemy of Kynell, and the creature beside him the spawn of Obsidian, yet he felt some pity for them. They, too, were caught in Amarian's web.

"Thank you for the courtesy, Corfe. The Commander had informed us of your post, but unfortunately, we have not had the pleasure of your company. Would you, both of you, care to dine with us tonight?"

Farlone stiffened. Lors ignored him while Corfe watched them both with feverish intensity. It was Tarl who spoke, his rough voice raking over the polite words. "Your generosity is much appreciated. But a Sentry would be a poor dinner guest. I will answer for my master." He stopped to wait for a cue from his superior. Corfe bowed slightly. "He would be honored to attend you at dinner, although he fears he does not have much to say."

Lors was so surprised at the creature's eloquence and humor that he laughed. Tarl continued, disregarding the interruption.

"My master will join you at orbset. Then, tomorrow morning all the generals will meet to discuss our plan for the commander's absence. Please inform General Tengar and the others."

Farlone finally decided to speak, if only briefly. "We look forward to your visit, Corfe. Until this evening."

They nodded and turned away, although Lors noted that Corfe stayed in Tarl's company no more than a few yards before abruptly veering off to the left. Funny how evil could not stand its own presence.

Corfe headed straight for his tent. He was at his desk before it occurred to him to check on Gair, unceremoniously bound several paces away and kept under close surveillance by a Mholi. The Sentry saluted as he approached. Awakened by the movement, the prisoner stirred from his uncomfortable afternoon nap.

"Corfe." His voice was barely audible, so weakened and dehydrated he had become.

Corfe nodded, stepped over the chains, then crouched down and looked closely at the unfortunate figure. This man had gained nothing by his treachery, but then, few men do. Corfe was no idealist, of course. He was not bothered by the betrayal itself, rather the stupidity of it. What could motivate this man to not only stay alive, but maintain his loyalty to the Prysm? Amarian had told him of the Gair's affection for Verial. Perhaps that was it. Certainly the sight of that woman was enough to drive any man to reckless behavior. But she had been gone for several fortnights now. If Gair had been bewitched by her beauty, he had had plenty of time, separation, and painful distractions to recover from the spell.

No, the look in Gair's eyes suggested that he was hoping for something more than a woman, even more than personal deliverance. Corfe wanted desperately to ask him what he was hoping for, but he couldn't bring himself to write such a question down. So he stalked off again, but not before motioning for the Sentry to get Gair some more water.

Relgaré's original fortification had shifted closer to the marshes ever since their great victory over the Cylini. Now Keroulian soldiers guarded the bridge, though they did not bother going deeper into the swamp. No one had any desire to discover its mysteries. It did not take long, therefore, before Corfe was alone with the damp undergrowth and foul orbmoss. His delirium deepened as the trees grew thicker. What was he doing out here? What had he ever been doing, other than trying to get by on his crimes? Why, in all those cycles since his mother had died, before he met Amarian, had he not considered becoming an honest worker? When had he decided to become a scoundrel? Was it when his father had abandoned them during his sixth cycle? Or when Kynell wrongfully took his mother from him a few cycles later? But where had any of his schemes got him?

He thought back on the night that Amarian had offered him the choice between bondage and death. Why didn't he choose to throw himself over the cliff into the sea? Surely that would have saved him a great deal of suffering. But when a man is offered life, he takes it, even if it means a life of silence. Now that silence weighed heavily on him. His dark mood thickened until all he wanted to do was shake his fist at both Obsidian and the Prysm. But what good would that do?

The orbs were setting by the time weariness overtook his frustration. He needed to return to camp, an impulse that became even more urgent when he remembered he had a meeting with the two princes. Why hadn't a Sentry been sent to remind him? Surely Tarl had sent a scout to keep an eye on him. No matter. He would issue a half-hearted apology to the young royals and then be on his way.

When night had fully descended, he still had a good distance to go. Yet to his dismay and surprise, his knees began to buckle with fatigue. His hips and arms soon followed. He began to feel as if his entire body was filled with lead. Before he knew it, he was forced into an unnaturally prostrate position on the swampy ground. Only with great effort was he able to lift his face up out of the mud so he could breathe.

He had no idea how long he lay in this uncomfortable position, but it seemed like an eternity before he felt a presence nearby. He suppressed a groan. Had Zyreio come to deliver punishment for his unfaithfulness? Fear gripped him, causing his breath to come in short gasps. Why didn't it say something?

After a while, he could sense it moving. He blinked the sweat out of his eyes and strained to look in the direction of the sound. His gaze fell on a swamp marmet, with greasy fur plastered against its small body and big eyes peering thoughtfully back at him. It was standing in the one spot accessible to the lunos-light. The entire situation appeared so ridiculous that Corfe couldn't hold back a chuckle. The creature blinked, then added some staccato squeaks to his laughter.

"It has been a long time since you laughed, Corfe."

Though its lips did not move, the tiny creature's voice echoed through his head. It was a little more than a squeaky whisper, but it an air of authority. Had it really just spoken to him? How did it know his name? And why couldn't he move his arms?

It continued. "I know much about you, young man. I know you have fled me many times, and even now you continue to make poor choices. I know that you keep your silence voluntarily."

Corfe shook his head, perplexed at the last statement, but unable to ask about it. The marmet nodded jerkily in response. "Why do you not speak?"

Corfe's patience with the little creature began to wear thin. "You know very well that I cannot speak."

The creature peered at him eagerly. Suddenly free to move, he clapped a hand over his mouth.

"Cannot what? Say again, young man."

Now on his knees, Corfe slowly removed his hand. "I can't speak. I'm mute. Amarian silenced me." His hand flew to his throat, searching for some sort of change, but found nothing except the urge to laugh. He jumped to his feet and shouted at the marmet.

"I'm healed! I can speak! Who are you? How did you do it? I owe you my life, little marmet."

The creature quickly became as solemn as its furry face would allow. "Be careful what you pledge, Corfe. In the end, you will be called upon to give it."

Sobered, Corfe splashed back down on his knees. "Who are you? Why have you come to me? You cannot be a servant of Zyerio."

"Ha! Zyerio could not contain me. But you will find out soon enough who I am. For now, go. The princes will be wondering at your absence."

Confused but obedient, Corfe rose and performed an awkward bow. Then the marmet was gone, leaving him to joyfully stagger his way back into the camp.

Gair looked up in surprise when he entered. He knew it was Corfe, but the man was hardly recognizable, covered in mud as he was, with a mad look in his eye. He lunged at him and Gair figured he was done for. But Corfe was frantically tugging at his ropes, hissing under his breath until Gair was freed. He then sat back on his haunches, admiring his handiwork.

Gair sat in shock for a moment (he was too weak to move, anyway), then finally dared to speak. "What's gotten into you?"

Corfe was glowing. "What do you notice different about me?"

"I don't know. You have mud all over you. Wait a minute! You're talking!"

Delighted that someone now shared his secret, Corfe jumped to his feet and clapped his hands. "I've been healed! There I was, in the marsh, and I couldn't move, in complete despair, then this marmet started talking to me, and I could taste the mud."

Gair tried his best to follow the narrative, but he had a difficult time making out what despair had to do with a talking marmet. He pleaded for Corfe to slow down long enough to make some sense. When Corfe did, Gair couldn't help but feel a little triumphant.

"Tell me again what the marmet said."

"He told me to speak again. And again!"

"No, after that. When you mentioned Zyreio."

Corfe winced at the name. "He said that Zyreio could not contain him. I don't have any idea what that means, but I really don't think that was Obsidian back there. It was something different, something much more intimidating."

Gair leaned back, rubbing his chafed skin and smiling like a fool. "It was Kynell."

He was surprised to see Corfe shake his head. "That's not possible. Why would he heal me? I'm his enemy."

"Not any longer, you're not. Look at the change he's caused in you after just a few minutes! You're alive, you can speak. By the Chasm, you're actually smiling!"

Corfe blushed. "I don't know. I don't know why he would heal me and I don't know why Zyreio hasn't struck me down yet. I don't even know why I'm talking to you, my prisoner, or even why you're talking to me, your captor."

Gair eyed his own mangled flesh, which was slowly, painfully, and incompletely healing. "The ways of Kynell are mysterious. But he has obviously set his sights on you. Maybe the Ages say something about it."

Corfe jumped, suddenly inspired. "That's it! That's why I've been healed! No, that's not possible. At least I don't think so." He started pacing, trying to dredge up forgotten scraps of information. "There was some debate about the timing, and I've hardly been a servant of the Prysm. Unless." He turned sharply toward Gair. "Where can I get a copy of the Ages?"

"A copy of the Ages? Well, you can go ask some of the Keroulian troops. Abridged copies used to be standard issue to officers. I heard that good King Relgaré stopped that practice a few cycles ago. But I bet most officers still have theirs."

Corfe did not stay to appreciate Gair's political commentary. As soon as he heard the word "officers," he rushed out of the tent. When he returned several minutes later, he was clutching a tattered copy of the Ages, hastily borrowed from Tengar. Like an eager child, he sat down cross-legged and flipped it open.

Gair watched him with interest, unable to hear what he was mumbling and suspecting that the excitement now overtaking him was something more than amazement at his recent healing. Corfe was obviously looking for something specific, though for the life of him Gair could not think what that might be.

The candles were burning low when Corfe, frustrated and exhausted, leaned back and looked at his friend. "Have you read the Ages?"

"Of course. My mother had a smuggled copy. Though I don't know as much about them as I'd like. What are you looking for?"

"I don't know, really. Maybe something about how Kynell treats his enemies."

"Somewhere in Folio Seven it says that the Prysm will shatter those who oppose it. But then later there's something about Kynell extending hand of mercy even for those who have cursed him. I've never quite made sense of the two. "

Corfe stared thoughtfully at the open book. "'For those who have cursed him.' Guess I would fall into that category." He looked gloomily at Gair's scars. "And I've harmed his servants. What would he want with me?"

Gair's heart went out to him. He had felt a similar desolation when he had first learned of Kynell. Why would a god taint himself by associating with his rebellious self?

"I don't know much about the Ages. My life in Amarian's camp prevented me from studying them like I should." He laughed grimly. "The only reason I know they used to be standard issue was from going through the pack of a captured Keroulian. But I do know that Kynell can do anything. Even, somehow, overlook the offenses of Zyreio's servants, if they should ask him to do so. And it looks like he's done the same with you."

"Except I didn't ask him to."

"But you're feeling the full weight of those crimes now, aren't you? Even the crimes you committed before you met Amarian? Trust me, several cycles ago I was in the same position, and I learned that Kynell honors a confession. Beyond that, I don't know what he has in store."

Some of Corfe's confusion lightened at Gair's words, but his smile was still weak. "I guess I'd better start with confession, then. This could take a while."

Gair looked at the light beginning to stream in under the canvas walls. "I'm sure Kynell will take the abbreviated version. It's almost dawn. The princes will be wondering what happened to you."

CHAPTER NINETEEN

Chiyo watched Telenar pace nervously, running his fingers through disheveled hair and angrily cleaning his spectacles.

"I just don't know what we're supposed to do now," Telenar complained for the fourth time that morning. Finally seating himself next to the general, he began to pick at the grass.

Chiyo was not unsympathetic. "I don't know that we're supposed to *do* anything, my friend. Isn't best to wait for Vancien's return? Besides, I told you that I've already sent runners back to the princes' camp. Since King Relgaren is in Lascombe, he should be spared Obsidian's influence. The two young princes, however, will be firmly under Amarian's thumb by now. Hopefully, my scouts can tell us how the rest of the troops fare. If Vancien has gone to the Dedication, then it's likely Amarian has gone, as well, meaning his men are on their own. Perhaps we can retake the army before it becomes entirely the property of Obsidian."

Telenar nodded grumpily. "When are the scouts likely to be back?"

"In the next few days. In the meantime, we must be careful not to let our impatience affect our men."

"Spoken like a true soldier. But you're right." He jumped again to his feet. "Besides, my focus needs to be on Kynell, not Vancien. Maybe I can consider this a forced spiritual retreat."

Despite his momentary stoicism, Telenar found it difficult to stay still, to wait, or to pray. Even his conversations with N'vonne, usually the highlight of both of their days, were short and stilted, involving repeated glances in the direction whence Vancien had disappeared. What he hoped to see on the horizon, he had no idea. But it had been half a week since Vancien had slipped out of his care. Who knew what could have happened in that time? The Dedication could have happened, the battle could have been fought, Vancien could be dead. How would he know? These worries gnawed continually at him as he stalked the camp, sending up half-hearted prayers for patience and looking for something to distract him.

The distraction finally came in the form of Chiyo's scout, who returned a few days later than expected, right when Chiyo was considering relocating and Telenar was considering going mad. But the news he bore was certainly worth waiting for: Amarian's second-in-command, the young mute named Corfe, had miraculously had his speech restored. Now he was asking the Keroulians to back him not just as a servant of Kynell, but as the Prysm Advocate. And the Keroulians, according to the scout's report, were listening.

Telenar nearly fell over at the news. Had the boy lost his head? How could he possibly think himself to be the Advocate? Worse still, how could the Keroulians believe him? His mind tried to reconcile the image of that scared young man in his office so long ago with the reports he was now hearing. Was it some trick of Amarian's to rob Vancien of his glory? But why would Amarian allow his own army to change allegiance from Obsidian to a Prysm pretender? No, it was unlikely that Amarian was behind this. Unlikely that Amarian even *knew* about this. Something else must be going on.

Chiyo spoke first. "We have to return. Somebody must knock some sense into him." He turned back to the scout. "How have Amarian's forces dealt with the change?"

The scout, a scraggly wisp of a man, gave a raspy laugh. "They don't know what to do. They were told to obey Corfe, and until they hear otherwise from Amarian, I think they'll do just that. It seems that some of Amarian's men are quite taken with the idea. The Sentries and fennels are, of course, very suspicious."

"And Relgaré's sons?"

"That's the strangest thing, sir. The boy priest is backing Corfe's claim, waving around the Ages like he's some sort of great prophet. So from the looks of it, Corfe has the full support of the House of Anisllyr."

Telenar shook his head, instinctively grabbing N'vonne's hand to steady himself. "This is insane. A Patroniite should know better." Then he thought back to his meeting with the Supras so very long ago. The man had been completely unwilling to listen to reason. "Or perhaps not. Chiyo's right. We're not doing anyone any good here. Corfe must be stopped before he turns the world upside down."

Vancien awoke with a start, having yet again fallen asleep between Thelámos' moving wings. The great beast flew relentlessly west, leaving Vancien with no doubt as to their destination. By his sketchy calculations, they were very close to Jasimor. He yawned, rubbed his bleary eyes, and surveyed the landscapes passing below. They were above Chiyo's territory now, flying south of the region's capital. He could just make out the spires of the trading post turned metropolis. Ktai was certainly a destination in its own right, and for half a moment, Vancien wished his Dedication would take place there, where he could at least get a good night's rest beforehand.

A squawk from Thelámos distracted him from his self-pity, bringing his attention to a small flock of gryphons directly below them. He admired their grace, watching one of them look up to screech welcome to the Ealatrophe, who responded in kind. Just as the lead gryphon was about to respond again, a dark form appeared, streaking straight toward the beast. Thelámos cried out a warning, but it was too late: the dragon barreled into the gryphon, scattering the flock and clutching its leader with fatal intensity. With an outraged shriek, Thelámos dove to its aid.

"Thelámos, wait!"

The wind whipped his words away, so as the wind whistled past him, he tried to get a closer look at the malicious beast. To his surprise, he saw that the dragon had a rider. To his horror, he saw that the rider was Amarian.

"Pull back, Thelámos! Back!"

But Thelámos was not listening. Vancien was just able to make out Amarian's expression before the two creatures crashed into each other, jostling the lead gryphon free, but entangling the Ealatrophe in a fury of talons and claws. Ovna's roar competed with the cries of Thelámos as the two clawed at each other. Their riders could do little more than hold on for dear life through the jets of flame mingled with flashes of stabbing cold. Vancien stayed buried deeply as possible in feathers, avoiding what he could of Ovna's rage and wondering why in the Chasm Amarian had provoked such a premature attack. Surely he knew an early success was impossible. Or maybe his strategy was simply to separate him from Thelámos.

Despite the intentions of all combatants, the beasts were straying closer and closer to the ground, until Ovna caught her wingtip on a tree branch, which briefly spun her away from the Ealatrophe, exposing her back. Thelámos took advantage of the opening and lunged for the killing stroke. But Amarian was ready. Cursing to ward off the blast of cold he knew was coming, he prepared to plunge his sword into Thelámos' heart. Thelámos saw the attack and slipped enough to the side to avoid the fatal blow. But Amarian's blade still bit deeply into his wing. Shrieking, the Ealatrophe rolled steeply to his right, colliding with the ground and sending his rider rocketing out of his seat.

Obsidian had not escaped unharmed. Thelámos had managed not only to propel Ovna further into a small cluster of trees, but had gashed her belly in the process of his own escape. Now she thrashed among the tree trunks shattered by the weight of her body, roaring in fury and almost crushing Amarian, who had also been ejected from his perch. At the moment, he was busily trying to avoid her thundering tail.

Vancien was not conscious enough to take note of his brother's difficulties. The last he remembered was skidding across an open field and colliding with something hard. Then his world went black.

When he awoke, neither Thelámos nor Ovna were anywhere to be seen, although the evidence for their landings was abundant: blood-stained, broken tree trunks creaked where once, Vancien imagined, there had been a small grove of peaceful trees, while a streak of flattened prairie grass marked where Thelámos had crashed to the ground. To Vancien's surprise, there was no trace of blood in the open field. He wondered through his hazy consciousness if an Ealatrophe does not bleed like men and dragons. Or else Amarian had not wounded Thelámos as badly as he thought.

Amarian. The name and its associations returned to him in full force as he staggered to his feet. Fortunately, his sword had skipped across the plains with him and was now laying only a few paces off. He picked it up, warily looking around for any trace of his antagonist, who had managed to disappear as completely as the two beasts. His blurry vision did manage to register the rest of his surroundings, however. The cluster of trees devastated by the dragon was an anomaly, just one of the few small groves scattered over the largest, most daunting stretch of prairie Vancien had ever seen. Indeed, except for those clusters, which huddled together as if alarmed by their surroundings, there were no distinguishing landmarks. Sky and prairie divided the entire world into two spheres of earth and sky, each one as dry and uncongenial as the other.

Where was Amarian? Perhaps he was hiding with the trees, or tucked down beneath the long straw-colored stalks. If so, Vancien suspected that he himself must look very foolish, standing out in the orblight, the only shape on the horizon. He quickly crouched down before contemplating his next move. His first step, of course, would be to figure out where he was. Peeking his head above the cover, he considered again his surroundings. In some ways, the prairie he found himself in was similar to the plains he had left behind. But the air here seemed more oppressive, as if he were not welcome here. Had he finally made it to the Plains of Jasimor? As soon as the idea occurred to him, he knew it to be true.

Feeling slightly nauseous, he broke off his search for Amarian. There was a faint throbbing beneath his boots that he had not noticed before: it felt like it was gently trying to take over his heartbeat. Against his better judgment, he pressed his ear to the soil to listen, just as he had done as a child when a large carriage passed through town.

He heard nothing except the rustling of the grass, but his heart reeled under a surge of hopelessness that swept over him like a cloud bank. Scrambling to his feet, he looking accusingly at the dirt. The despair was so palpable that it fogged his vision. From the moment his head touched the ground, the world had become a much darker place. His situation became unreal. What was he doing there, anyway? The purpose for his coming seemed unclear, or worse, ridiculous. Telenar, N'vonne, even Kynell seemed far off to him, so remote as to be irrelevant. His stomach started to tighten. Perhaps Kynell had abandoned him. No, that wasn't it. Kynell did not exist in the first place. How could he, when all mankind ever saw was what he was seeing now: trees, stone, and air? And if Kynell did exist, why did he never show himself? Obviously because there was nothing to show.

Feebly, Vancien batted a hand to ward off such fatal truths, which were radiating up through his boots, into his gut, and taking up residence in his spirit. Kynell was just a figment of his imagination. He saw that now, as clear as day. Telenar had been seriously mistaken, N'vonne gullible, and Verial was just a dream. He took a deep breath, his feet glued to the ground, his mind still attempting some sort of free movement. But Verial was not a dream. She *did* exist, and she was certainly in Amarian's grasp. Amarian must therefore exist. If so, then surely he must be as Vancien had understood him to be: a servant of Zyreio. That left two possibilities: either Amarian was mad or Zyreio was real. Vancien knew enough, even in that field of deception, to know that Amarian had all of his wits about him. Zyreio must therefore be both real and active (he focused hard on the tenuous logic, ignoring the surges of denial that assaulted him). Consequently, he was the likeliest candidate as a cause of the evil that infected all of Rhyvelad, just as his buried tongue tainted the ground itself.

Vancien stared at the ground beneath his feet in awe, swaying from all the lies of Obsidian that raced under his feet. Was deceit really so tangible? His beleaguered mind assured him that it was, while warning him that he, too, would soon succumb to this constant onslaught. He had to get out of here, had to break contact with the tainted soil. Pathetically, he prayed for Thelámos to reappear. But the Ealatrophe was nowhere to be found. So Vancien staggered over to a tree in the hopes of climbing it for a moment's respite. But as soon as he rested a hand against the trunk, he drew back in pain. The bark burned so intensely that it seared his palm. Was the tree on fire? He glanced up and down: it certainly looked like a regular tree. But when he looked at his hand he could not deny the singe marks. At the risk of more pain, he touched it again before pulling quickly back. The tree, which looked so innocent from a distance, was in truth burning furiously, angrily. Here in this horrible place, nature had bowed to Zyreio's wrath, absorbed it, and now exuded it.

He shuddered and moved away from the grove, which continued to silently accuse him. Still praying for aid, he looked around for any possible relief. His weak grasp of reality was beginning to slip again: his earlier conclusions about Verial now seemed complete foolishness. Who was to say that she wasn't some figment of his imagination? Alone in the plain, with no other soul in sight, the possibility seemed more than likely. Once again, the truth about reality overwhelmed him. How could anyone, looking out over these beautiful grasslands, believe in gods or prophecy? The plain truth was that this was all there is: ground and sky, himself and the throbbing soil underneath him. There was no Kynell who was watching him, no Zyreio who was chasing him. He, Vancien, was just a guy who had taken his childhood dreams too far.

He fell to his knees at the realization. Just a man, who, when he died, would disappear, as all other men did. While some men would have greeted this new awareness with relief (after all, the absence of deity could be considered rather liberating) Vancien wept. The truth of the matter was clear: he could no more dispute it than he could cease to breathe, although he would have gladly taken the latter option. He was left only with lamenting the loss of higher things, be they good or evil. In the course of his grief, he stretched himself out in the grass, allowing the sickening truth to flow fully over him. His surrender was almost complete, but before darkness claimed him, he asked Kynell—the Kynell that didn't exist—for help one more time. He received no answer, nor did he expect one.

Amarian had never felt so alive. Despite his thrashing from Ovna's tail, which left him bruised and cut, he greeted the sight of the prairie with unconcealed enthusiasm. He had no doubt as to where he was. The Ages said that it was here Zyreio had planted his tongue and so infected all of Rhyvelad. Infected. Bemusedly, he rolled the word over in his mind. Here was life. Here was the one source of truth in all the world and they had the gall to call it an infection. Well, they had been given their just rewards, he had no doubt, and they deserved no more of his attention. Here, he was finally alone with his god. Here Zyreio would meet him, face to face, god to man. And here he would finally be consumed with Obsidian's power. He saw again the chair that he had seen as a child: the chair from which he could see and control all things. He had finally made it, and all the Plains served as his throne. He smiled at the soft thrumming under his feet.

Quickening his step, he pushed deeper into the prairie, although where he was going, he could not say. Where does a man go when he is already at the center? But to stay still seemed like blasphemy. Better to explore all the corners of Zyreio's fields. Who knew what surprises might turn up? If he walked over to that far grove, would new truths reveal themselves? Was Zyreio waiting for him further in? The energy coursing underground pushed him on, and as he went, he attempted to process all the knowledge that pulsed from this holy place. Unlike Vancien, he was not bombarded with doubts about the gods' existence. Far from it: he was elated with the certainty that Zyreio was here with him and very soon they would both destroy the only one who stood in the way of their full consummation. Even Vancien was a distant concern. Distant, that is, until Amarian almost tripped over him.

He looked down in surprise, his pale features twisted in outrage: what other creature would dare to enter this sacred plain? It took a few moments for him to recognize his brother, whom he kicked lightly, more out of curiosity than malice. Vancien groaned and did not move. Unfortunately for him, his indolence offended Amarian, who kicked him again, harder and in the ribs. When Vancien still showed no inclination to move, Amarian, trembling with rage, drew his sword and pressed it against his throat.

"Get up," he growled, digging in the point until it drew blood. Only then did Vancien stir, raising his head and shifting away from the source of his discomfort. This proved difficult to do, since now the discomfort was coming from two directions: the ground beneath him and the figure above him. At first he merely squirmed, then, recognizing Amarian's silhouette in the orblight, started to his feet.

"It's you!" he stammered.

"Find your sword," Amarian said, ignoring his exclamation.

Vancien continued to stare. Then he knelt abruptly, pressing his ear to the ground. Amarian almost cut him at that point, but something stayed his hand. His young brother had always been dense, but now it seemed possible that he wasn't even right in the head.

Meanwhile, Vancien's expression turned triumphant. Jumping again to his feet, he looked on Amarian as a lover might look at the sudden appearance of his beloved.

"You're real."

"Of course I'm real, you fool! Did you think I would simply disappear, leaving all of Rhyvelad to you?"

But Vancien wasn't listening. With growing confidence, he picked up his sword and wiped it on his tunic. "You're still real, 'Ian. I can't get rid of you. I don't want to get rid of you. I love you. But," his smile vanished, "you must be delivered from the lies that surround you."

Amarian opened his mouth then shut it as Vancien continued. "Do you remember when Zyreio came to you? You did not want to go with him, but you chose to anyway. I knew then, as I know now, why you made that choice. But you have forgotten. Obsidian has stolen your heart."

Like Vancien's speech, Amarian's response was not his own. "You seek to confuse my servant, but it is too late. He is mine and has been mine since the day he chose me. He cannot hear you any longer. Now you speak only to me and I will never listen."

"Then I shall cut you out of him."

With that promise, Vancien lunged, Amarian parried, and the fight began. To any casual observer, it would have appeared quite ordinary, perhaps boring. There were no dramatic leaps or twists. The sound of clanging metal was flat as it echoed over the prairie grass. At one point, Amarian tripped over a spot of uneven ground, but Vancien could not follow up the advantage because he had become momentarily tangled in a knotted section of grass. By the time their swords met again, both had shown themselves to be less than graceful, but so consumed with their desire to kill each other that they wasted no time on theatrics or even threats. Except for the clash of the blades and the grunts of exertion, the Plains were silent.

Finally, after an eternity of combat, one fell. Vancien, the weaker and less trained, lost his footing. Then Amarian struck the blade out of his hand with such force that the blow sent him staggering backwards. In less than a breath, Amarian was over him, with the sword again pressed to his throat.

"To the Chasm," he said, pushing down.

Several leagues away, in the middle of his trek to stop Corfe, Telenar crouched down. His voyoté had bruised his paw on a rock and some quick bandaging was necessary to stop the beast's whimpering. While he was kneeling, pleading with Lansing to hold still, he heard somebody come up behind him. He greeted N'vonne without shifting his position, but to his surprise, she did not answer. He turned to see Verial, blindfolded, standing with her hand resting on N'vonne's shoulder.

"Telenar, I think something has happened."

Though it was N'vonne who spoke, Telenar did not hear her. He was gazing instead at Verial. Her skin was ashen.

"Take off her blindfold."

When N'vonne removed the cloth, Verial blinked rapidly, then looked down at Telenar. For a moment, she did not say anything. It seemed then to Telenar that all the cycles of her bondage dropped from her, leaving exposed a terrified young lady.

"Oh Telenar," she whispered, "I'm so sorry."

Telenar jumped to his feet. "Sorry for what? What do you know?"

The color had drained even from her lips. But Obsidian would not let her keep silent.

"Vancien is dead."

His form lay lifeless, a pool of blood staining the ground. Amarian took a moment to savor the sight. If only Rhyvelad knew the significance of this quiet scene, it would already be trembling. But Rhyvelad did not know yet. It would not know until he came riding back in triumph. Even then, some of the stupid ones would not guess until a Sentry sat on the throne of Keroul and the Patroniite order was expelled to the far reaches of the Chasm. Then, maybe, some of them would realize that a new age was coming upon them. And if they did not, what harm would it do? They could stay in ignorance for all eternity. It was no matter to him.

He puzzled a moment longer over what to do with the body. Should he leave it to gather flies? Carry it back in triumph? Bury it? He laughed at that third option. No, he'd best haul it back to camp. The protests of any die-hard Prysmites would be stilled by the vision of their decaying champion.

With a sigh, he shouldered his brother's heavy bulk and set off to find Ovna. Despite his new burden, each step grew more energetic until he reached her, still suffering from her wounds. He watched her without sympathy. Healing her was an inconvenience, but he could hardly walk back to Cylini territory.

He felt again the power of Zyreio course through him as he pressed a hand against her scales. If she had been in pain before, she screeched in agony now, writhing away from his touch as her torn skin pulled itself back over the wound: all the stretching, aching, and itching that accompany a slow convalescence concentrated into one excruciating moment. Then it was over. She lay there, scales glinting in the orblight, whimpering from shock and exhaustion. But Amarian, quickly refitting the harness and securing Vancien's body, paid no attention to her discomfort. A soft tap and a threatening command encouraged her to take him airborne, clear of the Plains' intoxicating presence and on his way to a triumphant return.

CHAPTER TWENTY

Telenar was going to be sick. How could this have happened? He was so sure, so *certain* that good would overcome evil, that Vancien would prove to be the stronger. Had Amarian resorted to foul play? Had Vancien simply made a mistake in an honest sword fight? He pressed Verial for more information, but her responses were terse and unhelpful. If she had made any progress at all during the past fortnights, she was now regressing, withdrawing into the shell of her former self. He and N'vonne tried to turn to each other for comfort, but even the most gentle of touches seemed pointless.

So the small army marched on in silence. Of course, the men had not been told what had happened, but they could sense the sobriety of their leaders. It did not take much intuition to know something was terribly wrong. But if they had known the depths of their commanders' confusion and anguish, they might have considered retreating back into the cozy marshes.

"We could stay out here," Chiyo suggested absently the night after they had heard the news. "Not much sense going back to camp, or to Lascombe."

Telenar shook his head. News of the tragedy had wrought a dangerous change in his friend. Chiyo could no longer be thinking clearly if he was considering abandoning the House of Arisllyr to the enemy so quickly.

"What about the princes? They may put up a fight, since they think Corfe is the new Vancien." N'vonne spoke bravely, though she choked as she pronounced Vancien's name.

"I don't understand it," Chiyo continued, ignoring her. "What happened to the armies of the dead that were supposed to come to his aid? Weren't all of us supposed to fight?" His head dropped. "I failed him. I should have killed Amarian when I had the chance."

Telenar glanced irritably at his friend. "You would have failed, then he would have killed you."

"Better dead than see us come to this."

"Perhaps. But you're not dead. And your men need you. I hadn't figured you for a man to give up so easily, Chiyo."

Chiyo would have gladly responded to this accusation, but his attention was diverted by a figure circling above them, its wings lopsidedly beating the air. Telenar saw it too and jumped to his feet, waving energetically.

"It must be Vancien's Ealatrophe," he cried, "and it's wounded."

Seeing that he had caught the humans' attention, Thelámos screeched wearily, folded its wings, and executed a graceless landing. Both Chiyo's men and the Cylini, with no little commotion, hastened to what most of them considered a safe distance. Not even Telenar dared approach; no one in their group was immune to its fatal cold. Still, the beast was obviously in pain. Whereas its left wing was folded tightly against its side, its right flexed erratically, as if the Ealatrophe desired to fold it in, but was unable to.

Telenar bit his lip as the Destrariae cold seeped into him. Did the creature's arrival mean anything? Perhaps Vancien was still alive somewhere. As much as he longed to believe such a thing, he knew otherwise: Verial's death-knell proclamation still echoed in his mind. With Vancien gone, Kynell's cause was lost for another five hundred cycles. His heart was torn between grieving for his young friend and for all of Rhyvelad.

Yet here was Vancien's Ealatrophe, watching him expectantly. All hope may be lost, but there were still some duties left to perform. He took a hesitant step forward, but the cold would let him go no further. N'vonne and Chiyo had tried to do the same with the same effect. Verial was nowhere to be seen.

Suddenly, at his elbow, he heard a boy's voice.

"He's wounded, sir," Bren said.

"Yes, I can see that."

"Can't we do something about it?"

"Such as? It's part Destrariae, boy. Don't you feel it?"

"Sure. But we can't just leave that wing torn as it is. Isn't there some way to fight off the cold?"

Telenar shook his head. "None that I've heard of. Vancien is the only one who could get near the thing."

"But Vancien's not here. Permission to try, sir."

Telenar had to admire Bren's pluck, but such an idea was foolhardy. "There's no way: its cold has killed men twice your size."

"Maybe Kynell will help me."

"Perhaps." Why not let him try? What did any of them have to lose? "All right, go on. May Kynell keep you safe."

Bren nodded and turned to Chiyo. "Do we have any extra cloaks or jackets, sir?"

Chiyo, who had been watching the exchange in interest, silently went to his pack and pulled out his riding jacket, which he gently put over Bren's shoulders. The great wool garment dwarfed his small frame, but at least it would offer a little protection.

So armed, Bren advanced toward the Ealatrophe, who was beginning to paw the ground. Telenar watched anxiously as the young man came within a few paces, stopped, drew the jacket nearer around himself, and moved forward again. Soon, he was at the creature's side, shivering but still alive. The Ealatrophe looked at him warily, then stiffened as Bren, whispering soothing, inarticulate words, began to gently appraise the wound. His teeth were chattering by the time he finished and hastened back to the others, who had blankets ready to receive him.

"It's a c-c-clean c-cut. Looks like it's f-from a sword."

"That must have been Amarian and his dragon." Telenar was staring thoughtfully at the beast, secretly relieved that some of his ache was turning into simple curiosity. "Nothing else would have attacked him. The blow might have sent Vance tumbling. Did you see any other marks?"

"N-n-o, sir. Only that. And if-f you give m-m-me a few minutes and the right s-stuff, I'll go back and s-see what I can do."

Chiyo clapped his hand on Bren's shoulder, not a little ashamed at his earlier behavior. "We will dress his wound, Bren. You've done enough for today."

But Bren shook his head. "P-please let me do it, if it's all the s-same. It's the least I can do for V-Vancien."

Chiyo nodded, then abruptly turned to the rest of his men. "Back to work! This boy has shamed all of us." They stared blankly at him, so he continued. "We can only restore our worth by redoubling our efforts to return home. As most have you have guessed, the Advocate of the Prysm has perished in his fight against Obsidian. Now we go to fight the one who killed him. To avenge him."

Telenar watched Chiyo during the speech, certain that such a thing was impossible, but unwilling to crush what little hope the man had left. Kynell willing, they would all die fighting for the Prysm and join Vancien in the hereafter.

It was a grand gathering. Gair, with clean bandages, was proudly mounted on a voyoté, patrolling the front lines of the assembled forces. He looked with justified pride over the congregation. The Keroulians were bright as always, with their shining blue and gold banners. No surprise there. It was their neighbors who drew Gair's attention. Sentry after Sentry stood at attention, their arms polished, their faces gleaming with a resolution Gair had never seen before. Behind them stood the rest of Commander Hull's multitudes, all of them, even the fennels, with their gaze fixed on one figure.

Gair saluted as Corfe ascended the makeshift stage. The past few days had wrought an astonishing transformation in the young man. Less than a week before, he had carried himself like a slave: disdainful toward his master but too scared to resist him. Now he was almost otherworldly. Even the Sentries and fennels were powerless before him, and the Keroulians welcomed his charisma as they welcomed the orblight. All knew that Kynell's chosen stood among them, rightfully receiving the homage of prince and pridehead alike.

Lors and Farlone bowed deeply as Corfe approached them, although Farlone did so with some reluctance. He had expected to find his glory in Cylini blood out here on the frontier. Instead, he had been dismissed by a taciturn Commander who then abandoned the camp, now he was being forced by popular will to submit to some upstart mystic who found himself "healed." His brother Lors, on the other hand, had discovered his life's calling. Here was the Advocate, the chosen one of the Prysm, and he as a Patroniite had the distinct honor of serving him. Ever since Corfe had emerged from his tent with the Ages clutched in his hand, Lors had known. Who else but the Advocate could have his speech torn out by the Dark One and then have it restored by Kynell himself? Who else could command the loyalty of Sentries and fennels? Granted, the fact that Corfe was not Amarian's brother was a problem, but that seemed like a technicality in the face of such momentous events. Besides, had the two not been "brothers" in their service to Obsidian? Now this same young man stood on the stage, ready to address his legions and call down the wrath of Kynell on all who would oppose the Prysm. It was a stirring sight.

"Men of Keroul," Corfe began, "Men of the West, Sentries, and fennels.

Most of you, like me, have spent your life serving Obsidian. You have killed many times in its name and were often prepared to die for it. Sentries, I speak most directly to you: Zyreio has persuaded your entire kind to enter into slavish devotion to Obsidian and its servants. You have been branded as henchmen of evil, children's worst nightmares." Some of the Sentries shifted at this last statement, uncertain that these labels were objectionable, while others fanned their ears wide to catch every word.

Corfe noted their response. "You see? Even now, you're not sure what to do with yourselves. What would life be without the slavery to which you've been accustomed? Is there life outside Obsidian? I am living proof that there is. Fennels," he shifted his gaze to the brooding felines. "You chafe at Obsidian's rule and rightly so. Kynell made you brilliant, free, and independent, but Zyreio has kept you enslaved. Now you must shake off cycles of stifling service to the evil one. Enjoy the freedom Kynell gave you and give him thanks for it."

He stopped to let the words sink in. Then, as he expected, the fennels began to slowly shed their armor, stretch their agile limbs, and disappear one by one. Soon only a few remained of what had once been a full-sized regiment. Then those, too, nodded respectfully toward Corfe and left. The Sentries watched all of this with scorn. No matter what Corfe said, they were soldiers. Corfe only hoped that he could enlist them to fight on the proper side.

A fight was soon coming, of this he had no doubt. The Ages were clear that a violent battle inevitably took place between the two Advocates. His brief but intense scrutiny of the book these past few days had revealed that such a conflict could take place anywhere and at almost any time after the Dedication. Amarian's return was imminent, but when he arrived, he would find an army arrayed against him. Battle would be unavoidable, and Corfe prayed fervently that the Sentries would not revert back to their old loyalties.

In truth, their support had been an unlooked-for blessing. When he had first returned, he had spent several hours in confession, during which he had pleaded with Kynell for forgiveness and direction, and had emerged from the tent fearing the worst. Surely any Sentry or fennel passing his way would notice a change, and if any subordinate heard him talking, he might request an explanation, which Corfe felt obliged—and excited—to honestly give.

Yet he expected no pleasant reaction to the news, and as the chief Sentry approached, he had steeled himself for any level of hostility.

After a respectful salute, Tarl had given his report. "The generals are assembled, sir. They await your presence."

"Good. Tell them I'll be with them shortly."

Tarl began to bow his assent, then stopped, his leathery ears fanned. "Pardon me for asking, sir, but it appears your voice has been restored."

Corfe nodded, then impulsively placed his hand on the Sentry's shoulder. "You are a good soldier, Tarl. You value candor, so I will be perfectly honest with you."

Tarl gazed at the offending hand with a dark expression, but Corfe continued.

"When I was in the marshes last night, my silence was broken."

"By whom, sir? By the Dark One himself?"

"Amarian is gone. Off to be with his god. No, the power that healed me is greater than anything under Obsidian."

"I was not aware such power existed."

"You knew of it, although I doubt you knew its strength."

Tarl snorted, sweeping his claw in the general direction of the Keroulian troops. "You mean the caper those men call a religion? Kynell?" He spat out the name in derision.

"That is the one who healed me, yes. And in my presence, I would be grateful if you did not speak of him with such disrespect."

Tarl's yellow eyes narrowed in disbelief. The human had certainly acquired new confidence over the night. "I am sorry, sir. I had not realized your opinion of the Prysm had changed so drastically. I will refrain from further offensive comments."

Swallowing hard, Corfe shocked even himself with his next words. "I need more than your silence, Tarl. I need your support in this. I need the Sentries to change their allegiance."

Tarl did not move. Had the human gone mad? Never before had a chief of the reptiles bowed knee to the Prysm. He wondered if he should strike Corfe down or just neutralize him until the Dark One returned. But he could not do either. Corfe was still his commanding officer and no religious conversion would change that. Still, abandoning Obsidian was not something to be done lightly.

"Sir, you must realize what you're asking. Even if I were to do this thing, I cannot speak for my regiments. They have opposed the Prysm for thousands of cycles."

"They will listen to you, Tarl. *That's* what they're made for: obedience. And it would not hurt to remind them that Obsidian has offered them no great rewards: a lifetime of unappreciated service, usually ending in painful death. Your kind are some of the most intelligent creatures that walk Rhyvelad. Surely your soldiers will see what service for Obsidian has done for them. Besides, I'm not asking you. I'm commanding you."

Although Corfe's logic did nothing to convince the Sentry, his insistence did. "As you will, sir. I will inform my regiments."

And so the transformation of the camp had begun, spearheaded by the Sentries, who, having been informed of the change, fixated quickly on their new duties. What their personal thoughts were, few could guess, although Corfe suspected that some of them had not been displeased with Tarl's words.

Amarian's pulse raced as the camp came into sight. It would be a small step to eliminate those useless Keroulian soldiers and their princes. The Sentries could dispatch them with little problem. The next move would then be to track down Telenar's roving band. After that, the throne of Keroul. Then, perhaps, the domains of the West. He could almost taste the victories as he urged Ovna forward.

To his surprise, it appeared that the troops were already assembled. That was interesting. Perhaps Corfe suspected his arrival and decided to be prepared. That would be all the more appropriate for the entrance he wanted to make. But when heads began to turn as he came into view, he sensed confusion rather than pleasure. Were those princes up to something? Why call the army together, if not to herald his arrival?

Corfe, for his part, was not alarmed by the dragon's shadow. He knew this hour would come. In truth, he was more interested in the reaction of his men than in Amarian. He did not move from his position on the platform, nor did his speech miss a beat. "Look!" he shouted, pointing to the descending beast. "Here is your chance to express your gratitude to Kynell. He has revealed to you the face of evil, the face of your oppressor! He sits astride that dragon and sneers down on us, believing us all to be pawns in Zyreio's game. You, Sentries, who have never known a day of happiness in your lives, he is the cause of your misery! Men of Obsidian, be men, not the slaves he expects you to be! Men of Keroul, this man has always been your enemy. Now is the day to defeat him once and for all!"

He was interrupted by a low pass from Ovna, who tried to silence him with a jet of flame. He leapt out of the way, but her attack ignited the small stage, sending himself and others scrambling. Immediately Gair shouted for the archers and the ballistae to fire when ready, but the dragon did not repeat her attack. Instead, she was hovering thoughtfully above the Sentry companies, which had not moved in all the tumult. As the dragon waited, Amarian's calm voice floated down over them.

"Sentries, what are you doing? Have you so lightly abandoned me? What has this traitor promised you? Wealth? Happiness? Why do you, my greatest servants, let these men raise up arms against me? Why do you not defend—by the Chasm, you miserable stump of a man!"

His outburst was directed at Gair, who had interrupted his silken speech with a shot so close it nicked Amarian's ear. The Sentries looked at him in astonishment as he drew another arrow, crying, "I said 'Fire'! Archers, fire!"

Amarian was immediately besieged with arrows. With another oath, he moved Ovna out of range, but not before commanding the Sentries to attack the archers. To Corfe's dismay, some of them actually did draw their weapons and lunge at the men. A melee broke out, and as the Keroulian infantry tried to force its way between the undefended archers and their attackers, a large group of Sentries under Tarl's command turned relentlessly upon their own kind.

Amarian would have viewed the bloodshed with satisfaction, except the archers kept firing and the ballistae were now operational. Besides, it took little military acumen to ascertain that the battle was already going against him: the Sentries who had obeyed his command were few and surrounded, while the men of Obsidian appeared to either disinterested or on the side of the traitor. Where had the fennels gone? Barking a retreat for the few soldiers who still stood by him, he impulsively scanned the chaos for the one who must be the cause of all this trouble. He found Corfe mounted on a voyoté, sword in hand, slashing at the attacking Sentries. Snarling, he ordered Ovna into a dive. The beast cleared her way with a jet of flame, igniting attackers and defenders alike, and before Corfe could escape, she was upon him. He managed to dodge the flame a second time, only to find his way into her claws, which she closed forcefully. She had barely pulled up above the fray, however, when she screeched, dropped her load, and whirled her great head around to look at her underbelly. There was lodged a ballista bolt, fired at close range and digging itself deeper into her stomach as she frantically flapped her wings. But the shot was lethal. After a deafening roar, she plummeted to the ground, striking hard and pushing the bolt directly into her heart.

Corfe landed with a thud, unharmed. Amarian, too, was intact, feverishly unstrapping Vancien's body before Corfe could regain his feet and attack. Hampered by the corpse, he could only flee toward his loyal Sentries, who immediately formed a protective circle around him and began the tortuous process of retreat. By sheer desperation the small group eventually managed to extract itself, rushing into the marshes. Tarl shouted for pursuit. Corfe would have seconded his command, but for a regiment to pursue the small band into the swamp was simply not feasible. He had to settle for sending a small battalion after them, although he had little hope of their success. Who knew how powerful Amarian had become after this Dedication of his? This first attack had caught him off guard, but the next battle would not be so easy.

CHAPTER TWENTY ONE

After sending a few Sentries off to deal with the pursuit party, Amarian could only slog through the swamp water, wondering at the last few moments. The power he had felt coursing through him was fading, as was his awareness of Obsidian inside of him. What in the Chasm had just happened? How had his triumphant return turned into a rout? Why hadn't Zyreio struck down the turncoats? He shifted Vancien's body, which was becoming intolerably heavy. Motioning for a Sentry to come relieve him of it, he tried to keep a wary eye on the creature to make sure it didn't eat his prize while he figured out his next move.

In truth, he had not felt so confused since that day so long ago, when that wild-haired instructor had tried to pawn off his lies of figurative Advocates and two gods who were really one. As Amarian remembered it, he had been so confused by the lesson that when Zyreio came to claim him, he had gone willingly with him, just for the gift of knowing that Zyreio wasn't a figment of his imagination.

At least on that day he had been presented with a clear course of action, however unpleasant. Now, he had nothing and nobody. Even Zyreio had left him. No, that was impossible. How could Obsidian abandon its own Advocate after Kynell had been so roundly defeated? Why would it? There must be another answer. Perhaps he was being tested. Perhaps Zyreio remembered the truth about that day. Amarian shook his head. What *was* the truth about that day? He suspected that there was something important he had forgotten about it, something that would give him a clue what to do next.

He looked over at the dead body of his brother bouncing gently on the reptile's back. Suddenly everything seemed so complicated, more complicated than it had been since, well, since that day again. Why did it always come back to that?

The corpse was beginning to smell, so he inhaled its fragrance like a perfume. There was still his victory at the Plains. No one could deny that. He had defeated his brother with ease. Little Vancien was no longer around to trouble him. He was gone.

Amarian slumped against a tree, uncaring about the water, uncaring whether he was still being pursued. He had murdered his little brother. Disgust swelled within him, bringing with it fragments of his past: visions of Vancien as a child, learning how to fish; a thunderstorm, a rain-soaked shirt, and making fire for a stranger; Vance with straw in his hair, attempting to buck a bale of hay; the stranger by the fireplace, making Amarian shiver.

A splash soaked his left side. The Sentry that was carrying Vancien's body had let it fall into the marsh: the pursuit party had caught up with them and was now attacking with the zeal of converts. The scuffle was extremely violent, but fortunately the attackers were too engaged with their fellow Sentries to keep track of Amarian or the body. Silently, and without fully examining his motives, Amarian crept over to the spot where Vance had disappeared. Feeling for the cold dead arm, he grasped it and began to pull it slowly through the water until the battle was several paces away. Even then he dared not allow it to surface, but rather submerged himself up to his neck, moving swiftly until all he could hear were distant sounds of the skirmish, muffled by the water lapping against his ears. Only then did he rise, lifting Vancien up out of the sludge as he did. He had to find some high ground where he could dry off.

Not too far away was an old, abandoned Cylini platform. Its wood was almost rotted through, but all he needed was a patch large enough for himself and his burden. He hauled himself up, but Vancien, now completely water-logged, was a little more difficult to manage. Only after a great deal of grunting and effort did they both make it onto the dry surface.

Now that they were situated, Amarian took his chance to glare at the body. His little brother, murdered. By his own hand. What would Vance say? Though Amarian would never admit it, Vance had been the only thing close to a moral compass in his life. Now that he was gone, Amarian half wished that he was back again, if only to talk about these new developments. What would he advise? Probably something laughable, like praying to Kynell.

The name of the god made him growl low in his throat. Kynell. He was the reason for this whole mess. If Kynell had been a little stronger, Amarian would have been dead on the battlefield, not Vancien. Then all would have been right. Rhyvelad would have been a happy place once again with Vancien in charge, Keroul would be as mighty as ever, and only one person would ever be the wiser. Only one person would know of the horrible choice forced upon a twelve-cycle old boy. Only one person sacrificed on the Plains of Jasimor. That was what should have happened.

But it had not happened. Kynell was the weaker, Zyreio the stronger, and Amarian, who had once made a choice to protect his brother, had now killed him in cold blood. Amarian shook his head: a sad story with a sad ending.

He stood up, not quite sure what he was going to do but determined to do it anyway. He might as well leave the body here, slumped gracelessly on the rotting wood. Graceless, like Amarian's own life. The word stuck in his throat. Would there ever been any grace for him? Probably not. Self-pity? Absolutely. Fear? In boat loads. But grace was reserved for the Prysm and the Prysm did not traffic with Zyreio's Advocate. The only grace for him was a dangerous one: one that brought the dead to life. Amarian did not trust it. He liked to think of himself as one of the most careful of Obsidian's Advocates, so he certainly knew enough not to bring back one of his servants from the grave. Imagine what that would have done to a subordinate's ego! No servant should think himself indispensable to his master. That's why they're called servants: to serve and be disposed of.

But Vancien had never been his servant. Vancien was merely his brother, neither his servant nor his master. It had been so long that Amarian had been pinioned between the two that the idea struck him hard. Vancien was not dependent on him to follow or to lead. He was simply there, separate from Amarian's world but indispensable to it.

He knelt down, irrationally grasping the wrist of the corpse to check for a pulse. There was none there: most of the blood had long since been drained out through the wound and washed away by the marsh waters. Still, he pressed his thumb harder against the tendons, pretending that the possibility of life still existed.

As he did, the image of Zyreio next to the fireplace sprang up in front of him so sharply that he rocked backward. He could see Zyreio looking at him, judging him. Then, the house—his father's house—was up in flames. Hull was trapped inside, bellowing for help. Vancien, too, was trapped. His boyish cries could be heard clearly above the roar of the fire. The crisis was so real that Amarian shouted out, attempting to put out the flames with his bare hands. But it was no use. Soon the house and all who were in it were reduced to cinders.

Amarian collapsed to the platform, sweating. There was no hope. Obsidian's Advocate could never bring something good into the world: Zyreio wouldn't allow it. The god had the power to destroy everything Amarian loved, not just once, but several times over. If he used a Grace to bring Vancien back from the dead (as he was now sorely tempted to do), Zyreio would simply destroy the boy again, and then where would he be? More alone than ever before.

The violence of the vision had caused him to disturb the body again. Now Amarian could see something bulky strapped to its back: no wonder it had been laying in such an odd position. It was large and rectangular, like a book. Curious, Amarian rolled the body gently onto its side to cut loose the bindings that held the object on.

It was the Ages. They were bloody and soaked, but still, there they were. He flipped them open to a familiar passage: "The day of the advocates always comes. . . .Ten thousand score of mornings and of evenings, then Rhyvelad will tremble again. The brothers will fight as enemies and one will die." That last line he knew well: it had been burned into his brain since the day he left home. But he had never bothered to read the next line. He looked closer, gently wiping away the mud that threatened to smear the ink.

"But the love of Kynell is eternal. It overlooks the crimes of brothers and enemies. It waits for repentance."

He read it again, certain that he was mistaken. Kynell did not overlook crimes. He judged them and executed punishment, when he had the power. Still, there it was: "'Overlooks the crimes of brothers and enemies. It waits for repentance.'"

He didn't understand. It looked like this passage was holding something out to him. Something like hope. But it went against everything else he knew about Kynell and Zyreio. Unconsciously, he moved his hand again to Vancien's wrist. *If you could just come back for a second, Vance,* he thought to himself, *you could help me understand this.*

The body stirred, but Amarian was too busy looking at the Ages to notice. Only when it propped itself up on its elbow and gave its head a shake did Amarian see what was going on. When he did, he dropped the book with a cry of terror.

"Vancien?"

Vancien shook his head again. It felt like he'd never get the water out of his ears.

"Amarian, what are you doing here?" He looked around, taking in the moist, insect-laden swamp. "What am *I* doing here? I was in the most amazing place." He frowned, trying to recall the memory.

Amarian, meanwhile, had recovered the Ages with a trembling hand. "I, uh, was hoping for your help." Then he remembered his hasty wish. "Do we have much time?"

Vancien rubbed his neck, which had begun to itch. "Time for what?"

It was an innocent movement, but it caused the full truth to dawn upon Amarian. The fatal wound was gone. Vancien looked healthy, as if the battle had never happened. He had done it. What would Zyreio say?

He must have muttered the question out loud, because Vancien's head snapped up.

"Zyreio? What's he got to do with anything?"

Amarian had a hard time finding his tongue. "He, uh, well, since I brought you back, I thought that maybe he did it."

"*You* didn't bring me back. Last thing I remember, you were plunging a sword into my throat." He stopped to scratch again at his neck. "But now I'm here again. Like N'vonne. You must have claimed your Grace." He looked sharply at Amarian. "Why? Why did you bring me back?"

Amarian was still flustered, but he did not take kindly to Vancien's tone. "I said, I wanted your help. There's a passage here. " He pointed to the open Ages. "I don't understand it."

Vancien stopped rubbing his neck long enough to look at the page in question. When he finally realized what line it was that was bothering Amarian, his attitude changed considerably.

"You want forgiveness?"

"Forgiveness? No. What do I need forgiveness for?"

"Killing me, for start."

Amarian flushed in anger. Here was the old self-righteous Vancien, back in full force. "For doing what I was born to do? I could have let *you* go with Zyreio, you know."

Vancien nodded. He had long suspected Amarian's motivations on that day. Amarian's words, though harsh, spoke of a great sacrifice.

"I know. And I'm grateful, believe me. You gave me the freedom to serve the Prysm. Kynell knows it well. But then you gave yourself over to evil. You persecuted and murdered Kynell's servants and killed his Advocate.

He should strike you down, but instead he offers you himself. Again. What will you say?"

For several moments, Amarian did not respond. History was replaying itself, except this time there was no young child for whom he had to answer. Two paths still stood before him, and this time if he chose against Kynell, it would be for his own reasons. He shivered at the thought of crawling back to Obsidian, of living completely alone, of serving a god who must despise him. Yet his pride balked at taking Kynell's offer. Did he dare trust the same one who had abandoned him that day next to the fireplace? He glanced again at Vancien, who was sitting patiently. Kynell's love waits for repentance, the Ages said. One thing Vancien had said was right: he certainly had a great deal to repent of since that day, if Kynell cared to hear him.

"He is still waiting for you, Amarian. He's still asking you to serve him."

Amarian bowed his head. How could he refuse Kynell a second time?

CHAPTER TWENTY TWO

Telenar and the others were still a few days away from the Keroulian camp when the Ealatrophe startled them all by screeching and gnawing at its bandages. It was early morning. Most people were still asleep in makeshift tents, heads resting uncomfortably on their packs. Before anybody could offer groggy intervention, the beast had torn off its restraints and launched itself lopsidedly into the air. Telenar alone did not wonder much at its behavior, having assumed it to be completely wild now that Vancien was gone. Bren, however, had appointed himself its primary caretaker and was very upset. In just a few minutes, he had organized a search party, including Chiyo.

Telenar grabbed his friend by the arm.

"Chiyo, this is foolishness. The creature has a mind of its own. Let it go."

Chiyo shook his head. "Tell that to Bren. He'd be off on his own if we didn't go with him. Besides, that thing could turn out to be useful."

"Not if it keeps behaving like that. Let Bren go and send some men with him. But you should stay here."

Chiyo, whose heart wasn't in the task anyway, nodded and hurried off to make arrangements. Telenar, meanwhile, went to find N'vonne and inform her of the new development. She would not be happy. Ever since the news of Vancien's death, she, too, had acquired an attachment to the creature. It was, after all, the last one of them to have seen Vancien alive. Now even that small comfort had disappeared. Telenar shook his head, still at a loss. How could Kynell have let this happen? Was the fate of Rhyvelad really just a gamble? How could a man have faith in a god who would allow (or worse, couldn't stop) the death of his own Advocate?

These and other dark thoughts hounded him as he made his way through the little encampment, the soberness of which mirrored his own grief. The Cylini warriors, usually given to song, were now huddled miserably around fires, staring at the embers in the cool morning light. The remnant of Chiyo's soldiers were just as disconsolate. Many of them had already slipped quietly away to rejoin the main force under Corfe. Except for these deserters and Bren's little search party, the entire camp seemed numb.

The search party was gone all day and into the next night. They returned torn and dirty the next morning, reporting that they had encountered no sign of the Ealatrophe. Telenar gathered his strength to offer them encouragement, but he was interrupted by one of them pointing abruptly to the sky. "Look, sir! Toward the south!"

They all followed his gaze and sure enough, there was a dot above the tree line that was growing larger and larger. Telenar held his breath while Bren shouted that it was the Ealatrophe and that it was carrying somebody. Two somebodies, in fact.

It did not take long for Thelámos to draw near enough for them to see whom it was carrying. N'vonne was the first to recognize the rider.

"Vancien!" She ran forward, nearly hysterical. "It's Vancien!"

Telenar stood rooted to his spot as everyone around him burst into cheers. Vancien himself was beaming like a proud parent. Everyone gathered around him as close as they dared. In their excitement, it took a few moments for them to notice the shivering figure behind him.

Amarian had drawn his jacket around him as much as he could, hiding his face in the depths of his hood. He hurriedly dismounted, stamping his feet to regain warmth and trying not to draw attention to himself. His entire body ached with cold. The crowd around him instinctively drew back, though few of them guessed his identity. Without a word of clarification to them, Vancien grabbed his brother's arm and walked over to Telenar, who still had not moved.

"Telenar, we need to talk."

It was difficult extracting themselves from the jubilant crowd, particularly N'vonne, who refused to let Vancien get out of arm's reach. Finally, Vancien promised them all a party of celebration and explanation that evening, which at least gave them an avenue for expressing their joy. They all eagerly set about the preparations, with the exception of N'vonne, who would not be put off.

Finally, the four of them were gathered in the tent, with Chiyo standing guard outside. Amarian sat quietly against the canvas wall, Vancien sat protectively just in front of him, with N'vonne immediately to his right. Telenar, meanwhile, had to pace. His delight over Vancien's return was mingled with a high level of confusion.

"You're telling me that you were *dead*?"

"Yes. Amarian killed me."

Telenar stared at the silent figure in the corner. The former Obsidian Advocate had not said a word since his arrival. Telenar resumed his pacing.

"How is this possible? There's nothing like this in the Ages. I don't even know where to begin."

He sat down with a heavy sigh and looked at Vancien helplessly. What in the world was Kynell up to?

N'vonne, however, had no such confusion. "How can you be upset at a time like this? Vancien is alive! What more could we want? And we should be grateful that Amarian has come home too. Welcome back, sons of Hull!"

———————

The return of Amarian pa Hull to the faith was welcomed by very few. Only Vancien and N'vonne were personally delighted with his deliverance. The rest were impressed merely from a theological viewpoint. Kynell's mercy was great indeed, but what were they to do with this sulking convert?

Their reception of Vancien, on the other hand, was little short of ecstatic. Not only had their champion returned from the grave, but the shadow that was descending over Rhyvelad had dissipated. What remained, however, were some unusual problems.

Corfe was still entrenched as a high priest of both men and Sentries. Although he might have welcomed Vancien as a religious oddity, Vancien would not allow Amarian near his old camp, since Corfe would consider it his duty as the Prysm Advocate to have Amarian killed on sight. Their only option was to return to the marshes for the moment, where the Cylini could offer some protection until they decided on their next move.

Besides, far greater concerns were battling for their attention. What had happened to the armies of the undead? Had they been summoned? If so, where were they? How would Amarian's actions affect the cycle of ten score thousand cycles? And what was Rhyvelad going to do with two Advocates?

Verial, meanwhile, hid like a frightened child after Amarian's arrival. The morning the recovering Ealatrophe had disappeared, she had rejoiced, only to be dismayed at its return and horrified at its passenger. Even sick with cold, Amarian terrified her. Now, although they all assured her (Amarian with a little less enthusiasm than the others) that he no longer posed a threat, she avoided his presence at all costs, even when he had told her the good news that Gair was still alive, though much damaged. After that point, it was only her fear of him that kept her from deserting the camp and running to Gair's side.

Vancien himself was unsure how to proceed. He felt no need to challenge Corfe, although he knew that was what Amarian expected of him. In his own mind, the work of the Advocate was completed. Zyreio had been defeated, albeit by somewhat unorthodox means, and was somewhere in the cosmos licking his wounds. The chaos that had threatened Rhyvelad never came to be. Relgaren, Relgaré's eldest, had succeeded the Kerculian throne. Farlone and Lors were still backing Corfe, but what was that to him? If Corfe wanted to claim Advocacy, let him. He would find out soon enough that he was lacking a worthy opponent. For the moment, Vancien was content to live with the Cylini.

Such peace was not granted to Amarian. His surrender to Kynell was, he knew, the greatest moment of his life. He lived in daily amazement at the Prysm god's mercy, while trying to absorb as much of his brother's tranquility as he could. But his cycles with Obsidian were not so easily forgotten. He had been closer to Zyreio than any mortal on Rhyvelad and that intimacy had left its mark. Fear had become his constant companion. Would Zyreio come after him? Would he be condemned to the Chasm for his betrayal? The knowledge of the Sentries' infidelity did little to ease his mind: they were his fellow deserters. Surely Zyreio would not let such a massive defection rest.

Although he shared these thoughts with no one, not even Vancien, they took a visible toll on him. Vancien watched with concern as his brother grew paler. Such unease was permitted by Kynell, Vancien had to remind himself, and it would pass in time. They were all readjusting.

Fortunately, a celebration distracted them from their concerns: Telenar and N'vonne were getting married. It was a glorious celebration, held in the orblit plains just west of the marshes and conducted by a Cylini priest. N'vonne was breathtaking. Surrounded as she was by late autore prairie grass and dressed in a brilliant white robe (a gift from the Cylini), she seemed like a gift from Kynell himself. Even Telenar cut a striking figure, and for once, he was completely happy. Guided by the priest, the two proclaimed their commitment to each other, and in so doing, they seemed to herald a brighter age than the one that had gone before.

End of Book One.

ABOUT THE AUTHOR

Lindsey is the youngest of the family—the fifth child—and youngest children like to think they have the most sensitive souls. When one of her older brothers introduced her to the fantasy genre, she was hooked and has enjoyed it ever since. It was her love of a full, mysterious, majestic world that led her to get an MA in Medieval Welsh history and then a PhD in Ancient History.

During her academic career she has written and presented several scholarly papers, but her heart has always been with creative writing: C.S. Lewis is her literary hero because he had a gift of helping readers understand and enjoy the most complex ideas.

Her websites, www.lindseyscholl.com and www.gooddiscourse.com, are dedicated to exploring truth in a colorful and sometimes humorous way. She is married to Dr. John Scholl, a fellow historian. Together they have eleven delightful nieces and nephews.

You can find more information about *The Advocate Trilogy* at www.theadvocatetrilogy.com.